Fortune's Soldier

Alex Rutherford lives in London and has travelled extensively in India. Alex is also the author of the Empire of the Moghul sextet of historical novels currently being filmed by Disney Plus/(Hot Star) in India for a six-series, high-budget TV production. The showrunner is Nikhil Advani. The Empire of the Moghul books are also under motion picture development in Hollywood.

FORTUNE'S SOLDIER

ALEX RUTHERFORD

CANELO

First published in the India in 2018 by Hachette India (Hachette Book Publishing India Pvt. Ltd)

This edition published in the United Kingdom in 2021 by

Canelo
31 Helen Road
Oxford OX2 0DF
United Kingdom

A CIP catalogue record for this book is available from the British Library.

Print ISBN 978 1 80032 283 7
Ebook ISBN 978 1 80032 240 0

The maps at the beginning of the book, illustrated by Pia Alize Hazarika, were originally created for the first edition of *Fortune's Soldier* by Alex Rutherford, first published by Hachette Book Publishing India Pvt. Ltd. in India in 2018. Reprinted with permission from Hachette India.

All maps in this work are pictorial representations, not to scale, and are not meant to represent exact political boundaries. They are for general illustration only, and are not intended to be used for reference purposes or reproduction elsewhere. It is clarified that the representation of a particular theme, or data set across regions with colour demarcations do not reflect political boundaries. It is also reiterated that such pictorial maps do not either represent or contradict India's national sovereignty, jurisdiction or the recognition of political regions as mandated by the Surveyor General of India for maps showing political boundaries.

Look for more great books at www.canelo.co

Printed and bound in Great Britain by Clays Ltd, Elcograf S.p.A.

*Power tends to corrupt
and absolute power corrupts absolutely.*

INDIA IN THE MIDDLE
OF THE EIGHTEENTH
CENTURY

NAWAB *of*
BENGAL'S
DOMINION

R. Ganges

R. Hooghy

MARATHA
TERRITORY

BENGAL

MURSHIDABAD

PLASSEY
×
1757

CHANDERNAGORE
Fort William CALCUTTA

NIZAM *of*
HYDERABAD'S
TERRITORY
HYDERABAD

BAY OF BENGAL

R. Palar MADRAS
Fort St. George
VELLORE
ARCOT
1751
R. Cauvery
MYSORE

PONDICHERRY
Fort St. David
CUDDALORE
DEVAKOTTAI
R. Coleroon
TANJORE

TRICHINOPOLY

COCHIN CARNATIC

TRAVANCORE

COROMANDEL COAST

N
E — W
S

Map not drawn to scale

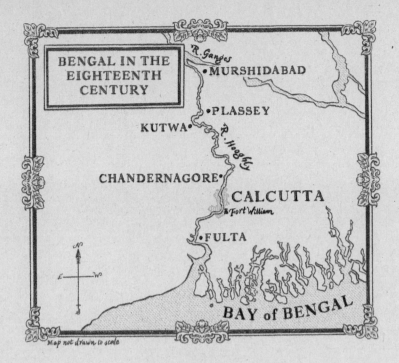

BENGAL IN THE
EIGHTEENTH
CENTURY

R. Ganges

•MURSHIDABAD

•PLASSEY

KUTWA•

R. Hooghly

CHANDERNAGORE•

CALCUTTA

Fort William

•FULTA

N

E   W

S

BAY of BENGAL

Map not drawn to scale

Cast List

Characters I have invented are marked with an asterisk. All others are historical figures of the time. – A.R.

*James Ballantyne, Laird of Glenmire, Scottish Highlands.

*Nicholas Ballantyne, James's nephew.

Cameron of Lochiel, head of the Scottish Clan Cameron and supporter of Bonnie Prince Charlie in the 1745 Jacobite Rebellion.

Bertrand-François Mahé, Comte de la Bourdonnais, senior French naval commander.

*George Braddock, recruit and later merchant in the East India Company.

Robert Clive, recruit and later senior official and commander of East India Company armies.

Thomas Broddyll, President of Bengal, 1739–1746.

Eyre Coote, officer in the British Army who served under Clive at Plassey.

*Hiralal Das, senior clerk in the British East India Company, Calcutta.

Roger Drake, President of Bengal, 1752–1756 including at the time of Siraj-ud-daulah's attack on Calcutta.

Rai Durlabh, one of Siraj-ud-daulah's commanders who defects to the British at Plassey.

Jeanne Dupleix, wife of Joseph François, Marquis Dupleix.

Joseph François, Marquis Dupleix, Governor-General of the French territories in India.

Warren Hastings, junior East India Company official in Calcutta at the time of Plassey and later the Company's first Governor-General in India.

John Hinde, Governor, Fort St. David, Cuddalore and briefly President of Madras, 1746–1747.

Mir Jafar, senior military commander of Siraj-ud-daulah's armies and later Nawab of Bengal.

*Khaled Kasim, cousin of Anwaruddin Khan, Nawab of the Carnatic, and ally of the French East India Company.

Anwaruddin Khan, Nawab of the Carnatic and ally of the British East India Company.

Lutuf Khan, a general in Siraj-ud-daulah's army.

Mohammed Ali, younger son of Anwaruddin Khan and the British East India Company's candidate for the throne of Hyderabad.

John O'Sullivan, Irish soldier and supporter of Bonnie Prince Charlie during the Jacobite Rebellion.

Stringer Lawrence, one-time commander Fort St. David, Cuddalore and subsequently leading military figure.

*John Martingdale, chief aide to Thomas Saunders, President of Madras.

Margaret Maskelyne, sister of Britain's Astronomer Royal, visitor to Madras and later wife of Robert Clive.

*Meena, dancer at the court of Anwaruddin Khan and Nicholas's lover.

Mirza Muhammad Siraj-ud-daulah, Nawab of Bengal, more commonly known as Siraj-ud-daulah.

Nicholas Morse, President of Madras, 1744–1746.

*****Harry Ross,** Lieutenant in the East India Company's Bengal Army.

Thomas Saunders, President of Madras, 1750–1755.

Chanda Sahib, senior military commander of Anwaruddin Khan and briefly Nawab of the Carnatic.

*****Raja of Silpur,** ally of the French East India Company.

*****Tuhin Singh,** Harry Ross's steward, later Nicholas Ballantyne's steward and closest friend.

*****Sohini,** ayah to Nicholas Ballantyne's and Meena's son James.

*****Ramesh Ramachandran,** Nicholas Ballantyne's language tutor in Madras.

*****Lucia Vendramin,** Venetian merchant's daughter rescued from pirates by Nicholas.

Charles Watson, admiral and commander of British naval forces in India.

Preface

In 2015, an antiquarian book dealer noticed a large metal box among the lots at an auction house near the Howrah railway station in Calcutta, now Kolkata. The catalogue claimed the box was an old campaign chest recently found in a house near Fort William and that it contained 'miscellaneous' papers. On impulse and because the price was low – no one else was interested – the dealer offered one thousand rupees for the box and his bid was successful.

Sifting through the contents, the dealer first found old but ordinary documents – bills and laundry lists – from the 1800s. But, delving deeper, he discovered papers dating back to the 1700s – letters, diaries – some mere scraps, but others in gold-tooled leather bindings. There were also tattered campaign maps, mildewed sketches, sheets of violin music, even. What struck him most was a name that occurred again and again – Ballantyne. Wondering whether there was any connection with the Nicholas Ballantyne who appears in my Empire of the Moghul books, he allowed me to read them.

There was indeed a connection. The contents of the box – the Ballantyne Papers I call them – revealed, sometimes in only tantalising fragments, further extraordinary events in the lives of a family bound body and soul to an India they loved – the Ballantynes. Even more intriguingly they provided glimpses of that unique, mercurial and controversial figure, Robert Clive at a pivotal time in the history of the Indian subcontinent. So compelling, so revealing were these insights that I decided the story deserved to be told.

It begins not in the heat, dazzle and dust of India, but in a colder, greyer clime.

A.R.

Part One

From the Highlands of Scotland to Calcutta, 1744–1745

1 – The Debt

Nicholas Ballantyne reined in and patted the neck of his sweating chestnut horse as he surveyed the familiar sight. The lime trees shading the drive – planted, his uncle had told him, in the time of King Charles I – were in flower, scenting the warm air of a summer evening. Pulling off his tricorn hat, he pushed back his long dark hair and wiped his brow with his neck cloth. His muscles ached. The ride from St. Andrews through the Highland glens had taken the whole day. Maybe it hadn't been the best idea to set out with a head still thick from a night's revelry with his fellow students to celebrate the end of their university studies.

Kicking his horse on again, Nicholas rounded the bend in the drive and there it was – Glenmire House, with its austere granite walls and slate-topped turrets, and behind it the green-blue waters of Loch Arkaig. Before he got any further, the oak doors of the house swung open and his Uncle James's dogs – Titus, a wolfhound, and Cicero, a springer spaniel – streaked towards him. Halting, Nicholas slipped from the saddle. Titus reached him first, almost knocking him over as he leapt up, exhaling hot, meaty breath, his tongue lolling, while Cicero ran in circles around them, barking joyfully.

As Nicholas led his horse towards the house, his uncle, waiting on the front steps, called out, 'The dogs are as glad you're home as I am. A Master of Classics now, eh, Nicholas? And not yet twenty. I'm proud of you... Come inside, you must be tired.'

Even on a mild June evening the flagstoned hall with its dark panelling hung with portraits of earlier Ballantynes felt chill as Nicholas followed the tall figure of his uncle to his study overlooking the loch. The sun, streaming through the deep sashed windows, had warmed this room. As the light fell on James's angular features, to Nicholas he looked as tired as if he were the one who'd just ridden all those miles from Scotland's east coast. His hair, once as dark as Nicholas's own, now had silver at the temples and the lines on his thin face had deepened.

At a gesture from James, Nicholas settled himself into a wing chair by the hearth. He watched his uncle take a long-stemmed pipe from the mantelpiece, pack it with tobacco, strike a tinder box to light it, then take a pull. As blue smoke curled into the air, James turned to him, 'Tell me everything. You've not been much of a letter writer... But then in recent months neither have I...'

–

A month later, hearing a rider canter up the drive towards the house, Nicholas put down his violin and went to the window to see a muffled man dismount, glance quickly around and hurry inside.

He was by no means his uncle's first visitor in recent days. The pace of life at Glenmire, as Nicholas remembered it, used to be measured, sedate – sometimes too much so for Nicholas's taste. But since his return from university, there'd been frequent comings and goings, sometimes at late hours and once waking him during the night. Nicholas was surprised his uncle hadn't introduced him to any of these visitors – not that they ever stayed long. Whenever he asked about them James fobbed him off with comments like, 'We'd things to discuss but nothing that need concern you.' Just the day before, as he'd walked up the drive after shooting pigeons in the woods, another rider had galloped so fast round the bend away from the house that Nicholas had had to jump aside. The horseman hadn't slowed but shouted an apology over his shoulder in what sounded like an Irish accent. Nicholas had only been away a couple of hours. Yet, within that time, the man had arrived, transacted his business and was departing again.

Odder still, a few evenings earlier he'd been crossing the hall when through the half-open door to his uncle's candle-lit study he'd glimpsed James talking to a thick-set man in a travelling cloak. They'd been speaking French, his uncle saying something like '*malheureusement, je dois...*', 'sadly I must...' At that moment, the clock in the hall had sounded, drowning his words and causing James to look up. Seeing Nicholas he strode quickly to the door and pushed it shut, but not before Nicholas had noticed the concern on his face.

Nicholas picked up his violin again but no longer felt the urge to play. Instead he continued to think. It wasn't as if his uncle was a particularly sociable man. He called their nearest neighbours the Murrays 'clacking, chit-chatterers' and refused their invitations as often as good manners allowed. So he clearly hadn't invited these recent visitors for pleasure. What could it all mean then? Was it something to do with the estate? Also peculiar – now that he thought about it – was that the previous week his uncle had set off early on horseback to visit another neighbour, one of his few real friends, Cameron of Lochiel, chief of the clan Cameron, at his estate of Achnagarry. Nicholas had known the chief all his life – had fished in the local rivers and stalked the hills with his sons. Normally he'd have expected his uncle to invite him to go too, but James hadn't said a word to him. In fact, he realised he'd seen remarkably little of his uncle since his return. James seemed distracted, anxious even, disappearing into his study for hours on his own.

Not until this latest visitor had galloped away half an hour later did Nicholas begin to play again – a Scottish air taught him by his mother that always relaxed him. Hearing the door open behind him, he assumed it was a servant coming to feed the fire – it was a chill day despite being summer – and he finished the short piece before looking round. To his surprise his uncle was standing in the doorway. 'You've a talent, I've always said that... Now come down to my study. I need to talk to you.' He was smiling but his tone sounded sombre.

James was silent until he'd closed the door of his study behind them and poured two glasses of whisky from a decanter. The peaty liquid warmed Nicholas's throat as he wondered what his uncle wanted. But James was studying the two oval miniatures on one side of the fireplace – one of a dark-eyed man in a blue coat with brass buttons and the other of a woman in a pink dress with a wide-brimmed straw hat, holding a spaniel – Nicholas's parents. They'd drowned nearly ten years ago when the East Indiaman captained by his father and returning home with a cargo of tea was wrecked in a storm off the coast of southern China. His uncle too seemed to be thinking of the tragedy that had brought Nicholas to live at Glenmire House. 'Your father's death was such a shock – I'd tried to persuade him the estate could support us both but he said Glenmire was mine. He was the younger son and would make his own way. He wouldn't take anything from me until you were born. Then he asked me to promise that if anything happened to him I would look after you – a promise I've done my best to honour...'

Not expecting any response – he always brushed away in embarrassment any thanks – James turned from the portraits, looked at Nicholas for a moment, then continued, 'Since you returned from St. Andrews, I've not been able to spend the time with you that I would have liked... I've been preoccupied and I'm sorry. But one matter that has absorbed my time concerns you and your future...' James paused to sip his whisky, then said, 'You're my heir, Nicholas. One day, you'll be Laird of Glenmire and its people will be your responsibility. But you're very young... You may know about Homer and Virgil but you've seen little of the world. That is why I've used what influence I have to secure you a position with the East India Company at its Bengal headquarters in Calcutta in Hindustan. You will sail from London in six weeks' time.'

For a moment Nicholas stared at him, not sure he'd heard correctly. Then as his uncle's words sank in, he blurted out, 'This is one of your jokes, isn't it? I've just returned to Glenmire. I don't want to go to Calcutta to work for the East India Company, or anybody else for that matter.'

James's face tautened. 'It's no joke, Nicholas. I know this must be a shock but do have some regard for my views as your guardian.'

6

'I'm sorry, Uncle. I just don't understand...'

'I'm not asking you to understand, Nicholas, but to trust my judgement and follow my wishes. I've not taken this decision lightly and I only have your best interests at heart.'

'But you're sending me away. At least tell me what I've done to deserve it. If you've heard stories about me at St. Andrews tell me! – I was a little unruly sometimes but no worse than most other students...'

For the first time since their conversation had begun, James smiled. 'No, no, it's nothing like that. Even I was young once. The reason is simply that this is an excellent opportunity that won't recur. Make your fortune in Hindustan and then – God willing – return here.'

Nicholas put down his glass. Through the windows he saw a fishing boat out on the loch and the familiar red-headed figure of one of his uncle's gillies bent over the oars. On the far side of the loch stretched the rolling, purple-heathered moors, every hill and gully almost as familiar to him as his own face. 'But I want my life to be here – to help you run Glenmire as you always said I would. Improve the grazing and... and... all the things we talked about. If I can't do that, at least let me decide my own destiny.'

'Of course I'd like you to be here with me but I mustn't be selfish. You need to experience the world. And of course I can't dictate your life to you, but the East India Company is the most powerful trading company in the world. A clever young fellow like you can prosper in its employ.'

'But what do I know about trade – or Hindustan for that matter?'

'That's not the point. As a Company clerk – a "writer" they call it – you'll learn what you need to know.'

A sudden thought struck Nicholas. Was this about money? His uncle had never been a wealthy man – perhaps his mysterious visitors were creditors. 'Forgive me, Uncle, but are you in debt? Is that why you want me to go to Hindustan? To recoup the family fortunes?'

James hesitated a moment. 'My finances are sound if that's what you mean. But we all have debts of one sort or another and I beg you to repay yours to me by not questioning me further and trusting in my judgement.' As he spoke he went to the great mahogany desk behind which he sat to transact the business of the estate, opened a drawer and pulled out a bundle of papers bound with green ribbon.

'And as for Hindustan, it has been the making of the Ballantyne family before.' He flourished the bundle at Nicholas. 'These letters were sent home by your great-great-grandfather – another Nicholas Ballantyne, as you know. He went there as page to Sir Thomas Roe, ambassador to the court of the Great Moghul in James VI's time. Though Roe came home, your great-great-grandfather didn't, at least not for many a year... Read them. They should encourage you. We'll talk again tomorrow. Now, I'm sorry, Nicholas, but I must ask you to leave me – I've much else to attend to.'

Taking the bundle Nicholas stood and walked slowly to his room. There, his mind still in a whirl, he examined the letters – sixty-three in all. Someone had numbered them. Unfolding the first, dated 12 February 1616, he smoothed out the yellowing paper. Although the ink had faded, his namesake had written in a flowing legible hand. Why should his uncle think that anything written so long ago would convince him to desert the Highlands for Hindustan? But he might as well read the letters... Lying on his bed propped up on his elbow, he began.

The first told of the long voyage to Surat on the west coast of Hindustan – mostly a tale of sea-sickness and tedium but then excitement as one night, off Madagascar, pirates attacked. His great-great-grandfather related how the sailors beat the pirates off as they tried to board their vessel at the stern. 'I joined in and knocked one – a giant black-bearded fellow – into the sea and then calmly despatched a second!' Nicholas smiled at this pretended nonchalance. In reality his great-great-grandfather must have felt anything but calm...

Reading on, Nicholas noticed how once his namesake reached Hindustan, the letters became longer, describing a world plainly beginning to captivate him – the embassy's long, dusty journey on elephant-back from the coast to the Great Moghul Jahangir's red sandstone capital of Agra, the exotic ceremony when the Great Moghul was weighed on giant scales against gold and jewels and his courtiers were showered with flowers of beaten silver, voluptuous dancing girls whirling to the beating of drums, tantalising glimpses of the Emperor's favourite concubines behind the harem's dark latticed windows. Sometimes his ancestor sketched what he described – Nicholas laughed out loud at a drawing of a spindly-shanked Sir Thomas Roe, slumped across a table, plumed hat askew, after a night-long drinking bout with Emperor Jahangir.

As time passed, the tone of the letters again altered. In one, his great-great-grandfather explained to his parents why, after Roe's return, he remained in Hindustan. 'I am not ready to come home – I must see what is going to happen here, whether those I care for will prevail in the coming troubles.' He described bloody rivalries between the Moghul princes. 'Though of the same blood, they do not scruple to fight each other for the throne, even to death.' He admired one prince in particular – Khurram – and became captain of his bodyguard, fleeing with him and his family when the Emperor Jahangir, the prince's father, turned against him.

He'd been with this Khurram when the prince had become the Emperor Shah Jahan and had still been serving him when his wife, the Empress Mumtaz Mahal, died giving birth to her fourteenth child. One letter described the Emperor's raging grief and his decision to build Mumtaz 'a white marble mausoleum such as you might see in paradise – they call it the "Taj Mahal".' His forebear had watched that 'milk-white tomb so cunningly constructed that it appears all of one piece' – rise up and even sketched it.

In a later letter, Nicholas's namesake described fighting for Shah Jahan's eldest son, Dara Shukoh, during the war that had ensued between the Emperor's sons. Nicholas read in wonder how at a great battle at a place called Samugarh, Dara Shukoh, 'riding in a crystal tower atop his favourite war elephant', had been defeated, and how his ancestor had witnessed Dara's public humiliation and execution at the hands of his bigoted brother Aurangzeb.

Intriguingly, the very last letter, despatched from the port of Surat began, 'My dear brother, by the time you receive this I will be on my way home to Glenmire. Will you recognise me I wonder, after forty years? You will think me an old man, I am sure. Perhaps you wonder why I'm returning? Though it breaks my heart, I have no choice. It is my only way to protect someone I love. Though she is his sister and dearer to him than any other being, the Emperor would kill her if he ever suspected our intimacy and if I remain he may uncover the truth.'

A glance at the loudly ticking clock on the fireplace told Nicholas he'd been reading for hours. Around him, the old house – almost unchanged since his great-great-grandfather left for Hindustan all those years ago – seemed still and quiet. Getting slowly to his feet he went to the window and looked out. Bats flickered through the falling dusk and the first stars appeared in the darkening sky. His imagination buzzed with new sights and sounds as if he already felt the hot Hindustani sun, heard the rhythmic beat of drums as dancers whirled, tasted hot spices, watched ranks of trumpeting war elephants in glittering steel armour march, tusks painted blood-red, into battle.

These images decided Nicholas. He had long hankered to visit the classical sights in Italy and Greece. Instead, he would trust his uncle and follow his own namesake to Hindustan. After all, before too long, he would return home to familiar and much-loved Glenmire, wouldn't he?

2 – A Passage to Hindustan

'Come on, sir, this way!' The ragged man who had offered to guide Nicholas through the bewildering forest of masts in London's Wapping Docks to his ship, the East Indiaman *Winchester*, beckoned urgently. Nicholas pushed after him through the crowds. He had slung across his back the large leather satchel which contained his most precious possessions – his uncle's parting gift to him of a pair of silver-mounted pistols, his money, of course, and his great-great-grandfather's letters. In his right hand he gripped the handle of his violin case. He was glad he'd sent his sea trunk ahead.

His guide, still gesturing to him to follow and shouting that it was a short cut, swerved down a cluttered, rubbish-strewn alley between two warehouses. Turning into it himself, the first thing Nicholas saw was a red-headed woman standing in a doorway, skirts raised as a sailor thrust urgently into her. Ahead, the alley branched into two narrower lanes. Nicholas stopped and looked around. Which way had the man gone? As he hesitated, a youth suddenly leapt from behind some wooden crates and lunged at him. His assailant's knife flashed as he sliced through the strap of Nicholas's satchel and snatched at it.

Dropping his violin case but hanging on to the satchel, Nicholas aimed a punch at his attacker which landed square on the youth's jaw forcing him to release his grip on the satchel and fall backwards onto the cobbles. He was still clutching his knife and as Nicholas leapt towards him he flung it. Nicholas ducked and the knife flew past his right ear to clatter harmlessly against a wall. With blood trickling down his neck from where he'd cracked his head on the cobbles, his assailant glared up at Nicholas. Then, suddenly, he switched his gaze to look over Nicholas's shoulder and shouted 'Clobber him, Tom!'

Nicholas whirled around, expecting to see his would-be guide about to bludgeon him, but no one was there. The youth was back on his feet. Darting round Nicholas and ducking beneath his belated attempt to throw out a restraining arm, he dashed towards the entrance to the alley. Nicholas raced after him, hurdling a coil of tarred rope the youth flung into his path from its resting place on some packing cases. Nearing the alley entrance, Nicholas made a grab for the youth's tattered jacket. The rotten fabric gave way but he'd slowed the thief enough to allow him to seize his shoulder, spin him around and smash his fist full into the boy's face, splitting his nose which immediately began pouring blood. 'That'll teach you to thieve!'

His assailant lay doubled up at his feet in what seemed genuine agony, blood dripping through his fingers as he cupped his nose, all fight gone from him. He must have been in cahoots with the guide, even if the older man had abandoned him. What a naïve and credulous bumpkin he'd been to accept the offer to help him find his ship, thought Nicholas. If he couldn't negotiate London's docks, what chance would he stand in even less familiar Hindustan?

Looking carefully around to see if the guide was still lurking somewhere, Nicholas found the alley quiet – even the sailor and the whore had disappeared. He was about to yell for help to haul his attacker off to the magistrates, when scrutinising him more closely he saw how young he was – a pitiable creature with his bare feet and pinched face, deserted even by his accomplice. Why send such a poor devil to the gallows – his almost certain fate. Pulling the youth to his feet, he gripped his shoulders and stared into his eyes. 'Promise never to do that again! Do something useful. Become a sailor or a drummer boy!'

'Y… Yes, sir… I promise,' the youth stuttered before Nicholas released him and he darted away.

Glancing round, Nicholas saw that thankfully, no one had made off with his violin case which still lay where he'd dropped it. Retrieving it and gripping his satchel tightly, he walked quickly from the alley and back into the crowds. He'd little doubt the youth would soon be thieving again and be hanged for it, but at least his own last action on leaving Britain wouldn't be condemning someone so young.

Twenty minutes later, having been more reliably directed by a custom's official to the East Indiamens' berth, he stood looking up at a carved wooden figurehead of a stout fellow with bulbous blue eyes. Some nobleman, perhaps, or maybe the ship's owner? Halfway up the rigging a sailor was testing the knots with a big hook. 'Is this the *Winchester*, bound for Calcutta?' Nicholas shouted to him.

'She is, right enough.' The sailor pointed to the faded gold lettering on her bow that Nicholas hadn't noticed. 'We sail on tonight's tide.'

With three tall masts and a solid-looking hull, his home for the next months appeared impressive, not that he knew as much about ships as the son of a sea captain should. She was widest at the waterline and along her main deck were a row of wooden hatches – presumably the gun ports. The air smelled of tar. A succession of sailors – most bending under the weight of sacks, but one gripping a bleating goat and another with a crate of fluttering hens on his shoulder – were going on board. Nicholas waited for a gap and then sprang quickly up the swaying gangplank onto the deck.

'Hello! Who are you?'

A loud, confident voice behind him made Nicholas turn. It belonged to a young man, perhaps slightly older than himself and certainly a good four or five inches shorter with a wide heavy brow, prominent nose and penetrating chestnut eyes. Some of his springy brown hair had escaped its ribbon, giving him a windswept look, and he was grinning.

'I'm Nicholas Ballantyne.'

'Ah, yes. I saw your name on the muster roll. Another poor devil sold into slavery to the Company by relations who can't wait to see the back of him, no doubt! I'm Robert Clive but call me Clive. I don't like Robert or, even worse, Bob. We're sharing a cabin. Can you play that thing?' Clive gestured to Nicholas's violin. 'Any caterwauling and I'll heave you and it into the sea to entertain the mermaids… Come on, I'll show you where we are.' Without waiting for Nicholas to reply, Clive headed for the stern.

Following him into the ship's dark interior, Nicholas bumped his head on a low beam – something he'd have to watch out for, he thought, if he wasn't to arrive in Calcutta with a major headache.

'Here we are. I hope you're tidier than me.' Clive beckoned him into a windowless canvas-sided cubicle just large enough to house two high wooden bunks on either side with scarcely four feet between them. Glenmire House had larger broom cupboards than this, Nicholas thought glancing round. In the shadowy light of a lantern he was relieved to see his brass-bound sea-chest beneath one of them. 'We passengers get squeezed in wherever there's room. We're much less valuable than the cargo,' Clive said, reading his thoughts. 'Let's go up on deck again. The air down here's as foul as a carthorse's fart but I suppose we'll get used to it…'

'How old are you?' Clive asked once they were outside.

'Nineteen. And you?'

'Twenty-two.' Clive gave a wide grin. 'My family would have liked to parcel me off to Hindustan years ago – I got into debt playing high at the Cocoa-Tree – a gaming house in London,' he added, seeing Nicholas's puzzlement. 'Then they were concerned I'd make a misalliance – there were these dancers at the Theatre Royal but my favourite left me for a richer man, so they needn't have worried. Then a merchant newly returned from Calcutta bought land adjoining my parents' estate, Styche in Shropshire, for double what it was worth, or so they said, and built himself a palace. When I saw how wealthy he was – riding about like some florid-faced Croesus in a fine carriage with his belly straining against the ruby buttons of his velvet waistcoat – I thought why stay in England and risk poverty and the pox? If he could do it so could I! He's clearly an idiot. He splashes his money on ridiculous entertainments like 'fete champetres' – his name for outdoor parties – with the local milkmaids bribed to dress as wood nymphs! And all to impress his neighbours. The only thing that impressed me was his money and a few of the better-looking nymphs, of course.'

Nicholas burst out laughing but Clive continued, 'Laugh if you want but I'm serious. I decided to do what my family had been urging me to for so long – but because *I* wanted to! They may think I'm going to waste my youth and energies bent over a high wooden desk penning accounts like most writers or "griffins" as I gather they call us newcomers and all for a miserly five pounds a year. But I mean to grab every opportunity to make my name and fortune. If the chances don't come quickly enough, I'll engineer them. And when I've succeeded I'll return home to show my sainted family how much they've underestimated me.' Nicholas glimpsed triumph on Clive's face as for a moment he ceased his relentless pacing and looked at Nicholas expectantly, like an actor anticipating the audience's applause.

'I'm sure you'll achieve everything you wish.' Nicholas smiled, inwardly wondering how anyone could be so certain of his future, so convinced of his destiny, to expound it to someone he'd known for only a few minutes. No one could predict what life held in store. Less than three months ago he'd foreseen no other life for himself than riding and stalking in the hills, playing his violin and one day succeeding his uncle as Laird of Glenmire. Would his new acquaintance have sufficient resilience to cope with whatever twists of fate assuredly awaited?

But Clive's restless thoughts had already moved on. 'Come on – I'll take you round the ship,' he said. 'I came on board at first light so I've seen most of it.'

Clive certainly did know his way around, conducting Nicholas everywhere from the messroom to which, he informed him, a roll of drums would summon them to their meals, to 'the heads' – the ship's latrines – noisome little wooden cubicles overhanging the water in the bows. He already knew the names of some of the crew and pointed them out to Nicholas. The pock-marked young man binding a sailor's gashed wrist on deck was Ben Lyon, the *Winchester*'s surgeon, and an old man with a bald head and filmy eyes, sitting on a pile of rope, seemingly oblivious to the bustle around him, was the ship's half-blind fiddler, Nat Berryman. With a grin he also told Nicholas, 'As junior Company officials we're required to salute the captain whenever we see him and be in bed with our lanterns extinguished by 10 p.m. But that's only what the rules say. They can't treat us like children – we're grown men!'

They were inspecting one of the *Winchester*'s cannon on what Clive explained was 'the orlop deck', when the ship's bell clanged and they heard orders being shouted to weigh anchor. They joined the small group of passengers at the rail on the quarterdeck as sweating sailors strained at the spokes of the capstan and the anchor on its long chain began its clanking rise. On the quayside, dockers waited to slip the hawsers. So this is it, Nicholas thought, no turning back now. What would the voyage be like? No one was even sure how long it would last – 'four to six months', a sailor had told them, before adding, 'and who knows what weather we'll see'. To Nicholas the prospect of storms was daunting but Clive only seemed to find it exhilarating.

As the *Winchester* nosed into mid-Thames, a light breeze taut-ening her sails, Nicholas noticed Clive talking to another young man, thick-set with a ruddy complexion and straw-blonde hair. He had lace at his throat and his cuffs, and beneath his red-velvet coat gleamed a brocade waistcoat. Something Clive had just said had made him laugh loudly. As Nicholas joined them, Clive said, 'This is George Braddock, another recruit for the Company.' Braddock made him a bow. 'Clive tells me you're a Scot, from the Highlands. All very good but we Braddocks are proud Englishmen, from Buckinghamshire – Prestwood House, near Great Missenden. It's close to Charteris Castle where my grandfather, the Earl of Marlow, lives. His brother died a hero, fighting for King William at the Boyne, you know.'

'I didn't think the East India Company was for grandees like you... Why hasn't your grandfather found you a comfortable little sinecure at court like licker of the royal boots or emptier of the majestic chamber pot?' Clive interrupted. Braddock's small eyes looked at him suspiciously but then he laughed again. It struck Nicholas that Clive had that rare gift of being able to say what he wanted and not only get away with it but also make people like him while he was at it. Within minutes Clive and Braddock were vying with each other over whose youthful misdemeanours had been the more outrageous.

'My dear Clive, actresses and women of pleasure are all very fine,' Braddock began, before glancing around and lowering his voice. 'What if I were to tell you that I've celebrated the rites of Venus in company with some of the most illustrious names in the land? At Christ Church – the University of Oxford, you know – one of my fellow undergraduates, I can't tell you his name, but if I say he's addressed as "Your Grace" you'll know his rank, did me the honour of inviting me to join a club, but again I must be discreet. Only its members know its name and it's a condition of our initiation never to reveal it.'

'But you can at least tell us what happens at the initiation?' Clive prompted.

Lowering his voice yet further, Braddock confided, 'It involves drinking from a chalice of pig's blood and inserting ones privities into the mouth of a severed goat's head as a sign that in sensual pleasure nothing should be forbidden. Every month, on the night of the full moon we met in a pavilion on the grounds of His Grace's estate. Sometimes we dressed like Romans, lying on gilded couches while naked beauties served us food, poured our wine and danced for us. Any woman who pleased our eye, we took there and then, in any way we wished. In two years I never required the mercury cure for the diseases of Venus – His Grace always made sure the women were virgins...'

'Why then aren't you still worshipping at the "altar" as you call it?' Clive asked.

'Being a member of the club was expensive. I ran into debt, turned to card-playing and lost, and when my creditors arrived trying to dun money out of me, my father found out. If I were the eldest son, he'd have turned a blind eye, but I'm not. So here I am, being sent to recoup my debts and make my fortune in Hindustan.' For a moment, what seemed a genuine sadness crossed his broad face. Then quickly recovering himself, Braddock said, 'May the women there be as pleasing and compliant as the ones I'm leaving behind.' Producing a silver hipflask, he took a swallow then held it out. 'Come, let's drink to the voyage ahead!'

–

'Beat you both!' Nicholas exclaimed. Since arriving in the tropics six weeks ago, the intense heat and humidity had been like nothing he'd encountered before and he was sweating violently. Taking a wooden scoop, he splashed water from a butt over his head.

'You were tiring, Nicholas. One more circuit of the deck and I'd have had you!' Clive said, heading for the water butt as well.

'Perhaps, but we agreed the contest was five times round, so pay up. You too, George.'

'You're fleecing me,' Braddock complained, his face an alarming shade of plum.

'Nonsense, Clive and I even gave you a head start. Last time you lost you blamed feeling seasick. It's calm as a millpond today so what's your excuse this time?'

Braddock said nothing, but pointedly examined his right ankle which was bleeding from a scrape against the scuppers.

'Come on, we'll give you a chance to get your money back. Name your challenge,' Clive slapped him on the back, grinning, 'Jumping out of one barrel into another…?'

'I'm not such a fool as to take that bet, I've seen how good you two are at it,' Braddock replied grumpily.

'Fence with me, then. You're always saying that your father got you the best instructor money could buy,' Clive said.

Braddock considered this for a moment. 'Very well – Ballantyne, you referee.'

For a bulky man Braddock was quick on his feet and to Nicholas's eye more skilful, but as the mock duel continued Clive looked so determined, his jaw set hard and his brows knotted in concentration, that Nicholas was sure he'd win. But darting in suddenly, with a clever, rapid twist of his wrist, Braddock forced Clive to drop his sword.

Just then a shout from the *Winchester*'s mate, standing by the main mast, made them look round. 'Calling all Johnny Raws and Polliwogs! King Neptune commands your presence. The longer you keep him and the shellbacks waiting, the worse for you!' Beside the mate stood the ship's barber in his long leather apron, razor in hand and a bowl of suddy water on a stand next to him. At a signal from the mate, two sailors placed a large butt filled with some liquid in front of the mate. Even from 10 feet away Nicholas could smell a stink worse than that from the urine vats in a tannery. The *Winchester* must be about to cross the Equator. Recently there'd been much eager speculation about the timing of the crossing and the nature of the initiation the 'Johnny Raws and Polliwogs' crossing for the first time would receive at the hands of the 'shellbacks' – those who'd crossed before.

As sailors and passengers gathered round, the mate shouted 'Make way for the King!' and a bearded figure appeared on the quarterdeck. Beneath the high crown made from a cooking pot covered with sea shells and the long cotton wool beard, Nicholas recognised the now familiar pitted features of the ship's surgeon Ben Lyon who was as great a practical joker as Clive. He was flanked by two pouting sailors in low-cut women's clothes, with false breasts made of coconut shells and long wigs woven from the split ends of rope which they tossed coquettishly as they simpered and called out ribald invitations to 'come lie with Neptune's mermaids'. 'Look at their faces – rouged like a Covent Garden whore's, if ever I saw one,' Braddock sniggered into Nicholas's ear.

Nat Berryman, perched on a water keg, struck up on his fiddle as, with the mermaids, Neptune descended onto the main deck and seated himself on a makeshift throne set up on a dais of planking. At a signal from the ship's master, acting as chief of ceremonies, a cabin boy handed a huge dead fish with bulging eyes to one of the mermaids who stroked it suggestively as Neptune roared, 'Bring the wretched initiates before me.'

Sailors were being lined up, hands bound, in front of the barber who seized the first, slathered his head with suds and then roughly shaved off his hair. Next the mate grabbed the man by the nape of the neck and plunged his head into the stinking contents of the vat before yanking him up again. Then he pushed his spluttering victim down on his knees before Neptune. 'Swear the oath! Say after me, "I, a miserable Johnny Raw until this day, swear allegiance to you, Great King of the Ocean. If I ever fail in my duty may I perish in Davy Jones's locker."' The man repeated the oath at which a cry went up, 'Kiss the fish! Kiss the fish!' Nicholas, Clive and Braddock watched, laughing and cat calling with the rest, as more initiates underwent the ceremony. While the last – a pale, thin-chested youth with straggling ginger hair – was receiving the barber's attentions, Clive slipped over to whisper something in the master's ear. When the red-headed sailor had kissed the fish, the master again addressed Neptune: 'My Lord, the ceremony is not yet over. We have among us three Polliwogs who have had the audacity not to pay due tribute to you.' He pointed to Nicholas, Braddock and Clive. 'What say you, my liege, what should their punishment be?'

Braddock turned to Clive. 'What on earth did you say? Passengers don't have to join in. I don't want my head shaved nor to embrace a slimy rotting fish...'

After conferring for a moment with the master, Neptune rose and, raising his arms with a theatrical flourish, addressed the three young Company men on whom all eyes were now fixed. 'You have defied me and must pay the price. My new shellbacks, to show your love for me, bind them and take them up the rigging!' Shaven-headed initiates rushed forward, tied long lengths of rope around the three men's waists and began pushing them towards the sheets. 'Climb! Climb! Climb!' the crowd roared as, slightly bemused, Nicholas began to mount the rigging, a sailor behind him gripping the end of the rope. He looked back over his shoulder to see Clive following. But on the deck Braddock resisted furiously until the sailors let him go.

When Nicholas reached the first yardarm, Neptune shouted, 'Get to the end of that!' Not looking down as he edged along the foot rope but guessing what was to come, Nicholas obeyed. Sure enough, a cry of 'Throw them down!' followed. The sailor with Nicholas quickly wound the rope a few times around the yardarm, then, still holding onto the rope, braced himself and gave Nicholas a push. Nicholas flew headfirst through the air before smashing into the water. It filled his nose and mouth. Choking and spluttering, he fought his way to the surface as the ship's momentum dragged him through the water. Then his chest scraped painfully against the ship's hull as he felt himself being hauled up over the rail and onto the deck. Moments later Clive was beside him, also gasping for air. Sailors undid the ropes around their waists and helped them to their feet to cheers as Neptune cried out, 'Truly these are worthy worshippers of the sea.'

'What did you say to the master?' Nicholas asked, still breathing hard as he pushed his dripping hair out of his eyes.

'A sailor had told me they sometimes ducked initiates from the yardarm. I bet the master five shillings you'd do it like me but that Braddock wouldn't!'

Had the competitive Clive made the bet to assert his superiority over Braddock after losing the fencing bout, Nicholas wondered. Probably – and he'd probably succeeded.

But at the 'Equator Feast' that evening, Braddock seemed in high spirits, especially as the port began to circulate. He was sitting opposite Clive and Nicholas and next to a thin-faced clergyman who looked in his forties and was on his way to Calcutta as a regimental chaplain. 'You should see the carriage horses my grandfather's just purchased – four perfectly matched greys,' Braddock was telling the clergyman. 'He's breaking them in himself, tooling them round the park of Charteris Castle, but next season he plans to stable them at his London home.'

Nicholas and Clive by now knew how much Braddock enjoyed boasting, not to say exaggerating, about 'my grandfather the Earl', and Clive gave Nicholas a quick wink. As soon as the clergyman rose – doubtless to piss, since he complained constantly of his 'leaky waterworks' – Clive leaned forward. 'Come on, Braddock. This is getting dull. Tell us some more about your "altar of Venus"!' The mysterious club was something else Braddock needed little encouragement to brag about. 'Did I tell you about the night His Grace came dressed – if dressed you could call it – as Bacchus and he had the fountains filled with claret. The women were dressed as nymphs and hid from us in the woods but we found 'em all right…'

'But all that's just play-acting for amorous boys,' Clive broke in. 'Did you never go to Mother Marshall's in London's Haymarket where they worship the dark arts? There's a high priestess with gold-painted nipples an inch long, who…' Clive lowered his voice to a whisper so Nicholas only caught the word 'serpent' but saw Braddock's eyes widen. It seemed to Nicholas that Clive's fertile imagination was conjuring something much more deeply decadent than Braddock's tales! By the time he'd finished, the gullible Braddock was regarding Clive with outright awe. But then Braddock jabbed a finger towards Nicholas. 'You're a dark horse, Ballantyne. You must have had adventures at St. Andrews but you never talk about them.'

'Fun though they were, my adventures weren't exotic. There's no point my trying to compete with you. Even if I have another glass of port – which I will when it comes round again – I won't be able to think of anything to impress you,' Nicholas said with a grin.

'You know, I don't think I believe you…' Clive said.

'You should. Aren't you always teasing me about my "book learning" as you call it? That's what I mostly did at St. Andrews.'

'And how will that help you when you reach Hindustan?'

'You never know. Perhaps more than the experience of pursuing painted priestesses. The Classics teach you about life, about people's characters and motivation, about strategy. Weren't you saying just the other day that the most important thing is getting people to do what you want and not the other way around?'

Clive looked thoughtful but only for a moment. 'Touché,' he said finally, 'but a bit priggish! Quick, pass me that bottle of vinegar, Braddock.' Glancing round to make sure there was no sign yet of the man returning, he added some to the port in the chaplain's glass. 'I'm growing tired of that clergyman's disapproving expression and stupid clucking noises when he overhears what we say. Let's give him a real reason for that sour face of his.'

—

Nicholas walked over to the *Winchester*'s rail to look out at the view. Noticing Clive and Braddock squatting beneath an awning, engrossed in a game of cards, he smiled and shook his head. He enjoyed cards as much as the next man, but not when there was so much new to see. The previous morning the ringing of the ship's bell – unusual at that hour – had woken them. They'd hurried on deck to find sailors high in the rigging trimming the sails and the helmsman responding to frequent shouted orders to alter course. A seaman told them the ringing of the bell was both a celebration and a thanksgiving to mark the *Winchester* swinging north from the Bay of Bengal into the Hooghly River. Calcutta was 70 miles upriver and the most hazardous part of their journey was over.

It was welcome news. After calling in at Cape Town, nearly two months ago, time had dragged – everyday the same heat, the same endless expanse of blue-green sea, enlivened only by silvery flying fish, arrowing through the spray and occasional groups of sleek-backed dolphins. But since entering the estuary, the sights – unlike anything he'd ever experienced – had captivated Nicholas. Scotland had great rivers, of course, but none as mighty as this. Moreover, the rivers of his homeland were mostly wild, solitary places, often veiled in mist and rain. The Hooghly teemed with life – fishing boats with sacking sails, stately high-prowed trading dhows, smaller boats piled with fruit and vegetables plying between small islands all looking lushly and luxuriantly green. As a settlement larger than any he had yet seen appeared on the Hooghly's east bank, Nicholas shaded his eyes for a better look.

'That's Diamond Harbour,' a voice behind him said.

Turning, Nicholas saw a thin man in his late twenties wearing a red army uniform, tall like himself, with a shock of fair hair, above a pale, rather pinched-looking face. Had they met before, Nicholas wondered. You could hardly avoid people within the close confines of the ship, yet he couldn't place him.

The man smiled, as if reading Nicholas's puzzlement. 'I'm Harry Ross. I came on board in Cape Town but I'm a bad sailor. Seasickness gets me almost immediately every time. It's only now that we've left the sea for the river I've felt able to leave my bunk. I'm lucky my family destined me for the army, not the navy, aren't I! What's your name?'

'Nicholas Ballantyne.'

'A Company man?'

'Yes, a writer.'

'And I'd guess this is your first time in Hindustan?'

Nicholas nodded. 'But obviously not yours?'

'No. I've been on furlough in Cape Town. Now I'm returning for a second tour of duty as a lieutenant in the Company's Bengal army. I can't say I'm in a hurry to get back but it's not that bad a life. At least here I can afford to play polo which I never could at home.' Ross stepped forward to stand next to Nicholas by the rail. 'Diamond Harbour used to be a stronghold for Portuguese pirates. You can just make out the ruins of their fort – Chingrikhali, I think it's called. Beyond it the river bends sharply to the left, then starts to narrow. My guess is we'll reach Calcutta by sundown.'

As they passed Diamond Harbour, Nicholas noticed the Hooghly changing colour. The higher upstream they sailed, the more yellowish-brown the river was becoming. 'Does the water always get this muddy?'

Ross nodded. 'Sometimes even more so. You should see it after the monsoon – the rains flush tons of earth and debris all the way down from the mountains in the north to be deposited on the mudflats.'

'The earth certainly looks fertile. What are those yellow plants, over there – crops or flowers?' Nicholas pointed to fields that looked as if a giant hand had gilded them.

'That's flowering mustard, almost ready to be harvested. People make oil from the seeds to favour their food. And see those tall, shiny-leaved trees over there – they're mango trees. The Hindustanis pickle the fruit when it's raw and also make it into a kind of jam – "chutney" some call it. But to my mind they're best eaten ripe and fresh. In June the trees drip with them… Believe me you've never tasted anything so good.'

For a thin man, Ross seemed to like his food, Nicholas thought. The deprivations of seasickness must have sharpened his appetite. The settlements along the mudflats were growing more numerous – cluster after cluster of flimsy-looking huts with walls of beaten earth and roofs of dried, plaited leaves. 'What happens to these villages when the rains come?' Nicholas asked.

'The monsoon sometimes washes them away completely, but with no shortage of materials to build from people simply begin again. If I've learned one thing about Hindustanis, it's their endurance, their patience. When I hear my fellow officers whining on in the mess, I think how much we could learn from these people if we only wanted to… If we only made an effort…'

By now, they were passing quite a large village and excited, near-naked children were running, shouting and waving, down towards the riverbank, some even diving into the water and trying to swim to the ship. Brightly clad women squatted at the water's edge, rinsing clothes and beating them on the rocks. Large horned beasts with pewter-coloured hides wallowed nearby, white birds waded daintily beside them or perched on their humped necks to peck insects from them. 'Water buffaloes,' Harry said, seeing Nicholas's puzzlement. 'The villagers use them for milk as well as for draught animals… And those birds are egrets.'

Nicholas could scarcely take it all in, from the vibrant reds, purples and oranges of the cloth wound around the women's bodies to the pyramids of large round cowpats drying in the sun – 'fuel for cooking,' Ross claimed. Nicholas caught his breath as a huge grey animal emerged from behind some palm trees, a man perched behind its great flapping ears, and swayed down towards the riverbank to drink. It could only be an elephant, Nicholas thought, as it lowered its trunk into the water. Though his great-great-grandfather's letters often mentioned elephants, even contained sketches of them, he had never imagined such stately creatures.

Everything was new and different. Yet, he was the one who was different, not these people and their world. If their places were reversed and the Hindustanis were suddenly in the Highlands, they'd feel they'd been transported to another world – and a colder one too! Yet again he wiped sweat from his face.

As the *Winchester* nosed round a further sharp bend, a complex of high red towers appeared from which three flights of broad shallow stone steps descended to the water's edge.

'That's a temple dedicated to one of the Hindu people's many gods, Vishnu. I visited it last year while on a hunting trip. If we were closer you'd see the façade is elaborately carved. Pilgrims come from all over Bengal to worship there and once a year – so I was told – there's a great festival that lasts nearly two weeks with torchlight processions during which statues of the god are paraded on huge carts they call juggernauts. The most important shrine in the complex is on that little island over there,' Ross pointed to a reed-fringed dot of rock on which stood a small cupola-shaped building. 'And see those stone platforms along the shore? People burn their dead there before scattering their ashes in the river.' Nicholas made out smoke spiralling from a pyre and through it figures dressed in pure white.

'Does everyone burn their dead?' Into Nicholas's mind came an image from Homer's Iliad of Achilles grieving by the funeral pyre of his friend Patroclus as orange flames consumed his body.

'No, only the Hindu people. The Muslims bury their dead, like us.'

'Why are all the people wearing white?'

'For the Hindus, white is the colour of mourning. They think it odd we dress in black at funerals.'

How much he had to learn, Nicholas thought, but the prospect excited him. As they sailed slowly on, the buildings along the riverbank were becoming more substantial – many constructed of brick, even sandstone. Encircled by walls like any great house at home within its parkland – like Charteris Castle, George Braddock would doubtless say – Nicholas glimpsed a domed and pillared mansion. 'Who does that magnificent palace belong to?' he asked.

'The Nawab of Bengal,' Ross replied. 'You're right it is magnificent, but it's no palace – just a hunting lodge and only one of many. I doubt the Nawab visits it more than once a year! He's as wealthy as he's powerful and the Company works hard to keep on good terms with him.'

Nicholas was about to ask more questions about the Nawab when a shout from the crow's nest, followed by the frantic ringing of the ship's bell, distracted him. He and Ross ran towards the bow to find that one of the small, roofed boats that he had watched ferrying people back and forth across the Hooghly was directly in the *Winchester*'s path. The men at the oars were pulling frantically and after a few heart-stopping moments just managed to work the little vessel clear.

Glancing up at the sky Nicholas saw the red ball of the sun was starting to sink with the rapidity he'd grown used to in the tropics. A light breeze had risen, relieving the earlier heat and bringing with it something else. Above the fetid, earthy aroma of the river, Nicholas detected an aromatic fragrance, pungent and sweet, that he couldn't identify. 'What's that I can smell?' he asked.

'That's Hindustan,' said Ross with a laugh. 'See those buildings along the bank – they're warehouses, "go-downs" they call them, where the Company stores sacks of spice ready to be shipped to Britain. But the scent's other things as well. Flowers and plants are giving off their fragrance. People are lighting their dung fires and cooking their evening meals – you can see the smoke rising – and fishermen are drying their catch on racks. No other place

27

on earth smells like this, particularly at this time of day. Wherever else life may take you, you'll never forget it…'

The expression on Ross's face, the affection in his voice, belied his earlier comment about being in no hurry to return. Clearly Ross loved something about this place. Interrupting Nicholas's reverie, he held out his hand and said, 'Do excuse me. I must go and prepare. I intend to go ashore tonight if I can. Perhaps we will meet again.' Handshake over, Ross walked briskly away along the deck.

Half an hour later, what Nicholas realised must be Fort William finally came into view on the Hooghly's eastern bank. By now, great bats were sweeping low over the water and the deck was crowded. Clive and Braddock had at last abandoned their cards and were standing in silence beside Nicholas as they took their first look at their employer's headquarters in Bengal. The setting sun softened the outlines of the two-storey grey stone building, its projecting wings protected by walls and bastions mounted with cannon. The Company's red and white striped flag fluttered from a flagstaff and from somewhere within the fort the sound of a bugle was borne faintly on the wind.

'Well,' Clive said, slapping Nicholas on the back, 'For better or for worse, here we are.'

3 – Two Monsoons

Though it was only just after dawn, Nicholas felt sweat trickle down his spine as he climbed into the saddle in the stableyard adjoining the Writers' House, where junior Company officials had their lodgings. Each day since he'd arrived in Calcutta three months ago seemed hotter and more humid than the last. Taking out his gold pocket watch – an eighteenth birthday gift from his uncle James – he saw that he had twenty minutes before he was due to meet Harry Ross for one of their rides.

Nicholas had been pleased when, towards the end of his second week in Calcutta, Ross had sought him out at the Writers' House. Ross, with his enthusiasm for Hindustan, was good company and some compensation for the fact that, almost immediately on arrival both Braddock and Clive had been sent 1,000 miles south to the older Company Presidency at Madras.

Nicholas set off at a leisurely pace towards their usual rendezvous point outside the Company barracks about half a mile away in the north of the city. As he approached, he saw Ross waiting on his handsome bay horse. With him, checking the hooves of his own mount, a fidgety grey, was his steward Tuhin Singh, a tall young man with a neatly clipped moustache, who often accompanied them on their jaunts.

'Nicholas, good to see you!' Ross smiled. 'Let's go before it gets any hotter!'

As they kicked their horses on, Nicholas wiped more sweat from his streaming brow with his neck cloth. 'What a place to build a city – why did they choose somewhere so far upriver instead of on the coast?'

Ross laughed. 'Good question. Two Englishmen are to blame. You must have heard the story?'

Nicholas shook his head.

'It started with Gabriel Broughton, surgeon aboard the ship *Hopewell* trading in the Deccan over a century ago. The tale goes that a daughter of the Moghul Emperor Shah Jahan was badly burned when her dress was set alight by an oil lamp and Broughton helped save her. As his reward, Broughton asked that the English East India Company be allowed to trade free of duties and to establish settlements here in Bengal. The Emperor agreed. But the man who actually established Calcutta some years later was Job Charnock – a Company official in Bengal. The Company had set up a trading station in the village of Hooghly. Charnock settled and throve there until an attack by some local rulers forced him and his Company comrades to flee downriver. They took refuge in three villages close together on the Hooghly's east bank – Kalikata, Satanuti and...' Ross paused for a moment, 'Govin... yes, Govindpur, if I remember correctly. Anyway, local people say Kalikata got its name from a story about the Hindu goddess Kali, consort of Shiva the Destroyer. The story goes that when the goddess, in another manifestation, sacrificed her life, Shiva was so distraught he put her corpse on his back and rampaged through the world, almost destroying it in his grief-stricken rage until another god – Vishnu – caused Kali's body to be cut into fifty-two pieces which flew through the air before landing on earth. The places at which they came to rest were regarded as sacred and people built temples there to honour the goddess. The little toe of her right foot is said to have landed here, on the banks of the Hooghly. That's why people named the site Kalikata and founded a village here.'

An interesting story, Nicholas thought, and one his friend seemed to find engrossing as he continued, 'When peace was finally restored and the Moghul Emperor had reaffirmed the Company's right to live and trade in Bengal, Charnock, for reasons best known to himself, chose Kalikata – or Calcutta as we call it – as the site of a new settlement. That was in 1690 and it's prospered ever since. Not bad for a city built on a swamp, eh?'

'I suppose not.'

Ross shot Nicholas a thoughtful look. 'Do I detect you're not entirely enamoured of Calcutta?'

Nicholas considered for a moment, then said, 'The truth is I'm disappointed. It's not what I expected – not that different from home, in fact. Our people, the British... their habits... have remained exactly the same here. It's so incongruous. The same clubs, the same formalities, the same petty etiquettes and hierarchies. We even dress like we're at home. Look at you in that ridiculous red jacket buttoned up to the neck. And we civilians are no better, sweating in our worsted stockings and woollen coats – and some of the older ones boiling their brains beneath their wigs. Yesterday at dinner, one of the President's guests keeled over as the port was being passed. Footmen loosened his neck cloth, doused his face with soda water and brought him round, but no one looked in the least surprised. Even worse, we still talk about the weather.' Nicholas looked up at the sky piled with mulberry clouds. 'Everyone keeps assuring me this heat will end as soon as the monsoon arrives. They seem obsessed with the rains. Some men are laying bets on which day they'll start, even the precise hour.'

'But surely your job doesn't disappoint you? Your uncle must have pulled some strings to get you appointed as an aide to the President of Bengal.'

'I doubt my uncle had anything to do with it. The President told me it was because I'd studied the Classics – they assume I'm good at languages. I spend two hours a day studying Bengali – it's the only thing I really enjoy.'

'Well, that's something. An ability with languages can take you far. Not many make the effort. I've never regretted learning Bengali. You've really no reason to mope. Most people would be glad to be in your shoes.'

Ross was right. Both Braddock and Clive would have leapt at the chance he'd been given – especially Clive who'd made no secret of how much he envied Nicholas. 'I'm being ungrateful, I know,' Nicholas acknowledged. 'But my job's so tedious. You should see the people I have to deal with! Company officials squinting over their spectacles at me, bow-fronted merchants steeped in port and the finer points of trade. The President told me on the very first day that my main duty was to stop them wasting his time, to listen to their pleas for special favours but not to make any commitments. Not the easiest task, you'll agree. The officials – "political experts" they like to call themselves – either bad mouth each other or suggest they're the ideal or indeed the only sensible candidate for the next promotion or prose on about our rivalries with the French or the intricate sparrings between Hindustani potentates like the Moghul Emperor in Delhi and the Maratha Confederacy. The merchants – admittedly often more astute than they look – insist on telling me about the Company's trade. How they calculate purchase and shipping rates for indigo or cotton or opium or saltpetre... How they could ensure a good profit for the Company – and in the form of commission for themselves of course – if only the President would relax this or that rule. One or two have even offered "to see me all right" if I can fix it for them. Perhaps I'm not cut out for it. Perhaps I should be in the army like you, Harry.'

'Believe me, it's not so different. D'you think our mess dinners are much more entertaining? When you've heard one old major's long-winded pig-sticking story you've heard them all.'

'But at least you get away from Calcutta on exercises. I'm stuck here among people who lack curiosity about this country. In fact, most can't see anything good about it. All they discuss is when they'll be able to go home, the estates they'll buy, the horses they'll have, the beauties they'll woo and marry – although given how bloated and red-faced most of them have become they'll have a lot of difficulty with that. I've already seen enough to know that to most people Hindustan's just a golden goose. Once they've made their loot here they're off home to enjoy it...'

With a rueful grin, Nicholas broke off. 'I'm beginning to sound like one of them, aren't I? Ranting, moaning and complaining like an old dowager. There are good things, of course. I've found a couple of like-minded musicians to play the violin with, and I like the Bengalis themselves and their country when I have the chance to get out into it, as I have today with you. Look at it, it's beautiful.' And it was. The dusty city was behind them as they trotted north through the countryside. Pale sunshine played across a lush landscape and a flock of green parakeets flew squawking overhead, causing Nicholas's horse to skitter sideways.

'Ah! So many discoveries and self-revelations in so few weeks!' Ross sounded more than a little amused. 'Let's pause under that banyan tree for a few moments. Then it's time for a gallop!' As they reined in beneath the tree, he turned to his steward who was already holding out a water bottle. 'Thank you, Tuhin Singh. You read my mind as always.' Taking a swig, then pouring a little over his head, Harry said, 'Come on. I'll race you both to that clump of trees near those huts over there.' Then he was off, dust flying from his bay horse's hooves.

Nicholas urged on his own horse, a temperamental chestnut that had already given him a couple of painful kicks and wasn't proving worth the five guineas he'd paid for it at auction. As on previous occasions, Harry won and Tuhin Singh was second. Nicholas suspected the young Hindustani with the self-effacing smile was a better horseman than either of them – once or twice he'd detected him reining back a little so as not to overtake Harry.

As all three wiped the sweat and dust from their faces, Nicholas noticed people emerging from the palm-thatched huts, just a hundred yards away, to stand watching them. Then, as an old man in a white dhoti appeared, they surrounded him and seemed to be having some kind of discussion. After a few minutes, the old man hurried towards them. After hesitating a moment, noting Ross's scarlet uniform, the man addressed himself to Ross, speaking what Nicholas recognised as Bengali. He could even understand some of it since the old man was speaking slowly and gesturing with his hands, presumably because he was talking to a European.

He seemed to be explaining he was the village headman. His village was being terrorised by a man-eating *bagh* – a tiger. 'We have no muskets to defend ourselves against the beast,' he was saying. 'Only last night it carried off a young man – a father of six children – who had gone into the fields to bring in his two cows for the night. We have no weapons with which to kill the beast. You are an officer, Sahib. Officers have guns. Help us.'

'We will, I promise. We'll return tonight,' Harry responded without a moment's hesitation.

The headman looked from the two Europeans to Tuhin Singh, and at a slight confirmatory nod from the latter, his shoulders visibly relaxed. 'Thank you, Sahib,' he said.

'If you've been studying Bengali as hard as you say, you'll have understood most of that,' Harry said.

'I did,' Nicholas nodded.

'You'll come tonight, won't you? It'll be good sport. We'll have a full moon to see by. And if you like, you can imagine you're taking pot shots at some of your old bores, not at a tiger.'

'I'm sure some have got thicker hides than any tiger, but of course I'll be there.'

'In that case, let's meet here an hour before dusk. And don't forget your musket.'

Turning their horses, the three headed slowly back towards Calcutta. Although it was still early, the temperature was already building and a heat haze forming along the distant banks of the Hooghly. As they rode into the city, through the narrow streets where the ordinary Bengali people lived, men still lay sleeping in the open on string charpoys. A few women, the edges of their bright saris pulled down over their faces, brushed dust and leaves from their doorsteps with bundles of twigs and woke and chased away pale-furred stray dogs dozing nearby.

Nearing the barracks, they entered the broad avenues of the wealthy Europeans' quarter. Liveried servants were unlocking gates and flinging them wide open. Through one rolled a horse-drawn carriage – there weren't many in the city – carrying a bewigged grandee to an early engagement. As they passed a particularly handsome mansion with busts of Roman and

Greek heroes topping the walls enclosing its grounds, they saw approaching a gilded hearse drawn by six-plumed black horses. A funeral. At once they reined in and Nicholas and Harry doffed their hats as the hearse went slowly by followed by a long column of dark-clad mourners, many wiping sweat from their brows in the heat.

'D'you know who's being buried?' Nicholas asked in a low voice.

'I'm afraid I do. Nathaniel Worthington – a Manchester cotton merchant. He died quite suddenly – apoplexy I think,' Harry replied. 'His nephew Jack's in my regiment. He told me.'

–

The heat was ebbing as late that afternoon Nicholas set out for his rendezvous with Harry. He enjoyed this time of day most when, with the sinking of the sun, all the smells – the warm earth, the waxy frangipani flowers, incense from the temples and shrines, the smoking dung cooking fires – fused into what seemed the very essence of Hindustan. Just as Harry had told him as the *Winchester* nosed up the Hooghly, no other place on earth smelled like this. As he trotted into the village, children watched from the doorways of huts. The small boys had shaved heads so their hair would grow strong and their eyes were rimmed with kohl as protection from the evil eye – or so Harry had told him. There was no sign yet of his friend. He must have been delayed on the parade ground, Nicholas told himself. The troops always seemed to be drilling.

However, the elderly headman was waiting for him, seated on a wooden stool beneath a tree. As Nicholas approached, he stood up and other villagers gathered round. Nicholas smiled and mumbled a greeting. Then dismounting, he secured his reins to the trunk of an almost leafless tree and untied the two muskets which he'd strapped to his saddlebag. He'd bought them – both Brown Bess flintlocks – from a Calcutta gunsmith soon after his arrival as fowling pieces to go duck and pigeon shooting when the opportunity arose, which it had done only once.

Under the curious eyes of the village children, Nicholas squatted down and began priming and loading the first of the muskets, opening the pan, and pulling the hammer to half-cock. Normally he loaded it with shot but that would hardly fell a tiger. Biting off the end of a paper cartridge containing gunpowder at one end and a round lead musket ball at the other, he tipped a small amount of the powder into the pan. Next, he poured the rest of the powder down the long muzzle to be followed by the musket ball and some wadding. Finally, taking the steel ramrod, he pushed everything – wadding, musket ball and powder – down to the breech. He'd just finished priming and loading the second gun when he heard hoof beats and glanced round. In the growing gloom a horseman was approaching. It must be Harry, Nicholas thought, getting to his feet. But as the rider came closer, he saw it was Tuhin Singh.

'Where's Lieutenant Ross? Isn't he coming?'

'He is not well and asked me to come alone. Where I grew up in the hills, tigers trouble our villages too – I've often tracked them,' Tuhin Singh replied in his good if careful English.

'Which hills are you from then?' Nicholas asked, thinking that with his height, prominent cheekbones and light brown eyes he didn't look like most Bengalis.

'The kingdom of Nokila in the foothills of the Himalayas, far to the north of here... A beautiful place,' Tuhin Singh added after a pause, his voice soft with what Nicholas took for melancholic longing. But before he could ask anymore, Tuhin Singh said briskly, 'Lieutenant Ross says to tell you he wants me to bring the tiger's skin back to Calcutta so he can see what sport he missed and – in his words – so we can't exaggerate its size, even if we exaggerate our skill and bravery!'

Though Tuhin Singh spoke gravely, Nicholas saw his lips twitch as he dismounted and slung his musket and a canvas bag across his back. After conferring with the headman, who gestured towards the far side of the village near some scrub and trees bordering a field of stunted corn, Tuhin Singh turned back to Nicholas. 'Lieutenant Ross asked them to build a wooden hide in a tree. It's over there. Follow me, if you would. It's all right – the villagers will bring your muskets.'

Nicholas accompanied him to the trees and the scrub, coloured orange and pink by jungle flowers. Thank goodness Tuhin Singh seemed both happy to take charge and to know what to do, considering he had never hunted a tiger himself – something he'd keep quiet about. In fact he'd never even seen one, unless you counted that stuffed beast in the entrance hall of Government House, all snarling lips, protruding yellowing incisors and glaring glass eyes, magnificent if it weren't for the moth-eaten patches around its haunches.

In the spreading branches of the tallest tree, the villagers had positioned some sturdy wooden planks, lashed together with jute rope some 10 feet above the ground. Tuhin Singh opened his canvas bag and took out a leg of meat. Nicholas caught its acrid stink as Tuhin Singh placed it on the ground about 15 feet from the tree. 'Rotting goat,' he responded to Nicholas's quizzical look. 'If we're in luck, the smell will lure the tiger to us. But we must be patient – tigers often like to hunt just before dawn. And remember the beast has recently feasted on that villager. With its belly full it may not even come. We can only wait and watch. Anyway, let's climb up.'

Nicholas followed the lithe figure of Tuhin Singh up into the branches with his muskets across his back. Finding it a much easier climb than the *Winchester*'s rigging, he relaxed. Squatting on the platform beside Tuhin Singh he felt a pleasurable thrill of anticipation. Would the tiger come? Two hours passed and the moon rose, full, ripe and yellow... still there was nothing except the distant bark of a jackal. Then, hearing a slight rustling in the undergrowth, Nicholas grasped his musket, ready for action, only to see a small dog emerge, scratch its testicles vigorously and trot slowly off into the village.

After another couple of hours, when the villagers had long doused their cooking fires and retreated inside their huts – no one dared to sleep outside with a man-eater on the prowl – Nicholas himself began to feel drowsy. He slapped at a mosquito that had just bitten his neck and inspecting his fingers found blood. Beside him, Tuhin Singh suddenly sat up and stared intently into the moonlit undergrowth opposite the platform. Now fully awake and with his heart beating faster, Nicholas followed his gaze but could see nothing. 'What is it…?' he whispered. Tuhin Singh put his finger to his lips, rose, picked up his musket, pulled the lock to full cock and put the butt to his right shoulder.

Then Nicholas did hear something – a breathy panting sound and the cracking of a twig or two. The bushes began to shake and toss and suddenly a great striped head pushed through. Nicholas stared mesmerised as for some moments the tiger stood, eyes gleaming in the light of the full moon, looking at the meat. Then, slowly, it emerged into the open, white-tipped tail swaying as it padded on great velvety paws towards the bait, saliva dribbling in silvery threads from its half open mouth. As Tuhin Singh leant purposefully forward Nicholas remembered what they were here to do. Seizing one of his muskets he cocked it and trained it on the tiger and, a split second after Tuhin Singh, fired. The tiger slumped, blood welling darkly from two wounds, one in the shoulder, another in the neck.

Tuhin Singh leapt agilely down from the platform. Nicholas followed, grasping his second musket. Tuhin Singh approached the tiger's prone body cautiously and prodded its lolling head with the end of his musket. But at that moment the bushes trembled again, and with a ferocious roar a blurred streak of orange and black hurled itself at Tuhin Singh. He leapt backwards, only to slip and tumble to the ground. A second tiger! As Tuhin Singh tried to scramble away on all fours, the beast was on him.

Instinctively, Nicholas yelled to attract the tiger's attention. As it raised its head to look at him, he levelled his second musket and fired, hitting the animal full in the chest. At first the tiger didn't react. Nicholas shouted again. Blood was beginning to leak from the tiger's mouth. Surely it must be about to collapse. Suddenly, the muscles in its shoulders bunched and it launched itself towards Nicholas. Grasping the barrel of his musket and swinging it like a club, he stood his ground. The tiger was almost on top of him when its great striped body twisted and fell to the ground to lie still at his feet, its eyes open but unseeing.

A dazed-looking Tuhin Singh was getting back on his feet, brushing earth and leaves from his once-white tunic, now torn and reddening as blood streamed from a gash in his shoulder. Tugging off his neck cloth, Nicholas bound the wound tight to staunch the blood flow, then shouted to the villagers who'd come running at the sound of musket fire to bring water.

'My fault, I should have known better,' Tuhin Singh confessed ruefully. 'In my excitement I forgot there could be a second tiger…'

'It's just lucky I brought two muskets. Anyway, Lieutenant Ross will be impressed when he sees we've not just one but two skins to show him…' Nicholas put his arm around Tuhin Singh's shoulders.

Back in his lodgings, Nicholas despatched his young Bengali houseboy with a jubilant message to Harry in the barracks and then, with the dawn light coming up, took a long soak in his tin bath. Resting the back of his head on the bath's edge as the water eased the itching, irritating mosquito bites he closed his eyes and breathed a sigh of satisfaction. Not only had he and Tuhin Singh rid the villagers of their man eaters but somehow he felt he'd undergone a rite of passage.

'Sahib!' It was his houseboy.

'Yes, what is it?' Nicholas sat up. Not a message from Government House at this early hour surely?

'A note from the barracks, Sahib.'

It must be from Harry congratulating him… Nicholas got out of the bath, wound a towel around himself and taking the note from the boy opened it. It was indeed from Harry. 'I'm sorry I missed it all. You're quite the hero, I understand. As soon as I'm feeling more the thing, I want to hear everything. Let's meet soon. I'll write again later.'

But the next note to arrive from the barracks – delivered just after noon next day – came not from Ross but from Tuhin Singh.

It told him Ross was dead, overcome by diurnal fever. Nicholas stared at the words, unable to take in their meaning. It couldn't be true... not Harry Ross! His friend had been so full of life and energy just hours ago...

–

'Why do they bury people so fast here? As if they can't wait to get the dead into the ground so they can forget about them.'

The stick-thin, silver-haired major seated by Nicholas's side in the rosewood pews of St. Anne's Church, close by the east wall of Fort William, gave him a sympathetic look. 'You're shocked. I can understand that. I used to feel exactly the same way when I lost a friend. The sad truth is that death is commonplace here – it often comes quickly, without warning. You get used to the transitory nature of existence because you must. You grow accustomed to looking forward, not backwards. God knows I've lost count of the funerals I've attended these past twenty years. The only advice I have is *carpe diem* – enjoy your life while you can. Tomorrow you may be gone like poor Harry. Most Europeans don't see out more than two monsoons before they're in the earth. But you may be one of the lucky ones – like me. And to answer your question more precisely, you must remember this is Calcutta, not Colchester. Bodies rot so fast in the heat that the sweet stench of decay becomes awful, sometimes even if you only leave them till the afternoon, and however many scented lilies you strew round the coffin.'

An hour later, Nicholas – still reluctant to grasp the reality of Ross's death, let alone that he had been buried and a farewell musket volley fired over his grave by his comrades – passed with the other mourners through the cemetery gates to the street where a line of palanquins and horse-drawn tongas waited to take the officers back to their stations. Glancing round he noticed Tuhin Singh standing across the street from the cemetery and went over to him.

The steward's face looked drawn and his eyes barely met Nicholas's as the two shook hands. 'I'm sorry, Tuhin Singh. We've both lost a friend. How is your wound now?'

'Healing well. The hakim who sewed it up complained it was hard work because tiger claws go deep but he did it well, I think.' Tuhin Singh managed a smile.

'Good. I…' Nicholas wanted to say something about Harry but couldn't find the words. Instead he said, 'I wish you well. Perhaps we'll meet again in better circumstances.' He was already turning away when he felt a hand on his arm and heard Tuhin Singh say, 'Don't go yet. I have something to ask.'

'What is it?' Nicholas looked at Tuhin Singh who lowered his hand to his side.

'You saved me from the tiger… I owe you a debt. Take me into your household to allow me to repay it.'

Tuhin Singh's words were so unexpected that Nicholas scarcely knew what to say. Feeling more than a little embarrassed, he replied, 'I only did what any man would have done – what you would have done for me.'

'Perhaps, but where I come from, when one man gives another back his life, it creates an obligation. If Lieutenant Ross had not died I would have found another way to discharge mine to you.'

Into Nicholas's mind came the thought that the Highland clans shared a similar code of honour – how strange that places as far apart as Hindustan and Scotland should have such a bond. 'I absolve you of any burden of debt. You owe me nothing,' he said gently. 'Why not return for a while to the hills of your homeland? Don't you miss it?'

'I do, dearly, but I can never go back there. Though my father was its ruler, my mother was a concubine and from a poor family. She died giving birth to me. As long as my father lived I had his protection but five years ago, while he was crossing a high pass, his horse slipped on the ice, tumbled into a ravine and he was killed. My two half-brothers – children of my father's principal wife – made it very clear there was no place for me in Nokila, so I left the mountains for Calcutta. Wherever life takes me is my home now.'

Seeing the sadness in Tuhin Singh's eyes, Nicholas suddenly realised that in many ways their histories weren't so different. Both of them had left their homes to make their way in places and at times not of their own choosing. The thought decided him. 'If you're sure, I'd be glad if you joined me.'

Tuhin Singh nodded in what looked like satisfaction. 'If you wish, I can come today. I will collect my belongings and bring them to your lodgings.'

Nicholas nodded in turn. 'Good. I will see you later then.'

Walking away, Nicholas pondered what he had done. Though he'd acted on impulse he didn't feel any regret. He had already seen Tuhin Singh's courage and resourcefulness. He didn't know much else about the man, but his loyalty to Harry had been obvious. And it could only be good to have a companion who could help him understand some of the many things about Hindustan that still puzzled him.

–

Her breasts gleamed with sweat as she straddled him, her eyes misty with a pleasure as deep as his own. 'Remember "*sthan*" is the Bengali word for breast and "*bagh*" the word for the tiger you're becoming,' her husky voice whispered.

A soft hand was on his shoulder caressing – no, shaking – him, and Nicholas slowly emerged from what he realised with some regret was a dream. Fragments of his conversation the previous night with Tuhin Singh returned to him. They had been discussing how he could improve his Bengali, make it more colloquial, just as Tuhin Singh wished to improve his English further.

'An option you have that's not open to me,' Tuhin Singh had said, 'is to take a "sleeping dictionary" to warm your bed and be your teacher to improve your language. A number of your countrymen do this and one will be easy to find. Her father will only require you to feed her and give him a few annas a month, and the girl will be glad to avoid a life of drudgery.'

Tuhin Singh's suggestion had surprised Nicholas, even shocked him a little. He had mumbled something about considering the option and not given it further thought, but this dream... Clearly his thoughts were heading in a certain direction... However, it was not a naked woman but his houseboy who was shaking his shoulder ever more insistently. 'Sahib, Sahib, wake up! The President's steward has sent a message requesting your presence in the President's office at 6 o'clock and it's already dawn.'

Struggling into consciousness, Nicholas tried to compose himself. 'Yes, yes, I understand. I'll dress at once. Have my horse brought to the door.' Why did the President need him so early? A rebellion? The sinking of an East Indiaman? Or was the President ill? The message had come from his steward after all. Since receiving news of Harry Ross's death three months earlier, Nicholas had become somewhat wary of sudden messages and summons.

Although he didn't appear ill, Thomas Broddyll didn't look his usual cheerful self as Nicholas entered his high-ceilinged white-washed office. The papers in the mahogany trays on the carved desk behind which Broddyll was seated stirred in the draught created by the punkha sweeping back and forth above his head like a giant butterfly wing. Broddyll was twisting the lace of his left cuff with the long fingers of his right hand. He looked up at Nicholas and began speaking slowly and deliberately as if he'd carefully rehearsed his words. 'I asked you here at this hour because I've a matter of the greatest sensitivity to discuss and wanted as few people around as possible. Have you had any news from home recently, Ballantyne?'

'Nothing for several months.'

'Are you sure?' Broddyll scrutinised him for a moment. Then, resting his hands on the arms of his chair, he continued, 'You'd better sit down too. It seems this will be as much of a shock to you as it was to me. Late last evening I received extraordinary – indeed alarming – news from London by the *Trincomalee* which had come

43

up on the evening tide. Prince Charles Edward Stuart has landed on the west coast of Scotland with the intention of raising the Highland clans to help him seize the throne from King George and restore the house of Stuart as Britain's monarchs. The French – perfidious as usual – are supporting him. They even provided the frigate that brought him and his conspirators to Scotland from where, it seems, they intend to march on London. The militias of every city between Edinburgh and London have been called to arms to defend our realm. At the same time, traitors are rallying to the banner of the Stuart. The Company's directors have sent me a list of those known to have answered the Prince's call. I'm sorry to have to tell you that the name of James Ballantyne of Glenmire is on it. Of course, the news is already months old. Heaven knows what's happened since.'

Nicholas could think of nothing to say. Once, while swimming off St. Andrews, a freak wave had broken over him and for some moments he'd found himself utterly powerless. The same feeling overtook him now...

Broddyll took a breath, then continued. 'The despatch asks me to root out anyone with even the suspicion of Jacobite connections in the Company's service. The Court of Directors don't want to do anything that will cause them to lose the favour of the King and of Henry Pelham's Whig government which remains so essential to our continued success.' Broddyll's final words came out in a rush. 'I hope you will understand that the nephew of an acknowledged traitor to our country and our king can no longer continue as my aide. Some might say I should dismiss you entirely from the Company's service but I will not. Personally, I don't doubt your loyalty and I think that would be a waste. You've worked hard and diligently... already shown a natural talent for languages and become nearly fluent in Bengali.'

Broddyll paused, straightening himself in his chair. 'I've decided to send you to Madras to study the southern languages. You'll be able to translate documents for our merchants and act as an interpreter during their negotiations. If anyone challenges my action in retaining a man whose family's loyalties to the

Crown have been compromised, I can point out that in your new role you'll no longer have access to sensitive information about Company policy. You must leave as soon as possible – today if there's a ship.' He stood up abruptly and held out his hand. 'Good luck, Ballantyne.'

Nicholas also got to his feet and took the President's hand, too stunned to say more than, 'I understand.'

Nicholas walked back to his lodgings in a daze, nearly colliding with a tonga whose angry occupant shouted 'Look out, you fool, we could have killed you!' but Nicholas paid scarce attention as he went over Broddyll's words. Could the reports about his uncle be true? As far as he could recall, James had never shown much interest in the Stuart cause. Portraits of Charles Stuart, 'the young Pretender', and his father, 'the old Pretender', hung in the houses of neighbours like Cameron of Lochiel but not on the walls of Glenmire. He remembered his uncle saying that the divine right of kings on which the Stuarts based their authority to rule as they alone pleased, unfettered by the wishes of their people and parliament, had no place in the modern world. Why then would he risk everything for such a cause? The reports had to be wrong. For a moment, Nicholas's spirits rose, but only for a moment. What about the occurrences that had so puzzled him after his return from university? The unexplained visitors, some French, some Irish... His uncle's furtive meeting with Cameron, his preoccupied air, the sense of secrecy and tension, his refusal to answer Nicholas's questions and his own sudden despatch to Hindustan. It all made sense if his uncle had indeed been involved in planning the rising...

If so, what was he to do now? Return to Scotland to be by his uncle's side, though he himself had absolutely no sympathy with the anachronistic Jacobite cause? James had talked about everyone owing debts of honour. If he himself had a debt, it was to his uncle... Yet, would James welcome his return? He'd clearly gone to great lengths to keep him out of the rising. Wouldn't it be for the best to follow his own, and what was probably his uncle's, wish and remain in Hindustan? He would write to James explaining what he was doing and why, and seek his blessing. He would send the letter care of his cousin, Lucius Forbes, a Dundee merchant trading in jute and oranges, whom he could trust to get the letter to James wherever he now was.

Until a reply came – and that would take some months – he would go south to Madras, as Broddyll had asked, and wait… At least he'd be leaving Calcutta's stuffy formality behind while his new employment, especially the chance to learn further languages, would perhaps be more to his taste – and he would be reunited with Clive and Braddock after many months apart.

As he entered his lodgings, his spirits began to revive a little. 'Tuhin Singh,' he called, 'I need to ask you something…' Would his steward agree to come with him to Madras, he wondered. Somehow Nicholas didn't doubt that he would.

Part Two

Madras and Cuddalore, 1745–1747

4 – A Reunion

'Rumour had it you were destined for instant glory. What did you do wrong? Cuckold the President?' Clive asked.

'I bet you didn't,' said Braddock. 'You haven't got my gift with women, Ballantyne.'

'A gentleman never tells,' Nicholas smiled.

'Ha! All the same, I'm glad to see you, even if it's a surprise. Clive's been terrible company, constantly moping that no one in Madras seems keen to recognise his natural genius,' Braddock continued.

'Shut up Braddock,' Clive cut in, a nerve clearly touched. 'At least you'll never be disappointed in your expectations. You're an ass, you'll always be an ass and everyone knows you're an ass – you included!'

'But I'm an ass that's making money. You may snigger, but I'll have the last laugh, just you wait and see.'

Nicholas's smile broadened. He was glad to see Clive and Braddock again, and unchanged too. He'd sought them out as soon as he'd disembarked in Madras. He was fortunate, too, in that there was space for him in the same bachelors' lodgings, where his two friends were now watching him arrange his various possessions as they ribbed each other. Glancing at Tuhin Singh, standing a little to one side, Nicholas could tell he too was amused, though discreet enough to hide it. Between them, his two friends had just told Tuhin Singh as much as there was to know about them.

'We heard about Harry Ross,' Clive said, his voice grave now. 'A real shame. Diurnal fever wasn't it?'

Nicholas nodded. 'Tuhin Singh here was with him when he died. He was Harry's steward. Now he's with me.'

'In that case, welcome to Madras, the pair of you, though I'm sorry to see you've still got that violin of yours, Nicholas!' Clive grinned, putting his arm round Nicholas's shoulders. 'We'll give you time to settle in but let's dine together later. Braddock claims he's got a decent bottle of brandy that he's going to open in your honour but I'll believe it when I see it. The last one was worse than vinegar!'

In fact, the brandy was nearly as good as Braddock had promised though Braddock drank most of it himself before rising blearily to his feet, muttering something about a 'romantic assignation' and staggering off into the warm night.

'Romantic, my arse. What he means is he's going to the bazaar to find a woman. We're not allowed to bring them back here – Company rules – though he's drinking so much these days I doubt he'll be able to get value for his money. One thing I must give him, though. He's proving an astute trader, God knows how,' Clive said, stretching out his legs.

'What about you?' asked Nicholas. 'Tell me how you've been. What did Braddock mean when he said you'd been moping?'

'He's right. I have been. As you'll find out soon enough, this place is a backwater. I don't see any point in my being here. No one in the Company – least of all the desiccated old fossil I work for – seems the least bit interested in my ideas for expanding the Company's reach and scope. In fact, quite the reverse. Several of the bigwigs have made plain they'd rather I didn't have any ideas at all or if I had to have them, I'd have the decency to keep them to myself. Sometimes I feel I'm going out of my mind with boredom, slowly dying of it... At least you were posted to Calcutta where things actually happen... But tell me the truth, now. When Braddock asked why they'd sent you here, you didn't answer. He's too thick to notice. I'm not.'

'I was going to tell you, but I'm surprised you haven't already guessed. I thought you'd have heard the news by now.'

'What news?'

'That a few months ago Prince Charles Edward Stuart, the young Jacobite pretender, landed in the Highlands to rally the clans. With their help and that of the French he means to take back the throne for the Stuarts and see his father crowned in Westminster.'

Clive gave a low whistle. 'No, I didn't know. We haven't had a ship from Britain these past months. Yours was the first from Calcutta for some weeks. The last two arrivals were from Canton in China.' He paused for a moment, then went on, 'Well, well, well. There'll be some nervous faces and loose bowels in London, I bet... But there's not been a Stuart king for over fifty years. Even with the French shoving in their noses as usual, who in their right mind would support the rising? Only a few Catholics and malcontents.'

'Well, my uncle, for one. It seems he's joined the rebels – and he's neither,' Nicholas said quietly.

'Why's he done it, then?'

'I don't know... I wish I did. I've gone over and over it in my mind. I've even wondered if the report about him is a mistake but I don't think so. Before I left Scotland he was preoccupied, not at all himself. I think he sent me to Hindustan because he knew what was afoot and wanted to keep me out of it. But to answer your question, the Company doesn't want me in Calcutta anymore because I'm – what's the expression? – "tainted by association". They've no proof I'm a traitor, but as the nephew of one they don't want me around.'

'It just goes to confirm that the Company bosses are idiots, but at least they weren't stupid enough to boot you out entirely.' Clive gave Nicholas a sudden sharp look. 'But perhaps I'm the idiot and making too many assumptions. You don't support the Stuarts, do you, Nicholas? You're not that daft are you?'

'I never thought about them much till now, but no, I don't support them. They believe in absolute monarchy and would suppress Parliament and our hard-won freedoms... Their time's over. They belong in the past.'

'I'd drink to that if Braddock had left us any brandy. But you don't belong in the past. You've your future to think about and you should. What are you supposed to do here?'

'Study the local languages so I can interpret for the merchants. It was President Broddyll's idea. He believed he was doing me a favour and that I'd be grateful. I suppose I am. I need something to do while I sit things out. I've written to my uncle explaining why I've decided to stay in Hindustan and asking his blessing. I hope the letter finds him...'

'You're just going to have to be patient till you hear something further – keep your head down and play that dratted violin of yours...'

'How can you of all people say that? I've never met anyone with less patience in my life.'

'True. But then I'm not you.'

'No,' Nicholas acknowledged, 'but even so waiting is hard. It takes months to get any news out here. For all I know, the rising's already over or maybe it's succeeded and we have a new king.'

'In that case Nicholas, I shall expect you to put in a good word for me at court. Your uncle will have considerable influence and perhaps he'll be prepared to listen to my ideas,' Clive replied.

–

'*En guard!*' Clive had clearly been practising his fencing, Nicholas thought. His expression exuded both concentration and confidence. Dancing on the balls of his feet he teased Nicholas with the tip of his foil, trying to lure him into a false move. Nicholas let him think he was deceived, encouraging Clive to attack, intentionally committing little errors and then saving himself by pulling back and parrying just in time. Just as Nicholas intended, Clive's thrusts grew bolder and wilder as, abandoning all thoughts of defence, he pressed forward. Suddenly Nicholas shifted his weight onto his front foot and, extending his arm fully, feinted left, avoiding Clive's thrust. Then, swiftly twisting right, he slid the point of his foil beneath Clive's belated and clumsy attempt to parry. '*Touché!*' he exclaimed.

Breathing heavily, Clive pushed out his lower lip like a schoolboy about to complain of unfairness and rubbed a hand through his tousled, wiry hair. 'I've never seen that move before. Where did you learn it?'

'My uncle taught it to me. Even at his age he's a better swordsman than I am.'

From behind them came a voice. 'And a traitor to boot! If there's one thing I can't abide it's a Scottish traitor. And that thrusting style of yours — French, isn't it? Now why doesn't that surprise me?'

Nicholas spun round to see who the speaker was — George Braddock, face red and swaying slightly in the doorway of the panelled practise room. As Clive regularly enjoyed reminding him, Braddock was becoming far too fond of arrack, the raw local spirit that burned the throat of all but the most hardened. But even for him it was early in the day to be drinking. Perhaps he'd been celebrating pulling off another of the so-called 'astonishingly profitable' deals he loved to boast about.

Braddock came nearer, squinting at Nicholas. 'How long did you think you were going to get away with it before someone found out? Do you think we're all fools?'

'Shut up Braddock. You, at least, are a fool!' Clive said, stepping forward.

'No, let him speak. What do you mean, George?' Nicholas asked, putting down his foil and picking up a cloth to wipe the sweat from his face.

'Not a peep out of you these past weeks while we were all talking about the Stuart rebellion. You were keeping quiet about your uncle, weren't you, hoping we might not find out that the reason the Company sent you here was that they don't trust you. I had it all from Harold Chadwick when he arrived from Calcutta by the *Charlotte* today. You know him, don't you? What I'd like to know is whether your uncle's a deluded fool or just intent on English plunder as you barbarian Scots have been for centuries...'

'What my uncle's done or hasn't done — and why — is his affair and his alone. I'll not judge him and you've no right to either. And as for your stupid insults to the Scots, well...'

'Let me deal with him, Nicholas,' Clive interrupted. 'George, you've been drinking far too much. Go and sleep it off. And by the way, Nicholas told me about his uncle the day he arrived in Madras. It isn't and wasn't a secret and there's no need to carry on about it – as Nicholas says it's nobody's concern but his uncle's.'

Braddock glared at Nicholas for a moment. Then, rubbing a hand over his face, staggered off, muttering to himself.

'Someone should shove his head into a water barrel,' Nicholas said. 'I hope when he's sober he'll regret what he's said, if he even remembers it.'

'Very noble of you but don't be too sure. I've seen more of him than you have.'

'If he's looking for someone to bully then he's picked the wrong man.'

'Let's waste no more time on him,' Clive said. '*En guard* again! I want my revenge. And then you're going to teach me that tricky move.'

Towards dusk that evening Clive put his head round Nicholas's door. 'Arthur Lewis has just announced he's going home on the *Charlotte*, leaving on the evening tide the day after next. He's getting married. He's standing everyone drinks in the mess,' he said. 'Come on!'

'Why not?' Nicholas got up from his desk and, adjusting his neck cloth, joined Clive in the corridor.

There was already such a crush that they had to push their way into the teak-panelled mess hall. At a long table at the far end, beneath paintings of bewigged Presidents and sober-faced luminaries, the mess's magnificently turbaned and moustached butler directed bearers in cream-coloured tunics embroidered with the Company's coat of arms, as they took bottles of Rhenish wine from crates packed with hunks of ice from the Company's ice house and tried to open them. Wine was rarely drunk in the mess and the bearers were unused to pulling the corks.

'Rumour has it that Lewis's bride-to-be is an heiress his parents have found for him. Perhaps she's already paying his bills. I don't remember him ever buying me so much as a glass of ale before,' Clive grinned. 'But maybe she thinks herself lucky. I also heard she's a voracious widow, twice married and twice Lewis's age with even less hair on her head than he has!' He took two glasses from a silver tray held out by a bearer. 'Anyway, let's drink to him, whether in condolence or congratulation!'

As he drank, Nicholas smiled. Clive's sense of the ridiculous and his outrageous embroideries of the facts always amused him, even if he didn't feel much in the mood for jokes this evening. Braddock's words had eaten away at him all day, reviving his worries about his uncle who, for all he knew, might be wounded, a prisoner or even dead by now. These past weeks he'd tried not to think about what might be happening at home, avoiding discussions speculating on the progress of the rebellion. From what Clive had said the consensus was that the rebels had little chance and deserved little sympathy. Whenever he wasn't immersing himself in his language studies, he released his pent-up emotions and frustrations as best he could by fencing with Clive or riding with Tuhin Singh.

As Clive moved off to talk to Ewan Stokes, a recently arrived young officer of engineers he knew from Shropshire, Nicholas looked round the crowded room. Braddock was standing by Arthur Lewis, surrounded by a group of other young men. Head thrown back, Lewis was drinking from the mess's two-handled silver tankard, brought out only for special celebrations, while Braddock shouted encouragement to drain it in one. Suddenly Braddock, seeming to sense Nicholas watching him, turned his head and looked straight at him. Then he said something that caused the rest of the group also to look round at Nicholas. Even from 20 feet away, Nicholas sensed their curiosity, their hostility. He watched as Braddock began elbowing his way through the crowd towards him, wine spilling from his glass as he approached, several others, including Arthur Lewis, following right behind.

'You've got a nerve showing up here, Ballantyne.' Braddock's face was redder and his words even more slurred than earlier.

'Why shouldn't I be here? Arthur invited all of us.'

'He didn't invite traitors, did you Lewis?' Swaying unsteadily, Braddock jabbed his host in the stomach with a gold-tinged finger.

Lewis, a quiet, self-effacing man, looked awkward and embarrassed. He put a hand on Braddock's shoulder and said, 'This is meant to be a celebration. Let's leave any arguments till tomorrow. And Nicholas is right. He's my guest.'

'You wouldn't say that if you knew what I knew!' Braddock muttered. 'This Jacobite bastard wants to destroy you, me, all of us, and everything we hold dear – everything my great-uncle fought and died for at the Boyne under King William. For all we know Ballantyne's a bloody French spy.'

'Braddock, you're talking rubbish. And Arthur's right. This is neither the time nor the place. We'll talk tomorrow.' Nicholas forced himself to speak quietly, hoping Braddock would take a cue from him and calm down.

But Braddock was having none of it. 'Don't tell me what to do. I'll decide when and where to speak and I say this: Now is the time and here is the place! I want everyone to know you're a Highland traitor, so don't you try to shut me up!' Braddock was shouting so loudly now that, raucous and noisy though the rest of the room was, people were turning to see the cause of the commotion. Several guests even came in from the veranda, where they'd gone to smoke their cigars and hookahs.

'I'd thought he'd have calmed down by now!' Nicholas turned to find Clive behind him.

'He's drunk as a lord still,' Nicholas said in a low voice. 'For his sake I'm trying to convince myself he doesn't know what he's saying.'

'He'd enjoy being compared to a lord,' Clive muttered, but Nicholas's whole attention was concentrated on the swaying Braddock who, fumbling in his pocket, pulled out a folded newspaper and shook it open. 'Listen all of you. This'll prove the truth of what I'm saying. While Arthur is letting Ballantyne down his hock, his flea-ridden Highland relations and their fellows

56

are probably already in London dancing around King George's head which they've stuck on a spike in Whitehall or queuing to lick the Stuart's reeking arse. I can almost hear Ballantyne's uncle beseeching, "Let me be the first to insert my tongue, Your Majesty,"' Braddock said in a woeful attempt at a Scottish accent.

Unable to restrain himself any longer, Nicholas stepped towards Braddock, fists clenched but Clive's hand was firmly on his shoulder as he said, 'Stop this at once. You've no more information about what's been happening at home than the rest of us, Braddock.'

'You're wrong there. Look what Chadwick's lent me! It's from London. He brought it with him from Calcutta. It's called *The True Patriot* and there was never a truer title.' Ignoring Clive he flourished the newspaper in Nicholas's face just long enough for him to read the title — printed in bold black letters — and beneath it a name, Henry Fielding.

'Look,' Braddock was bellowing. 'It's dated August 1745 — just after the rising began. And here's what this man Fielding has to say.' With the rest of the room now entirely silent, Braddock began to read aloud, wet-lipped, and sometimes stumbling over or having to repeat a word, but with vehemence and passion.

'Londoners sleeping in your g... g... goose down beds, wake up! You do not know the per... rril you and your loved ones are in. You believe in the rule of law. You believe in progress. You believe in civilisation. You believe in the Protestant faith. You b... b... believe in the peace and pros... prr... prosperity we enjoy under our lawful ruler King George. Yet all these things that every English man, woman and child holds dear may soon be taken from you by invading hordes.

'A de... degen... degenerate' — Braddock could hardly get the word out — 'prince of a de... generate line has landed on our shores. Even as you read these words, he is gathering a b... b... barbarian army to march south into England to attack our cities and our citizens. Fathers and mothers conceal your children — the Highlander likes nothing better than to f... f... feast on young human flesh! Hide your daughters if you do not wish to see them ravished before your eyes. Hide your sheep as well for if they cannot find women, they will not hesitate to sate their uncontrollable lusts on your livestock.

'And as if that was not enough, our enemies have allied themselves with our ancestral foe from across the English Channel – the French, envious of our gr... gr... growing empire and always ready to plot our downfall. With their armies will come Catholic priests and red-hatted cardinals – gloating agents of the infamous Inquisition – to eradicate our faith. If they have their way the fires of Smithfield will blaze again with Protestant martyrs. Do I exaggerate? No! In recent weeks, f... f... foreign ships have been wrecked off our coast. B... b... barrels have been discovered washed up on our shores. What was found within? Catholic tracts and rosary beads... Everything we hold dear – our very lives perhaps – may be taken from us if we do not rouse ourselves from our torpor... r... and act! Eng... Eng... Englishmen awake!'

As Braddock finished he fixed his bloodshot gaze on Nicholas. 'So what have you to say to that, Ballantyne?'

'Only to warn you not to push me further.'

'You've no defence, have you, because it's all true. And I expect you can hardly wait for your uncle and his stinking cronies to have their way. And here you are, skulking in Hindustan till the time you can go home and share in the loot... You haven't even got the guts to take part in the rising!' He pushed his round, flushed and sweat-drenched face into Nicholas's.

'Braddock! For God's sake man what's got into you?' Clive began but before he could say any more, Nicholas had broken free of his grasp and landed Braddock a crunching blow on the point of his chin which sent him flying backwards to strike his head on the polished wooden floorboards. 'Get on your feet and fight me like a man. I've had enough of your bile, you ignorant sack of shit.'

All eyes were on Braddock as he sat up, rubbing his jaw. There was a gasp as he said 'I'll fight you all right, but not here. You've insulted my honour and, to a member of a f... f... family such as mine, honour is everything. I ch... ch... challenge you to a duel.'

'I'm more than willing to meet you anytime, anywhere,' Nicholas replied. 'That is if you're man enough to go through with it when you've sobered up.'

The next morning, mounting their horses in the pale pre-sunrise light, Nicholas and Clive rode swiftly through the almost deserted streets of Madras towards the shore. Nicholas was concealing, away from prying eyes, the box containing the silver mounted pistols his uncle had given him on the eve of his departure from Glenmire. The Company strictly prohibited duelling.

'Disease kills enough of their employees, without letting them fight amongst themselves,' Clive, who had readily agreed to be Nicholas's second, had said when he reappeared in Nicholas's room just before midnight. He had told him Braddock wanted the duel to go ahead that very morning with pistols as the weapon. Clive had agreed with Braddock's second the meeting place on the shore.

'I wondered if he would back out,' Nicholas had said. 'How could he?' Clive had replied. 'Your quarrel was so public he knows he'd be a laughing stock if he bottled out...' Though he had tried, Nicholas hadn't been able sleep and he'd been glad to hear the tap on his door and Clive's whispered, 'Come on, time to go.'

Passing Fort St. George and leaving Madras behind, they rode briskly along a broad white sand beach to the agreed meeting place near a long-abandoned Hindu temple. As they dismounted and entered the temple precincts, a troop of monkeys, interrupted in the business of stripping a lone mango tree of its lush yellow fruit, dropped to the ground and scampered off, tails erect. Sitting on a pile of tumbled stones near a carving of Nandi, the bull venerated by the temple's worshippers, on which someone had placed a wreath of marigolds, Nicholas unlocked and opened the case containing the two pistols, thought for a moment then selected the one that always seemed to feel better balanced in his hand. It had an eight-inch steel barrel, engraved with the gunsmith's name, David McKenzie, Dundee, and a heart-shaped walnut butt that gleamed.

'Let me see it.' Clive flicked open the well-oiled flintlock firing mechanism, then raising his arm and pointing the pistol, squinted down its barrel. 'Impressive.' He handed it back to Nicholas who began to load it. 'You seem pretty cool about all this. Have you fought a duel before?'

Nicholas shrugged as he primed the pan, rammed black powder and a lead ball down the muzzle with the horn-capped ramrod and set the pistol to half-cock so it couldn't go off by mistake. 'Appearances can deceive and, no, of course I haven't fought a duel before. But I'm a good shot. Braddock's the one who should be worried. After all, he's hardly had time to sober up.' Nicholas took a swig from his water bottle then pulled out his pocket watch. He'd told Clive it was his if he died, an offer Clive had laughed away. Still twenty minutes to go to the agreed time. Clive, as often, read his mind. 'He'll be here, on time or before. Like you, he'll want to get it over with.'

Clive was right. Within five minutes, Nicholas caught the sound of muffled hoof beats in the sand as Braddock and his second, an angular, ginger-haired merchant called Andrew Andrews, rode up. Braddock dismounted, his normally red face beneath his butter-blonde hair decidedly pale. He nodded to Clive, glanced briefly at Nicholas without meeting his eye, then said, 'Well, let's get on with it.'

Nicholas and Braddock stood aside some yards apart, both staring fixedly out to sea, while their seconds observed the etiquette of confirming that the other side's weapon was acceptable.

Then Clive, speaking with unusual formality, advanced to Nicholas and Braddock and said, 'The duel you are about to fight may have fatal consequences. As your seconds it's our duty to try to avert it.' Turning to Braddock he continued, 'You are the one who has asked for satisfaction. Do you still insist upon it?'

After a moment's hesitation, voice quivering slightly, Braddock said, 'I do.'

'In that case, Andrews and I will now mark the two points where each of you must stand.' Drawing his sword Clive stuck it into the ground. Then advancing with Andrews across the flat ground, he counted out twenty-five paces at the end of which Andrews too stuck his sword into the sand. Then, Clive said, 'Gentleman, take up your weapons. Braddock – you have the right to decide which position you prefer.'

George Braddock thought for a moment then walked across to where Andrews' sword was still swaying and where he would have the light of the morning sun behind him. As Nicholas took up his own place and handed Clive his jacket, he could feel the increasingly rapid beating of his heart. In a minute or two, for better or for worse, the duel – and perhaps his life – would be over.

Andrews took a large white handkerchief from his pocket and shook it out. 'The moment I drop this to the ground will be your signal to fire. Any questions?' Nicholas and Braddock shook their heads. 'In that case gentlemen, I wish you good luck!' Andrews stepped back, well out of the line of fire.

Standing sideways to make their bodies the smallest possible target, Nicholas and Braddock raised their pistols. A breeze blowing off the sea was making the handkerchief in Andrews's hand dance like a living thing. Come on, Nicholas thought, squinting into the sun, every nerve, every muscle tensed. Come on, drop the thing! What was Andrews waiting for? Then he heard a loud report, something hot nicked his cheek and he caught the acrid smell of powder.

'Braddock, you coward! Andrews hadn't given the signal to fire!' Clive shouted as Nicholas touched his face. Nothing. Just a scratch…

'Ballantyne, according to the rules you may now fire at will,' Andrews said hoarsely, his expression as shocked as Clive's.

George Braddock dropped his arm to his side and, with his smoking pistol still dangling from his hand, just stood where he was. As he saw Nicholas raise his right arm, he started to shake and sweat came running off him. Even so, he continued to stand his ground as Nicholas raised his arm a little further, again narrowing his eyes against the rising sun, and prepared to fire. He squeezed the trigger and heard the sharp report. Braddock slumped to the ground. Andrews ran over and dropped to his knees before his sprawled figure.

'Save yourself the trouble,' Clive said contemptuously. 'He's not hurt. He's just fainted from fear. Nicholas deliberately fired over his stupid head. Any fool could see that.'

Turning away without a backward glance at his former friend Nicholas called out, 'Never forget you owe your life to a "Highland savage", Braddock!'

As he replaced his pistol in its case, he felt Clive's arm around his shoulders. 'That was generous of you. I only hope it wasn't a mistake. Debts of gratitude don't always sit well with the likes of him.'

'Maybe so. Last night my blood was hot. But this morning it had cooled. There was no way I was going to yield but I didn't want his blood on my conscience. Probably better for both of us if he lives as a known coward than dies a martyr to a hard-hearted Jacobite "traitor".'

5 – The Letter

Seated at the back of the mess hall in the late afternoon, Nicholas frowned as he studied the hand-written passage in Tamil, the principal language of Madras, that his tutor, Ramesh Ramachandran, had asked him to translate. Until the Company had employed him to teach its employees, Ramachandran had been a munshi in the bazaar, waiting cross-legged beneath an awning to write or read letters for the illiterate.

With Ramachandran as his guide, Nicholas often walked through the narrow alleys of the bazaar past pyramids of brightly coloured spices, herbs fresh from the fields, garlands of white jasmine and orange marigolds for worshippers to take to the temples, glittering gold-painted glass bangles and bales of the calico cloth that George Braddock claimed to be making such large profits from buying. He and Ramachandran sometimes squatted on their haunches to eat fried samosas stuffed with spiced potatoes and peas or idli – steamed cakes made from fermented rice powder – that they dipped into sambhar, a spicy lentil and vegetable preparation flavoured with tart-tasting tamarinds. Clive had warned him more than once that if he continued to eat in the bazaar he'd soon be dead but he loved the tongue-tingling flavours.

Tuhin Singh, a stranger like himself to Madras and the ways of the south, sometimes came with them. Having discovered how few people spoke Bengali or any other language he understood, he too was learning Tamil, often complaining about how different it was from anything he knew and how difficult it was to learn yet another script.

Nicholas himself liked the graceful swirling Tamil script. Ramesh Ramachandran had explained that because it was originally written on palm leaves, curved strokes had been used to avoid ripping the leaves. It had thirty-one symbols – each representing a syllable and combining into compounds – which took concentration and a good memory to learn. If he was translating it correctly, the text before him was a love poem. 'Your lips are red like...' What was that next word? Yes, 'rubies'. 'Your eyes shine like diamonds...' 'Your breasts are round and firm like pomegranates...'

This must be his tutor's idea of a joke, Nicholas thought. Only yesterday, a half-smile on his face, he'd asked if Nicholas had a woman. Or perhaps he just thought Nicholas needed a change from passages about battles between the Vijayanagara dynasty that once ruled Madras or the exploits of the bewildering panoply of Hindu gods and legendary heroes.

'Your lime juice and water, Sahib.' Nicholas took the glass from the bearer and continued trying to make sense of the words in front of him but rapidly approaching footsteps distracted him. He looked up to see Clive's friend Ewan Stokes in the doorway. 'The *Queen Anne* from London's mooring. Some of her passengers will be here in a moment. Now we'll get some news from home...!' Those who'd been reading put down their books and papers and the billiard players laid down their cues as everyone started talking at once. An East Indiaman direct from home hadn't reached Madras for some time. As more men piled into the mess, Nicholas remained quietly where he was. Since his duel with George Braddock, he'd sensed people were careful not to talk about the rebellion in front of him, never mind speculate about its outcome.

As the first arrivals off the *Queen Anne* – a portly man with well-polished boots sporting a red brocade waistcoat and a younger more plainly dressed companion – came in, Nicholas saw Clive and Braddock among those crowding behind them. Without more ado, Ewan Stokes said, 'Forgive us mobbing you like this, but we've had little news from England for some time.

What's happening there? What can you tell us about the Jacobite rebellion?'

'The rebellion?' the elder man looked surprised. 'It's over. When we sailed, Charles Edward Stuart was on the run and the first executions of rebels were taking place.'

Nicholas saw a triumphant smile on Braddock's face as Stokes said, 'Please, tell us more, Mr...?'

'Weeks, Josiah Weeks – I'm a cloth merchant. This is my nephew, Samuel. I'll tell you what I know... The Prince brought his rebel army over the Esk River and advanced south into England, brushing the English armies aside. They say that in London the wealthy citizens were loading their jewels and silver plate onto barges, ready to flee – even that King George's yacht was kept constantly manned and ready to carry him down the Thames and back to Hanover. I do know that the London militia was mustered to defend the capital but, of course, it never came to that...' Weeks paused to accept a tankard of ale from a bearer and take a long drink. 'Ah, best I've tasted in months! To my mind beer doesn't keep well aboard ship. Anyway, where was I? Derby was where it all went wrong for the Prince. After his army had occupied the city, the Highland chiefs told him they would go no further. Why so, you may ask, with London only 120 miles away?' Weeks surveyed the room, clearly relishing his rapt audience. 'Well, the reasons were these. The Prince had promised that King Louis would send French troops to help him but none appeared. The Frenchies had broken their word – well, what else would you expect of them? The Prince had also promised that the English would rise for him – that his journey to London would be a triumphal procession, not a campaign. That didn't happen either. To give you an example, when the Jacobites marched into my own town of Manchester, most of us barred our doors. Only three hundred men – unemployed riff-raff mostly – volunteered to march with the Prince.

'When the Highland chiefs refused to continue, they say the prince ranted and raved like a mad man. He even banged his pretty head against the wall but the chiefs wouldn't relent. So he had no option but to retreat back over the Scottish border. The Duke of Cumberland – England's hero, God bless him – followed the Prince and finally brought him to battle at Culloden, near Inverness. His troops cut the rebels down in their hundreds as the brave fools, hopelessly outnumbered, made a final charge on foot against Cumberland's cannon. The Prince fled into the heather but I'm betting they'll catch him. His head and his shoulders may well have parted company by now and I for one will drink to that!' As a cheer went up around the mess, Weeks raised his tankard again and drained it.

'And I'll drink to it too and toast King George!' shouted Braddock.

As the mess hall erupted in celebration, Nicholas stayed where he was at the back of the room. After a few minutes, Clive made his way towards him. 'I'm sorry, Nicholas. This must be hard for you, but for all you know your uncle may well be alive.'

'Who knows?' Nicholas said getting to his feet. 'I'm going down to the harbour to see if they've landed the post off the *Queen Anne*. There might be a letter from my cousin in Dundee. I told him I was coming to Madras.' Before Clive could say anything further, Nicholas hurried out, leaving his Tamil translation forgotten on the table.

Ten minutes' swift walking brought him to the waterfront where the *Queen Anne*, a handsome three master, was moored a few hundred yards offshore. In the rigging, seamen were furling her sails while others laboured to swing nets full of cargo over the side to be lowered into rowing boats waiting below. More and more passengers were coming ashore, some walking a little unsteadily at the unfamiliar feel of firm ground beneath their feet. Porters, ragged cloths wound round their heads, were besieging them for custom. Seeing a ship's officer, Nicholas edged through the crowd towards him and called out, 'Is the mail landed yet?'

'You're not the first to ask me that. We've several sacks of it – loaded in London and at the Cape – but the purser still has them aboard.' His attention claimed by an elderly man in a tight-curled wig complaining that he couldn't find his valise, the officer turned away. Seeing the crew of a boat that had just landed some passengers about to cast off again, Nicholas ran over to it. 'Take me out to the *Queen Anne* with you, if you would. I have business with the purser.'

At a nod from the sailor in charge, Nicholas climbed into the boat and seated himself in the bows. The sailors had to row hard against the tide and surf and it took them over a quarter of an hour to reach the ship. Standing up in the rocking boat, Nicholas grabbed the rope ladder dangling over the *Queen Anne*'s side and scrambled aboard. Cargo cluttered the main deck – barrels of wine, bales of woollen cloth, even a case marked 'Medical Instruments'. Two greyhounds gazed soulfully through the struts of a wooden crate into which they'd been placed ready to go ashore. A tall, weary-looking officer called to Nicholas, 'Are you the Company agent? Have you brought the customs documents? You've kept us waiting long enough...'

'No, I'm not the agent, but I need to see the purser urgently.'

The officer's face fell as he said, 'You'll find him at his paperwork in the great cabin,' and pointed to a companionway at the stern. Nicholas hurried inside, knocking his head against a swaying oil lamp before his eyes adjusted to the gloom. The door to the great cabin was open. A young man of about Nicholas's age was sorting with ink-stained fingers through a pile of papers.

As he looked up, Nicholas said 'Do you have the mail from London? I need to see if there's a letter for me.'

A frown of irritation creased the purser's forehead. 'A lot of people in Madras want their letters. The post will be ashore by tomorrow when all the documents have been signed. You must wait like everyone else.' He returned to sifting his papers.

'Please... It's important. I've a relation I'm concerned about. It's months since I've had news of him.'

The purser raised his head again and this time looked at Nicholas with more interest. 'You sound Scottish, like me. What's your name?'

'Ballantyne.'

The purser's expression softened. 'The private mail's in that jute sack in the corner. Go on, take a look.'

Nicholas hurried over. Opening the sack's neck, he tipped the contents onto the cabin floor and began searching. There were letters for Clive and for others he knew, Braddock included, but seemingly nothing for him. Then he saw it, almost at the bottom of the heap – a square envelope addressed to him care of the East India Company, Madras. Thrusting it into his pocket, he piled the rest of the letters back into the sack.

'So you found what you wanted,' said the purser who'd been watching him.

'I think so.'

'My name's Murray. I'm from Perth and I think I understand your anxiety. I hope your letter brings you good news.'

Out on deck again, Nicholas sat on an upturned barrel and oblivious to the bustle around him, took out the letter, opened it and began reading.

My dear cousin,

I received your letter from Hindustan and sent it on to Edinburgh where, as I'd heard, your uncle was with the Prince. By the time you read this you may already know that the rebellion is over. Government forces under the Duke of Cumberland routed the rebels at Culloden. The Prince's whereabouts are unknown, but there is a reward on his head. Some say he is hiding in the islands, others that the French sent a frigate to rescue him and he is already safe on French soil.

As for your uncle, I wish I could give you firm news but, despite many enquiries, I cannot. It's said he was with the Prince at Culloden. His name was not among the dead but whether he has fled with the Stuart or made his own escape I cannot say. But sadly I do have news of Glenmire. Government troops have seized the house, cut down the avenue of lime trees and driven the estate workers from their homes. The papers have published lists of those estates declared forfeit because their owners committed treason. Glenmire is among them. It is now in the hands of Fergus Campbell who fought with the Duke of Cumberland at Culloden.

This news will grieve you but the Government is not in a forgiving mood. It is taking reprisals against anyone suspected of supporting the Prince. In the Highlands, villages have been destroyed. The poor clansmen – their wives and children – have been driven out to starve in the heather; their cattle seized and their crops burned. English soldiers are hunting down Jacobite fugitives in the glens. It must be said that Cumberland and his soldiers deserve his nickname of 'Butcher'. Some of the rebels have already been executed, condemned to the traitor's death by hanging drawing and quartering though some, because of their great rank, received a more merciful death. Some rebels are to be transported to our American colonies.

It's a sorry state of affairs. That vain, callow foreign wastrel of a Stuart should never have come to Scotland and asked others to risk their all to satisfy his vainglorious ambitions. We've no love for the Stuarts in Dundee. Most of us here – myself included – feel only relief that such an ill-judged rebellion failed. The Stuarts would have ruined Scotland's prosperity, which relies so much these days on our trade with our English neighbours.

But I am sorry for James. Whatever he did, it's hard to lose everything at one stroke. I know how much he loved Glenmire and cared for those on his estate. But what possessed him to risk himself – and them – in such a cause? All he has achieved is to plunge our family name into ignominy. I only hope it will not affect my own trading ventures.

I will write again if I learn more.

In the meantime, I remain your affectionate cousin,
Lucius Forbes

That evening, alone in his room, Nicholas opened a bottle of Madeira and took a long pull. Had his uncle always suspected the rising would fail? Looking back, in those last weeks at Glenmire despite all the bustle and the comings and goings there'd been a quiet melancholy about him. Where was James now? Would he himself ever again see the only member of his family with whom he had a close bond? Not since he'd learned of his parents' drowning had he felt such an emptiness.

He re-read the letter. The final paragraphs showed Lucius as the merchant he was, selfishly concerned only with the profits from his oranges and jute... For a moment Nicholas felt a sudden surge of anger, but it ebbed just as quickly as it arose. He was being unfair. Lucius was just being honest, and weren't his own feelings about the rebellion in general much the same? Nicholas took another swallow of the Madeira. If what Lucius had written about reprisals in the Highlands was true, the government was committing murder. The chiefs had raised their clans for the Prince because – like his uncle – they'd believed it was their duty and they owed a debt of honour. But the chiefs had at least had a choice. What choice had the ordinary clansmen had? None but to obey the call of their laird as they'd done through the centuries. And what a price all of them – high or low, his uncle included – were paying for their loyalty to the Stuart cause, while – just as George Braddock had said – he himself was safe here in Hindustan.

But what could he, should he, do now? Stop being a cog in the Company machine? Why was he helping to make profits for its directors in London who probably thought of Highlanders – as Braddock did – as less than human and were happy to see the government use its share of Company profits to fund their repression. Yes, he'd resign. There were other ways to see the world. He could go to sea in the China trade like his father. Though he'd no experience of sailing, he was a quick learner. On the *Winchester* he'd observed how the seamen handled the sheets, adjusting the amount of sail to the force of the winds, and an officer had taught him the rudiments of using a sextant.

It was nearly eleven by the time Nicholas sat down at his desk and dipping his quill in his brass inkpot began to write, his hand less steady than usual thanks to the Madeira: 'I, Nicholas Ballantyne, hereby tender my resignation to the East India Company because...'

There was a tap on the door and, without waiting for Nicholas to call out for him to enter, Clive strode in. 'You know what a night owl I am. When I saw candlelight beneath the door I knew you were still up.' Nicholas saw him glance at the nearly empty Madeira bottle on the desk. 'I'd have dropped in on you sooner but a whole group of us were called to the office – some problem with the *Queen Anne*'s lading bills. It looked like they'd lost a dozen barrels of cheese and some cases of claret for President Morse... You'd have thought they'd mislaid the crown jewels. Did you find a letter for you when you went down to the ship?'

Nicholas nodded. 'Here.' He passed it to Clive who, after reading it, handed it back, saying, 'Who are you writing to? Your cousin?'

'No. I'm resigning from the Company. By this time tomorrow, I'll be gone from Madras. Tuhin Singh too – if he wants to come with me...'

'But where will you go? You can't just run away...'

Nicholas's head was starting to ache. 'I'm not running away but I'm sick of the Company and the Braddocks of this world and everything they stand for. There's no point my going home to Scotland – I no longer have a home there – but neither is there any point in my staying here...'

'When the effect of that almost empty bottle of Madeira beside you has worn off you'll see things differently. I won't let you make such a fool of yourself,' Clive said. Before Nicholas could stop him, he grabbed the half-written piece of paper off the desk, ripped it up and sent the pieces fluttering in the air. 'Think man!' he went on. 'If you leave the Company what future will you have? Where will you go? What will you do? And what will your resignation achieve? It will be nothing but an empty gesture.'

When Nicholas didn't reply, Clive persisted. 'Wandering about in the wilderness like that fellow Ulysses you're always talking about... Being alone outside society wouldn't be heroic, wouldn't alter anything. The only way you can change things is from the inside. Develop a thicker skin and stick it out. It'll be worth it in the end. If you leave, George Braddock will say he was right about you all along – that your loyalty was suspect and so in future should be that of any Scot he happens to dislike or envy. Is that what you really want?'

'Perhaps my loyalty is suspect. Why should I serve the Company when it serves a government that's savaging my people?' Nicholas said at last.

'A government backlash against the Highlands is inevitable. What did you expect? After all, the Jacobites were not only trying to seize the throne but inciting France, our greatest enemy, to invade Britain on their behalf. But the reprisals won't last. And you can't condemn the entire Company out of hand. Isn't each director, each employee, capable of thinking and acting for himself? And think of all the Scots who work for the Company. Yes, of course, they'll be keeping their heads down just now, but they'll hardly be eager to repress their own compatriots!'

Clive paused for a moment, then continued, 'Don't look at me like that. I'm no Braddock. I'm only thinking about you when I tell you that if you resign the only person you'll be damaging is yourself. Braddock would love it, of course. But, much more importantly, imagine what your uncle would say... You've told me how anxious he was to keep you out of the rebellion, how he strove to get you into the Company. If he's still alive – as he probably is – imagine how he'll feel to discover everything he's done for you was for nothing.'

Nicholas sighed, suddenly feeling exhausted. 'You've had your say, Clive. Now please leave me alone,' he said quietly.

'I'm not leaving. You know what an insomniac I am. I'm going to stay here till morning to make sure you don't write any more stupid letters. Tomorrow, when you're sober, if running away is what you still want to do, then on your own – probably aching – head be it.'

All Nicholas wanted to do was sleep, but Clive wasn't finished. Gripping Nicholas by the shoulders he said, 'You can do well, but only if you stop being sorry for yourself – and so proud that you think manipulating the Company for your own ends is beneath your oh-so-elevated principles. You need to be more like me – determined above all to succeed – letting nothing and nobody stand in your way – using the Company as a means to your ends instead of letting it rule you and accepting its valuation of you. Then, once you're wealthy and powerful enough, you can put the world to rights any way you want!'

Something of Clive's logic resonated in Nicholas's mind. Perhaps Clive was right. Maybe resigning wasn't the noble gesture he'd thought it to be. Perhaps it took greater courage to face the world as it was than to reject it for its shortcomings. 'All right, I promise not to write any letters of resignation, but only if you leave me in peace to sleep… Please…'

Clive smiled. Any triumph, however small, gratified him immensely, Nicholas thought.

–

'Are you sure you heard right?' Nicholas asked, as a few days later he, Clive and Tuhin Singh rode their horses into the shallows of a small stream running down to the sea to let them drink.

Clive nodded. 'Absolutely certain. President Morse's door was open and I caught every word. The President certainly believed it – he was god-damning – calling the French every name he could think of.'

'Who brought the news?'

'One of our most reliable agents, apparently. And he wasn't just reporting bazaar gossip. He'd been in the French settlement down the coast at Pondicherry this past month and noted the French transports and warships coming and going from Mauritius – their names, size, number of guns – the quantity of troops and type of cannon being disembarked. From everything he saw – the drilling, the artillery practice on the parade ground in Pondicherry, – he's convinced it's only a matter of time before they attack us here. After all, we're only 100 miles north up the coast from them – a plump sitting duck.'

'But are they really such a threat? Surely we could hole up in Fort St. George until reinforcements came from Calcutta?' Nicholas said.

'Only if we have time to lay in supplies and fortify it properly. But if what the agent says is right, we haven't.'

'Why should the French want to attack the British in Hindustan?' Tuhin Singh looked puzzled. 'They have their own settlements here to trade from. Why would they risk disrupting their own commerce by fighting the Company?'

'Because they're hungry for land and trade and don't want competition. They're already at war with Britain in other parts of the world, like North America,' Clive replied. 'They'll reckon that if they stir up enough trouble we'll divert troops from elsewhere to Hindustan which will only be to their benefit. Alternatively, if we don't, they can just walk in and take over our trading stations and procure for themselves a virtual monopoly of the trade with Hindustan. After all, the Portuguese in Goa are a spent force and the Dutch in Chinsurah are insignificant. Ever since I arrived in Madras I've thought the Company directors were too complacent – spending their days hunched over their ledgers, gleefully counting their profits instead of thinking about how to expand our influence or even to defend ourselves against those with grander ambitions. Not that anyone senior would listen to me, of course.'

'So you're always claiming,' Nicholas replied. 'But as Tuhin Singh says, the French would be taking a risk. Maybe you're being too pessimistic.'

'That's what the Trojans kept telling Cassandra when she predicted the fall of Troy. And we all know what happened next... Anyway,' Clive's tone lightened, 'I've also heard the French have a secret weapon.'

'What's that?' Turning his horse, Nicholas rode up onto the bank. Sliding down from the saddle and holding his reins in one hand he squatted at the water's edge to splash cool water on the back of his neck.

'Not so much a "that" but a "who"' – Clive smirked – 'the wife of the French Governor-General in India, Marquis Dupleix. Her name's Jeanne but they call her *la voluptueuse*. She's said – with her husband's full knowledge – to be deploying her charms to seduce Hindustani rulers to support the French. I even heard she had herself wrapped up in a Persian carpet and smuggled into the Raja of Tanjore's command tent naked except for a few diamonds and pearls adorning her body.'

Nicholas burst out laughing. 'Somebody's been reading too much of Shakespeare's *Antony and Cleopatra*!'

'Maybe. Or maybe it's all true and she is a modern Cleopatra or Lucretia Borgia. Wouldn't you like to find out…? French women are reputedly rather skilled in the arts of love.'

'And you've a lurid imagination, Clive. Come on, it's time to go if we want to be back in Madras before nightfall.'

With five miles still to cover, the sun was already dipping low on the western horizon when above the rhythmic pounding of the surf rolling in along the shore Nicholas heard increasing sounds behind him and glanced round to see galloping up from the south in the purpling dusk a squadron of Company light cavalry, sand spraying from their horses' hooves.

As they drew nearer, Nicholas, Clive and Tuhin Singh reined in, their mounts whinnying and skittering in excitement. Nicholas noted that the face of the leading rider – a captain, he thought – was dust-covered and his tight fitting scarlet jacket dark with sweat. 'What are you doing here? Haven't you heard?' the captain shouted as he rode up. 'President Morse sent us out on a reconnaissance and do you know what we found? Bloody French troops from Pondicherry only 40 miles from here and advancing fast on Madras. Ride with us and don't spare your horses. We've not a moment to lose.'

6 – First Blood

'You're right. All five ships that appeared at dawn have the *fleur de lys* on their sails. They must be part of Admiral de la Bourdonnais's fleet from Mauritius,' Clive collapsed the brass telescope and handed it back to Nicholas. The sun, well-risen now, beat down on them as, two days after their dash back to Madras, they stood with Tuhin Singh on the walls of one of the series of small stone watch towers that guarded the approach to Madras. With news of an imminent French attack, Company labourers had worked feverishly to erect makeshift barricades linking them to other strong points to form a defensive perimeter around the city and Fort St. George. 'It looks as though they're planning to land more troops, doesn't it? Probably on the beach near that grove of palms a mile or two beyond our defences. They'll have to use the ship's boats to get them through the surf though,' Clive said.

'Pity the surf's not pounding as high as on some days. I've seen it overturn even boats manned by experienced sailors but it'll still give them trouble,' Nicholas replied.

'What I don't understand,' Clive continued, 'is why President Morse won't deploy troops to the shoreline to confront the French as they land. A few good volleys of musketry would see them off. I said as much to one of our commanders who just waved me away saying civilians should leave such matters to those with military experience. Fat lot of benefit their military experience has been so far! The army commanders left Madras almost undefended when they ordered the 66th Foot home three months ago in case they were needed to fight in Europe or in the wars in Nova Scotia. What's more, the admirals sent the two largest ships of the line with them. Fools! If it wasn't for their mistakes they wouldn't have had to recruit the likes of us into this rag-tag militia.'

A few minutes later, Tuhin Singh, who had taken the telescope from Nicholas, said quietly, 'I believe I know why the army officers don't want to deploy troops from our defences down to the shore.' He had the telescope trained on some fields of high corn about half a mile from where the French now appeared certain to attempt a landing. Several boats had already been lowered from the transports and apparently ant-sized men were swarming down ladders into them. 'The Company commanders fear an ambush and they're right. I can see lance tips just behind that corn. They must belong to the French horsemen from Pondicherry. Their commanders probably hope that even though we're outnumbered we'll send men out from our breastworks towards the landing beach so that their horsemen can ambush and massacre them on the flat open ground near the shore.'

'Are you certain? Let me look!' Clive seized the telescope and raised it to his eye. Despite the seriousness of the situation Nicholas smiled. Clive hated to be wrong. Moments later, Clive snapped the telescope shut and handed it back to Tuhin Singh. 'I think you're right. You must have damned good eyes, even with that thing!'

'He does,' said Nicholas, who found himself continually amused by how many people underestimated Tuhin Singh, most often simply because he was Hindustani. His expression grew serious again as he said, 'What are we going to do about it? Shouldn't we at least send a messenger to the nearest army commander just in case they haven't noticed?'

'I doubt even they're that stupid,' Clive said. 'But I'll go down and tell one of the Company servants assigned to us to take the message. While I'm there I'll see if there's anything else – old carts, charpoys, tree trunks, ale barrels, anything – that can be dragged up to reinforce these pitiful barricades.'

Clive's mission seemed to take him a little longer than he'd anticipated since he didn't return for nearly an hour. By then, despite one of the smaller boats being upset as it came through the surf, spilling its occupants into the foam, about two hundred blue-clad French troops had landed and were forming up on the shore in neat ranks under the command of men wearing tricorn hats and waving swords, presumably officers or sergeants.

Meanwhile, with their attempt to entice the Company's heavily outnumbered forces out from their defences to attack them by the shore having failed, the French cavalry from Pondicherry in their blue coats with white facings were emerging from the cornfields. Among them were several squadrons of more brightly clothed riders from the Hindustani allies of the French. These included, as Nicholas pointed out, some troops from the Raja of Tanjore, identifiable by their large blue banners emblazoned with silver tigers – their ruler's emblem.

Before long, several large elephants came into view through the now mostly flattened corn, the morning sun glinting on the metal plate armour shielding their heads. They had open howdahs on their backs and through the telescope Clive made out that each howdah had a small swivel cannon mounted in it, manned by three gunners. 'But I didn't see any other cannon,' he said.

'They probably couldn't haul them up sufficiently fast from Pondicherry nor land them through the surf,' Nicholas replied. 'Their absence may be Madras's saviour.'

By the time Clive, Nicholas and Tuhin, squatting on the ground at their post, had eaten a meagre lunch of flat bread, stewed lentils and bananas, it was obvious the French commanders were planning an immediate attack. Drummers had appeared at the head of the ranks of both the French and their allies. Trumpets were sounding and more banners being unfurled. Clive had succeeded the day before in persuading one of the officers to put him in command of their small watch tower. Now, throwing away the last of his bread for an ever-vigilant black crow to carry off, he quickly made a tour of the tower's few defenders – a mixture of Europeans and Hindustanis – all civilian employees of the Company, not soldiers. Nicholas could see him encouraging the nervous-looking and checking with them the loading of their muskets to ensure their ramrods had pushed the powder and ball sufficiently far down the barrel.

When Clive returned, Tuhin Singh and Nicholas were standing in the only small patch of shade they could find checking their own weapons, including the muskets which they'd used to shoot the tigers in Bengal and Nicholas's pistols. Nicholas looked up to see a broader smile on Clive's face than in a long time, his whole frame alive with the excitement he constantly craved – the epitome of the born warrior and adventurer he claimed to be. 'I've had the bearers bring up full water skins and make piles of what muskets balls and cartridges we possess where they can get them quickly to our men when they run out. I don't think there's much more we can do,' Clive said.

'Or much more time to do it in,' Nicholas responded as the elephants with the cannon began to lope forward, surrounded by a screen of cavalry. When they were within a few hundred yards of part of the outer defences about half a mile from Nicholas's position, puffs of white smoke and loud bangs indicated that the artillerymen in the howdahs had opened fire. A rattle of ragged musketry followed from the Company defences. A *fleur de lys* banner dropped from the hand of a leading French cavalryman as he was hit and fell to be trampled into the sandy earth beneath the hooves of his companions' horses. The banner wrapped itself around the legs of another horse causing it to stumble and fall, pitching its rider – a sword-flourishing officer – over its head to smash into the ground.

Several large explosions signalled that the Company's few mostly ancient cannon were coming to the defence of Madras. An artillery elephant swerved away from the attack, dislodging its mahout from behind its ears, and ran, trunk raised and trumpeting loudly, towards the position Nicholas and his companions were defending. As it came closer he saw a great gash in its belly from which its intestines were spilling. Before the animal could reach their sandstone tower, its legs gave way and it collapsed sideways, crushing its howdah and the one frightened artilleryman who had managed to cling on during its dying rampage.

The French horsemen were now sweeping along the barricades firing their pistols as they went. The remaining elephants too appeared to be moving towards Nicholas's watchtower, the gunners in the howdahs oblivious to musket fire as they struggled to swab and re-load the swivel cannon to fire at the makeshift defences. Pieces of wood from an overturned cart shattered by one of their cannon balls flew into the air. In turn, a French artilleryman, hit in the back by a musket ball, collapsed onto the side of his howdah and then, losing his balance completely, toppled headfirst from it to sprawl seemingly lifeless on the sandy ground.

Quickly, Nicholas and his two companions levelled their muskets and took careful aim at the onrushing French horsemen. Nicholas targeted not a rider but one of the leading horses, calculating that bringing it down would cause more disruption than killing a single man. Waiting until he was certain he was in range he gently squeezed the trigger. The musket fired and its butt recoiled against his right shoulder. His target – a tall white horse – collapsed in a heap of flailing legs and hooves, bringing down two others and leaving three riders in the dust. Two lay still but the third scrambled to his feet and was limping back to the French lines when he was hit in the back by another defender's ball. He flung up his arms and fell forward into the dirt. Several other men and horses were down. One rider had his foot entangled in his stirrup as he fell. His bolting, frightened horse dragged him along until he hit his head against a rock, spilling out his brains in a bloody mess, and the stirrup leather snapped.

Clive was on the parapet now, yelling defiance at the enemy and encouragement to his fellow defenders as he hastily rammed powder and ball into his musket to reload. Nicholas had already reloaded and was squinting down the barrel of his musket, picking out his next target when trumpets again sounded from several points along the enemy line. Nicholas watched as the leading ranks of blue-coated French horsemen began to rein in, then to wheel away from the Company defences, picking up speed again as they went. One or two bravely paused to pull up a wounded or dehorsed comrade behind them.

As they withdrew, pursued by musket and cannon shot until out of range, and the acrid white gunpowder smoke began to disperse, Nicolas was surprised to see how few casualties there had been among the French and their allies. The artillery elephants had suffered the worst. Three were down, as far as he could see all dead, the head of one split like a ripe watermelon by a cannon ball. The horse that Nicholas had shot, its white coat now streaked with blood and dirt, was gamely trying to stand on its three legs, its fourth hanging limp and clearly broken, only to collapse each time it did. Nicholas took careful aim at its head and, moments after he fired, it finally sank to the earth and lay still. 'What are you wasting powder for? We'll need it when they return as they surely will,' Clive demanded as Nicholas set down his musket.

'Putting the animal out of the misery I caused it,' he explained. 'But worse than me wasting powder, you nearly wasted your life! Why stand on that parapet, exposing yourself to enemy fire as recklessly as you did?'

'Caution is for cowards,' Clive responded, then seeing Nicholas bridle added, 'I don't mean that you are a coward. It's just that I don't believe I'll be killed – at least not until I've achieved my ambitions. If I am wrong, I am… Well, you only die once and I will die a hero and what happens after that, let the devil take it…'

'Whatever your reasons, sometimes you need to think before you act.'

Clive smiled. 'What makes you believe I don't? Didn't I know you could lead our men as well as I, if I fell?'

A little later, Nicholas watched the vultures beginning to cluster around the bodies on the ground below, pecking at eyes and tearing off strips of skin and flesh with their strong curved beaks and talons. A mass of blue-black flies covered the carcass of the elephant which had spilled its intestines and which was already beginning to stink in the torrid afternoon heat. Then Nicholas saw three riders – each with a large white flag of truce – ride out sedately from the French lines.

'They can't be coming to discuss terms for a withdrawal, can they?' Nicholas asked.

'Not after only one attack,' Tuhin Singh replied.

'And that wasn't even an all-out assault,' Clive said, 'more like a reconnaissance in force – they scarcely used any of their hundreds of infantry.'

A red-coated Company officer, identified through the telescope by Clive as a major he knew, rode out through a gap opened in the Company barricades and escorted the three towards Fort St. George. An hour later they re-emerged and were conducted through the barricades before riding quietly back to the French lines. There, as Tuhin Singh who now had the telescope saw, they dismounted and walked into a large, newly erected tent, clearly their commander's. Less than ten minutes later, to Nicholas's great surprise some barefoot, white-turbaned workers under the command of two or three Company sergeants began to pull away a cart and other materials from the Company barricades about a quarter of a mile away from his watchtower.

'What in God's name are they doing?' he asked. As Clive and Tuhin Singh came to his side, more workers appeared to begin dismantling other parts of the barricades. A minute or two later, Ewan Stokes rode up to the watchtower where the three men were looking on with growing disbelief. 'The President's surrendering Madras to avoid unnecessary casualties in what he says would be a fruitless battle against overwhelming numbers,' he shouted up to them, confirming their worst fears.

'God damn him as a coward to every hell known to man or devil,' Clive shouted, flinging down his musket. Nicholas could only nod in agreement as he and Tuhin Singh put down their weapons.

An hour later, under the raised muskets of a ring of French soldiers, Nicholas, Clive, Tuhin Singh and their companions came down from the watch tower to join a group of other dejected defenders of Madras.

'*Posez vos armes à terre!* Pile your weapons on the ground!' a tall, bearded French sergeant shouted.

As they laid down their swords and muskets, Nicholas congratulated himself that he'd hidden his silver-mounted pistols beneath some rubble in the watchtower. Once the prisoners had been disarmed, the French soldiers began dividing them – the British into three groups, officers, other ranks and civilians, and making a fourth group of the Hindustani soldiers. Seeing by their clothing that Nicholas and Clive weren't regular soldiers in the Company army, a young French corporal pushed them towards the civilians but when Tuhin Singh tried to join them he shouted, '*Pas toi! Va-t'en!* Not you! Be off with you!' When Tuhin Singh didn't move, the soldier looked puzzled, then shouted even louder, '*Allez!* Go!'

The French must have decided they could only cope with a certain number of prisoners, Nicholas thought, seeing other Hindustani civilians including Ewan Stokes's groom also being dismissed. 'I'd get out of here, Tuhin Singh, and quickly before they change they minds,' he said in Bengali. 'And do me a favour. Retrieve my pistols from the watchtower before anyone else finds them and keep them safe for me.'

The young soldier now had his hand on Tuhin Singh's chest and was pushing him. 'I will,' Tuhin Singh shouted as he turned and walked away. 'And I'll do whatever else I can.'

'*Mains derriere le dos!* Hands behind your backs!' soldiers were shouting to their captives, then binding their wrists loosely with rope. Once they'd finished, they formed their prisoners into a column and began to march them towards the fort. As they trudged, heads down in the heat, more and more captives joined them from other defensive positions so that by the time they entered Madras's narrow alleys, there were about eighty of them. Nicholas noticed that a sweat and dirt-streaked George Braddock was among the last to join, descending with several others from another watchtower.

The prisoners' route lay through the crowded bazaar, where Nicholas glimpsed a familiar face among the onlookers – Ramesh Ramachandran. The minute his tutor spotted him, he pushed forward to thrust a small book into Nicholas's jacket. 'I heard you were a prisoner. Some Tamil poems for you to translate to pass the time,' he said quickly before a soldier pushed him back.

Nicholas tried to turn to call out his thanks to Ramesh Ramachandran but a musket butt jabbing him in the small of his back forced him on again. Ten minutes later, the captives passed through Fort St. George's stone gatehouse into its broad courtyard, where other British prisoners – a few supported by their comrades, one using a large branch as a make-shift crutch and several with crudely bandaged wounds – were already assembled. Under the eye of a spruce young French officer, whom Nicholas heard addressed as Capitaine de Roquefeuil, soldiers began lining them up. Ignoring a soldier motioning him to stand elsewhere, Nicholas positioned himself next to Clive.

As they stood for some time sweltering beneath the hot late-afternoon sun, French troops recorded their names and positions in the Company and checked them for concealed weapons. Then, on the young officer's orders, his men began herding the prisoners towards two doors – one on either side of the courtyard – to cries of 'Vite! Vite! Quickly! Quickly!' Nicholas, Clive and about twenty others including George Braddock found themselves channelled through a door in the fort's north wall. Descending a narrow spiral staircase with his eyes only slowly adjusting to the growing gloom and his hands still tied, Nicholas struggled to keep his balance, stumbling against Clive.

At the bottom of the stairs, torches of tar-dipped rags burning in sconces illuminated a passageway lined with cells. Nicholas had only once visited the fort's dungeons when Ewan Stokes had insisted on showing him and Clive the antiquated weapons – long sharp pikes, blunderbusses, matchlock muskets from the time the fort was built – stored there. The Company hadn't used the cells for prisoners for some time.

'Vous deux, tournez vous! You two, turn round!' Nicholas and Clive faced the damp wall as soldiers cut the ropes tying their hands, then propelled them into a windowless musty-smelling cell no more than about eight feet by ten feet with just a pile of straw – presumably intended as their bedding – on the flagstone floor against the back wall. As the iron door slammed shut behind them, the only light that remained was from the torches burning in the passage filtering through the eighteen-inch square grille in the door.

'Bastards!' Clive shouted as their captors thrust the others into the remaining cells in twos. He turned to Nicholas, 'How long d'you think they'll keep us here?'

'It depends what happens elsewhere. I suppose we're valuable as bargaining chips.'

'Hostages, you mean! I told our fools of commanders our defences were too weak and our numbers too few! Why didn't they listen to me?' With a cry of frustration, Clive flung himself down on the straw.

–

'What's that?' Clive peered through the grille. 'I'm sure I heard something coming from above, from the courtyard.'

'Probably just the French drilling again,' Nicholas said.

'No. It's more than that.' Clive was listening intently now. 'I can hear horses' hooves on the cobblestones – quite a number of them. Maybe, the Company's sent an envoy to negotiate our release.'

Clive was in one of his optimistic moods, Nicholas thought. During the ten days that they'd been locked up – only allowed outside to empty their latrine buckets or for occasional exercise in the courtyard – Clive had alternated between anger at the shortcomings of his seniors, black despair when it was almost impossible to talk to him, and extravagant hopes of an early release.

But, perhaps this time, Clive was right. Something certainly seemed to be happening. Going to the grille, Nicholas too heard the clatter of hooves, but it probably meant nothing more than the arrival of fresh troops to reinforce the garrison. He looked out into the shadowy corridor to see what he could make out. In the cell opposite, George Braddock was also peering out, face drawn, his chin covered with stubble. A barber from the bazaar had only been allowed down to the cells once. For a moment their eyes met. Since their duel, Braddock had been careful to avoid Nicholas. Then, at the sound of footsteps descending from above, both looked away.

The passage grew brighter as a man – an officer by his dress and holding a lantern in his hand – came towards the cells. Someone else – a little shorter and wearing a cloak with a hood concealing the face – was behind him. A few feet from the cells, the officer – Nicholas recognised de Roquefeuil – halted to exchange words with his companion, then stood aside. The cloaked figure approached the grille of Nicholas's and Clive's cell and pushed back the hood. A woman!

Unfastening her cloak, she handed it to de Roquefeuil. Above the tight-laced bodice of her blue silk gown, the round tops of her breasts gleamed pearl-like in the half-light. Sapphires hung from her ears and around her neck. Curling auburn hair framed a face whose most striking feature was a pair of dark lashed eyes, more brilliantly blue than either her dress or her jewels. As she stepped closer – so close Nicholas could smell her perfume – those eyes looked straight into his as she said in excellent though heavily accented English, 'I am Madame Dupleix, wife of the commander of the French forces. I asked to inspect the cells so I could assure myself of the welfare of our prisoners.'

So, the noise in the courtyard had been the arrival – obviously in some style – of the famous, or rather infamous, Jeanne Dupleix, Clive's '*la voluptueuse*'. When Clive had talked about her, the idea of a French siren smuggling herself naked into the presence of princes had seemed laughable. Now – held by those bold mesmerising eyes – Nicholas wasn't so sure. She was truly voluptuous – that soft skin, those generous lips, the creamy curve of her near-bare shoulders…

'You don't speak. Do I frighten you? Is there nothing you want to ask of me?' Madame Dupleix looked amused.

She perfectly understands the effect she's having, Nicholas thought. She's planned it, she's enjoying it and she intends to exploit it. The realisation broke the spell. 'The only thing we want is our freedom,' he said shortly.

'I regret I cannot give you that. The French are not to blame – merely the fortunes of war. But I have brought you all something.' Turning to de Roquefeuil she ordered, '*Donnez moi ma corbeille.*' He handed her a basket covered with a cloth which she pulled back. The musty heavy air suddenly held the scent of ripe oranges. She was holding an orange in the palm of her hand. 'Look! I will prepare it for you to sweeten your imprisonment.' She dug gently into the peel with her long painted nails and pulled it back slowly and delicately from the soft flesh beneath. Nicholas's mouth watered. Though they were given enough to eat, their diet of bread, coarse rice and stewed vegetables with the occasional piece of scraggy chicken was as monotonous as it was unappetising. When she'd stripped off the peel, she broke the fruit into segments then held out her hand like the keeper of a menagerie about to feed a wild animal. Her smile grew wider as she reached through the grille bars. 'Give me your hand. These are for you.' She tipped the segments into Nicholas's right palm.

Then shifting her gaze to Clive, standing close behind him, she said, 'And this is for you, Monsieur, though I cannot peel a fruit for every prisoner.' Smiling, she passed him an orange through the bars. 'Were you... *blessé*... what is the word? Yes, "wounded" in the fighting?' she asked Clive, 'I see your right hand is bandaged.' Clive nodded, though, as Nicholas well knew, the wound – four days old – was the result of him slamming his hand against the wall in a moment of frustration at his situation. 'What is your regiment?' she asked. 'Was your entire regiment posted to Madras or are some of your comrades elsewhere?'

'I'm not a soldier. I'm a civilian,' Clive said shortly.

'Ah,' Jeanne Dupleix gave a little sigh. 'Nevertheless, I am sure you fought bravely. And you?' She looked again at Nicholas. 'You are also a civilian? Even so, I'm sure you too were a hero.'

'A hero to you French perhaps. To me he's a bloody Jacobite traitor,' Braddock called out. 'Ask him where he's from.'

'Shut up, Braddock!' Clive shouted, 'I thought you'd learned your lesson the last time you insulted Nicholas!'

'Where is your home, monsieur?' Madame Dupleix asked Nicholas, as if in obedience to Braddock.

'Scotland.'

'Ah!' Those blue eyes held his again. 'A Scot. From the Highlands?'

'Yes.'

'Where, may I ask?'

'A small place. You'll not have heard of it.'

'The men of the Highlands are valiant fighters, my husband says. I hope that when this sad war is over you will see your homeland again.' Then, without pausing, she continued, '*Les Ecossais sont les bons amis des Français. Je suis desolée de ne pas pouvoir vous aider, mon cher monsieur, et que votre pays souffre à cause des Anglais...*'

'Sorry. I don't speak French,' Nicholas – suspecting some kind of a trap – instinctively replied. In fact, he'd understood Madame Dupleix perfectly. She'd said, 'The Scots are good friends to the French. It grieves me that there's nothing I can do to help you, my dear sir, and that your country is suffering at the hands of the English...' But why had she said that? And why had she been interested in what regiment Clive might be in? Was she trying to extract information that might be useful to the French?

'He's lying! All Jacobites speak the lingo of England's enemy!' came a shout from the cell opposite – an emboldened Braddock again.

But Nicholas said no more as an impassive Madame Dupleix moved on to the next cell where he heard her softly quizzing Ewan Stokes about his role in the fighting and the strength of his regiment and Stokes doing his best to tell her nothing.

–

Feeling something run over his foot Nicholas kicked out. Rats often squeezed through the small rusting hole in the bottom of the door to sniff about for crumbs of bread or grains of rice dropped into the now mouldering straw of his bedding. Stretching out again, Nicholas tried to sleep. Clive moved restlessly beside him, clearly awake. Neither spoke.

The offer the French had made five days ago to free any prisoner who gave his word not to take up arms against them and to leave Madras had come as a surprise. Most – including George Braddock – had accepted. By now they'd be well on their way to Calcutta or maybe Bombay. For those who'd refused – Ewan Stokes and a handful of others, all soldiers, as well as themselves, the only civilians now left – the conditions had become a little harsher: food only once a day and no more visits to the courtyard to see daylight and feel the sun on their skin. Then, two days ago, the French had moved the soldiers elsewhere, leaving Clive and Nicholas alone on the corridor.

What was that? Not the scrabblings of some rodent this time but footsteps. Nicholas sat up. Guards had brought their food hours ago and it couldn't be far off midnight. Who'd come at this time and why? A flicker of orange light entered through the grille. 'Clive!' Nicholas whispered as he got quickly to his feet.

'What?'

'Someone's outside.'

'You're imagining it', Clive muttered, turning on his side. 'Or perhaps it's *la voluptueuse* naked and coming to seduce you.' He chuckled. But at the sound of a key being inserted into the lock he too scrambled up as the cell door swung open and a shadowy figure peered in.

'Who are you? What do you want?' Nicholas said.

The figure said nothing, but stepping forward raised his lantern to reveal a familiar face.

'Tuhin Singh!' gasped Nicholas.

'How on earth did you get into the fort?' Clive asked, equally amazed.

'No time now for explanations. Come on…' Tuhin Singh said.

Nicholas and Clive followed him swiftly from the cell, along the passage and up the winding staircase that led to the courtyard.

But at the top, instead of leading them outside, Tuhin Singh motioned them to follow him down a passageway to the left. It led past a guardroom where, through the open door, Nicholas glimpsed two soldiers slumped over a table on which were the remains of their meal and two overturned glasses. He assumed they were dead but then one let out a guttural noise somewhere between a grunt and a groan.

'Hurry up!' Tuhin Singh whispered.

As they moved swiftly on, the flickering light from Tuhin Singh's lantern casting their shadows on the stonework, all seemed reassuringly quiet – the only sound the distant barking of a dog. Reaching a heavy iron-studded wooden door, Tuhin Singh halted. As he pushed it open, Nicholas felt a soft breeze on his face.

From behind them came a noise. Turning they saw a burly French soldier, blue jacket hanging open and a guttering torch in his hand, standing in the passageway staring at them. After a moment he shambled towards them, swaying a little drunkenly and muttering words Nicholas couldn't understand. Then, suddenly realising something was wrong, the soldier shouted '*Au secours!* Help!' and, turning, began to lurch on unsteady legs away from them. Instinctively Nicholas, the nearest to him, sprang towards him, leapt onto his back and knocked him to the floor. Straddling him, he seized his head and banged it hard against the flagstones. Though blood flowed, the soldier still struggled in his grip. Nicholas yanked his head back again and thumped it down once more. This time the man gave a low groan and passed out to lie in a growing pool of blood.

Getting quickly to his feet, Nicholas rejoined Tuhin Singh and Clive by the door and the three of them went outside. They were in a small compound with a stone well in the centre around which several dogs were sleeping. One raised its head from its front paws to look at them but after a few moments settled down again. By the light of two torches burning in brackets, Nicholas made out a wide archway at the compound's far end and beyond it the fort's main courtyard. But what caught his attention were the two bullock carts near the archway, each loaded with some six or seven giant wicker baskets. Tuhin Singh hurried over to their turbaned drivers and whispered a few words. The men nodded and climbed up onto the seats of the carts, whips in hand.

Tuhin Singh gestured to Nicholas and Clive to come closer. 'Quickly! Into a basket, each of you – one on one cart, one on the other. Hide yourselves inside as best you can. I'll put the lids back on.' Nicholas jumped onto the nearest cart, pulled off the round lid of one of the baskets and got into it. In the darkness, he could smell only rank linen – they were laundry baskets! He guessed where he was – the compound from which the garrison's linen was collected daily to be taken down to the water to be washed and bashed against the stones by the dhobis!

As Nicholas crouched down, he felt Tuhin Singh tug more linen over him, then replace the lid. Almost immediately, at a crack of the whip, the cart began to rumble over the flag-stones. Nicholas braced himself against the sides of his basket which swayed wildly as the cart grazed against some obstruction. Hearing the driver curse, Nicholas realised his cart must have clipped the archway into the main courtyard. Several more nerve-jangling minutes passed before a voice – presumably a soldier in the gatehouse – called 'Arrêtez! Halt!' Brisk footsteps approached. Instinctively Nicholas's fingers curled as if he had a pistol or dagger to reach for but of course he had nothing. What could they do if they were discovered? Run for it and hope not to feel a musket ball between the shoulder blades? He heard one of the drivers shout back, 'Seulement le linge sale, comme d'habitude. Only the usual dirty laundry.' Nicholas breathed more easily as the guard responded, 'Allez, pass,' and the carts moved off again.

Fifteen minutes later the carts stopped. 'It's all right. You can get out now,' Nicholas heard Tuhin Singh say. Heaving themselves from their baskets and dropping to the ground from the carts, Nicholas and Clive looked about them in the moon-light. They were outside a low white-washed house shaded by a tamarind tree that Nicholas recognised. As soon as Tuhin Singh had paid off the drivers and they'd trundled off, whipping up their bullocks, Nicholas said, 'You took a great risk for us. And if this house belongs to who I'm sure it does, we also owe Ramesh Ramachandran our thanks.'

'Come inside quickly before you're seen,' was all Tuhin Singh said. He led them into the house, past a small shrine where incense sticks smouldered before a brass statue of the pot-bellied god Ganesh, to a small room where Ramachandran was waiting. 'I'm glad to see you all safe,' he said, a relieved smile spreading over his face. Then from a table he picked up a calico-wrapped package and handed it to Nicholas. 'Your pistols. Tuhin Singh brought them here for safekeeping, together with your violin.'

'I'm very grateful.' For a moment Nicholas thought of his uncle, so many thousands of miles away and possibly a fugitive, as he himself was now, or a prisoner as he'd been only an hour or two ago. He could only hope that James had friends as good as his...

'What next, Tuhin Singh?' Clive asked.

'Well, you need to get out of Madras as quickly as possible.'

'But where to?' Nicholas looked from Clive to Tuhin Singh.

'What about Fort St. David at Cuddalore?' Clive suggested after some moments. 'It's only 130 miles south of here and the nearest Company post. If it is attacked, we'll be much more useful there than if we go to Calcutta or Bombay.'

'But the French settlement of Pondicherry's between us and Cuddalore. We'd have to skirt round it. Isn't that risky?' Nicholas asked.

Clive shrugged. 'Not necessarily. In fact it could work in our favour. Heading south is the last thing any pursuers would expect us to do.'

'All right. Let's do it then. I can't think of anything better. Can you Tuhin Singh?'

'No. But you'll need good disguises. I thought you might, whatever you planned to do. Yesterday I bought those in the bazaar.' Tuhin Singh pointed to two striped cotton robes of the type merchants wore, folded on a chair. Once Nicholas and Clive had put them on, he wound turbans round their heads, then stepped back. 'Ramachandran, what d'you think?'

'They're much too pale – especially after days in prison. Smear some earth from that pot of marigolds on their faces.'

Taking handfuls of damp soil, Tuhin Singh rubbed their faces, throats and the backs of their hands.

Ramachandran looked at them hard, then nodded. 'That's better! All the same, I hope no French soldier you meet inspects you too closely. Try to keep your faces well covered and to travel by night if you can.'

Half an hour later, riding the three skinny but serviceable horses that Tuhin Singh had also procured the day before, they were well beyond the city and galloping along the shore. Nicholas tasted salt spray on his lips. As the sun came up, with no sign of anyone except a shepherd driving his herd of bleating goats, they felt safe enough to halt and rest their horses in the shade of a palm grove.

Dismounting and fastening his reins to a trunk, Clive said, 'So come on Tuhin Singh, tell us how you managed it... I've been puzzling over it from the moment you came into our cell.' Tuhin Singh was usually both modest and reticent with Europeans other than Nicholas, even with Clive, but there was now pride in his voice as he said, 'After the French soldiers refused to let me into the fort with you, I went to Ramachandran's house and together we debated how best to help you. I realised that there was nothing I could do unless I got into the fort. The obvious solution was to get employment there. With Ramachandran's assistance, that wasn't so hard. The French have retained many of the Company servants and he knows one of the chief cooks well. He persuaded him to employ me in the kitchens, where he allowed me to help prepare food for the soldiers and also to take it to them when they were on guard duty. The guards got used to seeing my face, they trusted me.'

'When I heard that some prisoners were being released I watched to see who they brought up from the dungeons, but of course you weren't among them. So I continued to keep watch. Three days ago, when I took them their food, I overheard some of the guards talking about the French naval commander's birthday – I think they said his name was de la Bourdonnais – that there were going to be big celebrations – grand dinners aboard the fleet and in a huge tent set up on the shore. All were invited – other ranks as well as officers. Since the French think they've little to fear from the British or their allies just now, I reasoned that most of the fort garrison would attend. The guards were complaining that their officers were making them draw lots to decide which of them must stay behind to guard the prisoners. That's when I knew that the night of the celebrations would give me my chance.

'I asked Ramachandran to bribe the drivers of the laundry carts to carry you out of the fort concealed in the laundry baskets they collect each night. He found them willing enough – the French are paying them even less than the British were! Once I knew I had the means to get you out of the fort, all that remained was for me to drug the soldiers left behind to guard you. After those attending the celebration had left, I brought the guards large cups of wine in which I dissolved pellets of opium, asking why shouldn't they too celebrate their commander's birthday? They drank the wine without question and the opium loosened their tongues. When I mentioned your names – I pretended I had a grudge against you, Nicholas, for cheating me of my wages – they told me where your cell was, even showed me the key. Then I brought them some more wine. After the second cup, they passed out. I waited until I was sure no other guards were coming to relieve them, then took their keys and went to find you.' Tuhin Singh shrugged. 'That other soldier was a surprise. Otherwise, it went better than I'd hoped. We were very lucky.'

'Nonsense,' Clive slapped Tuhin Singh on the back. 'Often we make our own luck, but not this time. Our escape was all your doing. We are indebted to you, my friend!'

7 – The Siege

'When he was President of Madras, Elihu Yale named Fort St. David after the Welsh saint. Now it'll need a miracle from the saint himself to save it from the French!' Clive muttered, shading his eyes as from a low ridge he, Nicholas and Tuhin Singh surveyed the small sandstone fortress about two miles ahead. Built on rising ground, it was bounded to the south by a wide river and to the east by the glinting expanse of the Bay of Bengal, but its other two sides were vulnerable. Erected in the Company's early days, the builders of the fort, settlement and port had been less concerned about defence than safe anchorage for trading vessels and easy inland access for merchants.

'Whatever it's called, it's good to be here.' Nicholas unwound his turban from his head, and sliding from the saddle tugged off the striped robe he'd been wearing over his shirt and breeches these past three days. 'We won't be needing these anymore...'

'Anyway,' continued Clive, 'the governor of the fort will be glad to see us when he hears our news from Pondicherry! It'll be a chance to make a good first impression!'

'It's Tuhin Singh the governor will have to thank for the news, not us, and "glad" is not quite the word for his likely reaction to the kind of information we bring,' Nicholas reminded him.

Insisting Nicholas's and Clive's disguise would fool no one if they were seriously challenged, Tuhin Singh had left them with the horses, concealed in some scrubland just outside Pondicherry, and had entered the city on foot. There he'd witnessed much activity with troops drilling and inspecting equipment and a large baggage train being assembled. Mingling with some of the mule and bullock-cart drivers eating at the small stalls in the bazaar he'd learned that soon – very soon – they expected to head south. This could mean only one thing – that the French intended to seize Fort St. David and Cuddalore as well as Madras and, thus, extinguish the Company's presence in southern India.

The sun was setting and the first bats skimmed the air as the three of them cantered up the slope to the iron-studded gates of the fort, already closed for the night. Cupping his hands, Nicholas shouted up to the guards on the ramparts, 'We're Company men who've escaped from Madras. We've news for the governor.' A minute or two later, a smaller gate set into the main one opened and after a brief scrutiny the guards ushered them into the fort.

After pausing to wash, the three were taken to the quarters of the governor, John Hinde – airy rooms set high on the battlements where he was eating his evening meal. Hinde, an elderly man whose sallow, mottled skin spoke of many years of service in Hindustan, pushed aside his plate and listened quietly to Clive's and Nicholas's account of the fall of Madras, of which he'd already received some reports. However, he began to look grave as Tuhin Singh described what he'd seen and heard at Pondicherry.

'Of course, I knew an attack was likely. It's the next logical step for the French. But I've very few men fit enough to fight – barely two hundred and fifty soldiers and half a dozen officers. Three months ago, we had a bad outbreak of cholera which took a heavy toll. More recently we had an outbreak of fever. I've requested replacements but with no result... My best hope is that Anwaruddin Khan will send troops to assist us.'

'Anwaruudin Khan?' Clive queried.

'You'll know him better as the Nawab of the Carnatic. I've sent messengers asking for his help. I've heard nothing so far, but he's been a loyal ally to the Company for some time. As ruler of much of southern India he has the ability to put a well-equipped army quickly into the field. But if a French attack is as imminent as you say, even he may not be in time.' Hinde sighed. 'Of course, I've been doing my best to prepare – we've plenty of drinking water from our well and therefore no need to rely on the river. And

I've brought in all the grain and livestock I could so we could survive a siege for some weeks. But if the French and their allies discover how undermanned our defences are, they'll launch an all-out attack to swamp us. I may be forced to surrender, just like they did in Madras, to save lives. I won't sacrifice men in a battle I can't win.'

'But if we allow the French another easy victory who knows where their ambitions will lead! We can't give in so easily,' Clive burst out. Glancing at his friend, Nicholas saw the raised chin and feverish expression characteristic of him when his passions were roused, and he knew that in a moment he'd insult the governor. 'Surely you...' Clive was beginning again, but before he could continue Nicholas cut in. 'I've an idea. If we can stop the French from discovering how few we really are, we can buy ourselves time until either the Company's or the Nawab's troops get here.'

'A laudable suggestion, but tell me how, young man.' Folding his thin hands, Hinde looked at Nicholas with the expression of an indulgent but world-weary schoolmaster.

'Even if you don't have soldiers, you must have spare uniforms?'

Hinde nodded. 'Yes, but I don't see how...'

'What if we make dummies out of straw, dress them up in uniform and position them around the battlements to pretend our numbers are greater than they are? To make it more realistic we can keep moving them around.'

'Why not?' Clive broke in. 'We've the time to do it. From what we know of the French preparations, even if they push hard they probably can't get here for at least three or four days.'

'The French may not be as easy to trick as you think. They may even have infiltrated agents into the fort to report on our situation,' Hinde said.

'Or maybe not,' Clive insisted. 'We fooled them once! We escaped from Madras under their noses in laundry baskets.'

'Beware of over-confidence, young man,' Hinde cautioned, his voice grave.

'That's what people say when they're afraid to take risks. In a situation like this, if you don't take some risks you can't succeed. You said as much yourself. Do you want to be remembered as the man who surrendered Fort St. David or the man who saved it?' Clive persisted.

Nicholas laid a restraining hand on Clive's shoulder but not before he saw Hinde's eyes flash. 'You forget yourself,' the Governor snapped. Rising from his chair he strode to a window overlooking the parade ground. For some moments, he looked out before finally saying quietly, 'Well, I suppose we'll lose nothing by trying,' before adding, 'as to practicalities, take as many soldiers as you need to help you. To reinforce your authority you'll need a military rank. I'll appoint you ensigns in the Company army and inform my other officers. Now, you must be tired. My butler will arrange accommodation for the three of you. I only hope you won't regret your decision to come here.'

–

Who'd have thought straw could weigh so much, Nicholas thought as he dragged yet another stuffed dummy along the battlements overlooking the gatehouse. They had been at it for five days, wedging them into position, then resting pieces of wood, roughly carved to resemble musket barrels, on the stonework – spare muskets were less plentiful than spare uniforms. Elsewhere along the battlements, Company soldiers were doing the same, while down in the courtyard others were sewing bags on which they were chain-stitching eyes, noses and mouths with thick dark thread, stuffing more uniforms and also filling sandbags stitched from any material that was to hand, even damask tablecloths from the officers' mess.

'Better-looking than you, most of our mock soldiers,' said Clive, grinning at Nicholas. 'But let's see if we can't improve on them! Here, take this!' He held out a piece of charcoal. Gripping one of the dummy heads, Nicholas added lavish moustaches and a large mole, while Clive made the eyebrows on two others more pronounced. Next, along with Tuhin Singh, they cut lengths of hessian from old sacks and silk from cushions they'd found and wound them like turbans round the heads of some of the dummies. Could his idea possibly work, Nicholas wondered, tucking in the ends of a green turban. Though neither Clive nor Tuhin Singh had said anything, they were probably wondering the same thing...

Later that night, with the dummy soldiers in place, the three of them walked the battlements. Southwards, cooking fires from the town of Cuddalore pricked the night. To the east, along the Bay of Bengal, all was dark except for the bobbing lanterns of a few fishing boats returning home. As they walked the northern section of the walls all seemed too tranquil. There were no sounds beyond the occasional hooting of owls and barking of dogs fighting beneath the battlements. In the moonlight, Nicholas could just make out the ridge from where he and his friends had first glimpsed Fort St. David. But, as he watched, specks of light began to appear all along the ridge like distant fireflies.

'The French are coming,' he announced to his companions.

Immediately on hearing the news, Hinde called a council of war to which, given the few officers among the defenders, he invited Nicholas and Clive. As soon as he could, Clive broke into the discussion. 'If we just sit back on the defensive for more than a day or two, even with our dummy soldiers it won't be long before the enemy realise they outnumber us. We must make them uncertain about our intentions so they'll always feel the need to hold troops in reserve to counter the unexpected rather than commit everything to an all-out attack.'

'That's all very well, but how are we to achieve that?' Charles Clarke, an elderly major scarcely recovered from the cholera, which had reduced him to little more than a skeleton, and Hinde's most senior officer, asked.

Clive replied instantly, 'Make a sally when they least expect it.'

'When and against whom?'

'Their main body, just as they're forming up for an assault. If we ride hard at them, we can inflict considerable casualties and damage to their equipment and even more damage to their morale at little cost to ourselves. As for timing, our best chance is in the early morning when the French are most likely to prepare an attack.'

'How many men would you need?' Hinde asked.

'Fifty,' Clive replied.

'That's a fifth of our fit men.'

'With forty I can still guarantee success.'

'They'd all have to be volunteers. If you can recruit forty I will agree we should take the risk since you're right – unless we do something we're unlikely to be able to hold out until reinforcements arrive.'

'I will volunteer,' Nicholas told Clive as they left the conference. So too did Tuhin Singh when he learned of the plan. But Clive, backed up by Nicholas, refused his offer. Tuhin Singh could still scarcely bend his sword arm which had been caught between a cannon limber and a stone wall as he'd helped manoeuvre a cannon into its firing position on the ramparts two days earlier. Within less than an hour, Clive had collected the other thirty-eight volunteers he needed – a combination of Hindustanis and Britons.

To ensure he had the earliest possible warning of the French preparing an attack, and thus an opportunity for his own sortie, Clive secured permission for a doubling of the sentries on the ramparts in the hours around sunrise. He also had half his volunteers awake, fed and stood to arms at this time.

Only two days after he'd instituted this regime, during which only limited exchanges of musket and cannon fire had taken place, Tuhin Singh, who had insisted that because of his outstanding eyesight he should be one of the extra sentries, shook Nicholas awake with his good arm just before dawn. 'Wake up! The French have lit their cooking fire at least half an hour earlier than usual. It could mean an assault's imminent. Clive's already waking the remaining men.'

Tipping water on his face Nicholas quickly roused himself. Ten minutes later he joined Clive to hear Tuhin Singh, who had again descended from the ramparts, report that the French appeared to be preparing to move some of their cannon to a more advanced position to increase their chances of battering down the strong walls of the fort.

'An ideal time to attack them then,' Clive said.

A grizzled artillery sergeant named Henry Armstrong, one of the volunteers, who had overheard Tuhin Singh's report, spoke immediately in a thick Northumbrian accent, which at first both Clive and Nicholas found almost impenetrable. 'You'll want to take spikes to hammer into the cannons' firing holes to disable them.'

'Yes,' said Clive when he'd understood what Armstrong was saying. 'And we'll take some ropes, spare horses and harnesses to pull one or two of the small cannon back into the fort if we can. Even if we can't do that, spiking some will remove quite a part of the French advantage. Let's get the extra equipment and horses, and go!'

A quarter of an hour later the main gates of the fort opened, creaking on their hinges after days of inactivity, as the defenders quickly and temporarily removed the beams that reinforced them. The forty volunteers charged through them on their mounts, most of which were now so underfed that their ribs were showing. Clive and Nicholas were in the lead, heads bent over their horses' necks, swords extended and yelling encouragement to those following. In the still dim light Nicholas's horse stumbled over the stinking headless corpse of a French soldier decapitated by a cannon ball in the previous fighting. Thrown up onto his horse's neck Nicholas clung on for a while, then pulling back on the reins he regained his saddle. The horse galloped on, but the incident meant he'd fallen back a little from the foremost riders.

Even so, after less than a couple of minutes he was in among the French, whom the sortie had taken completely by surprise, as they tried to move six cannon forward. Clive, bending from the saddle of his tall chestnut and swinging his sword, had already slashed down two of the gunners. Three of Clive's men, including Sergeant Armstrong, had thrown ropes over one of the smaller cannon while another had dismounted and was hammering an iron spike into the firing hole of the largest.

Suddenly, Nicholas was aware of a French horseman spurring towards him, his heavy sword already raised to strike. Nicholas ducked as quickly as he could and the sword passed harmlessly over his head. Swiftly wheeling his nimble mount, the Frenchman was on him again. This time Nicholas was ready. He again dodged beneath the man's wild swing but, with his arm extended and firm just as when he fenced with Clive, he thrust his sword deep into the Frenchman's stomach just beneath his ribcage. The man's blood spurted at once and spattered Nicholas's hand and arm as he twisted his sword to withdraw it before the Frenchman collapsed sideways from his saddle.

For a moment Nicholas reined in, overcome by the reality of battle – the realisation that he'd killed a man in hand-to-hand combat for the first time, only to hear Clive shout, 'For God's sake, Nicholas, look out!' Jerked back to the battlefield, Nicholas saw another Frenchman riding at him. He had just enough time to raise his sword to deflect the blow which was aimed at his head but the force of the stroke was so great that glancing off his sword hilt, the blade carried on to strike his arm a glancing blow, ripping his jacket and slicing into his flesh. Nicholas quickly parried another, then thrust his sword deep into the man's thigh, causing him to cry out and swerve away into the press of battle.

Blood trickling down his arm from his wound, Nicholas pushed on towards the cannon where more Company men had dismounted and were endeavouring to attach the harnesses of two spare horses to the ropes already bound around the small cannon, no more than a three- or four-pounder. Within a minute or two they had succeeded, remounted and were urging their horses forward while attaching other ropes to the pommels of their own saddles to utilise whatever spare energy these animals had. Slowly, the cannon on its wooden carriage began to move. As it did, Clive yelled, 'Close up around the cannon and head back to the fort!'

Others passed on his cry as they tried to disengage, and Nicholas saw Clive slash down two French attackers to save one of his men from encirclement. Nicholas himself unhorsed another who had been attacking one of the Company men – a red-turbaned youth who had lost his own mount – with a blow to the abdomen. Nicholas grabbed the reins of the Frenchman's horse as he fell, then threw them to his comrade who, he now saw, was bleeding from a wound to his calf. Nevertheless, the youth hauled himself into the saddle and with Nicholas headed for the fort gates.

Clive's little force was back inside the fort with the small cannon within minutes, the French troops too confused and surprised to pursue them. As the gates closed behind them, soldiers rushed forward and lifted the heavy reinforcing beams back into position. As both men and horses gasped for breath, Clive dismounted and shouted to some of those not involved in the sally to heave the captured cannon up to the ramparts, find cannon balls to fit, and fire it at the French as a sign of their triumph.

Looking around and attempting a head count, Nicholas saw only three men had been left for dead outside the walls, but that several others, besides the youth he'd helped, were wounded. Henry Armstrong would have an additional scar for his collection from that sword slash to his right cheek. Blood was still running down Nicholas's own arm, dripping from his fingers to form a small scarlet puddle on the ground. Dismounting, he began to feel faint but immediately found Tuhin Singh at his side, supporting him with his good arm and leading him to a shady side room. By the time Clive arrived, Tuhin Singh had helped Nicholas remove his blood-stained shirt and jacket and Nicholas was biting his lip as Tuhin Singh poured alcohol into his wound to cleanse it before the surgeon stitched it up.

Clive watched for a moment, then said, 'You're lucky to get away with that scratch, Nicholas. After your first encounter you looked like a man in a dream. You can't pause for reflection in combat. Too much thinking'll just get you killed!'

'Perhaps you're right. But instead of criticism how about a word of thanks for my part in the raid?'

'Yes, congratulations are due all round, not least to myself as leader,' replied Clive, grinning now.

Nicholas looked at Tuhin Singh. 'Modest as usual, isn't he, our Clive?'

—

'Haul it up!' Nicholas watched as the two men operating the winch on the ramparts slowly pulled up the carcass of Clive's horse by the rope attached to its hind legs until its head, with its lolling tongue and reproachful round brown eyes, was off the ground. The chestnut had not recovered from a wound in its flank received during its master's successful sortie to capture the cannon. This was hardly surprising. With the French now appearing ready to wait to starve the defenders out, Hinde had severely reduced rations over the past weeks for men, and animals had received almost nothing. Nicholas looked on as Henry Armstrong – gaunt and the wound to his cheek still red-raw and weeping pus at one end – walked up to the horse's dangling corpse. With a single expert stroke of his sword he slashed its belly wide open, releasing a sigh of foul gas and spilling its blue-grey intestines and much of the rest of its empty guts.

At his orders, two other men carried away the offal and intestines, nearly all of which would be eaten in some form. Then they began skinning the beast, paring away the chestnut hide with sharp knives. Nicholas could see scarcely any creamy fat between the skin and the dark red muscle and white sinew that covered its skeleton. With two heavy strokes of his sword Armstrong hacked off the horse's head. It would be used for soup, boiled up with water from the fort's deep well, which still showed no sign of drying up. One of Armstrong's helpers caught the rush of blood which had collected in the neck in a wooden bucket – that too would have a use – while the third man began slicing off the flesh. Hearing footsteps behind him, Nicholas turned to see Tuhin Singh and Clive.

'Tuhin Singh has an excellent idea for another sally,' Clive said, his expression eager. 'You know how sharp his eyes are, particularly with the help of a telescope. Well, he's noticed something unusual about the French camp. Go on, Tuhin, you tell him. For once, don't let me steal your thunder.'

'The French's makeshift grain store and one of their two gunpowder stores are surprisingly close together, and a little distance from the main camp. That makes sense for storing the gunpowder, of course, to ensure it is well out of our cannon range and also far enough from the main camp in case of an accidental detonation.'

'Interesting, but what's the significance?' asked Nicholas.

'The two stores are quite near to the rocky gully that runs down from the fort towards the river. Tomorrow is a near-moonless night. A small band of us could reach them undetected if we slink down the gully. Once there, we might be able to carry off a few sacks of grain and detonate the gunpowder store. The explosion will create such confusion it's unlikely anyone will pursue us.'

'I can't see any obvious flaw. Why not give it a try?' Nicholas said. 'We might gain a few more rations to eke out our supplies until the Nawab's forces arrive and losing half their gunpowder would be a real setback for the French. Let's go up to the ramparts, check the lie of the land around the gulley again and then, if we're satisfied, go to the Governor.'

–

The next evening, two hours after sunset, fifteen men – the maximum number of the now further depleted garrison Hinde had sanctioned – gathered. The Governor had also forbidden Clive's participation – much to the latter's annoyance – on the grounds he would only permit one officer, Nicholas, to accompany Tuhin Singh and the fifteen, and that Nicholas had the cooler head. Most of the men were Company sepoys. All were wearing dark clothing and each carried a jute sack in which to put whatever plunder they could from the grain store. Henry Armstrong and two comrades carried the tinderboxes, fuses and three small barrels of gunpowder to be used to ignite the gunpowder store.

Rather than leave by the small gate set within the large main one that the French might be watching, the Company volunteers scrambled down a rope ladder dropped from the ramparts beside a tower standing at the junction between the river and landside walls. Ten minutes later all were safely down and, with Nicholas in the lead, began to move around the base of the tower towards the place where the distance to the gully was the shortest – about 20 yards.

As he picked his way over some uneven rocks, Nicholas's foot slipped on something soft, sticky and stinking – a latrine drain must empty just above. Cursing inwardly, he continued, signalling as best he could in the darkness to the others to avoid the mess. Then, bending double, he ran quickly over the stony ground to the gully. Still undetected, he dropped into it, slumping, pistol in hand, against the side nearest to the enemy positions. Swiftly, the other men began to cross to the gully. The sixth stumbled over a rock and fell with what to Nicholas seemed a loud thump. Still nothing moved in the French lines. A few minutes more and the remaining men had crossed without further mishap. The group moved on down the gully, led this time by Tuhin Singh because of his excellent eyesight and his detailed knowledge of the topography built up by his study with his telescope from the ramparts.

All went well until, half way down the gully, Tuhin Singh disturbed a sleeping dog. Baring its teeth, it snarled and barked, then launched itself at Tuhin Singh who had just enough time to despatch it with his drawn dagger before it could sink its teeth into his thigh. The whole group halted, crouching low, alert for any sound from the French lines. Still there was none. Skirting the carcass of the dog they continued down the gully. In a little while, they reached the nearest point of the gully to the two stores, about 30 yards from the grain store and half that again to the one containing the gunpowder.

Nicholas caught the sound of voices from the direction of the grain store. The French must have had the sense to position sentries there. Listening intently, he heard a pair of feet moving towards the gully from that same direction. Nicholas froze as the sound stopped a little distance from its edge. Had the sentry spotted something? Was he about to raise the alarm? Moments later, liquid splashed on the ground. The sentry was just taking a piss. Soon the footsteps began to retreat. Signalling to Tuhin Singh to follow, Nicholas crept further down the gully, then, pulled himself over the edge and, crouching, ran towards the opposite side of the grain store from that on which the sentries seemed to be. Flattening himself against the wooden planks of its wall, he was quickly joined by Tuhin Singh. The sentries – probably only two of them – were talking again.

After a brief whispered word, he and Tuhin Singh edged around the wall. Peering around the corner, Nicholas saw that the sentries – there were indeed only two – were squatting at the door of the grain store, playing cards by the light of a small lantern and paying no attention to their surroundings. Their muskets were resting against the wall a few feet away. Without hesitation, Nicholas and Tuhin Singh flung themselves on the two men. The sentry whom Nicholas tackled, kicked out hard as Nicholas seized him under the chin with his left hand and wrenched his head back. But he could not prevent Nicholas from slitting his exposed throat with a single slash of the dagger he held in his right hand. Scrambling to his feet to see that Tuhin Singh had overcome the other sentry equally silently, Nicholas picked up the sentries' lantern and ran to the gully to guide the remaining men to the grain store.

When they reached it, Nicholas held up the lantern as Tuhin Singh levered off the flimsy doorlock with his dagger. It came away quickly and the two looked inside. The grain was mostly in sacks already. After another whispered conversation, Nicholas instructed eight men each to take a sack of grain on their backs and return up the gully towards the fort. Then, with the remaining seven, he and Tuhin Singh crossed to the gunpowder store.

A much more substantial construction than the grain store, it was made of rough mud bricks, roofed with palm leaves over which two layers of oilcloth had been stretched. The lock on the stout, well-fitting door was strong and firmly attached. Tuhin Singh took three or four minutes to prize it off while his comrades peered anxiously into the surrounding darkness, straining for any sight or sound that other guards had been alerted. But none came.

Once the lock was off, Nicholas and Tuhin Singh, carefully shielding the lantern flame, went inside with Henry Armstrong and his two comrades with the tapers, tinderboxes and small barrels of gunpowder. Inside, there was a thick smell of dust and saltpetre. Armstrong sneezed twice, only partially muffling the sound with his hand. The French had sensibly kept their gunpowder barrels well separated but, at a gesture from Nicholas, Armstrong quickly had the three barrels they'd brought with them placed by three of the French barrels. Carefully protecting the tinderbox with his hand, he lit in succession the tapers attached to the three Company barrels. The tapers' length was designed to give Nicholas and his men four minutes to make their escape. Once they were lit, Nicholas, Tuhin Singh and the others quickly left the store, Tuhin Singh pausing only to close the door in case a chance gust of wind got in and extinguished the tapers. Soon, all nine were moving swiftly up the gully, with Nicholas counting the seconds as he went.

He'd only reached one hundred and seventy when a musket shot rang out at the head of the gully, then a second. Those carrying the grain bags must have been discovered. He and the others had no alternative but to continue up the gully, pulling out and cocking their pistols as they went. In the next instant, a loud flash lit the darkness behind them. The boom of explosions in the gunpowder store immediately followed. Temporarily deafened, Nicholas reached the gully's end. By the light of the now-growing fire he saw four French soldiers running towards the body of another, presumably a sentry who'd fired the first shot and been killed by the Company men. Raising his pistol, Nicholas took aim and fired at the leading Frenchman who had paused momentarily to look towards the explosion. Hit in the head by the pistol ball, the man spun round and fell, his feet drumming the ground in his death tattoo. Soon, the other three Frenchmen were also down.

With the element of surprise now gone, Nicholas shouted to those carrying the grain sacks to abandon them and for everyone to race for the main gate. Nicholas himself began to run, legs pumping. A musket ball whipped past his ear. Moments later he stumbled over a protruding rock and fell heavily as two more musket balls passed where his head would have been. Winded and gasping for breath, he scrambled up and ran on towards the gate to see Clive emerge from it and fire a musket shot. Then he dropped his weapon and ran to help one of the Company volunteers who'd collapsed in a heap near the gate, seizing him beneath his armpits and dragging him back into the fort.

Tuhin Singh too had reached the gate, as had several others. Nicholas did not enter until the last two men – sepoys, burdened by the grain sacks which they had bravely refused to abandon – were inside. All fifteen men had returned, but Henry Armstrong had again been wounded, this time in the shoulder, while the man Clive had rescued would be lucky if the surgeon did not have to amputate his badly mangled left leg to avoid gangrene setting in. One of the sepoys who had retained his grain sack showed Nicholas and Tuhin Singh two musket ball holes through which grain was leaking. The sack on his back had saved his life.

'You're a lucky man as well as a brave one,' Tuhin Singh told the soldier, while Nicholas clapped him on the back. 'We'll be sure to recommend you and your companion to Governor Hinde for urgent reward. You've well deserved it.'

8 – Salvation

'Something's going on in the French camp. Here...' Tuhin Singh handed Nicholas the telescope and he looked towards what had now become a familiar sight: the protective perimeter of roped-together carts, the lines of tents – those of the French to one side, those of their Hindustani allies to the other – the cannon and the black scar in the red earth where the gunpowder store had blown up.

Tuhin Singh was right. In the early morning light Nicholas could see officers running from their tents, some still fastening their sword belts. Bugles were sounding, and more and more soldiers were milling around. Some were running towards the horselines and the compounds, where the oxen that hauled the gun carriages and the mules and asses that pulled the baggage wagons were penned. A few were starting to collapse tents.

'I can't believe it, but it looks as if they're leaving and in a hurry!' As Nicholas continued to watch, one officer – a tall man with the sun's first rays glinting off his braided epaulettes – urged on two soldiers as they struggled to carry a large campaign chest from his tent.

'Here, let me look,' Clive seized the telescope. 'They *are* going! They're hitching up the gun carriages and loading up their baggage. Their allies too... I can see some of the Raja of Silpur's men mounting up over there. But why do it in daylight when they could've sneaked off in the night without any risk of attack from us?'

'Perhaps they want to be seen. Perhaps they're trying to tempt us into making a rash sally.'

'A trick you mean, Nicholas? In that case, they don't know Governor Hinde! He's too cautious to fall for that.' Clive's tone suggested Hinde was too cautious for much.

Clive was right. Within a few minutes orders came from the Governor for every man to stand to his post in case the retreat was a ruse to disguise an imminent attack. Hinde also ordered Tuhin Singh to keep watch with his sharp eyes and telescope from the fort's highest vantage point – the top of a tower – in case enemy reinforcements had arrived from Pondicherry during the night and were concealed in the hills, waiting to join an assault.

But as the morning drew on and the garrison sweated as they stood to arms on the ramparts in the rising heat, their besiegers continued to break camp. By noon, the entire enemy force was on the move, heading not northwards back towards the hills and Pondicherry, but westward across the flat, sun-scoured plains. Kerchiefs bound around their foreheads to keep the sweat from running into their eyes, Nicholas and Clive watched from the battlements, flanked on either side by straw soldiers.

'Well, these seem to have served their purpose!' Clive said, nudging one beside him with his foot. 'With luck we won't have to keep lugging them round the battlements to fool the French. Probably just as well – this one's falling apart. Look!' As he kicked it again, its leg split and straw fell out.

Nicholas was growing drowsy in the heat when a cry of 'Up here! Quickly!' jerked him to full attention. It was Tuhin Singh. Nicholas and Clive ran up the steep stone steps to the top of the tower 20 feet above them where he was on lookout. 'There, on the ridge!' Tuhin Singh pointed northwards.

Taking the telescope, Nicholas squinted through it to see horsemen streaming down from the ridge, some carrying banners, others with long lances, their steel tips flashing in the sun. Who were they? French troops? Company cavalry? As the riders continued their descent he noticed that most had yellow turbans and that their banners were bright yellow too. Hadn't Hinde said yellow was the colour of Nawab Anwaruddin Khan, the ruler of the Carnatic? On the battlements below, others had spotted the advance and were cheering. Hinde himself was staring intently towards what was by now a yellow-turbaned tide sweeping towards Fort St. David.

'The French must've got word that the Nawab's troops were coming! That's why they upped and left in such a hurry,' Clive was exultant. 'Come on!' Nicholas and Tuhin Singh followed him down to the battlements, where Hinde was conferring with some of his officers. As he saw them, the Governor smiled. 'When you young men arrived, I didn't think we'd hold the fort against the French. I was wrong. Now, I need volunteers to ride out and greet our allies. No doubt you'd like to be among them…'

Minutes later, the fort gates were swung open to allow out twenty riders commanded by Hinde's most senior officer, the still frail Major Clarke. His orders were to rendezvous with the Nawab's forces and report the direction taken by the retreating French. It hadn't been easy to find horses still strong enough to carry a man. Nicholas could feel his mount's sharp ribs against his calves and hear its wheezing breath. However, they hadn't far to ride, barely three miles, before they encountered the first of the Nawab's horsemen.

Major Clarke signalled his little troop to halt, then trotted forward with a sepoy from Madras as his interpreter. All the time, more and more horsemen were galloping up, among them a handsome, luxuriantly moustached man flanked on either side by a *qorchi* – squire – each carrying a yellow banner. He must be the commander, Nicholas thought. Sure enough, Major Clarke was at once conducted to him.

Nicholas, Clive, Tuhin Singh and the other Company men waited while the two men conferred. 'I don't see how we're going to be able to join in any pursuit of the enemy. This poor nag's ready to drop,' Clive said, patting the scraggy neck of his bay. But it seemed that Clarke and the leader had already thought of that. After a few minutes, Clarke trotted back to them. 'That's the leader of the Nawab's troops, Chanda Sahib. He's going after the enemy. With their artillery and baggage trains to slow them down, they can't be more than 10 or 15 miles away, if that. I'm returning to the fort to report back to the Governor but any who wish can join the Nawab's troops. They have enough spare mounts.'

Half an hour later, Nicholas, Clive and Tuhin Singh were mounted on three fine horses which, despite the distance they'd already covered that day, skittered and pranced as if still fresh. To the booming of kettledrums secured on either side of a tall grey gelding, Chanda Sahib's men moved forward. As his horse broke into a smooth canter Nicholas felt the warm wind in his face. It was good to be in the open and on the move again. Chanda Sahib, riding at the head of what must be five hundred riders, didn't need to be shown the route the departing enemy had taken. Discarded possessions and equipment littered the dry, dusty, slightly undulating terrain – a split water bottle, pieces of webbing, cooking pots, a metal tobacco tin with a French regimental crest and even a dead bullock that had been cut from its traces and on which vultures were descending.

In the early afternoon, a huge dust cloud appeared in front of them, thrown up by the retreating enemy. 'They can't be more than three or four miles ahead. But if we can see them, they'll be able to see us,' Nicholas said to Clive, riding at his side. 'What d'you think Chanda Sahib will do?'

'Attack straight away, I hope. Even though we can't surprise the enemy, we can at least deny them time to position their guns.' To Clive's satisfaction that seemed to be Chanda Sahib's thinking too. Orders came to prepare to attack at once. Watching his friend check his musket and pistols, it struck Nicholas that Clive was actually looking forward to the fight. As he drew one of his own pistols, he too found his blood pounding. Once Chanda Sahib had thrown out a protective screen of pickets to guard against an ambush, a trumpet – strident and high – sounded and the horsemen quickened their pace to a gallop.

Infected by the excitement of the others around them, their horses needed no urging and flew over the hard ground, eating up the distance separating them from their quarry. Within ten minutes they were up with the rear of the French column – a haphazard mass of gun carriages and baggage wagons. Attempts seemed to have been made to draw them into a defensive circle, then abandoned. All that lay between Chanda Sahib's men and the first of the carriages and wagons was a small detachment of French cavalry who, after firing a few panicky and badly aimed pistol shots at the oncoming riders, wheeled their mounts to flee, a few pausing to take up gunners who were pleading for rescue.

Storming through the abandoned cannon and baggage wagons towards the main column, Chanda Sahib's riders made short work of any soldiers in their path. The crack of muskets and screams of the wounded mingled with cries from hundreds of camp followers caught between the two forces, running hither and thither as they sought refuge from the fighters and their onrushing horses. A slight young woman with a baby bound tightly to her chest by a shawl was running hard, only to stumble and fall beneath the hooves of a fleeing French cavalryman.

The next Nicholas knew, he was in among the main French body which seemed in chaos, with some struggling to get away and others preparing to make a stand. To his left, three enemy musketeers dropped to their knees. Nicholas saw puffs of white smoke and orange flashes as their musket balls began to fly. One hit a rider a few yards ahead of him, knocking him sideways from his saddle, his arms flailing, to lie directly in Nicholas's path. As Nicholas gathered his reins, lent forward and gripped tight with his knees, his horse cleared the fallen man.

Somewhere ahead of him, to his right, he thought he glimpsed Clive, sword drawn as he hurtled onwards. Then he lost sight of his friend amid the swirl of drifting musket smoke. A French soldier crouching behind a jumble of rocks suddenly stood up and aimed his musket at Nicholas who ducked. The ball went over his head but close enough for him to feel it pass. Narrowing his eyes and aiming his pistol, Nicholas shot at his assailant who keeled over, sliding down between the rocks.

'Nicholas! Look out!' Tuhin Singh called.

Turning his head, Nicholas saw a spear arcing towards him. He pulled his mount sharply to the left and the spear swooshed by him to his right, embedding itself, shaft quivering, in the ground just ahead of him. The barefoot soldier who'd hurled it – a young Hindustani in a purple turban – turned and ran, but Tuhin Singh rode determinedly after him. Before the soldier had got far, Tuhin Singh, bending from his saddle, had sliced his young head off his shoulders with a single sweep of his sword.

Glancing round, Nicholas saw two French gunners – one an enormous bull of a man with a black beard, the other smaller – attempting to load a cannon, perhaps a three-pounder, among the very few the French had been able to turn to face the onrush of Chanda Sahib's horsemen. The smaller man had just lifted a cannon ball into the barrel and his comrade was preparing to ram it home with all his considerable strength. As Nicholas galloped up, the small man fled, but the other turned to face Nicholas, reversing his ramrod and wielding it like a weapon. Without warning, Nicholas's horse stumbled to its knees, sending him flying over its head to hit the ground almost at the feet of the gunner with the ramrod.

Stunned for a moment, Nicholas quickly gathered himself and rolled sideways, then somehow scrambled to his feet and threw himself on his assailant. The impact of his leap knocked the bulky gunner off his feet. As the man bucked and writhed and seemed certain to throw Nicholas off, Nicholas grabbed the man's hand that was still grasping the ramrod and bent it back with all the force he could muster until he heard the wrist bone snap. Howling with pain, the gunner went limp for a moment and Nicholas pulled out his dagger and thrust it twice up into his chest just beneath the breastbone. The gunner's body crumpled and scarlet blood dribbled from his mouth into his black beard.

All around Nicholas, Chanda Sahib's horsemen were fighting hand-to-hand with the enemy. As riders clashed around him amidst clouds of dust under the late-afternoon sun, Nicholas realised that, dismounted, he was in as much danger of being hit by flailing hooves as by musket balls or sword blades. He had to find a horse. 'Nicholas! Here!' a voice called. Clive was leaning towards him from the saddle, right arm extended. Grabbing it, Nicholas pulled himself up behind his friend and hung on tight as

Clive spurred forward, making not for one of the knots of fighting horsemen but for two baggage carts behind which were four Hindustani soldiers. One had just fired his musket and knocked a trooper from his horse. Another was levelling his weapon. The other two were crouching low, reloading.

As Clive galloped towards them, sword extended, Nicholas, peering over his shoulder, shouted a warning as the man who had just fired dropped his musket, drew a dagger from his belt, bent back his arm and flung it to thud into Clive's saddle just by his knee. With Clive almost on them, the remaining three soldiers dropped their weapons, turned and fled. As Clive lunged with his sword towards the one who'd flung the dagger, his nerve failed too and he stumbled after his comrades, only for Clive to slash him down with a cut to the head that opened his cheek to the teeth and bone.

Clive reined in by the now-abandoned baggage wagons. Looking around, Nicholas realised that the fighting was subsiding everywhere. The enemy soldiers were fleeing – some on horse-back, some on foot, abandoning their cannon and the baggage train – pursued by Chanda Sahib's men. It was a rout. As Nicholas watched, one of Chanda Sahib's riders thrust his lance into the back of a French cavalryman with such force that the tip went through his body and emerged from his chest. Screaming and with his clothing darkening with blood, the Frenchman writhed in the saddle for a moment like a boar spitted by a huntsman before falling to the ground.

Amid the chaos, Nicholas glimpsed Tuhin Singh, riding with a group of Chanda Sahib's men, seemingly unscathed except for a gash on his cheek. For a second their eyes met. Then Tuhin Singh galloped on. Moments later Nicholas saw him, holding his reins with his teeth, level his musket and fire at a blue-coated French officer 40 yards ahead of him, knocking him from the saddle and then gallop on again. Spotting a riderless horse – bloodstains on its saddle and down its right shoulder testimony to the probable fate of its previous owner – Nicholas slid to the ground from behind Clive, grabbed the animal's reins and vaulted into the saddle. 'Come on!' he shouted to Clive. 'Let's go!'

'No hurry.' Clive's tone was relaxed.

'What do you mean "no hurry"? The enemy are fleeing – we should join the pursuit. Tuhin Singh's already ahead of us with some of Chanda Sahib's men – I just saw him.'

'The battle's already won. We've more than done our bit. Let's pause a minute or two and investigate these wagons first.' Clive dismounted and, securing his reins to a wheel of one of the baggage wagons, pulled back its oilcloth cover and began to explore the contents. 'Nothing much here. A few sacks of grain and some boxes of musket cartridges. You know who these carts belong to?'

Nicholas shook his head, eager to be off.

'The Raja of Silpur. I recognised the markings on them.' Clive moved on to the second wagon and rolled back its cover.

'What are you looking for?'

'They say the Raja's as rich as Croesus. I'm hoping he brought some of his wealth on campaign,' Clive said, grinning. 'Ah, what's this?' As Clive turned towards him Nicholas saw he was holding something wrapped in a cloth. Glancing quickly round to make sure the fighting had indeed moved on and that they were in no danger, Clive pulled off the cloth to reveal a large box. 'Come and take a look. I'd bet there's more than the Raja's spare clothes in here…' Moving closer, Nicholas saw a sandalwood box inlaid with ivory flowers. The elaborately chased hinges looked like solid gold. It was locked and, after a couple of futile rattles at the lid, Clive took his dagger, inserted it beneath the lid and prized it open. As he saw the contents, he smiled.

'Look.' He held up a jewelled drinking cup inlaid with rubies that flashed blood red in the sunlight. 'This would have been a trifle to the Raja but it'll make a nice souvenir of our victory.' He tucked it inside his tunic then delved in again. 'And what about this?' He held out a silver dish inlaid with turquoises and pearls. 'Take it! We deserve a reward for all the blood and sweat we expended. If we wait till all the booty's pooled we'll never get anything worth having.'

Nicholas said nothing.

Seeing Nicholas's expression, Clive asked, 'Why are you hesitating? Didn't we play more than our part in the victory? We need to look to ourselves because no one else will... And we've a right to something. We're not like those freeloaders who are always last into the battle but first into the loot. Take it, and then let's join the pursuit if you must!'

Part Three

The Court of Anwaruddin Khan, Nawab of the Carnatic, 1748

9 – The Envoy

Nicholas smiled as he read Clive's latest letter, brought by a courier from Fort St. David. His friend was a good correspondent, especially when he had personal successes to report and since the routing of the French at Cuddalore, there had been several. Not only had Clive's commission as an ensign in the Company army been confirmed but he had been posted to Fort St. David where he had impressed, or so he claimed, the officer, Major Stringer Lawrence, now in command there. The letter's ebullient ending made Nicholas smile.

> *Yesterday, Lawrence asked my opinion on how best to reinforce our defences. He's also consulted me about a plan to take the attack to the French. I'd tell you more but dare not in case this letter should fall into the wrong hands. You are missing all the excitement.*
> *Yours till hell freezes,*
> *Your friend,*
> *Clive*

He'd certainly missed Clive since they'd parted three months ago, Nicholas thought, folding the letter. But that didn't mean – as Clive was hinting – that he regretted being seconded into the service of Anwaruddin Khan. Governor Hinde had taken him completely by surprise when he'd said, 'Ballantyne, it seems the Nawab has heard about your bravery in the defence of Fort St. David. He has suggested that we post you to his court for a while.' He'd surprised himself by how quickly he'd agreed – certainly not merely because the Company was keen, though it was. 'You'll be our man at the Nawab's court, Ballantyne. Not that we distrust him, of course, but we like to keep an eye on our allies and with the French at our throats these are dangerous times,' Hinde had urged. 'And it wouldn't be forever – probably two years at most.'

The reason Nicholas had agreed so readily was, as he had told Clive, that he saw this not only as an opportunity to learn more about this land where fate had brought him but also to liberate himself, for a while at least, from the constraints of Company life – and the doubts he still read in some faces about his Jacobite associations. Clive had looked dubious and tried to dissuade him, but Tuhin Singh had agreed without hesitation to accompany him, repeating that his loyalty was to Nicholas and no one else. Together they had ridden south from Cuddalore to the Nawab's sandstone fortress of Birangarh on a palm-fringed tributary of the Cauvery River.

Since then, Nicholas had spent his days observing the drilling of Anwaruddin Khan's soldiers and riding on manoeuvres with them. He had seen little of the Nawab himself, who remained a figure of distant magnificence. Only a few days ago, on the Nawab's birthday, Nicholas had watched as, in the hall of public audience, Anwaruddin Khan, sitting cross-legged on scales of pure silver, was weighed against bags of spices, chests of coins and rolls of silk. Fascinated, Nicholas had recalled how his great-great-grandfather had witnessed just such a ceremony at the Moghul court.

Pulling out his pocket watch, Nicholas saw it was time to join Chanda Sahib. After the fighting around Fort St. David, Chanda Sahib had returned to his estates, but the previous night, hearing kettledrums boom above the gatehouse, Nicholas had hurried into the courtyard in time to see the general sweep into Birangarh at the head of a troop of soldiers. This morning, an attendant had brought Nicholas an invitation to meet Chanda Sahib on the battlements at dusk for a tour of the fort's defences.

Nicholas checked his red tunic was properly fastened. Like Clive, he too had been formally commissioned into the Company army as an ensign which meant wearing the hot and uncomfortable uniform. With a final tweak at his collar, he headed up to the battlements. Chanda Sahib was already there. Diamonds flashed in his gold-embroidered turban and from the hand he raised in greeting, 'Welcome, my young friend. Let's walk.'

As the setting sun gilded the river below, they strolled along the battlements. 'My officers told me you and your comrades fought well in the defence of Fort St. David and in the pursuit of the enemy… but not quite like other Company soldiers…' Chanda Sahib said, pausing to inspect a tall, yellow-turbaned trooper who sweated visibly under the commander's penetrating gaze.

'What do you mean? How do Company soldiers fight?' Nicholas asked, as Chanda Sahib moved on again.

'Bravely but sometimes without imagination, simply obeying their orders.'

'Isn't that what soldiers are supposed to do – be disciplined? That's why the Company drills its men so hard,' Nicholas replied, unexpectedly piqued.

'Merely an observation, not a criticism. I didn't mean to offend you. As I said, you and your friend Clive seemed different.'

'Not really. We used our initiative as good soldiers should when circumstances change.'

'That is exactly what I find praiseworthy, but it's not why I suggested to the Nawab that you be seconded to his court.'

Nicholas started. He had assumed someone in the Company had proposed the idea to Anwaruddin Khan.

'Of course, we have plenty of good officers of our own,' Chanda Sahib continued, 'but when you and I talked after the fighting was over, I realised you're not like most of your countrymen. You've learned our languages. You're curious about your surroundings. I thought we might also learn from you.' When Nicholas said nothing for some moments, Chanda Sahib clapped him on the shoulder. 'Why so silent?'

'No reason,' Nicholas replied. Then, clearing his throat, he asked, 'What did you mean when you said "learn from me"?'

They had reached the top of a spiral staircase descending to the courtyard below and Chanda Sahib paused. 'I rose in the service of Anwaruddin Khan as much through my wits as my bravery. Now we will spend time together to the benefit of us both. I will explain something of how Hindustani commanders think while you will tell me more about the workings and ambitions of the Company. It's a difficult animal to predict – even its friends don't always know where it is going or why.'

And neither do its employees, Nicholas thought, but he kept the comment to himself as they descended the stairs.

Reaching the courtyard, Chanda Sahib spoke again. 'I believe that though you arrived some weeks ago you have not yet spoken privately with the Nawab?'

Nicholas nodded.

'Well, he will summon you soon. Other matters have been preoccupying him but he's curious to meet you. How much contact you have with him after that will depend on what he thinks of you. Experience has taught him to trust only a few.'

'Why? As Nawab of the Carnatic, he's the most powerful ruler in the region.'

'It's precisely his position that makes him vulnerable. Power and wealth incite envy and ambition even within his own family – and, of course, other rulers would like to destroy him. They see the rivalries between you Europeans as their opportunity... By supporting the French against the Company, the Raja of Silpur had hoped to damage the Company's ally, the Nawab. But that's enough serious talk. Before I go, tell me how you are finding things – you must miss your friends, Robert Clive, for instance?'

'I do miss them, but my friend and steward Tuhin Singh is with me.'

'Tuhin Singh? A Hindu, isn't he?' Chanda Sahib stroked his fine moustache. 'Are you sure you can rely on him?'

'I trust him with my life, if that's what you mean. He rescued me from captivity in a French dungeon.'

'Your confidence in him does you credit. But remember that the loyalties of Hindus can waver.'

'The Company has many Hindus in its armies, Rajputs, Tamils, Bengalis. No one could fight harder or more bravely or be truer to their salt. Their loyalty once offered is unshakeable. So is Tuhin Singh's.'

'Don't be angry. I'm only speaking from experience. Now, I've matters to attend to. But in the days to come we will see more of each other.'

A formidable man, Nicholas thought, as Chanda Sahib strode away, and the kind best stood up to. Why did he distrust Hindus so much? Yet, were his prejudices any different from those in Europe, where Protestants and Catholics had so recently fought and killed one another? It would be disappointing if his quest to learn more about Hindustan was only going to teach him that men's prejudices and suspicions were the same the world over – a dislike and distrust of anyone who differed from themselves in any way.

Chanda Sahib's prediction that the Nawab would soon summon Nicholas proved correct. Just three days later, he was ushered into the Nawab's presence. Anwaruddin Khan sat tall and upright on his throne, a dagger with an emerald-studded hilt at his waist and more emeralds in his yellow silk turban. A regal figure, Nicholas thought as he rose from his bow, if an elderly one. The Nawab's beard was silver-white and his broad face pocked like orange peel. But he looked vigorous for a man of some three score years and ten which Nicholas had heard was his age.

The Nawab was scrutinising him just as closely. Nicholas waited. Chanda Sahib had warned him not to speak until the Nawab addressed him.

'I have grown curious to meet the foreigner at Birangarh.' The Nawab spoke slowly and in English, his deep voice resonating in the richly gilded hall of private audience. Apart from two guards by the door and a further pair on either side of the throne, they were alone. 'What do you think of my court?'

'Very fine, Highness, though I've little experience of such things,' Nicholas replied in Tamil.

The Nawab blinked. 'Was my English at fault? Why didn't you reply in your own language?'

'You did me the courtesy of addressing me in my tongue. I wanted to return that courtesy by replying in a language of the Carnatic,' Nicholas said, this time in English.

The Nawab nodded in acknowledgement. 'That does you credit. Chanda Sahib told me one of your ancestors spent many years at the Moghul court in the service of your king. Perhaps he was just as silver-tongued. Your family must be a great one in your own country.' The quadruple strand of pearls around his neck gleamed as he spoke.

Nicholas smiled. 'No, Highness. My family are not important people. My ancestor was merely a page to the English ambassador to the Moghul Emperor. When his master returned to England, he decided to remain. He served the Emperor Shah Jahan and later fought for his son Dara Shukoh.'

'So you know what happened during that troubled time?'

'Yes, or at least what I've read in my great-great-grandfather's letters. He described how, when Shah Jahan became ill, his sons fought each other for the throne and Aurangzeb captured and executed Dara Shukoh. My great-great-grandfather witnessed it all.'

'The Emperor Aurangzeb was a guest here in my father's time. I remember him well. I was surprised by how plainly he dressed – no finery or gems – and how he refused to listen to our court musicians, declaring that though he loved music he had renounced it as vainglorious and therefore sinful. My father told me the Emperor was a hard man to like or know, that his standards were absolute. When his eldest son rebelled against him, he imprisoned him for the rest of his life, never forgave him. Never even visited him. His other sons and even his daughters also suffered his displeasure. Perhaps the only member of his family he truly loved was his sister Jahanara. They say that when she was badly burned in a fire he refused to leave her bedside until he was sure she would survive.' The Nawab paused and then said, 'I am an old man now and the past makes me sad. As a young one, I expect it bores you. Let us talk of other things. Tell me about your homeland. Why do so many of you leave it to seek your fortunes here in Hindustan? I can't decide whether you British are a race of warriors or traders...'

'Both, I think, Highness. Let me try to explain.'

Occasionally throwing in a shrewd question, the Nawab listened attentively for a while. Then, leaning back and raising a hand on which the top joint of the third finger was missing – an old battle wound, perhaps, Nicholas wondered – said, 'I've enjoyed our talk and we'll talk again. But I'm weary now so you must leave.'

As Nicholas returned to his quarters, a thought struck him. His great-great grandfather had written of his love for the Moghul Emperor's sister. Could that have been Princess Jahanara, whom the Nawab had mentioned? It was a tantalising idea.

–

Nicholas and Tuhin Singh swayed in their saddles as their horses advanced into the river up to their hocks and began drinking. They'd barely taken a few gulps when such a terrible scream split the air, that both horses raised their heads, skittering so violently that it was a few moments before their riders got them back under control. More screams, high-pitched and agonised like a chorus from hell followed. They seemed to come from further along the riverbank.

Nicholas and Tuhin Singh gathered their reins and urged their mounts into a gallop in the direction of the cries. What could it be? Rounding a bend in the river they had their answer – Chanda Sahib's soldiers were executing the fifteen dacoits they'd captured earlier that day. Nicholas had assumed they would be taken back to Birangarh to face justice but Chanda Sahib clearly had other ideas and the scene before him made Nicholas sick to the stomach.

Two of Chanda Sahib's soldiers had one of the robbers in their grip while two others were spreading his legs. They lifted the shrieking man up – thighs still splayed – above a pointed stake driven into the riverbank, then rammed him onto it so hard that the point entered his rectum. His agonised yells grew yet more desperate as with a couple more hard pulls on his ankles, with the man's own weight to aid them, the soldiers forced him further down the stake until its sharp tip burst through his abdomen. His eyes looked ready to pop from his head as a bloody gobbet of flesh, falling from his twisted lips, told Nicholas he had bitten off his own tongue.

All around, Chanda Sahib's men were seizing the limbs of the dacoit's wildly struggling and writhing companions and impaling them too. More and more blood was staining the ground as the cacophony of screams grew ever louder. Some victims were vomiting blood and the contents of their stomachs. Others had lost control of their bladders and bowels. Their clothing was streaked with their dripping urine and brown with their faeces. Meanwhile, vultures circled overhead, awaiting a feast of flesh.

Chanda Sahib, mounted on his black stallion, the rubies on its bridle flashing blood red in the sun, was calmly supervising the impaling of the dacoit leader. As Nicholas and Tuhin Singh rode up, they heard Chanda Sahib telling the man, 'I'm saving you till the last. Go on! Knock it into the ground!' The expression on the dacoit's bruised, battered face and in his rolling bloodshot eyes, was one of sheer terror as he looked up at Chanda Sahib. Then with violently shaking hands he began hammering into the hard-baked ground with a rock the stake that would be used to kill him.

Why didn't Chanda Sahib just have these wretches shot or beheaded, Nicholas thought, horrified. They deserved death for what they had done, but not this.

It had all begun the previous day when, returning from a hunting trip into the hills, they had encountered groups of frightened villagers fleeing a band of dacoits terrorising their community.

'So we have a fresh hunt!' Chanda Sahib had told his men.

Within twenty-four hours they'd tracked the band down and captured them as they made camp alongside this wide river. Nicholas had seen the dacoits' work with his own eyes – the trampled fields where the bandits had wantonly destroyed crops and animals they'd not been able to carry off, the women they had raped. The blank face of one – she couldn't have been more than twelve or thirteen – kneeling on the ground, arms wrapped tight round herself, rocking back and forth and singing something to herself over and over haunted him still. But this was no less inhuman. A glance at Tuhin Singh's face told him his friend felt the same.

'Is the stake ready? Then make him squirm!' Chanda Sahib ordered.

'Stop!' Nicholas shouted, but Chanda Sahib's men ignored him, grabbing their victim by the shoulders, lifting him up then forcing him down onto the stake. The man's frantic writhing was only worsening his agony. 'No!' Nicholas called out again, only to hear Chanda Sahib say, 'This is justice my young friend, do not interfere.'

Ignoring him, Nicholas slid from the saddle. Drawing his pistol, he strode towards the dacoit leader, levelled the weapon at him and just had time to register the gratitude on the man's contorted face before firing. As the ball penetrated his skull, the dacoit's head slumped on his chest.

'Enough, please! Show mercy. Put the rest out of their agony too,' Nicholas pleaded looking up at Chanda Sahib. The commander's eyes flickered. 'Very well but only as a courtesy… because you ask it.' At his nod, soldiers ran towards the stakes and swiftly slit the throats of those still alive until, finally, the screaming stopped. Shutting his eyes, Nicholas lowered his head and let out a sigh.

'Let's go,' Chanda Sahib shouted to his men. As Nicholas remounted his horse and rode by his side, Chanda Sahib shot him a glance. 'Why so queasy and soft-hearted? I've seen you kill on campaign without hesitation.'

'That's different.'

'You mean soldiers should only kill in battle?'

'Something like that, I suppose.'

In recent months Nicholas had twice been on campaign with Chanda Sahib and the Nawab's troops – the first time against a wealthy vassal attempting to establish himself as an independent ruler and the second against a neighbouring ruler who'd plundered caravans carrying silks and spices to the Nawab's court. Both campaigns had been short but violent. He'd learned to face new weapons – daggers whose serrated double blades sprung open like scissors inside a man ripping through sinew and flesh, multibarrelled pistols that fired four balls at a time, trumpeting war elephants wearing steel-plate armour glittering in the sun with spikes on their headgear and scimitars tied to their red-painted sharpened tusks. Yet, the horror he'd felt at seeing those impaled figures on the riverbank surpassed it all.

'Bandit scum! They only got what they deserved. And it's important that the people see with their own eyes that the Nawab will avenge them when they are wronged. Long after the vultures have stripped the dacoits' flesh from their bones, people will remember that their ruler's justice is swift and terrible.' Chanda Sahib's voice had an edge as he added, 'None of my own soldiers has ever questioned my actions…'

'I didn't mean they didn't deserve to die. It was the manner…'

'They were infidels. The people they violated were true believers. Their executions were God's vengeance on them. They don't deserve your pity.'

Nicholas was glad Tuhin Singh, riding behind, was out of earshot. 'You talk about Hindus as if they're your enemy.'

'Many are.'

When Nicholas said nothing, Chanda Sahib kicked his horse into a gallop and shot forward in a cloud of pale dust. Behind him, on the riverbank, vultures were already tearing at the bodies of the dacoits.

Nicholas had seen enough of Chanda Sahib to know he was a brave and capable commander. His self-confidence and the scale of his ambition reminded him in many ways of Clive. He was a skilled tactician, too, but, unlike Clive, he was cautious, never making a move before he was sure of his force's superiority over the enemy and always consolidating his conquests before moving on. He also seemed to believe in conciliating his opponents – at least some of them – after defeating them. The campaign against the neighbouring ruler had ended in a treaty. 'Nothing stays the same in Hindustan,' Chanda Sahib had told Nicholas. 'Alliances shift and fortunes fluctuate. My former enemies may in future be useful to me... And, of course, to the Nawab.'

Yet, Nicholas noted, Chanda Sahib only applied such ideas – so similar to the Company's policies – to men of his own faith. His contempt for Hindus was something Nicholas couldn't fathom. Did Anwaruddin Khan feel the same? Perhaps he should ask him?

The Nawab's remark at their first meeting that he wished to talk further with Nicholas had proved genuine, and not mere politeness. Scarcely three or four days passed without the Nawab calling for him. Nicholas dutifully reported their growing acquaintance to Governor Hinde, in his monthly despatches, knowing he would be pleased that he was gaining the Nawab's confidence. However, Nicholas knew he would be less happy to know they seldom discussed the Nawab's political and military aspirations or his attitude to the Company. Anwaruddin Khan was a man of great erudition, curious about other cultures and especially about Nicholas's Classical studies. Nicholas had sent to Madras for an English translation of Homer's *Iliad*, which the Nawab had been devouring. The story of Troy reminded him of a great siege he had taken part in in his youth.

Now that Chanda Sahib had ridden ahead, Tuhin Singh cantered up to take his usual place by Nicholas's side and they exchanged glances. After what had happened to the dacoits, they would have plenty to discuss tonight. What would Clive have made of it, Nicholas asked himself. Perhaps, like Chanda Sahib, he would think him over-squeamish.

In fact, nearly a week passed before the Nawab, preoccupied with a visit from an envoy of the Nizam of Hyderabad, whose vassal he was, asked Nicholas to come to his private apartments and, as he sometimes did, to bring his violin. As Nicholas entered, Anwaruddin Khan was sitting cross-legged on the floor, his ivory-inlaid sitar beside him. 'I'm glad to see you. These past days have been full of nothing but talk of taxes and troop levies. Let us play that Scottish melody you taught me. It will soothe my mind.'

The plangent sounds of the sitar married remarkably well with the violin's softer tones. Anwaruddin Khan was a skilled musician and as he played, eyes half-closed, his expression relaxed as if music indeed drove away the cares of ruling. As the last haunting notes died away, the Nawab put down his sitar, reclined against an orange bolster and took a nut covered with gold-leaf from a silver dish. He gestured to Nicholas to take one from the same dish, a sign of high favour. Emboldened, Nicholas raised the topic that had troubled him since Chanda Sahib's cruel killing of the dacoits.

Two nights ago, from the battlements of Birangarh, he'd noticed white-clad pilgrims heading for what a soldier told him was a small Hindu temple north of the town. The next morning he'd ridden there. Paying a loitering small boy a few annas to hold his horse, he'd walked through the high temple gateway surmounted by brightly coloured, intertwined figures – warriors, demons, gods and goddesses – into the compound beyond.

'Highness, yesterday I visited a Hindu temple. I'm curious about the Hindu religion and wanted to learn more,' he began.

Nicholas saw the Nawab's eyes fixed intently on him. 'Many of your subjects are Hindus and no less loyal to you because of it,' he continued, choosing his words with care. 'Yet, some of your commanders seem suspicious of them. I don't understand why.'

'So you thought visiting a temple might help explain the reason? Did it?'

'No. The temple was very peaceful, with only a few worshippers. No one challenged me or even looked at me. A woman was hanging strings of jasmine and marigolds around the neck of a statue of a deity. In the inner sanctum, a white-robed priest, forehead marked with ash, was lighting incense. When he finished

I asked him to explain what he'd been doing. He put oil and ash on my forehead and invited me to sit with him. He talked about the perpetual balance in the cycle of life, about the gods Shiva, Brahma and Vishnu. From what he said, Hinduism seems a gentle, spiritual faith.'

'As indeed it is.'

Nicholas looked at the Nawab in surprise.

Anwaruddin Khan smiled as if he understood Nicholas's puzzlement. 'I'm no Aurangzeb. He reimposed taxes on the Hindus – the jizya – abolished by his great-grandfather, Emperor Akbar. He pulled down temples and constructed mosques on their sites. Why? He believed he was doing God's work, I suppose. Yet, all he achieved was to divide his empire and make it impossible to govern. He spent most of his reign on campaign here in the south and must have died knowing the Moghul empire would soon fall apart, as indeed it has, allowing outsiders – and forgive me if I include the Company in their number – to fight over its carcass.'

The Nawab's expression was very serious now. 'My father taught me to believe – like the Emperor Akbar – that many paths lead to God. It is not for mere human beings, even a great ruler, to say which is right or wrong. It is also not good policy. By treating all his subjects fairly, regardless of religion, Akbar created a mighty empire. Although today the empire of the Moghuls is disintegrating we should never forget what made it great and gave it strength.'

'Then why do commanders like Chanda Sahib behave as they do?' Nicholas could not stop himself from blurting out. 'When we captured some Hindu dacoits, instead of just beheading them – as I've seen him punish Muslim robbers – he impaled them...'

'Chanda Sahib is an excellent and brave officer but not a great thinker and certainly not a man of philosophy. That sometimes leads him to confuse acts of cruelty with acts of loyalty. I've tried to curb his excesses but he's too valuable to be overly harsh with. But be assured that I allow my subjects freedom to worship as they please unless their customs violate principles of common decency and humanity. Have you heard of the practice of sati?'

Nicholas shook his head.

'Some Hindus believe that when a man dies and his body is laid on the funeral pyre it is the duty of his wife – young or old – to die with him. Some widows willingly sacrifice themselves. Others are forced screaming into the flames – I've seen it with my own eyes. It is a barbarous practice that I will not tolerate in my lands,' the Nawab paused. 'But, otherwise, why should a man's religious faith concern me so long as he is loyal to me, his earthly ruler? You still look troubled but when we celebrate the Nauroz you will see with your own eyes that, just as at the court of the great Akbar himself, all are welcome here.'

–

The Nauroz festival that marked the start of the lunar new year was not far off. Only a month later, oil lamps swaying on gold wires strung across the main courtyard of Birangarh danced like shining stars. The Nawab had told Nicholas he prided himself on his magnificent Nauroz celebrations but he hadn't imagined anything like this. In the centre of the courtyard stood a vast tent of amber-coloured silk with gold-laced awnings that had taken a week to erect, surrounded by smaller tents in every colour from ruby red to sapphire blue.

This particular night marked the start of festivities that would last a week. All manner of celebrations lay ahead, from feasts and fireworks to elephant fights and tiger hunts. Sandalwood from incense burners scented the air while from the fort kitchens came the smell of roasting meats and fragrant spices. All the Nawab's vassals and allies would attend to offer and receive gifts. When Nicholas entered the amber tent, the Nawab's vizier – a tall, thin man normally dressed in plain brown robes and carrying a ledger but today wearing a purple kurta embroidered with pearls – gestured him towards a long, low table. It was placed just beneath a gold cloth covered dais on which stood the Nawab's throne of state, carved from ivory to resemble a giant peacock. Nicholas realised he was being given a place of honour because all the other tables – except the one at which Chanda Sahib was already seated – were farther from the dais.

Nicholas lay back against the cushions, sipped the chilled sherbet poured for him by a servant, and then surreptitiously pulled out a hipflask to add a good measure of arrack to his glass. It tasted much better that way. Glancing round, he was amused to see an elderly courtier doing exactly the same thing before concealing his flask again in the long fur-trimmed sleeve of his green robe. Nicholas noticed fretted wooden screens on the far side of the tent and guessed the Nawab's wives would be behind them, able to observe the goings on unseen.

The tent quickly filled up and the noise level rose until a sudden blast of trumpets brought instant silence. 'All hail His Highness, the mighty Nawab Anwaruddin Khan, lord of the Carnatic,' proclaimed the vizier as everyone stood and looked towards the wide entrance to the tent. Eight yellow-liveried servants entered carrying an open silver palanquin upon which sat the Nawab, egret feathers swaying in his cloth of gold turban as he looked right and left acknowledging his guests.

Reaching the dais, the bearers lowered the palanquin carefully. As the Nawab stepped out and mounted the shallow steps, attendants showered him with seed pearls and rose petals. Seating himself on the ivory throne, Anwaruddin Khan said, 'I welcome you all here to celebrate Nauroz. May the new year bring fortune and favour to all.'

'And to you, Your Highness!' the guests roared back in what Nicholas realised must be a time-honoured response.

At a clap of the Nawab's heavily jewelled hands, a long line of bearers streamed into the tent carrying golden platters piled with cooked chickens, quails, pheasants, haunches of venison; brass cooking pots holding delicately sauced stews of chicken and lamb from which emanated the scent of cardamom and coriander seeds; platters of pulao stranded with golden threads of saffron and gleaming with almonds wrapped in gold and silver foil; and fragrant bread steaming from the tandoor.

Nicholas ate with relish, tearing off hunks of bread to scoop up gobbets of stew, and skewering pieces of roasted meat with the tip of his dirk. Glancing up at the dais he saw the Nawab watching the scene with quiet approval.

The meal finally over, the Nawab's vizier stepped forward and, raising his hand, called for silence. Nicholas sensed the expectancy as the vizier opened a scroll and intoned, 'To mark the Nauroz, the Nawab wishes to bestow his favour on his loyal subjects and allies.' He began to read a list of names. The first was Chanda Sahib, who stood to be presented by an attendant with a silk robe and a green leather pouch that by its obvious weight contained coins.

And so the presentations continued. To his surprise Nicholas heard his own name. As he stood a young attendant handed him a crimson robe stiff with gold embroidery and a silver box. Inside was a heavy gold ring inset with an emerald carved with a peacock – the Nawab's personal emblem. He slid the ring onto the fourth finger of his right hand. A perfect fit!

Presentations complete, attendants carried away the tables while the Nawab's guests positioned themselves around the edge of the tent to make space for the entertainments about to begin. Nicholas had just found a place near the entrance to the tent when suddenly the torches were extinguished, plunging the tent into darkness. Instinctively, Nicholas's hand went to his dirk but he relaxed as, almost at once, four men, each carrying two burning brands, ran into the tent. Naked except for their loin cloths, their hair bound in top-knots and their muscled bodies gleaming with oil, they started juggling the brands and tossing them to each other.

'They're from Madurai,' a man next to Nicholas whispered. 'The Nawab summons them every year. This is just routine for them – but more is to come.'

He was right. After a few minutes, the juggling ceased and one of the performers approached the dais, still holding one of his flaming brands. Slowly, deliberately, he applied it to his chest. There was a sharp intake of breath all around. Nicholas leaned forward – surely the man had burned his skin? – but his face remained impassive and, as he lifted the brand away, his skin was unmarked. He repeated the action several times and then, advancing towards Chanda Sahib, held the brand towards him. 'Feel the heat, sir, the fire is real. Hold this piece of silk into its heart.' He handed Chanda Sahib a strip of material. As the general dangled it into the flames, the fabric caught alight, shrivelling up so fast that Chanda Sahib quickly dropped it to the ground. The performer ran lightly back to the centre of the floor, spread his legs wide for balance, threw back his head, and opening his mouth wide inserted the tip of the brand into it. Flames streamed from his lips, but as he straightened up and pulled out the brand, circling it over his head in triumph, his mouth remained unscarred.

As the fire-eaters departed, attendants re-lit the torches and more performers followed – acrobats so pliable and lithe their bodies seemed boneless, a snake charmer at the urging of whose wailing pipe a speckled cobra rose from a basket to sway before him and a magician who produced gold coins from men's ears and noses. Next came musicians, carrying flutes, drums and a sitar, who seated themselves opposite the dais. As they began to play, Nicholas noticed the other guests again craning their necks towards the entrance to the tent.

Above the plaintiff melody, Nicholas caught a rhythmic jingling and a tall young woman in spangled trousers and a tight-fitting silk bodice that left her midriff bare and with brass bells fastened around her ankles entered the tent, stamping her feet and curling her arms sinuously above her head. Her hennaed hair hung loose, so long it almost reached the curve of her buttocks, visible through the flowing diaphanous material of her trousers. Behind her followed six more dancers, each keeping the beat. The music, which had at first been slow, almost languorous, began to quicken and the lead dancer began to twirl. But it was the last dancer to enter – younger and slighter than the others – who held Nicholas's attention. Her movements were as graceful as if she was the music's very soul. Suddenly she raised her head and for a moment it seemed to Nicholas that her large, luminous dark eyes looked into his. With its high cheekbones, delicately ached brows, small, straight nose and full mouth her face was the most perfect he had ever seen – Helen of Troy in Hindustan…

The music grew faster and wilder and with it the dancers' movements. All around him the guests roared their approval. The lead dancer was now whirling so fast her hair swirled around her like a curtain of silk, while her companions had flung themselves to the ground and kneeling back before the Nawab were arching their backs, breasts out-thrust and hips gyrating. As the beating of the drums grew louder and there came a great clash of cymbals, the lead dancer too fell on her knees before the Nawab, as if surrendering to him in passion.

Through it all, Nicholas's attention remained fixed on the young dancer.

He couldn't take his eyes off her as she finally rose and accepted a bag of coins from the vizier as the other dancers had done. Her compelling, luminous beauty haunted him as the performances continued, including a man who led in a tamed leopard with his three-year-old son clinging to its tawny muscled back.

By the final evening of Nauroz, Nicholas felt light-headed from lack of sleep. Everything he had seen and done was a confused but glorious blur in his memory. But the last night would be the best, or so the Nawab had hinted in the note delivered to his room just before dusk. Neither he, nor Tuhin Singh to whom he showed the card and was good at picking up court gossip, could guess what the Nawab intended.

About three hours later, an attendant led Nicholas to a terrace projecting from the battlements over the dark river below. There a small but exquisitely decorated Nauroz tent had been erected. It was so heavily embroidered with golden thread that it glowed in the light of six torches burning around it. The awnings and entrance flap were secured with jewelled ribbons and from within came the soulful strains of a sitar.

As Nicholas entered, he saw Anwaruddin Khan reclining against a yellow bolster propped against one side of the tent. The Nawab raised his hand in greeting, then gestured to Nicholas to sit beside him. He must be the first of the guests, Nicholas thought, noting with surprise that no one else was present except for the sitar player seated in the corner. The tent – lit by candles in tiny gilt cages – was piled with brightly coloured cushions and bolsters. At one end a shimmering piece of blue silk shot through with silver thread concealed whatever lay behind. Food waiting to be served, Nicholas wondered.

Anwaruddin Khan seemed to read his mind. 'There are no other guests. I invited you here because I have a surprise for you. Sometimes you reveal more of yourself than you perhaps realise. On the first night of the Nauroz I suspected something which now I wish to put to the test.' Smiling, the Nawab rose, clapped his hands together three times, then to Nicholas's astonishment he turned and left the tent.

As Nicholas – more than a little startled – got quickly to his feet, he heard a sound from behind the silk screen. Then a small bejewelled hennaed hand emerged round the screen, caressing its edge. It took hold of the silk and pulled it aside to reveal the young dancer whom Nicholas had not been able to drive from his thoughts these past days.

Her pale green shift was so sheer it showed every contour of her slender body. As the sitar music grew louder, she advanced into the centre of the tent, her eyes never leaving his face. When she was just a few feet from him she said softly, 'My name is Meena. The Nawab asked if I would dance for you alone. I told him it would be my pleasure if I could give you pleasure... But perhaps we don't need the sitar player,' she continued after a pause. 'I can keep the rhythm myself.' Without waiting for Nicholas to reply, she turned to the musician and made a sweeping gesture with her hand, at which the man immediately rose and slipped out into the night.

Meena lowered the flap over the entrance to the tent, then turned to Nicholas again. He felt as bewitched as when she'd looked at him during the dance. His mouth had gone dry and he could find nothing to say. Eyes still fixed on his face, Meena shrugged off her shift to stand before him in the soft apricot glow of the candles lighting the tent. She was entirely naked except for a thin gold chain hung with tiny bells encircling her waist. Her shining hair, tumbling around her, could not conceal her small but perfect breasts, hennaed with small flowers around the nipples. Raising her arms above her head, she began to dance, slowly, sensuously, revolving her hips so that the bells shook like leaves on a tree in the wind. Meena was right. She had no need of a sitar player, Nicholas thought. Her perfect body, by its motion, made its own music. The tinkling of her bells matched the pounding of his beating heart as he felt desire greater than any he had ever known.

She came nearer, until her arms were around him, her finger tips teasing the back of his neck and running through his long brown hair while she pressed herself against him so that he felt the warm softness of her. Very slowly, she unfastened and removed his red army jacket, then his shirt. Now her fingertips were caressing his bare chest, running lightly over his battle scars and all the time her wide, shining dark eyes looked into his. He burned with the longing to take her in his arms and satisfy his passion, but he felt as awkward and uncertain as a teenaged boy about to make love for the first time.

'I am yours if you wish it,' Meena whispered softly.

'What do *you* wish?' Nicholas asked.

'To be your lover.'

'Truly? You don't have to do this. Don't be afraid. I'll say nothing to the Nawab, I...'

But he got no further. Meena's fingertip was on his lips, 'Ssh. Our bodies are gifts given us to enjoy. Come...'

Taking his hand, she led him over to a low divan, lay down and held out her arms. Nicholas needed no further invitation. Stripping off his breeches he lay down beside her and buried his face between her breasts. Her breathing was as rapid as his own. His hand stroked the smooth plane of her stomach before descending to caress the soft-downed mound between her legs. She gave a low moan, then whispered, 'I'm ready...'

As he entered her, Meena arched her back, pushing her hips against him, answering every thrust with a little cry of pleasure. At the very moment of climax he bent his head to kiss her and her lips opened beneath his. As he collapsed onto her, their bodies ran with sweat and their breathing was ragged. But it wasn't long before he felt her fingertips caressing him anew, and the eager response of his body that needed no urging.

10 — The Assassins

'Babur, the first Moghul emperor, used to have musk melons packed in ice brought all the way to Delhi from Kabul, swearing they were the sweetest and that nothing comparable was to be had in Hindustan,' Anwaruddin Khan said biting into the soft yellow flesh of a melon. Wiping the juice from his lips he continued, 'But I'm sure he was wrong, and that these melons from my shaded hot-houses are the best imaginable.'

Nicholas, seated cross-legged among a tumble of turquoise and scarlet velvet cushions, nodded. He and the Nawab were sharing a late afternoon meal after a successful morning's hunting. The Nawab had despatched the main hunting party back to Birangarh with the carcasses of the animals they had shot, but decided he wished to remain overnight in this hunting lodge and invited Nicholas to join him. Soft rays from the descending sun slanted through the stained glass in the dome topping the lodge's main room, causing a rainbow of colours to dance across the white-washed walls. The four tall, bearded bodyguards standing straight-backed and statue-still – two at each side of the great mahogany entrance doors – seemed to share the general languor. The head of one appeared to be drooping onto his broad chest.

'That shot with which you brought down the deer in the coppice this morning was a fine one,' the Nawab said. 'It must have been at the very limit of your musket's range.'

'It's really down to the weapon. I bought mine from one of the best gunsmiths in Calcutta. I'm sure I could obtain...' Hearing a movement, Nicholas broke off. From the corner of his eye he noticed two of the hitherto motionless guards slip quietly out of the room – a curious thing to do without seeking the Nawab's permission. He scarcely had time to register what was happening before the remaining two drew their swords and rushed towards Anwaruddin Khan who was seated opposite Nicholas and with his back to the door. Instinctively, Nicholas hurled himself towards the Nawab with his hands outstretched and pushed him out of the path of the two onrushing attackers. Then, rolling over, and drawing his dirk as he did so, he grasped the legs of the foremost assailant, pulling him to the floor among the cushions and immediately thrust his dirk twice into the man's groin, staining the guard's yellow pantaloons orange with a rush of scarlet blood.

Scrambling to his feet, Nicholas launched himself headfirst at the second assailant as he lunged towards the Nawab, catching him in the pit of his stomach, causing him to double up and fall backward, dropping his scimitar. Moments later, Tuhin Singh, alerted by the Nawab's cries, was beside Nicholas and had the man's arms pinioned behind his back. 'Where are the other two?' Nicholas asked as he scrambled to his feet, heart beating wildly. 'They tried to stop us from entering the room. The captain of the guard and his deputy and I were talking in the anteroom when we heard the disturbance. They are dealing with them. I'm sure they'll have them secured by now.'

'They're not secured,' the captain reported entering the room at that moment with his deputy. 'They're dead.' Stooping over the crumpled and motionless body of the first attacker, the captain felt the man's neck for a pulse. Suddenly the man jerked upright, grabbed his arm and pulled him down among the bloodied cushions. They rolled around grappling with each other as the Nawab's attacker tried to reach his fallen sword, but he was weak from the loss of blood and the captain, freeing his long dagger from its scabbard at his side, stabbed it into the man's throat. Blood welled from the gaping gash and trickled from his mouth. He lay still once more, this time truly lifeless.

By now, Anwaruddin Khan was on his feet, his own dagger in his hand but his expression composed and his voice steady as he said to his four saviours, 'Thank you. You will be well rewarded.'

Then, he turned to the only surviving attacker. Tuhin Singh had tied his arms behind his back and the deputy captain of the guard had a firm grip on his shoulders. The would-be assassin appeared outwardly calm and did not shrink back as the Nawab strode across to him. His face only a few inches away, the Nawab roared, 'You will die for this. But tell me now who put you up to it and your death will be speedy and painless but if not...'

The attacker said nothing, but just looked down at the floor.

'Have no illusions, traitor. You will speak before you die. Better to save yourself the pain,' the Nawab repeated.

'I will not, Your Highness. And you must know from my former service to you in battle that I can withstand pain,' the guard said through clenched teeth.

'We will see.' Anwaruddin Khan turned to the captain of the guard. 'Take this wretch back to Birangarh and apply the hot irons.'

After he had been removed, the Nawab said to Nicholas, 'He is indeed a brave man and I suspect he will tell us nothing. To give the best chance of extorting a confession, I will order him not to be tortured at once but in a few hours. Allowing him time to ponder his coming agony might loosen his tongue. We too must now return to Birangarh.'

Early the next morning, in obedience to Anwaruddin Khan's summons, Nicholas stood beside the Nawab who was seated in the courtyard of the Birangarh fort beneath a green and white striped awning to protect him from the rising sun. 'As I expected,' Anwaruddin Khan said, 'the surviving attacker told my men nothing, not even when hot irons were applied to his body. A search of his quarters and possessions and those of his co-conspirators revealed nothing either. However, a fellow guard said he had been worried about meeting debts incurred while gambling, of which he was inordinately fond, but had recently spoken of coming into money, as he claimed, after the death of a childless uncle. It seems that money – as so often happens – is the root of his evil. And now he must die.'

The Nawab shouted an order and the captain of the guard appeared through the main gateway to the courtyard at the head of his men. Advancing in double file and in step to the rhythmic boom of a kettledrum from above the gateway, they formed up in ranks behind the Nawab who clapped his hands. Moments later, two soldiers appeared, dragging the would-be assassin, his feet trailing in the dust. As they flung him to the ground before the Nawab, Nicholas saw that his bare back carried the raw and blistered marks of the burning irons. For a moment, Nicholas thought he could still smell burning flesh but knew it must be his imagination. The torture would have finished some time ago.

'Once more, I ask you to reveal your sponsor,' the Nawab demanded. The man, who was now struggling to stand, shook his head. 'Then tie him to the execution block.'

The two soldiers pulled the prisoner, limp and unresisting, to a seemingly rust-stained marble block a few yards away which had an iron ring at each of its four corners. They pushed their captive onto his back on the stone and tied his limbs, one to each ring. At a further command from Anwaruddin Khan, a large elephant – one ear tattered with age – entered through the main gateway and, guided by the iron rod of its equally elderly mahout seated behind its ears, slowly approached the stone where the assailant lay spread-eagled. At a touch of the rod from its mahout, the animal raised its large right forefoot above the man's stomach.

'One last chance to avoid the pain and indignity of such a death,' the Nawab called out. 'Reveal the identity of your paymaster!'

The prisoner's voice was barely audible to Nicholas as, through chattering teeth, he said, 'I can't. The man has my family hostage, Your Highness. He will kill them if I speak. I owe it to my innocent loved ones to die rather than bring them harm.'

'So be it.' The Nawab clapped his hands once more. At another touch of the rod, the elephant lowered its foot onto the prisoner's stomach. As its full weight bore down on him, the man let out a single long howl of agony. Then his belly and bowels burst, releasing a stench so nauseous that Nicholas had to swallow to avoid retching. Seeing his distress Anwaruddin Khan said, 'I cannot show mercy and must be seen by this man's comrades, lined up behind my throne, not to show mercy. If I did, what they would see as my weakness would encourage other rebels.'

Had Cumberland thought the way the Nawab did as he'd ravaged the Highlands, Nicholas wondered as he continued to struggle to retain the contents of his stomach. Had the judges who condemned Jacobite rebels to be hung, drawn and quartered had the same thought in mind?

That evening, the Nawab invited Nicholas to dine with him, but he had little appetite. After the attendants had carried away the silver plates still containing quantities of pulao, lamb and chicken – the latter in the creamy, spicy sauce which Nicholas usually so enjoyed – servants lit the oil lamps in the mirror-lined niches in the walls, producing a flickering light. They cast long shadows as the servers brought in bowls of fruit and then left the two men alone. Peeling a grape, Anwaruddin Khan said, 'I'm indebted to you for your part in saving my life yesterday.'

'Nothing more than my duty, Highness.'

'Maybe, but others do not show the same loyalty. A son of my cousin, Khaled Kasim, has left the court abruptly. Though I've no firm evidence, I suspect his departure is connected with the attempt to kill me.'

Into Nicholas's mind flashed Chanda Sahib's comment about Anwaruddin Khan: '*Power and wealth incite envy and ambition – even within his own family...*' Even so he asked, 'Is that likely? Your own cousin?'

'Why not?' the Nawab replied. 'I can never feel easy on the throne. If I relax my vigilance there will be other attempts and, as yesterday proved, I will never be able to anticipate all usurpers. When my ancestors came from the steppes around that fabled golden city, Samarkand, they brought much that was good with them, but also their code of '*ya takht, ya takhta*' – the throne or the coffin. To me it is a curse under which I must live and probably die. The code permits each family member to challenge for power, not only when the ruler dies but at any time.'

'Such behaviour seems to be in man's nature.'

'I don't deny that, but in Hindustan rulers of states take the same attitude to other rulers. Rather than cooperate, they weaken themselves by fighting with each other for supreme power, however transitory. Thus they lay themselves open to new invaders, just as they did to the Moghuls. Foremost among these newcomers, of course, are you Europeans as I've pointed out before.'

'You are correct in that, Highness,' Nicholas said, feeling a little uneasy. 'However, rebellions and fighting among ruling families bedevil many places in Europe as well as in Hindustan, not least Britain as I know to my cost. My uncle recently lost our family estate in one such civil war. And, of course, you know European states fight among themselves as the battles between the East India Company and the French in Hindustan show.'

'I hope the Company is grateful for my support against the French but I sometimes fear they will only support me as long as it suits their interests.'

Nicholas became silent, thinking how the French had cynically supported the Jacobites just long enough to ensure they distracted the British Government from its other campaigns in Hindustan and Canada and then abandoned them. Yet, things weren't always so. Throughout history, men of principle had sacrificed their personal interests – even their lives – in the name of honour and duty. Eventually he said, 'Sometimes loyalty runs deeper than self-interest. I pray that will be true of the Company towards you.'

'Perhaps. But those Company directors about whom you yourself often appear mistrustful should remember that with so few Britons in Hindustan their ambitions can only succeed if they respect their allies and the people of this land. In the long run, a reputation for probity and loyalty will serve them better than one for duplicity and deception. They should also reflect on the harm they do by importing their conflicts with their European rivals to Hindustan. I aided the Company against the French at Fort St. David because, for the sake of my people, I have allied myself with them and felt honour bound to do so. But wouldn't it be better if rulers like myself were not forced to take sides in your disputes and indeed if you Europeans did not interfere in our internal affairs?'

Nicholas nodded. He had seldom heard the Nawab sound so grave.

'The past thirty-six hours have exhausted me. I wish to retire for the night,' the Nawab said a few minutes later.

As Nicholas returned to his own quarters through the warm Hindustani night, an attendant materialised from the shadows with a letter. 'This came by the latest dak messenger from the coast, Sahib.' Nicholas entered his room and lit the wick of an oil lamp with his tinder box. The letter bore his Uncle James's familiar writing! Hurriedly Nicholas broke the seal and began to read.

> *Nicholas, my dear nephew,*
>
> *I can only hope and pray that this letter reaches you. If it does, you will probably think me foolish when I tell you that in my heart I knew how it would end when the Prince appealed to my honour to join him. My consolations for my predicament are that I paid our family's debt to the Stuarts, that I kept you out of it and that you are young and have your life ahead of you. I received your letter and you were right. I would never have wanted you to return from Hindustan to join a doomed rebellion. There is nothing for you in Scotland – make Hindustan your home and prosper there – and do not think too harshly of your loving uncle who has deprived you of Glenmire, your heritage. I fear I cannot tell you where I am at present in case this letter falls into Hanoverian hands but I will write again when I am sure of my safety.*
>
> *Your affectionate uncle,*
> *James Ballantyne*

Nicholas's hands shook as he put the letter down. It was some comfort to know his uncle was alive, but where was he? Was he truly safe? When would he hear from him again?

Steeling himself, Nicholas re-read the letter, dwelling on the lines, *There is nothing for you in Scotland – make Hindustan your home and prosper there – and do not think too harshly of your loving uncle.* He could not think badly of James, but it was a bitter thought that he might never see Glenmire again, never gallop along the drive or row on the loch or walk through its woods. Slowly, he folded the letter and put it among his other papers in his campaign chest. His uncle's words and the events of the past two days had shown him how similar human nature could be, whether here, in Hindustan, or in far-away Scotland, and how loyalty – whether that of the Nawab's assailant to his family or of his uncle's selfless loyalty to the Prince – could indeed overcome self-interest as he had tried to say to the Nawab.

For a long while, Nicholas paced about his room, his thoughts in turmoil, until around midnight a light tap on the door broke his reverie. Opening it, he saw Meena's face, illuminated by the soft light of the brass oil lamp she was holding in her hand.

'You said you would come to me tonight. I waited but you did not come...'

'I'm sorry.' Taking the oil lamp from her, Nicholas drew Meena gently inside the room and closed the door. Then, bending his head he kissed her lips. 'I have had much to think about.'

'You look troubled... But I can tell you do not want to talk... at least not yet... Let me take care of you.' With deft fingers, Meena unfastened his tunic, then pulled off his shirt and gestured to him to lie face down on the bed. 'If I had known, I would have brought sandalwood oil but you will just have to make do with my bare hands.'

Resting his weary head on his arms, Nicholas felt her begin to knead his shoulders with her fingers. Closing his eyes and drinking in the familiar warm scent of her he felt the tension slowly start to ebb. She was working with her palms now, sliding them up and down his spine, pressing now softly, now harder.

'That's better, isn't it? I can feel your muscles relaxing,' Meena said, then planted a kiss on the back of his neck.

Nicholas nodded. Meena had the power to make him feel better, whether during their joyous love-making or the quieter moments when they talked. Sometimes he tried to describe his life in Scotland to her. She asked many questions and he could see how hard it was for her to understand a place she had never seen. In turn, she had told him about her childhood – about her mother Anjali, also a court dancer who had trained her, and the father who, Anjali claimed, was a noble of Anwaruddin Khan's court, though she would never reveal his name. Anjali had died just as, at fourteen, Meena had begun to dance for the Nawab.

'Don't you mind?' Nicholas had asked a little awkwardly. 'I mean performing before strange men?'

Meena had laughed. 'You're so odd! Are all the British like you? I've told you before, I learned from my mother our bodies are a gift, not something to hide. And I've always loved to dance. It makes me feel truly alive. If men enjoy watching me, so much the better.'

'But what about the desire you rouse? Every man who sees you must want you.'

'As you did?' Meena smiled. 'It troubled me a little when I was still very young. But I am a performer not a slave. I have never been forced to take a lover. It has always been my choice.'

The more he had pondered her words, the more he realised that Meena led a freer and more honest life than many European women whose loveless marriages were mere financial transactions in which they had little say. How often in Calcutta or Madras had he heard whispers of brutalities and infidelities hidden beneath the veneer of seemingly respectable Company marriages? Meena could choose her own destiny, a fact of which she seemed joyfully aware. 'From our very first night, I gave myself to you freely as was my right. I will be yours, as long as we both wish it,' she had said.

And he did wish it. Indeed, he could scarcely imagine his life without her.

'Have I done my job well?' Meena whispered into his ear.

'You have. And now it's my turn.' Turning quickly over, Nicholas dislodged her so that she tumbled, laughing, onto the floor. He pulled her up beside him and held her tight.

'You don't look quite so sad now. I'm glad,' she said softly. 'But won't you tell me what's been troubling you?'

'You understand me so well... I received bad news from Britain this evening – news that shocked me. That's why I did not come to you as I had promised. I needed time to think.'

'Bad news? Has someone died?' Meena's dark eyes searched his.

'No, not that. But tonight, for the first time I've realised I'll probably never see my home in Scotland again.'

For some moments, Meena was silent, her fingers stroking his long hair. Then she said. 'Life is strange. News that makes you sad makes me happy. I know I am being selfish – too greedy for happiness – but I can't lie to you. I don't want you to go home, not ever.' Raising herself on one elbow, she put her finger on his lips. 'We've talked enough, now,' she whispered before her hands slid over his chest and stomach and her lips met his.

11 – Temptation

12 November 1748

Dear Nicholas,

Congratulate me! I write no longer a humble Ensign but a Lieutenant. As they say, it's an ill wind that blows no good. In this case fortune has blown nothing but fair winds in my direction. The reason for my promotion is this. One night, while we were besieging Pondicherry, the French sallied out against a trench that my platoon and I were defending. I'd anticipated just such a trick and we were ready for them, muskets primed and loaded. This is how my commanding officer reported the action: 'Clive's platoon, animated by his exhortation, fired with great courage and vivacity upon the enemy causing them to fall back in chaos and disarray with many losses.'

Though I thank the stars I was given such an opportunity to prove myself once more, the siege ultimately failed. It wasn't the French who forced us to retreat, but the violence of the monsoon rains. They say peace with France is coming. I pray it isn't true. There can be no true peace for the Company, no chance to reap the rich rewards of trade in Hindustan, if we allow our European rivals to remain. I, for one, will not rest until we have driven them into the sea!

Write soon with your news. They say the Nawab is preparing to advance on the French at Ambur? Is that right?

May you be prospering as I am,
Your friend,
Clive

Nicholas tucked the letter into his tunic pocket, smiling. Typical Clive! But he was glad for him. From the fragments he'd heard, the siege of Pondicherry had been ill-advised and the officer in charge inexperienced in siege tactics. Things might have gone better had a French cavalry patrol not captured Clive's mentor, Major Stringer Lawrence, while he was leading forces towards Pondicherry to reinforce the siege.

Clive obviously knew nothing yet about the assassination attempt on Anwaruddin Khan, but he was correct. The Nawab was advancing on Ambur, on the banks of the Palar river, 180 miles west of Madras. The Company was launching an attack on French positions there – a prelude to trying to win back Madras itself, and had called on their allies' troops. Nicholas had been surprised that the Nawab intended to go himself but he had told Nicholas, 'I may be old but I am still a warrior. And when I lead my troops into battle, my enemies will see that I am no feeble old man to be despatched by an assassin's blade.'

Nicholas would have liked to accompany him, as Chanda Sahib was, but to his surprise Anwaruddin Khan had a different mission for him. As the Nawab had suspected, his cousin Khaled Kasim – the ruler of a small state adjoining the Nawab's lands and his vassal – had indeed been behind the assassination attempt against him. Fear of detection had forced Khaled Kasim's hand. Within two weeks of the failed attack, he had proclaimed his allegiance to the French and declared war against the Nawab. Now he was leading his army to rendezvous with Dupleix's forces in French-controlled territory, just beyond the Nawab's north-eastern borders.

Learning of this, Anwaruddin Khan had given Nicholas command of a large detachment of cavalry including a company of fifty mounted musketeers. 'My cousin has a head start of six or seven days but he can only move at the pace of the slowest –

his foot soldiers and baggage wagons will delay him,' the Nawab had said. 'If you ride fast and light you can get ahead of him. To reach Dupleix he must go through the Marapur hills and there is only one route through a narrow defile. Get there first. Occupy the high ground above it and if Khaled Kasim attempts to pass through, delay him until the major force I'm assembling arrives. Then we'll crush the traitor like an almond in a nut-cracker...'

Twelve days ago, Nicholas, with Tuhin Singh beside him, had ridden out from Birangarh at the head of his men. At first, they had crossed flat dusty plains criss-crossed by dried-up creeks and river beds, giving a wide berth to the route along which, according to Nicholas's scouts, Khaled Kasim's forces were making dogged progress, marching only at night because of the high summer heat. The sun, beating down relentlessly, had punished Nicholas's men, too, as they travelled by day. On the fourth afternoon, several had been stricken by heatstroke. The first, a grey-bearded man with many years' service in the Nawab's army, had descended into delirium with bloated tongue and swollen lips before dying. Another – a youth – had fallen from his horse without previously giving any sign of distress. Several others had slumped in their saddles, semi-conscious.

Two days later, Nicholas's column had begun their ascent of the golden eroded sandstone of the Marapur hills and reached the vantage point above the pass that the Nawab had described. The shade of a sprinkling of trees and some large honey-coloured rocks honed by wind and rain into fantastical shapes, gave at least some protection from the sun and cover from the enemy. Nicholas had ordered the horses to be tethered in a saucer-shaped depression close to a spring from which they could drink. The modest baggage train consisting only of pack animals – carts would have been too slow – had caught up with them three days ago, bringing tents, cooking pots and more sacks of rice and grain. It had also brought Meena who had insisted she would follow him, overriding all his objections with the simple words 'When I am not with you I do not exist...'

A sliver of moon lay on its back in a plush indigo sky in which the first stars were appearing. The day's heat had been fierce, but the temperature was growing more bearable as Nicholas returned from inspecting the ring of pickets he'd stationed around the camp to keep watch through the night. Dupleix's forces were only 20 miles away and it wouldn't have escaped their notice that his own had been encamped here for six days. All armies had their spies… It wouldn't do to be caught unawares – especially since he'd outflanked the army of the rebel Khaled Kasim.

Now, as he walked slowly back towards his tent in the centre of the lines, his men were squatting round their cooking fires – burning charcoal, not wood, because it produced less smoke – and preparing their evening meal. How he'd enjoy plunging his head into a basin of water… Then for relaxation he might play his violin or challenge Tuhin Singh to a game of chess. Later he would ask Meena to come to him. His blood quickened at the thought and he was smiling as he ducked beneath the tent flap and went inside. In the darkness it took him some moments to locate his tinderbox. While he was still feeling for it he thought he smelled something – a sweet, potent scent, strangely familiar. Locating the box at last he struck it, lit a candle in a clay jar on an upturned wooden box by his bed and looked around. As the candle began to shed its soft light, the heady scent still filled his nostrils. Turning, he saw a woman wearing a long, dark cloak, her face hidden behind a veil, standing in the shadows.

'Meena?' No. This woman was taller, more statuesque. Before he could speak again she stepped forward, put a finger to her lips, then slowly lifted back her veil. It couldn't be, but yes, it was Jeanne Dupleix… He reached for the dirk in his belt but she stepped forward quickly, saying, 'Hush, no need for all that. Surely you aren't afraid of a mere woman? I am alone with you and entirely in your power…'

Nicholas stared, still not quite able to believe that this apparition was real. 'How did you get into my camp?' he asked curtly.

'Two of my husband's soldiers brought me close to the perimeter just after dusk. We've been watching you since not long after you arrived – we know at exactly what time your pickets take up their positions for the night watch. I walked openly up to one of them and told him I was your abandoned mistress, dying of love for you. You know how sentimental these Hindustanis can be. To save my poor heart from breaking and – I admit – in return for a few coins, he brought me to your tent when no one else was around to observe. Don't be too hard on him – he was anxious for your safety. At least that's what he told me as he ran his hands over my body to assure himself I was no assassin and had no weapon concealed about me…' Her purring voice fell silent and her eyes looked teasingly into his.

Nicholas strode to the entrance to the tent and was about to call for the guards, when behind him Jeanne spoke again. 'Don't you at least want to know why I've come? I remember you so well from those days after Madras fell to us – your *bon mien* – what is it you say in English, "good looks"? And I recall how you refused our offer of freedom, unlike so many of your companions. But, of course, they were unprincipled Englishmen. You, on the other hand, are Scottish – a Highlander – descended from a people with a fine tradition of honour who helped your young prince and who have always been friends to France.'

'I'm no more a friend to France than France was to the Jacobites.'

'Politics is a sad thing, *mon ami*. Charles Edward Stuart lacked strength – he is a pretty boy, but a weak one. We came to realise he could never succeed. So why risk our soldiers, our money, in a doomed cause? But the prince should not be bitter. We sent a ship to rescue him and bring him safely to France where our king has given him a fine palace to live in and doves with jewelled collars to play with…' Her complacent smile galled Nicholas as she continued, 'If the Highlanders feel betrayed, they should blame the English, not the French. Tell me, doesn't it offend your honour to serve a government that has so ravaged your people – even your own uncle who has lost everything and must live like a pauper, dependent on our French charity…?'

'My uncle? What do you know about him?' Nicholas grasped Jeanne Dupleix by the wrist so tightly he could feel its small bones, but she didn't flinch. Holding his gaze with her sapphire-blue eyes she said, 'Don't be concerned. At least he's safe – an exile in a garret in Boulogne.'

'What else do you know about him?'

'Nothing more, I promise you. Why should I? He's just one of many...'

Nicholas let go of Jeanne's wrist which, smiling to herself, she rubbed a little. 'What do you want?' he asked. 'You didn't come all this way to tell me about my uncle.'

'I have a proposition for you. You would do well to listen for such a chance may not come again. My husband knows the influence you have with Anwaruddin Khan – the high regard the Nawab has for you, especially since you saved him from assassination. We want you to use it to persuade the Nawab to abandon the British and become our ally instead.'

'Why should the Nawab break faith with the British?'

'Because we have something he wants. Khaled Kasim sent his own son to us in advance of his army for safe-keeping. And believe me we do indeed have him "safe". One word from the Nawab and we'll execute him or hand him over to the Nawab to torture as he pleases. Surely the Nawab would like to revenge himself against Khaled Kasim and what better way than to kill his son?'

'The Nawab has his own forces to fight his battles for him. In a few days, we'll have dealt with Khaled Kasim and if the Nawab wants his son, we'll take him from you. He doesn't need your gifts or pretty promises!'

'You speak with such authority, yet how do you know what is in the Nawab's mind? Send me to him with a safe escort. Let me argue my case with him in person.'

'He's a man of honour and so am I. I'd no more send you to him than I'd send a whore from the bazaars!'

For the first time Jeanne's eyes flashed with real emotion. She stepped forward and dealt him a stinging blow on his left cheek.

She was breathing hard and her full lips were half open as she looked challengingly up at him – a look more like that between two warriors on the battlefield than between a woman and a man. Raising both hands to her throat she unfastened the clasp of her cloak and let it fall to the ground. Beneath it she was wearing a low-cut gown, whose silk ruffles revealed the swell of her breasts.

Before Nicholas realised what he was doing, he was gripping her by the back of the neck with one hand and forcing his mouth down hard on hers. He felt a shiver run through her as she pressed herself closer against him before she sought his free hand and guided it to her breasts, murmuring 'I knew you wanted me. I always know… Your bed is of hard wood, like a peasant's. Take me here, instead, on the ground.'

Nicholas's head was spinning – Jeanne's potent scent, the softness of her flesh, her caressing words were bewitching…

'Wait… I have a gift – *un beau cadeau* – for you…' She pushed him gently away and then with a few deft movements loosened her gown and shrugged it from her. Her naked body, pale as the pearls in her ears, was true to the name by which she was known – *la voluptueuse* – with rounded hips and long, tapering legs. Taking his hand, she pressed it between her thighs. 'See, I'm ready for you… While I was peeling that orange for you in the prison, I imagined this and now I shall find out…'

Something in her tone, perhaps her absolute confidence in her power over him, broke the spell. He did remember her peeling the orange and the contemptuous, self-satisfied smile on her face as she'd inspected her husband's prisoners as if they were creatures in a zoo. Well, he was no prisoner now. He would not be mastered by so flimsy a weapon as this woman's charms. What had he been thinking of? He stepped back, picked up her dress – still warm from her body – and threw it to her before turning away and saying quietly, 'Get dressed!'

'Why?' she said, evidently puzzled, her words coming fast. 'You want me. I know it. I saw your desire, I felt it too. Surrender to it.'

'I won't be played for a fool!' Nicholas said shortly. 'As I said, get dressed!'

As she studied his face and read the resolution there, Jeanne Dupleix's expression grew colder. Shrugging her shoulders, she pulled on her gown. 'So good-looking, but such a prig,' she said. 'Perhaps you are like your English countrymen after all.'

'You understand nothing about me. I'm my own man. I serve the East India Company because it's what I choose to do. If ever I decide otherwise, I'll do so openly, not resort to squalid tricks or treachery. Madame, now tell me something. Why do you prostitute yourself as you do? Have you no honour, no shame?'

'Prostitute myself?' Jeanne's lovely eyes hardened. 'Like you, I also choose to do what I do. But I'm no common whore, giving my body for money. Would you believe me if I said I do it for the sheer thrill of it? Probably not. Aren't men supposed to be the only adventurous ones... I do what I do for my husband, whom I love, to advance his career and blunt the intrigues of his enemies, and I do it for my country, which I also love. But, yes, most of all I do it for myself, for the adventure, to show that as a woman I have the power to shape events just as you men do!

'You smile, standing there so high and mighty, thinking yourself safe behind your pompous, pious, conventional principles, but I nearly had you just now. I saw the desire in your hypocritical eyes. You're no better than the rest − scarcely more than brute animals, all of you, that I enjoy bending to my will. Does my behaviour make me any worse than you men who don't hesitate to exploit my sex if we let you? I don't think so!' She paused for a moment and then continued, her tone ever harsher, 'But I see from your face you have no comprehension of how I feel and have set your mind against me. *Mon Dieu*, you're a man of your time and I've been born outside of mine. I have wasted my breath. What happens now?'

Nicholas walked over to the tent flap and held it open. 'Now you leave. I'll send a soldier with you to the camp perimeter to make sure you're not molested. No doubt your escorts are waiting to take you back to French territory and your pimp of a husband.'

Jeanne gave him a scornful look but before she replaced her veil, he saw the heightened colour in her cheeks. Then she was gone.

For a few moments Nicholas felt dazed. The whole thing could have been a dream, except that Jeanne's heady perfume still scented the air. To clear his disordered thoughts, he plunged his head into a large brass bowl filled with water. Why hadn't he had her arrested? Was it because there'd been some truth in what she'd said? His uncle had suffered at the hands of England. His people, the Highlanders, were still suffering. Jeanne Dupleix had offered him a chance for revenge – but for what? And against whom? If he betrayed the Company, it would only benefit the French – the supposed allies who had abandoned the Jacobites in their moment of greatest need. Of course, he could have negotiated favours for his uncle – something to rescue him from penury. But how was he to know if Jeanne's stories about James were true? In any case, James was a man of scrupulous honour who would hold betrayal and deceit an unacceptable price to pay.

Yet, what about his own honour when for a few mad moments, gripped by lust, he had forgotten himself? Not once while he was with Jeanne had he thought of Meena whose young, trusting face now seemed to swim before his eyes. Relief that he had overcome temptation – if only just – that he could still take Meena in his arms knowing he had not betrayed her, over-whelmed him. And with it came the realisation of how much Meena had come to mean to him… How much more than simple carnal lust…

Stepping outside, he called to a servant to go to the women's tents and ask Meena to come to him. Ten minutes later, she was there. As he knew it would, her fresh, youthful beauty, her uncomplicated rose-scented embrace banished from his mind all thoughts of Jeanne Dupleix's attempts to use her powers of seduc-tion to tame him physically and his anger with himself at so nearly succumbing mentally. He felt a deep tenderness, as enfolded in each other's arms he and Meena made love, equal partners in the giving and taking of pleasure, until in the paling light of early morning they heard the camp begin to stir.

Among the documents in the campaign chest of the Ballantyne Papers found in Kolkata is a letter from the Nawab Anwaruddin Khan, congratulating Nicholas on the success of his campaign to prevent his cousin Khaled Kasim from rendezvousing with the French until the Nawab's main force arrived. He also commends Nicholas on his part in the subsequent battle during which the traitor Khaled Kasim was killed.

Meanwhile, as Clive had previously predicted, peace between the French and the British was indeed in the offing. In fact, the Peace of Aix-la-Chapelle had already been signed in Europe. However, the news did not reach Hindustan until too late to save Anwaruddin Khan, killed leading his men into battle against the French at Ambur. Nicholas's diary reveals his sorrow at the Nawab's death in a war that was already over, though he also wrote, 'To die sword in hand in battle, rather than in bed or by an assassin's knife, is what he would have chosen, I'm sure.'

Following the Nawab's death, the Company lost little time in recalling Nicholas to Madras, recently relinquished by the French under the treaty.

A.R.

Part Four

From Soldier to Secret Agent, Madras, 1749–1755

12 – Tanjore

Red dirt flew from the hooves of their horses as Robert Clive galloped alongside Nicholas down a steep valley towards the wide, tree-shaded Coleroon river below. Tuhin Singh was a few yards ahead, his outstanding skill as a horseman as usual giving him the advantage as they guided their mounts around rocks and a few scrubby bushes.

On his return to Madras, Nicholas had enjoyed being reunited with Clive, preening in his new lieutenant's uniform, his prominent nose almost twitching with enthusiasm and pent-up energy. 'The good thing is that the Company aren't interpreting the peace too strictly,' he'd told Nicholas, pouring him a glass of claret as they sat in Clive's cool quarters in Fort St. George. 'It's greatly to our advantage that news takes so long to travel between London and Madras or Calcutta. Before hearing of the peace, the Company had already agreed to a request from the usurped Raja of Tanjore to send an expedition to restore him to his throne. Besides the usurper being allied to the French, a major attraction was the large, not to say magnificent, reward the old Raja promised the Company, including the gift of the port of Devakattoi to use as we wish, if we restored him to the throne. As I heard, he has also made generous private promises to several of the Council members here. Anyway, the Company quickly sent out an expedition. And as you probably know, it was a disaster! We lost most of our baggage train while crossing a swollen river.

'But,' Clive said, eyes sparkling, 'the Company and its council members for once showed good sense and decided not to give up their fine opportunity for profit! They ignored the news of the peace and ordered Major Lawrence – just released by the French – to lead a new force to Tanjore. Yours truly is going – I've been posted to a detachment of cavalry in the vanguard. And you're just in time to come along too! I'll fix it with Major Warburton who's commanding the detachment. He's quite a character, red-faced and with a peppery temper to match. People say – though I don't know if it's true – that he's the illegitimate son of some minor bishop. What is certain is that he rose from the ranks through bravery and the sheer ability to survive battle wounds and disease. I like him!'

Warburton had readily agreed to include both Nicholas and Tuhin Singh in his detachment. But Nicholas had found it hard to part from Meena so soon – only ten days after arriving in Madras – especially since, to their joy, she had recently discovered she was pregnant. At least he'd had time to find them lodgings near the fort – a bungalow with a small courtyard well-shaded by a mango tree – and to employ servants to cook and clean. 'Will you be alright here?' he'd asked when the inevitable moment of parting approached.

'Of course,' she had replied, embracing him. 'I have everything I need. While you are away, I'll sit beneath the tree and practise playing my tanpura. The sound will soothe our baby…' Her silken hair had half-veiled her face as she looked down at her belly. Then, taking one of Nicholas's hands, she had laid it for a moment on the barely perceptible roundness. 'No movement yet, but when you return perhaps our child will kick in greeting.' She'd looked searchingly into his face before saying softly. 'You must go, I know – but come back safely to me, to us…' They'd kissed lingeringly. Then, as each tried to hold back a tear, he had turned and walked outside, mounted his horse and ridden away, trusting himself to look back only once to see Meena waving both hands in farewell.

Three weeks into the expedition, though the pressures of the campaign allowed little opportunity for reflection, there was not a day when at some time or other he did not think of Meena. Warburton was proving everything Clive had said. His language and command style were equally blunt and aggressive. 'Gallop hard! Find the enemy quickly! Charge them and send them to hell!' he'd ordered earlier that day as, just before first light, he'd led their section of the vanguard in pursuit of a combined scouting force of French and Tanjorean troops reported to be nearby.

But the task was proving far more difficult than Warburton, at least, had anticipated. They'd been riding for four hours already with no sign of the enemy. A scout had reported the tracks of numerous horses but closer examination of the horse dung as well as the poor definition of the hoof prints had shown that the tracks were not recent. 'From what I'm told, there should be a ford down there. Let's get across and then take a breather,' Nicholas heard Warburton shout from a little behind him. The major was not a thin man and even on his fine grey charger found keeping up with his leading riders a problem.

Five minutes later they were at the ford with no sign of enemy tracks in the mud around it. Even at the ford, the river, dark with silt, did not look that shallow. Warburton, wiping away the sweat streaming down his face with his neck cloth, ordered three men to ride into the water to check how easy it would be to negotiate. The three entered the river, cautiously probing the bottom with their lance-tips as they went. The current did not seem particularly strong and when they were halfway across, with water washing around their knees, their leader, a corporal, shouted back, 'It's possible to cross, though there are one or two potholes in the bottom to be wary of.'

'Let's go then!' Warburton urged his grey charger in. Clive, Tuhin Singh and Nicholas were among the first to follow. By now the three pioneers were emerging from the river on the opposite side, their horses shaking the water from their coats. The corporal turned and shouted back, 'The deepest point is three quarters of the way across. Take...' He got no further as a fusillade of musket fire erupted from the shadow of the trees fringing the far side of the river. The corporal dropped his lance and plunged from the saddle into the murky water as did one of his companions. The third clung grimly to the neck of his horse which, wounded in the flank by a musket ball, bolted in fright and pain up the riverbank, only for another musket ball to knock the rider sideways from his saddle to sprawl lifeless on the ground.

At the same time, forty or more French and Tanjorean horsemen spurred out from the trees and galloped into the river raising great splashes of water in their eagerness to attack the Company troops. One of the leading riders – a scimitar – wielding, blue-turbaned Tanjorean – rode straight for Major Warburton whom he had correctly identified as the commander. Warburton was distracted – his whole attention on controlling his fine horse which seemed to have stumbled into one of the pot holes in the riverbed. Nicholas yelled a warning and pulling on his reins turned his own mount towards Warburton and his attacker.

Hearing Nicholas's shout, Warburton just had time enough to raise his left arm to block the attack as the advancing Tanjorean swung his scimitar at his head. Warburton's arm caught the full weight of the stroke just below the elbow, and immediately dangled loose and useless. At that moment, Nicholas, sword drawn, reached the pair and with a swift thrust deep into the chest of the Tanjorean, who was intent only on finishing off the major, dehorsed him. Arms flailing, he fell backwards into the water with a large splash. Blood was pouring from Warburton's forearm as Nicholas shouted to one of the Company troopers to get their commander back to the bank while trying to tie off the wound with his own neck cloth.

While he was doing so, he suddenly became aware of two other horsemen – one French, one Tanjorean – bearing down on him. He parried the lance of the blue-coated Frenchman with his sword but the Tanjorean's lance penetrated the neck of his horse. The animal reared up and fell backwards into the muddy water, landing partly on top of Nicholas, trapping him beneath the dying animal. He struggled to release himself but could not free his left foot from its stirrup however hard he kicked. His lungs felt fit to burst and his cheeks were puffed out as he tried not to breathe in water while he tugged furiously at the stirrup. All of a sudden a hand with a knife appeared through the murk and cut the stirrup leather.

Nicholas reached the surface, desperately gasping for air. Simultaneously, Tuhin Singh's head appeared from the water beside him. His knife had saved Nicholas from drowning.

'Thank you,' Nicholas gasped, chest heaving as he regained his breath.

'Think nothing of it. A small recompense for killing that second tiger in Bengal.'

Pushing his wet hair out of his eyes, Nicholas looked around. 'I think they're going!' He was right. On the far bank, their adversaries were pulling back from the fight, some pausing to pick up a musketeer from the riverbank, then galloping away. A few Company troops were now across the river, more were in the water where several bodies were floating. A third remained on the bank from which they'd started. They were in no position to undertake an immediate pursuit as even the impatient, impetuous Clive – the most senior unwounded officer – recognised. He did, however, despatch two scouts to shadow the retreating enemy at a distance.

Major Warburton lay on the bank from which they had attempted to cross. A tourniquet seemed to have staunched his blood flow. As Nicholas and Clive stooped over his body to inspect the apparently semi-comatose major's wound – a mess of bloody flesh, sinew and splintered bone – Clive said to Nicholas, 'His arm's half off and it must come off completely if he's to survive. But we've no surgeon.'

'Then do it yourselves,' Warburton opened his eyes and barked. 'Give me some liquor – I'm sure one of you young blades must be carrying a flask. And if not, there's a half-full one in my saddlebag. Clive – you and my orderly hold me down. And you, Ballantyne, do the amputation. From what I know of Hindustan conditions you'll need to cauterise the wound if it's not to mortify.' With that, Warburton lay back, leaving Nicholas and Clive to stare at one another across his body in shock. After a moment, Nicholas said to Clive, 'Well, I suppose there's nothing for it but to get on with it.'

They set to immediately. Nicholas cleaned the mud and remaining blood and gore from his sword which he had recovered from the river. Clive pulled out a hip flask containing brandy from his own saddlebag and after taking a swig to fortify himself handed it to Warburton's orderly, a burly Welshman, to start giving the liquor to the major. Then he ordered two troopers to prepare a fire and, once it was burning, to heat the blade of the major's sword in it until it was red hot.

These preparations took nearly twenty minutes, after which Clive and Nicholas returned to where an ashen-faced Warburton was lying, his orderly, who had removed the major's bloodstained shirt and tunic, still feeding him brandy. As well as his clean sword Nicholas was now carrying a makeshift chopping block he'd fashioned from a piece of a large fallen branch from which he'd stripped the bark.

'Get on with it quickly, God dammit!' Warburton growled as he saw them approach. Clive and Warburton's orderly held the major down by his shoulders and the orderly placed a wad of cloth in Warburton's mouth to prevent him from biting his tongue. Nicholas positioned the major's left arm carefully on the chopping block and, forcing himself to focus his eyes on the exposed muscle and bone of the wound, raised his sword above his head. With a single stroke, he severed the forearm above the wound and below the elbow. Warburton's eyes bulged and his body spasmed in agony. In response to Clive's shouted order, a trooper ran up with Warburton's sword, the blade glowing red and the hilt swathed in cloth. Taking the hilt Nicholas held the blade twice against the wound which sizzled like meat on the griddle. For the first time, despite the wadding in his mouth, they heard Warburton's muffled groans.

A little later, as Clive and Nicholas were recovering from the stress of their efforts, and Warburton appeared to have fallen asleep, the two scouts who'd been shadowing the retreating enemy reappeared on the opposite bank and splashed back across the ford. Approaching Clive, they dismounted and saluted, and the foremost of them – a trooper named Vikram Narayan – said, 'The retreating horsemen joined a much larger enemy group camped about 10 miles away. As we left, nearly the whole force seemed to be mounting up and on the point of returning towards us.'

'How many of them are there?' Clive asked.

'About four hundred.'

'That's five times our number,' Clive said to Nicholas. 'We can't run before them – we've too many wounded men and horses. We need reinforcements from our main body but they're at least 15 miles off...'

'Why not send Tuhin Singh for them? He's our best horseman.'

'Agreed. But before he sets out he must know where to bring them. Our present position is indefensible.'

'Do you remember the conical hill we skirted at the head of that steep valley as we rode down to the river? We could occupy the hill top and hope to hold the enemy off until Tuhin Singh returns with help.'

'Yes, I remember. It's barely a couple of miles away. It looked fairly rocky so there should be some good cover. I can't see how we can do better. I'll give the necessary orders – you brief Tuhin Singh and get him on his way as soon as possible. Tell him to take any of our horses if he thinks they're fresher and will be faster than his own.'

Tuhin Singh was soon galloping back up the valley, head low to his horse's neck and urging the animal on with hands and feet. Scarcely a quarter of an hour later, the rest of the small force was following him, moving more slowly, carrying their wounded with them. Major Warburton at first insisted that he could sit unaided on his charger but after only a few hundred yards he slumped over the horse's neck and Clive ordered a trooper to climb up behind him and hold him steady on his mount. Clive rode at the head of the troops. Nicholas, riding at the rear with ten soldiers, frequently wheeled his horse around to scan the ford and the land beyond it for any sign of pursuit.

He saw none before they reached the hilltop. There – after a quick discussion with Nicholas – Clive ordered the wounded to be taken to the side of the hill away from the enemy's likely direction of approach. He had half the troops dismount and position themselves behind the many jagged rocks with their muskets and a good supply of powder and ball. He stationed the remaining horsemen on the reverse of the hill, out of sight but ready to be called into action when required.

Then, after eating any food they had in their saddle bags and gulping water from their bottles – Clive warned the men not to drink it all, they might have greater need of it later – everyone waited anxiously in the midday heat, their eyes on the valley and now somewhat distant ford.

About an hour later, they spotted several blue-clad French horsemen appear at the ford and begin to cross swiftly, followed by a large number of the Raja of Tanjore's men. 'I'd guess there are two hundred and fifty or so of them,' Clive said to Nicholas.

'They must have left some of their soldiers at the camp,' Nicholas replied.

'Or sent them on some kind of encircling movement.'

'Probably not. Those with local knowledge say that's the only ford for many a mile.'

'Let's hope so – two hundred and fifty is better than four hundred.'

Immediately, they made a tour of the dismounted musketeers, checking their weapons and telling them to hold their fire until given the order. The two had little doubt that the enemy would soon be heading towards them – their tracks were all too obvious – and so it proved. Within minutes, enemy riders were cantering up the valley without even taking the precaution of throwing out a screen of scouts. Soon their leading elements were only a quarter of a mile from the hill on which the Company men were now positioned. Would they carry on past it, Nicholas – who had agreed with Clive that he would command the dismounted troops while Clive commanded those on horseback – wondered.

Might they simply follow the tracks made by the Company men as they'd originally approached the ford? He could only hope so.

But even as they watched, one rider – bending from his saddle to examine the ground – pointed towards the hill. He had clearly seen the tracks moving towards it and not returning. Rather than the whole force wheeling towards the Company position, a tall officer wearing a blue tricorn hat led a detachment of a hundred or so men to investigate. They quickly approached the first of the rocks behind which the Company troops were concealed. Knowing there was no time to waste, Nicholas yelled 'Now!', and thirty muskets crashed out in unison.

The French officer spun round and fell from his saddle. So, too, did four of his men. The horse of a Tanjorean trooper hit by a musket ball reared, throwing his rider backwards to the ground, then bolted in panic through the enemy ranks, disrupting them further. Almost immediately, Nicholas heard the pounding of hoofs behind him as Clive and his horsemen crashed into their enemy. The momentum of their downhill charge felled the horses of two French troopers, taking their riders crashing to the ground with them amid flailing hooves. Clive spitted another rider with his lance, carrying him out of the saddle. The enemy advance was already faltering, with several riders turning back down the hill.

Several of the dismounted Company troopers with Nicholas succeeded in reloading their muskets and began a ragged fire on those still bent on the attack. Nicholas picked out a Frenchman on a black horse and steadying his long musket on the rocks behind which he'd taken cover took careful aim and fired. The man threw up his arms and collapsed to the ground, striking his head on a rock, and lay still, neck clearly broken. However, one of his comrades must have seen the flash and smoke as Nicholas fired. Pulling on his reins he turned his horse towards Nicholas's position, then charged hard at him, clearly banking on the assumption that Nicholas would not have had time to reload and bent on avenging his fellow. Nicholas, however, had his pair of pistols loaded and by his side. Seizing one, he cocked it and resting the barrel on his left arm waited until the horseman was no more than 20 yards away, well within pistol range, then fired.

He seemed to have missed, since the rider still came on, sword extended. When he was only a few feet away, as Nicholas reached for his second pistol, he slipped sideways from his saddle, hit after all. Nicholas threw himself down as his attacker's riderless horse continued its charge and leapt over the rocks behind which Nicholas had positioned himself. One of the horse's back legs caught Nicholas a glancing blow to the shoulder before the animal careered back down the hill.

By now, in response to shouted orders, the rest of the enemy were retreating quickly down the slope. As he rubbed his shoulder, Nicholas heard Clive yell to his horsemen, 'Don't pursue them too far! If we get strung out they'll be able to pick us off.' The troops obeyed, beginning to rein in, wheel and return uphill. The defeated enemy soldiers retreated only as far as their main body which was still congregated on the track leading down the valley towards the ford. There, Nicholas could see their comrades helping the injured from their horses and binding their wounds. What appeared to be the commanders, both Tanjorean and French, were conferring, occasionally pointing up the hill. One was making sweeping gestures. 'Perhaps proposing a circling movement to attack us from all sides at once,' Nicholas suggested to Clive.

'That's certainly what I'd do. Let's reposition our men to thwart such an attack if it comes – but I'm not sure how long we can hold out if they make a concerted assault...'

Twenty minutes later, with the dismounted musketeers now positioned more equally around the hilltop, Nicholas and Clive scrutinised their enemies' movements carefully. At least one hundred and fifty men had dismounted and were moving on foot around the base of the hill. Then they began to climb the slope slowly, keeping in a rough line as they ascended.

As Nicholas checked on his troops once more, he heard Major Warburton shout to his Welsh orderly from where he'd been placed in the shade, 'Get me a loaded pistol Williams. If they break through, even with one arm I'll be able to wing one of them.' Some attackers were now crouching just out of musket range waiting for others to catch up. As Nicholas stood on a rock to get a better view, a Tanjorean musketeer ran forward a few yards, took aim and fired. The ball struck the rock by Nicholas's feet, sending small splinters flying into the air, two of which penetrated Nicholas's calf. As he bent to pull them out, he heard a French officer shout an order to continue the advance up the hill.

Immediately his men ran forward, bending double to make themselves the smallest possible targets. Then Nicholas heard a sound from beyond the head of the valley. Could it be a bugle? The enemy soldiers had heard it too, and several had paused, turning to look in that direction. There it was again, a little closer and, yes, it was definitely a bugle. Tuhin Singh must have located the main Company army. Help had arrived! Two Tanjorean scouts were riding hell for leather in a cloud of red dust down from the ridge at the head of the valley. Pulling on their reins, they halted by some of their officers. Almost immediately the French sounded their bugles and the Tanjoreans their trumpets. The attackers began running full pelt down the hill. One stumbled over a rock and, dropping his musket, rolled over and over down a steep, muddy incline.

'After them!' Nicholas yelled and at the same time Clive charged with his troopers. Soon some of the latter were up with the last of the fugitives, bending from the saddle to slash at their backs. One Tanjorean, keeping a cool head, ran in a series of tight zigzags, evading his pursuers, before scrambling through some bushes to safety at the base of the hill. Four or five, braver than their fellows, turned and dropping behind some rocks fired at the onrushing riders. A musket ball brought down a young trooper riding so close to Clive that specks of his blood splashed Clive's face. Then he and his men were on the musketeers, cutting them down as they reversed their muskets in a vain attempt to fend them off. By now, most of the attackers were back with their main force and beginning hastily to mount up and gallop west down the valley into the late afternoon sun. Soon the leading riders were re-crossing the ford.

Quickly mounting, Nicholas rode down to the main track to join Tuhin Singh and Clive who were talking to the senior officer of the newly arrived Company column, Lieutenant-Colonel Alexander Graham.

'Sir,' Clive was arguing, 'let me lead the pursuit! From what we've learned, their camp's no more than a dozen miles away. We should be able to push them beyond it and seize their supplies and equipment.'

'But it'll be dark in two hours or so, Clive,' the lieutenant-colonel said.

'There's a full moon tonight, sir,' Tuhin Singh broke in quickly.

'Ah, yes, of course there is,' Clive said. 'Even if we take longer than I anticipate, that should give us enough light, sir.'

'I suppose so, Clive. You may go. But make sure the detachment you take is strong enough and don't fall into any more ambushes.'

After Graham had departed, Clive said to Tuhin Singh, 'Thanks for reminding Graham and indeed me about the moon, otherwise I don't think we'd have got permission for the pursuit.'

Nicholas, Clive and Tuhin Singh were soon across the ford and, guided by the two scouts who had originally found the enemy camp, were making good progress with their strong detachment of troopers. Each time they came to a place such as thick bushes or coppices, which provided cover for a potential ambush, they slowed down and gave them a wide a berth. However, the only enemy they encountered were several prone bodies, a lame and riderless horse and two wounded Frenchmen lying with their backs to a tree to whom Nicholas threw a full leather water bottle as he rode on. To one side of the detachment now was a small lake whose waters reflected clouds pinkening in the sunset.

'There can't be more than three miles to go,' one of the two scouts responded to a question from Nicholas.

'And the terrain?' Clive asked.

'There's some marshy ground at the end of the lake, then there's a narrow valley for half a mile or so.'

'A potential ambush spot?' Nicholas asked.

'Perhaps,' the guide replied, 'but the climb to the ridge above one side of the valley didn't look too difficult.'

'Better than taking the risk of being attacked from above or blocked into the valley,' Nicholas said.

'Let's lose no more time. We can't decide until we see how the ground lies,' Clive replied.

With the scouts leading, the column moved along the lakeside and began splashing through the marshland with its pools of green-scummed water. Mosquitoes buzzed around Nicholas's sweat-soaked face and he tried to brush them away with a hand on which the knuckles were already sore and red with bites. Ahead of him, the horse of the leading scout, Vikram Narayan, suddenly reared amid a great commotion in one of the pools. Its rider, clinging to its neck, yelled, 'Crocodile!' as he lost his grip and fell into the water. His horse splashed away, neighing in fear. The other scout lowered his lance and charged towards his comrade who was flailing in the water, trying to fight off the crocodile which had its jaws open and was lashing the pool with its tail. Within less than a minute he had spitted the crocodile with his lance.

As Nicholas rode up he saw the pool was turning rusty-red with blood, not only that of the crocodile but also of Vikram Narayan who was bleeding from a gash in his calf as he was pulled onto one of the troopers' horses. Nicholas's horse plunged and bucked as another crocodile emerged from a nearby pool. Taking careful aim with his pistol Nicolas shot it between its great protuberant yellow eyes but the ball seemed scarcely to penetrate the beast's leathery skin and thick skull and it still came on, eager for a meal. Then, seeing the stricken body of the first crocodile, it turned away, clamping its great pointed teeth on the beast – not averse, it seemed, to cannibalism. Nicholas fired again with his second pistol, this time into its pale underbelly. The reptile relaxed its grasp, mortally wounded.

The whole detachment swerved as fast as it could towards the nearest dry land, which they reached without further trouble. There the leading riders halted to examine the bite to Vikram Narayan's calf. It had not penetrated to the bone, and after his wound was tightly bound he insisted on resuming the lead with his comrade. The column soon reached the entrance to the steep valley about which the two scouts had warned. Luckily the ascent to the ridge above one of its sides appeared gradual and relatively easy for men on horseback, just as they had said.

Cautiously, the riders ascended the ridge, which was quite wide, allowing at least three riders to proceed abreast. They could see no sign of the enemy in the V-shaped valley below, just a well-trodden track of beaten earth beside a trickle of a muddy stream amid some scrawny trees. Flocks of birds which to Nicholas looked like crows were settling down to roost in their branches. Then, about a quarter of a mile ahead at the valley's end, the crows suddenly rose into the air, a black cloud silhouetted against the pink evening sky. There must be an enemy position there and the troops occupying it must have spotted the Company soldiers. Immediately, Nicholas spurred his horse forward, shouting to the men to gallop along the ridge to the valley's end and, as soon as the slope had levelled sufficiently, to descend and attack the enemy from the side and rear.

Five minutes later he was slashing at a group of Tanjorean foot soldiers attempting to defend a makeshift barrier of brushwood blocking the end of the valley. They abandoned their post soon enough and ran for their lives.

'Bypass them! The enemy camp is our target!' Clive shouted, urging his horse along the track leading from the valley. As Company soldiers rode, heads bent low to the necks of their tiring, sweat-scummed horses, sporadic musket shots rang out from mounted marksmen sheltering in the darkening shadows beneath trees. Firing from the saddle at moving targets and eager to turn and evade the onrushing Company troopers, most of their shots missed but one ball caught the black horse of a Company rider square between the eyes, causing it to slump immediately to the ground, trapping its rider's leg beneath it as it fell. A comrade reined in to aid him.

Emerging onto a plain, Nicholas saw, through the descending gloom, the enemy camp now being abandoned with its fires still burning, with food still cooking on spits over them. Those enemy troops who could, were mounting up and fleeing in a disorderly retreat. As Nicholas approached, a rider in a blue tunic pitched headfirst from his horse as it stumbled in the semi-darkness over the rope of a tent. The tent itself collapsed into one of the cooking fires and was burning brightly when what must have been some powder horns stored inside exploded, lightening the darkness and sending sparks and debris high into the sky.

At the sound of the explosion, Nicholas's horse began to prance and rear but he quickly brought it under control. As he spurred on again, the group he was chasing suddenly halted and as their leader shouted, '*Nous nous rendons!* We surrender!' threw down their weapons. Throughout the camp, more and more of the enemy were doing the same.

That evening, as they sat together round one of the camp fires, eating the food abandoned by their routed enemy, Nicholas noticed that Clive's saddlebags, on which he was sitting a little precariously, were bulging. 'What have you got there?' he asked, though he already suspected the answer.

'Just a few little rewards from the baggage in the officers' tents. I'm sure you noticed me disappearing into them once or twice.'

'Rewards for what?'

'For my initiative, my courage... Oh, don't look so virginal, Nicholas! Haven't you seen others who've done far less than us doing the same? D'you think I'm the only one?'

Nicholas shook his head as Clive went on, 'D'you believe the senior Company men who buy up estates in Britain get the money to do it by following all the rules? No, the Company expects them to use their initiative. Don't you have to be a little selfish to prosper? How do you think George Braddock has been so successful? The Company expects its employees to be that way.'

'Think me foolish or naïve but I don't want to behave only as well as others do. I want the Company's forces to behave better than others – certainly better than Cumberland's men in the Highlands – rather than descending to their level at any chance they get.'

Clive bristled. 'I know what the army did in the Highlands. I'm no saint – no soldier can afford to be – but I've driven no women and children out to starve, burned no one out, burned no homes or crops, nor will I ever do it.'

Silence reigned for a minute or two before Nicholas stood up and said, 'Be that as it may, reflect on what I've said. It's been a long day. I'm tired and going to turn in.'

'Before you do,' Clive responded, 'you might like to know that among the French officers we've captured is an Irishman – O'Sullivan I think his name is – who apparently fought with the Jacobites in the rebellion. He might just have some news of your uncle.'

Some of Nicholas's exhaustion evaporated. 'Where is he?'

'In the compound with a few other officers. I'll have him brought here if you wish.'

A few minutes later, a trooper led a slight figure in an ill-fitting blue French officer's uniform up to the tent which Nicholas had commandeered from Clive who had absented himself. The officer had a clean bandage round a small wound on his hand. His ginger hair was speckled with white and his green eyes looked nervously about him as Nicholas gestured to him to sit.

'Why have I been separated from the others and brought here?' he asked before Nicholas could begin. 'I'm not a man to betray trust, if that's what you're hoping. I'll not be answering your questions, whatever devilry you apply.'

'Steady on and take a drink.' O'Sullivan took a swallow from the flask Nicholas held out, as Nicholas continued. 'This spirit is the only devil around here. I do indeed have some questions. You may choose whether you answer, but I hope you will when you hear their nature, which I'm sure won't be what you expect...'

O'Sullivan's expression was noncommittal, but as Nicholas began to explain about his uncle's part in the Jacobite rebellion and his own wish to learn more about his fate the Irishman's shoulders dropped and his expression softened. 'James Ballantyne you say his name is?'

'Yes, he was born with the century, so he was forty-five at the time of the '45 neatly enough. He's a tall, thin man.'

'Was he a comrade of Cameron of Lochiel?'

'Lochiel was his neighbour and friend,' Nicholas said eagerly.

'Then I think I may have met him once or twice in the aftermath of the rebellion during the chaos when those of us who could escaped to the French ports. If he's the man I'm thinking of, he decided not to stay with Lochiel in France – a nation he didn't seem too fond of – but to make his way to the Americas. The Carolinas or Nova Scotia, I think he said. A quiet man, I remember, and not a die-hard supporter of the cause. Would that be right?'

'Yes. I'm sure that was my uncle. I'm very grateful for news of him. At least I know he's alive. Take some more of the brandy, won't you?'

They drank a little more and the officer told Nicholas some details of the Jacobites' ultimately disastrous campaign, though he had nothing more to tell of James's part in it. With O'Sullivan's tongue beginning to loosen a little, he lamented the French treatment of the Jacobite exiles. 'The broken promises. The condescension from their arrogant nobility and their lack of loyalty.' Taking another sip, he added, 'Not that loyalty or honour seem to count for much anywhere anymore, if you ask me. Look at some of your own Company people, why don't you? Colluding with the French, doing dirty little side-deals of their own, even selling them arms.'

Nicholas was suddenly alert. 'What do you mean? Who do you mean?'

Seeing his change of expression, O'Sullivan drew back. 'No. No names. Nothing like that. I've said enough. I'll preserve my honour. It's about all I've got left. Just remember, no group – certainly not your East India Company – has the monopoly of virtues or indeed vices. Venality and corruption know no frontiers.'

However hard Nicholas pressed, O'Sullivan would reveal no more, which, in truth, Nicholas admired. However, as they drank a little more O'Sullivan relaxed again. 'There is something I don't mind telling you,' he said, his words slurring a little. 'The French commanders are at each other's throats... I've no love for them as you'll have realised... Dupleix and La Bourdonnais detest each other. In fact, Dupleix thinks La Bourdonnais is in his way.'

'His way to what?'

'Dupleix has grand ambitions. His heroes are the Spanish Conquistadors in South America, all-powerful and kings in all but name. He wants to crush the British and make southern India a French possession not because he cares about trade but because he wants to be Viceroy. I've heard him say so.'

'Doesn't Dupleix have enough influence not to have to worry about La Bourdonnais?'

'Not any more, at least so I've heard... Dupleix is greedy and corrupt, all too openly taking bribes from anyone foolish enough to pay him and quarrelling with his fellows. And that's not to mention that Circe of a wife of his – he pimps her out to further his ambitions. Doesn't seem that she's unwilling, though... as someone said he wouldn't have got as far as he has without her, and with her he'll get no further. Together they're making themselves a laughing stock among the French and the Hindustanis alike...' Catching the uncomfortable expression on Nicholas's face, O'Sullivan paused but then continued. 'Ah, I suspect that you may know something of the lady? Has she had her pretty little fingers in your breeches?' As Nicholas blushed like a schoolboy but said nothing, O'Sullivan grinned. 'So there are things that you too don't want to talk about. But heed what I say about Dupleix.'

After O'Sullivan, a little unsteady on his feet after the brandy, had been escorted back to his comrades and Clive had returned to the tent, Nicholas told him of O'Sullivan's claims of Company officials colluding with the French and their allies. Clive's response was vehement disbelief. 'Can you really believe any Company official would betray his country to its greatest enemies? I can't! I suspect that your Irish friend was being more loyal to his French comrades than you think and throwing sand in your eyes. He probably picked up some of your scepticism about the Company and the behaviour of its employees – myself included – and was trying to foment discord and suspicion in our ranks.'

Nicholas said no more. O'Sullivan had seemed honest enough but clearly there was no point in pursuing the matter with Clive. He would keep his own ears and eyes open. He yawned, weary again – not just from the exertions of the day, but from something deeper.

But why allow himself to feel cast down? Soon he would be back in Meena's arms and in a few months' time, God willing, be a father.

13 – Love and Loss

As on so many recent nights, Nicholas found sleep impossible. He flung back the cotton sheet and, rising from the bed, splashed his face with water from a large brass bowl. Then he went out into the courtyard of his bungalow in Madras. The beauty of the silvery moonlight filtering through the branches of the mango tree and fireflies in the dark meant nothing to him as he walked slowly around the courtyard. A sudden vigorous wailing from a side-room caught his attention and he hurried towards it. Stooping beneath the room's low wooden lintel, he stepped inside.

Sohini, the middle-aged Bengali woman he had employed as an ayah, was leaning over a carved wooden cradle in the corner, making clucking, soothing noises and the crying was subsiding. Hearing Nicholas, she looked around and straightened up. 'Your son is restless again tonight,' she said. 'I will stay with him. Go back to your bed, Sahib.'

'No, Sohini, I'll stay with him. I can't sleep either,' Nicholas said, just as the child began to cry again.

By the orange glow of an oil lamp burning in a niche in the wall, he saw her hesitate. She had grown very protective of his son, almost possessive, and didn't seem to trust any man, certainly no European, to know what he was doing. 'It's all right,' Nicholas said gently. 'And don't worry, I'll call you at once if I need you.'

Sohini pulled her cotton sari more tightly around her, nodded and left him alone with the child. Approaching the cradle, Nicholas peered down at the tiny crying creature. Cupping the little head as Sohini had shown him, he carefully picked up his son. As he did so, the baby stopped crying though it continued to thrash its limbs, causing him to tighten his hold.

He carried the child outside to the seat beneath the mango tree where Meena had loved to play her tanpura and sat down himself. As he gazed down at the infant's delicate features, his son grew quiet and, it seemed to Nicholas, looked intently back at him. Was that possible at only three months old? Perhaps it was. 'James,' he said softly, 'James Ballantyne. What are you thinking?' It had been Meena's suggestion to name their son after his uncle but the child resembled her more than any Ballantyne. Those dark, luxuriantly lashed eyes were already so like hers. Nicholas took a deep breath. Every time he looked at James the child reminded him of Meena, both a blessing and a curse. As time passed, perhaps it would be only the good times he remembered, not the pain of losing her, but for the moment her death was too recent, too raw.

As he watched, James's eyes began to close. In a few moments he was asleep. What a light burden to hold in his arms, but what a weighty responsibility to have to carry through life... He'd never anticipated how fatherhood would feel, but then how could he? How could anybody, until they actually held the flesh of their flesh in their arms? From the moment Meena had first passed their son to him to hold, he had felt such love, such a fierce desire to protect that it had startled him. At that moment he'd known he would do anything to shield both mother and child from harm.

Yet, some things were beyond any man... Once again, in his mind Nicholas was back by Meena's bedside. The fever had struck suddenly, two months after the birth of their son, and she had survived only thirty-six hours, descending for a while into a writhing, sweat-soaked delirium before, towards the end, returning to herself. As Nicholas had gripped her small hand tightly in his own larger one, she had turned her dark eyes towards him and, voice almost a whisper, said, 'I love you Nicholas. Promise you'll never forget me and that you'll talk often to our son about me. My life with you has been good. I'm only sorry I will not live longer to enjoy more time with you and see our son grow to manhood.'

Nicholas had not tried to deceive her, to tell her that she would survive, but had said softly, 'I love you. I will never forget you and I will make our son a man you'd be proud of.' She had smiled gently and closed her eyes. A few minutes later as Nicholas wiped beads of perspiration from her forehead her spirit had drifted quietly from her body.

Just hours later, with a white-robed Hindu priest chanting at his side, Nicholas had carried Meena's lifeless body towards the pyre of wood he and Tuhin Singh, spurning all offers of help, had constructed on the beach, near the temple where he had fought his duel with Braddock. Weeping he had laid Meena gently on the pyre, composing her body as if in peaceful sleep. At a signal from the priest as he continued to chant, Tuhin Singh had poured ghee on to the sandalwood from a large brass pot. Then the priest had told Nicholas, 'The time has come. Take a brand from the small fire over there and let the flames consume her body.' With a shaking hand, Nicholas had applied the flame to the base of the pyre which in moments was a curtain of orange flame behind which Meena's body had disappeared.

James had wakened again and was squirming in his arms. He could only thank the gods that he had this child to remind him of what he had lost, Nicholas told himself. But what about James? He was so young; he would never have memories of Meena...

–

'Sit down, Ballantyne.' John Martingdale, chief aide to Thomas Saunders, the President of Madras, gestured Nicholas to a chair. Martingdale – a short genial-looking man whose prosperous belly was straining the buttons of his buff-coloured waistcoat – also seated himself.

'I've got good news for you.' Martingdale leaned forward and smiled. 'We're appointing you to the Political Department. Your knowledge of the local languages and rulers will be invaluable to us...'

The Company's Political Department? Nicholas stared at Martingdale.

'You look surprised and I think I understand why. It wasn't so long ago that the Company thought it might be...' Martingdale struggled for the right word, '... well unwise... to trust you close to the heart of Company affairs. But times have moved on, the Jacobite Rebellion is an irrelevancy now and in the interim you have amply proved your loyalty.'

'No, you don't understand. I'm much more of a soldier than an official now – and a soldier I hope to remain.'

Martingdale's smile broadened. 'In a way you will. Your bravery and military skill will be just as important as your languages in the role we have in mind. Look, let me speak frankly. We may be formally at peace with France but who knows how long that will last. Our rivalries with them grow more complex and more dangerous. They're systematically seeking to extend their web of alliances with the ruling families of Hindustan, recklessly promising power and wealth to any who will listen. The French strategy seems to be to intervene wherever and whenever they can in local politics, setting one ruler against another, setting son against father, brother against brother, securing any advantage they can. It's obvious that the French hope that if they can whip up civil wars in southern Hindustan and in Bengal, the resulting chaos will give them the opportunity to drive the Company out and achieve total mastery over Hindustan.'

Nicholas briefly smiled to himself as an image flashed into his mind of some French official in Pondicherry making exactly the same speech about the perfidy of the British.

The geniality had ebbed from Martingdale's voice as he continued. 'The truth is that to get the better of the French, to throw the beggars out of Hindustan once and for all, we need good intelligence and loyal local allies. We need much better information about what is happening in the princely states, the politics, the personalities. We need friends among the rulers and their courts. Otherwise we'll always be on the back foot until one day the *fleur de lys* and not the Company flag, will fly over Madras, Calcutta and Bombay and all our enclaves here. You understand what I'm saying, Ballantyne?'

'Of course.' So they want me to be a spy, Nicholas thought. For a moment, an image of Jeanne Dupleix's overflowing bosoms swam before him. At least intelligence-gathering would offer a distraction and a means of sometimes escaping Madras and its painful memories.

'You will attend the Council meetings. As such you'll know the Company's innermost business. If you agree to take this role, we must have your promise of absolute discretion.'

'You have it.'

'From time to time we will have missions for you – I assure you they'll require all your quick wits, resilience and courage. I can't emphasise enough how important this work that you – and others too – will be undertaking is.' Martingdale's face relaxed and he smiled again. 'If anyone asks about your new job, just say that you've been appointed a political officer and that you'll be assessing intelligence reports and advising the President – the partial truth, after all.'

Nicholas rose, assuming he was being dismissed but Martingdale waved him back into his chair. 'There's something else. I understand you have a young son?'

'Yes.'

'And the mother is Hindustani?'

'She was… She died four months ago.'

The edge to Nicholas's voice and the expression on his face, hadn't escaped Martingdale. 'I'm sorry. What I have to say may sound insensitive in the circumstances but bear with me. Many of us have had our "bibis". It's what young men do.' From his tone Nicholas guessed he was including himself. 'But – and I don't say this is right, it's just the way it is – I need to warn you. Your new role will make you more prominent. Be discreet, and don't make a show of your child, or you may damage a promising career…' He paused, then added, 'You look annoyed, Ballantyne, but I'm only telling you this for your own good – and your son's. Well, I must attend to other business now. Goodbye, but I'm sure we'll meet again soon.'

As Nicholas walked through the carved rosewood doors, held open by liveried Company servants, to the antechamber beyond, he pondered Martingdale's words. The idea that he should hide away the six-month-old James, all he had left of Meena, appalled him. He'd nearly told Martingdale that if the Company couldn't accept both him and his son, he'd refuse his new appointment… But he knew that would be rash, as Clive would surely tell him if he were here now, instead of away on campaign. Better to wait and see whether people were really as narrow-minded as Martingdale had hinted.

'Ballantyne?' A stylishly dressed figure seated at the far end of the antechamber stood up. George Braddock! He had changed little except for his somewhat increased girth. A large ruby ring flashed on one of his fingers and a handsome enamelled fob watch dangled against his embroidered silk waistcoat. What did surprise Nicholas was Braddock's friendly expression.

'I heard how bravely you fought with Clive. I was wrong to doubt your loyalty. I'm sorry. I admit it. We should let bygones be bygones. I also hear Clive's been promoted again. Quite the great man these days. That'll please him!'

Nicholas was saved the trouble of replying by a clerk who came to usher Braddock into Martingdale's office. 'We must meet some time. Then I'll tell you what I've been doing. I've pulled off some unprecedentedly ingenious deals I can tell you,' Braddock said over his shoulder.

As the rosewood doors closed behind Braddock's bulky figure, Nicholas walked outside into the sunshine. If Braddock thought the past could be swept away so easily, he was mistaken. Nicholas would ensure their paths seldom crossed.

–

In the soft candlelight Nicholas glanced at the longcase clock against the wall. It told him that nearly five hours had passed since he'd left his son with Sohini in the garden of his white-washed bungalow to attend a dinner at Martingdale's mansion.

The only good thing about the evening had been another of Martingdale's guests, recently arrived from England, who had been introduced to him as Miss Margaret Maskelyne, sister of Britain's Astronomer Royal. Dark-haired and violet-eyed, her quiet elegance had caught his attention. As they'd sat on the veranda among the other guests just before dinner listening to Mrs Martingdale – unflatteringly attired in a frothy white muslin dress more suitable for a woman half her age – lament the problems of training house servants, their eyes had briefly met. During dinner, seated on Martingdale's right, she'd shot him a knowing smile while she'd composed her face, as if listening attentively to their host's long-winded monologue on Company politics. Later, as Mrs Martingdale had shepherded the women away to leave the men with their tobacco, Madeira and port, he'd noticed her looking at him again.

'Well, gentlemen. Shall we rejoin the ladies?' Martingdale stood and led the way to his wife's drawing room where most of the women were grouped around a table admiring or pretending to admire some china ornaments that Mrs Martingdale was explaining she'd had shipped from England. However, Margaret was seated on a low couch by the open French doors reading a small book bound in green leather. As Nicholas approached, she looked up and smiled.

'I'm interrupting you, I apologise,' he said.

'What do you mean?' she said closing the volume. 'Conversation's surely preferable to any book.'

'That depends on the conversation…' he said, with a sideways nod towards the group of women.

Margaret's smile broadened. 'Won't you sit by me, Mr Ballantyne? I know who you are – by all accounts something of a hero…'

'Accounts can be deceiving… Tell me about yourself. What's brought you to Hindustan?'

'My cousin Anna is married to Claude Mulgrave, a Council member. Her letters made me curious about the place. My parents couldn't object – I'm of age. I have my own income. I can travel where I please, do as I please.'

'Are you staying with your cousin?'

'Yes. She's unwell or she would have been here. I worry about her. In England she was always so healthy, so strong... When I arrived I was shocked to see how much she'd changed in only fifteen months. She's... How can I describe it? Faded, lethargic... As if the hot sun is draining the energy from her. In England we used to walk and ride. Now I can scarcely get her to leave the house. She spends most of her day lying on a chaise longue and only dresses fully towards nightfall. Even then it's often only because her husband insists she preside over their dining table when they have guests or accompany him to some grand function. She doesn't even take as much interest as I'd expect in her two children, leaving them all day in the care of the ayah who only brings them to her for an hour or two each evening.'

'Hindustan isn't good for many Europeans. The climate, the armies of servants to carry out our every whim, make people indolent.'

'But not you, clearly.'

Nicholas shrugged. 'Life for a soldier is different. But even we – active though we are – can't protect ourselves against all the ill-effects of life in Hindustan. I'm sure you've already realised how quickly life can be cut short here.' For a moment memories of Meena's funeral pyre, burning so bright, and of standing by Harry Ross's grave flashed through his mind.

'Yet you've never thought of returning home?'

'No. There's little there for me.'

'I'm sorry. It was thoughtless of me to ask,' Margaret said quickly, her pale skin flushing.

'You know that my uncle was a Jacobite?'

'I've heard that your uncle lost all he had in the '45 but it seems unjust that you should suffer for his actions.'

'Suffer? I haven't suffered. The people who've suffered and are still suffering – for all I know – are the ordinary clansmen of the Highlands.'

'It seems to me you're wrong to say you've not suffered. I can hear it in your voice, see it in your eyes.'

'Perhaps to some extent. But I've been lucky. My uncle sent me to Hindustan before the rebellion to protect me. If I hadn't come to love this place so much I might have thought harder about returning to Scotland.'

Margaret's dark brows rose. 'Love, you say?'

'Yes. From the moment my ship rounded a bend in the Hooghly as we approached Calcutta, it captured something in me and hasn't let me go.'

'Then you're a romantic as well as a soldier. But I think I understand what you mean. What I like best is going out riding in the early morning just as the world's waking up. The flights of green parakeets screeching across the sky, the monkeys leaping through the branches, the sun as it first peers, a great white ball, over the horizon. Riding in Hyde Park under dull grey skies just can't compare, but' – she lowered her voice so as not to be overheard – 'I have to say the company in London's better. People here talk about nothing but who's going to get promoted next and how much money they've amassed. All very understandable but I think I'd hoped to find some grander vision – are we only here as traders and shopkeepers? I often wonder what the local people think about us, but I never meet any I can really talk to. My maid – when I try to talk to her about Madras – never tells me anything, certainly never expresses an opinion. She only says, "Yes, Memsahib" and "No, Memsahib" and plainly prefers me to keep silent.'

Nicholas smiled. 'I felt pretty much the same when I first arrived – wanting to learn more about what was going on around me and frustrated when I couldn't.'

'When did that change for you?'

'Two things happened, I suppose. The first was meeting a young Hindustani, Tuhin Singh. He became my steward, then my friend. At last I had someone who could answer my questions, help me understand the local customs and appreciate what lies behind them. The other was when the Company decided to exile me from Calcutta to Madras because of my Jacobite connections.

The war with France gave me my chance to become a soldier and later to join the court of an important local ruler. That's when I began to see the real Hindustan. But ask me if I understand it and I'd still have to say no. This is a complex land, an ancient society – far older than our own. It's suffered centuries of conquerors from the time of Alexander the Great and even earlier. For a while most of the country was united – mainly against its wishes – under the Moghuls but now their power is broken. Much of Hindustan consists of warring states driven by rivalries and shifting allegiances.'

'So what is the Company's ambition here?'

'The Company wants the areas of Hindustan where they have trading interests pacified. And they want the French out of the whole subcontinent so they can pursue their ultimate goal of making profits.'

'Not a particularly noble aim.'

'No, but if the Company can bring peace, then that can't be bad. After all, the Company as such doesn't care what religion or race the people with whom it trades are. In that sense at least it's tolerant – or so it seems to me. But at the same time part of me wonders why the British are here at all? Why do we – or indeed the French – believe we have the right to interfere here?'

'You may well be right but few in this room would agree with you.'

'No. And I'd not talk to them about such things.' That was true, Nicholas thought. He'd never shared such doubts before with anyone except Tuhin Singh, Meena and occasionally Clive, although Clive had little sympathy for Nicholas's 'niminnypim-miny scruples', as he called them. 'But I've more right than many to be in Hindustan,' he continued. 'I have a son whose mother was a Hindustani.'

She gave him a gentle smile. 'I know. I've already discov-ered how much people like to gossip. For all its pretensions and self-importance, Madras is just a big village… What's your son's name?'

'We called him James, after my uncle.'

'I also heard that his mother had died. I'm sorry. That must have been hard for you – and for the boy. Perhaps I could meet him sometime...'

Nicholas hesitated. She was intelligent enough to realise she was asking to do something others might disapprove of. Only last week, a senior official he knew from council meetings and his wife had driven in their carriage past the tonga in which he'd been riding with James and Sohini and cut him – the man studying the braiding on his cuffs and the woman gazing studiedly from beneath her parasol into the mid-distance. On more than one occasion he'd overheard dubious jokes about 'little brown by-blows'.

He was about to reply when a shadow fell over them. Glancing up he saw Martingdale beaming at them.

'Ballantyne, what on earth have you been saying to Miss Maskelyne to make her look so serious? My wife knows of your skill as a pianist, Miss Maskelyne. She begs that you will favour the company with a few pieces.'

'Of course,' Margaret said. Rising to her feet, she walked over to the rosewood pianoforte where Mrs Martingdale was sifting through some sheet music.

Martingdale hadn't been paying false compliments. Margaret Maskelyne's elegant hands flew over the keyboard as Nicholas and everyone else in the room listened with rapt attention. Music had always had the power to move him ever since as a small boy he'd sat listening to his mother play. It was she who'd decided he should learn the violin. He closed his eyes the better to appreciate the rippling notes.

–

The tonga halted by the gates of the President's residence. As Nicholas stepped down, a voice shouted, 'Sahib, look out!' He stepped hastily back as a carriage rolled past, the plumed head-dresses of the female occupants swaying like the crests of sarus cranes. Then he set off up the sweeping drive. He hadn't got more than a few paces before a boy in Company livery holding a flaming torch darted forward to light his way as if he could have missed the mansion illuminated for one of the grandest balls of the season. Through the deep-sashed windows he could see guests milling in the golden glow of giant candelabras.

In general he avoided the ostentatious parties that were a part of Madras life and which – when he did feel obliged to attend – usually involved him in deflecting proposals to join one Company faction or another or to participate in private trading ventures. All such proposals came with entangling ties and obligations – and these, above all, he wished to avoid. But tonight's ball was one he could not escape... Martingdale had made clear he expected all the senior officers of the Political Department to be there.

His mind went back to something Martingdale had said to him in private only that morning, a smirk rounding the corners of his lips. 'I hear you're to be congratulated, Ballantyne. She's quite a catch – brains, beauty and £500 a year. The Astronomer Royal for a brother-in-law! You're a sly dog. I'd never have guessed, but my wife suspected and had it from Anna Mulgrave that it's as good as settled! I wish you both every happiness.' He'd vigorously shaken Nicholas's hand and before Nicholas could say anything had hurried away, leaving him nonplussed.

The idea of marrying Margaret Maskelyne had never entered his head. These past weeks while he'd been waiting impatiently for his first mission, they'd quite often been in each other's company but not through any contriving of his. He had enjoyed talking to her, liked her independent spirit, her wry amusement at Madras and its ways, her gift for the piano. He liked and admired her but never once had he felt the stirrings of anything deeper.

But what about her? The shock of Martingdale's words had made him reflect on how many times she'd invited him to sit by her, turn her music for her, ride by her side on expeditions into the country. And how she'd asked again to meet his son, which he'd arranged by bringing James and Sohini to the maidan at the time she took her evening carriage ride. As for tonight, only the evening before at the Martingdales she'd laughingly flourished her dance card at him and told him she'd pencilled him in for the first dance. 'You're a musician like me. I know you'll not trample my feet like some of the great clodhoppers I've come across here. And you must take me into supper, I'm as much at risk from being bored to death as trampled to death…' He'd been only too happy to agree, never thinking he'd awakened her expectations.

'Come, Sahib,' the boy called out, doubtless anxious to be rid of him so he could find another guest to escort and win a tip from. Nicholas realised how slowly he had been walking – he'd rather face a battle than what might lie in store for him this evening. Telling himself not to be ridiculous, he strode forward into the pool of light beyond the great double doors. A servant took his hat while gesturing him to join the line of guests ascending the great staircase to where the President and his lady were waiting. Here he handed his card to a magnificently uniformed steward who shouted in rich bass tones, 'Lieutenant Nicholas Ballantyne.'

As wary as a soldier wondering where a marksman might be concealed, Nicholas scanned the ballroom and almost at once saw the tall, graceful figure of Margaret Maskelyne. Her dress was the same shade of violet as her eyes and her thick black hair was adorned by a simple wreath of white jasmine. She was comparing dance cards with another young woman and laughing. Looking up for a moment, she smiled and waved her card at him as if to say, 'Remember, I'm promised to you for the first dance…'

Nicholas nodded politely, then taking a glass of wine from a servant, he walked into an adjoining room where card tables had been set up for those who did not wish to dance. Four dowagers were already seated at a table – diamonds flashing on their practised fingers as they dealt – as were several groups of men among whom was George Braddock. Upon seeing Nicholas enter the room, Braddock gave him a genial nod. Nicholas briefly inclined his head and moved on. As he had hoped, they worked in such different spheres they'd rarely encountered one another since their first brief meeting.

He drained his glass more quickly than usual and took another. No time seemed to have passed at all before he heard the musicians strike up for the first dance. Gulping down the wine and squaring his shoulders, he made his way back into the ballroom and through the crush to Margaret's side. 'Nicholas, don't look so serious!' she said as he took her hand and led her to where the dancers were forming up.

The dance was a minuet and, for once, Nicholas struggled to remember the steps, familiar though they were, and he had to force himself to concentrate. 'What is it, Nicholas? What's wrong?' Margaret asked as hand in hand they advanced at a stately pace towards another couple.

'I must speak to you. Not here but alone, as soon as the dance is ended.'

Glancing at her he saw her smile softly as her pale skin flushed and cursed himself for a fool. He'd made matters worse. She must think he meant to propose.

For the rest of the dance he said nothing more, going through the steps as best he could. The sooner he could talk to her the sooner he'd know her feelings. Martingdale's words might just have been the product of ill-informed gossip. Perhaps in a few minutes he and Margaret would be laughing about the obtuseness of people who'd read their friendship as something more. The dance seemed to go on forever but finally the violinists – to Nicholas's ear far from gifted – fell silent.

'Come out onto the terrace with me.' Nicholas said as they bowed to one another. Margaret nodded and, drawing her fan from her purse to cool herself, led the way towards the doors at the far end of the ballroom that gave onto the terrace. A faint breeze was stirring and above their heads bats flickered. Glancing around, Nicholas saw to his relief that they were alone.

'Well, what is it you have to say to me, Mr Ballantyne?' Margaret's tone was teasing. 'Come now, it's not like you to be tongue-tied.'

'Margaret... Today, Martingdale said something to me... He implied that everyone expects us to wed.' Looking down at her, he saw her smile falter and his heart sank.

'Isn't that what you want Nicholas? I thought...'

'I'm sorry. I never meant to give you that impression. I liked you from the moment I saw you. Your presence in Madras has been one of the few good things about living here but...'

'But what?'

'In my heart, I still have a wife – Meena, the mother of my child... I'm sorry.'

'So am I.' Margaret shook her head, her expression stricken. 'You've made me a laughing stock.'

'That was never my intention. And a laughing stock in whose eyes? We've always laughed together about these people with their silly, petty, conventional ideas. I never thought you cared what they thought.'

'As a man you can say that.' Her violet eyes flashed. 'As a woman, even I – independent as I am – don't have that freedom. Don't you understand that after the way you've behaved towards me we're expected to marry?'

'Margaret...'

'No, let me speak. I admit I encouraged you. You're clever, out of the ordinary, you don't bore me. We would have been good for each other and I'd have cared for your son. But I'd never have done that if I'd thought for one moment you didn't feel the same attraction.' She paused to collect herself. 'But that's over and I must think of myself. Even the fact that I'm alone here with you now could damage me. I thought I'd be returning to the ballroom as the future Mrs Ballantyne. If that's not to be, I must go back inside at once.' She looked up at him, a last appeal in her fine eyes.

'Margaret, I never meant this to happen. I hope our friendship can continue.'

'If you think that, it only shows how little you understand women. I've been alone with you for too long already.' With a rustle of her silk skirts she was gone.

Alone on the terrace, Nicholas felt no relief. How much easier it would have been if he could have loved her. And was love even necessary where there was friendship, respect, empathy... But in Meena's arms he had known love – real love. For him, at least, there could be no compromises.

'You have played fast and loose with Miss Maskelyne!' Martingdale's usually genial expression was severe as he shook a long finger at Nicholas. 'I did not expect it of you – neither did my wife. She is shocked at your behaviour.'

'I never intended this to happen. If I have offended Miss Maskelyne, I'm sorry. Truly I am.'

'Well,' Martingdale's tone softened, 'You're not the first young man to get himself in such a tangle or worse and you won't be the last. And you're an absolute fool not to snap her up. She could have been the making of you. But perhaps some of the blame is mine. I kept you waiting for a mission... Too much time on a young man's hands breeds mischief.'

Nicholas was about to protest yet again that he had never intended to mislead Margaret – never even flirted with her in the accepted sense – but what would be the point?

'The thing is, Ballantyne, it would be better if you left Madras for a while. Let things settle until the ladies forget your misdemeanours and move on to some other scandal...'

'Where are you sending me?'

'To the far south – the kingdom of Travancore. Its ruler, Marthanda Varnar, defeated the Dutch some years ago and certainly has no love for foreigners. But he seems to think he needs the Company. Three weeks ago, his envoy arrived in Madras bringing a letter and asking our help in suppressing some rebellious vassals who have banded together against him. This might be our opportunity to gain a foothold in the trade in the spices grown in the region, especially pepper, and you know how profitable that is! But we need to understand what Marthanda Varnar really wants and what he's prepared to give in return.

'That's where you come in. Take ship for Travancore. See what you make of him. But also assess the strength of the insurrection against him. After all, it might be more advantageous to us to support the rebels... Never forget there is always more than one way of looking at a problem.' Martingdale gave Nicholas an appraising look. 'It's not what I would have chosen for your first major mission. But it has the advantage that it will take three or four months, maybe more, and will get you out of the way of the memsahibs...'

–

In fact, it was closer to five months before a trading vessel belonging to a Persian merchant they had boarded at Cochin brought Nicholas and Tuhin Singh back to Madras. The mission had not been successful. Marthanda Varnar had appeared keen enough on negotiating an alliance with the Company. But as the weeks turned into months and his forces appeared to be making good progress against their enemies, Nicholas had begun to suspect that the ruler was playing for time, hoping that his armies could completely overcome his enemies unaided, which would save him the need to make concessions to the Company. Finally, after writing to Martingdale saying what he was intending to do, Nicholas had called Marthanda Varnar's bluff and announced his intention to depart on the next available ship unless a treaty was concluded within a week. The ruler had made no effort to detain him and Nicholas had cursed his own stupidity for staying so long.

But now as the familiar outline of Madras with Fort St. George at its heart appeared on the horizon, Nicholas's spirits rose at the thought that in just a few hours he would see his son again. Arriving at his bungalow, he hurried inside in search of Sohini and James only for a bearer to hand him a folded note on which, in writing he was sure he recognised, was scrawled 'URGENT'.

He opened it to see it was dated three days earlier and was indeed from Clive.

> *Martingdale told me he expects you back in Madras within the next few days. Come and find me as soon as you get this. I'm surrounded by arrogant, ignorant imbeciles and if I can't make them listen to me I swear I'll go mad!*

The note showed every sign of having been written in a fury, with erratic handwriting, several blots and one crossing out where Clive substituted 'imbeciles' for 'fools'. Typical Clive, Nicholas thought. He'd said nothing about why he needed to see him so urgently. Well, he'd find out soon enough and in any case it could wait. His first wish was still to see his son. Refolding the letter, Nicholas went to find James.

How much he had changed, Nicholas marvelled, as a few minutes later, Sohini placed the child in his arms. His face had lengthened and below the eyes that would always be Meena's his nose was growing quite aquiline, like Nicholas's own.

'See how heavy he has become, how he wriggles. He is strong – always pulling my plait – and already trying to walk,' Sohini said.

'I'm sure he is,' Nicholas replied, smiling down at James. 'Let's see.' Placing his son gently on the floor, he knelt before him and took hold of his hands. Sure enough, James started pushing down and a few moments later was unsteadily on his feet. Supported by Nicholas, he took a tentative step, then another, before subsiding back on the floor and beaming at his father and Sohini. How proud Meena would have been, Nicholas thought. If only they could have shared moments like this together…

Two hours later, with dusk purpling the sky, Nicholas climbed out of the tonga, which had brought him to Clive's lodgings close to the fort. His friend might not even be there, Nicholas thought, rapping on the door. But, to his surprise, Clive himself, not a servant, opened it.

'About time!' said Clive ushering him in. 'I'd heard a ship from the south had landed passengers soon after midday. Another hour and I'd have gone to your bungalow.'

Clive's hair was wild, his neck cloth half-unravelled and he had two or three days' growth of stubble on his broad chin. 'It's good to see you, but you look terrible. What on earth's the matter?' Nicholas asked as he followed Clive inside.

'You probably haven't heard yet but the Nizam of Hyderabad has died entirely unexpectedly. We think he was probably poisoned,' Clive talked rapidly as he paced about. 'That's why I and others have been recalled to Madras. Rumours say a concubine slipped the poison into one of his aphrodisiacs. Whatever the cause, his death has sparked a war of succession and – what a surprise! – we and the French are supporting rival claimants to the throne. We both want to secure influence and favour in such a fabulously wealthy state and, in particular, access to the mines in Golconda – the world's only source of diamonds. The French, led by Dupleix, are backing Muzzafar Jang, the dead Nizam's grandson. Chanda Sahib is aiding him too. You know him well from your time with Anwaruddin Khan, I think?'

'Of course, I remember Chanda Sahib. He was always out for himself and more than confident of his own abilities. Even so, I was surprised when I heard his troops were among those that overwhelmed and killed Anwaruddin Khan. What a hypocrite. All the time I heard him disparaging the Nawab's enemies he'd been among them.'

'Well, while you were away he's gone further. He's imprisoned the Nawab's elder son, installed himself as Nawab of the Carnatic and switched support to the French. We've heard the French have promised him the largest payments and areas of conquered territory they've ever made to any ruler.'

Nicholas frowned. 'Who is our candidate for the throne of Hyderabad?' he asked after a moment.

'Anwaruddin Khan's younger son, Mohammed Ali. Did you meet him while you were at the Nawab's court?'

'No, both the Nawab's sons were away in the territories he had appointed them governors of. Where is Mohammed Ali now?'

'In the fortress of Trichinopoly and under siege by Chanda Sahib. Our scouts report his situation is desperate.'

'What are we doing to relieve him? Who has the President placed in charge?'

'Well may you ask. It's the usual dither, delay and damned be anyone who speaks out with a good idea!' Clive said, banging his fist against the white-washed wall. 'I can't get people to listen when I suggest what we must do! I have a good, clear plan. We should already be on the march. My head aches so much with the frustration of it all, I feel my skull is going to burst. Sometimes, I confess, I am in such deep despair, I wonder what the point is of living if no one will give me my chance to prove myself. I've become so overwrought that I'm only sleeping at all now by taking opium to calm myself. If things go on like this I really wouldn't be afraid to kill myself, you know...'

'Steady on, Clive... As you told me when I wanted to leave the Company's service after news of Culloden, what good would that do? It would merely be an empty, futile gesture and a much more final one than my stalking off in high dudgeon to be a sea captain or some such!'

For a few moments Clive said nothing. Then, for the first time since he'd begun his tirade, his face held the hint of a smile. 'I suppose you could be right.'

'Well then, enlighten me about your master plan so that I can at least assess it in all its glorious ingenuity and novelty. Then I can perhaps help you frame it in a way that might convince our seniors. But even without hearing it I can give you some advice. It's not too surprising that no one is taking you seriously, given what is, to put it politely, your unkempt appearance and the way you're marching about wild-eyed as you propound your theories.'

'You mean I should follow convention in all its superficiality?' cut in Clive. 'Where would we be without that impediment to progress, success and individuality? Any more pearls of homespun wisdom?'

'Yes. Don't interrupt people and don't hector them. You'll only antagonise them with your arrogance. And try to see the other point of view. Not everyone who dares question or disagree with you is in league with the devil. And finally, any suggestion that you're presenting your ideas out of a desire for your own glory rather than the Company's benefit won't help your cause.'

Clive's shoulders relaxed and his half-smile broadened into a grin. 'Surely my good and the Company's good are the same thing, aren't they?'

Knowing his friend's powers of self-deception, Nicholas still wasn't quite sure he was joking and replied simply, 'Well, come on. Let's hear the grand strategy then.'

'Essentially it is to draw away some of Chanda Sahib's forces from the siege of Mohammed Ali at Trichinopoly by attacking, taking and holding the fort at Arcot on the banks of the Pilar river. You'll know it, I'm sure.'

'Yes. It stands between the Javadi hills and the Mysore ghats and dominates the main trade route between Mysore and Bangalore. How strongly is the fort defended?'

'Not heavily, according to our agents' reports.'

'In that case I can see how your plan might work – and the local people may be inclined to help us too. From what I know of him, I suspect Chanda Sahib is not proving an unduly tolerant or generous new master. Not all of his forces may relish turning their coats and fighting against their old allies in the Company.'

'That's true. The President's holding a council of war tomorrow. I know they'll want you to attend because of your knowledge of the Carnatic. Help me present my case there. Perhaps, together, we can get them to listen for once.'

'Yes, and I think I'll be able to add some arguments of my own.'

At a quarter to eight the next morning, Nicholas accompanied Clive into the council hall of Fort St. George. Both were dressed in their newest Company uniforms and Clive, freshly shaved, was carrying beneath his arm a rolled-up map. They were the first to arrive. Sensibly, the President of Madras, Thomas Saunders, always held his meetings at that time to avoid the worst heat of the day. Clive and Nicholas each settled themselves on one of the straight-backed chairs towards the end of the long mahogany table. Despite the early hour, the room was warm and they were glad of the draught from the customary punkhas flapping overhead.

Soon, other Council members began to arrive. First came George Pigot, whom both Nicholas and Clive knew from their previous service in Madras. Although still only twenty-nine he had been in India for twelve years now and was spoken of as a future successor to Thomas Saunders on the latter's retirement which some people – Clive included – insisted could not come soon enough. Other men soon followed including several military officers. Major Warburton was among them, the empty lower left arm of his tunic pinned up and his face as rubicund as ever. He smiled at them in acknowledgement. A young man entered holding a sheath of papers. 'Thomas Ponsonby the President's new aide-de-camp,' Clive whispered to Nicholas. 'The only thing he's good for is shuffling those papers.'

Finally, everyone rose as Thomas Saunders entered – a tall figure dressed in a brown jacket and cream waistcoat over his white shirt. On arriving as President a year ago, after the French had handed Madras back to the Company under the terms of the Treaty of Aix-la-Chapelle, one of his first actions had been to rehang the portraits of his predecessors in the Council chamber that the French had taken down. Just behind Clive and Nicholas was one of Elihu Yale, with a brass plaque recording that he had governed Madras in the seventeenth century and later founded a college in the Americas.

Another of Saunders's early actions had been to commission a portrait of himself to join his predecessors on the walls. He now sat beneath it on a chair more richly carved and with a higher back than the rest. The painter had secured a good likeness. The long, sallow face, the high cheekbones, the thin lips that turned down at the ends with an expression of world-weariness captured much of what Clive had said about his character.

Saunders began with a few brief preliminaries about the movements of shipping, the replacement of one of the naval station's post captains who had died of dysentery the previous week and the apparent theft of Company stores: 'The worst loss we've suffered – if I remember right – since the loss of some weapons before our expedition into Tanjore.' Most present nodded in agreement with Saunders's view but none could provide enlightenment on the fate of the stores. Finally, Saunders said, 'I suppose we'd better get down to the main business – the battle with the French and their allies over the succession to the throne of Hyderabad. Major Warburton, would you report on the siege of Trichinopoly?'

'To be frank, President, our man Mohammed Ali is barely holding out against Chanda Sahib,' said the major. 'It's difficult to get reinforcements to him because Chanda Sahib is expecting us to send them and will ambush any column unless we send it in massive strength.'

'Something we don't have enough troops to do,' Saunders interrupted, 'without exposing Madras to the risk of capture again and that is something I'm determined I cannot – will not – permit to happen again! It was such a heavy blow to our prestige, both here with the Hindustani rulers and at home in Europe.'

'President, if we can't reinforce our position at Trichinopoly why not reduce the numerical imbalance there by drawing away some of Chanda Sahib's troops?' Clive broke in. 'As you know, I have some ideas about how to achieve such a diversion. May I explain?'

'If you must, Clive,' said the President, exasperation in his tone. 'But could you please be a little more reasoned and calm than you were the last time.'

Clive got quickly to his feet and unrolled his map on the table. Others – not including Saunders – rose and gathered round, as Clive went meticulously and logically over his plan for a diversionary attack on Arcot, indicating the route the Company troops would take. He seemed to have considered every eventuality, Nicholas thought, struck by his friend's ability to cut through detail and grasp the big picture.

'The best of it is we wouldn't need more than a thousand men,' Clive finished.

'Any comments on Clive's plan, gentlemen?' asked Saunders.

Before anyone else could respond, Nicholas intervened. 'From the knowledge of the Carnatic that I gained during my time at the court of Anwaruddin Khan, although it may at first seem rash, I believe Clive's scheme has merit. When I was at the Nawab's court I discovered that many of his fellow senior officers were suspicious of Chanda Sahib. Some may be reluctant to fight against their former friends and allies in the Company for a man in whom they have little trust. What's more, his character and beliefs are not such as to win the ordinary people over to his side. Finally, the relatively flat terrain would be in our favour. We could march our troops the 70 miles to Arcot quickly – in a maximum of a week – even with a baggage train. Once we've captured the fort, it would take Chanda Sahib's men some time to reach Arcot to deal with the threat – even when he hears of it – allowing us time to ready the fort for any impending battle or siege. Trichinopoly is much farther from Arcot than is Madras.'

'It still seems risky to me,' said Saunders.

'You can't win great victories without taking great risks. Don't you see that,' Clive responded with vigour, just as he had lectured Governor Hinde at Fort St. David. Clive hadn't gained in tact, Nicholas thought.

'My suspicion is that in your ardour you underestimate the risks and overestimate the likely rewards, young man,' said the President. 'But I would like to know what others here think.'

'I think it's worth a go,' said Major Warburton. 'On the campaign on which I lost my arm to the Tanjoreans, Clive and Ballantyne here convinced the commanders – me included – to give them their head and the result was the rout of the enemy and the capture of their camp. And one further thing, President,' he allowed himself a brief smile, 'my friend Clive is calmer on the battlefield, and in a crisis, than he is in the council chamber.'

'And what do you think, Pigot?' Saunders asked.

'I agree with Ballantyne's analysis of the politics of the Carnatic and its leaders. By judicious bribery we should be able to suborn one or two of them to our side, shouldn't we Ballantyne?'

Nicholas nodded his assent.

'Also,' Pigot continued, 'Arcot is strategically placed on the trade route to Bangalore, and Chanda Sahib will feel he cannot let us occupy it with the potential for us to advance further into his realm. Therefore, he will indeed feel the need to divert forces to recapture it.'

'Does anybody else have anything to say to the contrary?' Saunders asked.

Robert Dwarkins – the Company's bespectacled chief lawyer in Madras – spoke. 'Like you, I'm cautious, President. Although the scheme clearly has some merits, we must remember that our main care must be the protection of Madras, as you yourself said. Can we spare a thousand men from the garrison?'

'That is exactly my point,' said the President. 'Clive – what's the minimum number of men you'd require if I indeed took the risk and gave you command of such a mission?'

'Five hundred – say two hundred Europeans and three hundred sepoys – but I'd want to decide which men they were. And, of course, some cannon – perhaps four or five.'

Thomas Saunders sighed. 'Very well then. If you take only five hundred men and four cannon you may proceed with your plan. But take Ballantyne with you. From what I gather, he's been a restraining influence on you in the past.'

'With pleasure,' Nicholas replied.

'And you, Ponsonby,' Saunders turned to his aide, 'make damn sure you record in the minutes of this meeting to be despatched to London and Calcutta that my approval was based on the unanimous advice of my council.'

15 – Arcot

Two weeks later, Clive, with Nicholas at his side, rode out of Madras to the sound of trumpets with banners flying at the head of his column of five hundred troops, mostly cavalry supported by three companies of sepoys. At the centre of the column were four eighteen-pounder cannon on wooden limbers, each pulled by teams of sixteen oxen and each with eight spare animals trotting behind in case of disease or injury to those in the traces. A baggage train brought up the rear, which, although small, would govern the speed of the column.

Clive, with advice from Nicholas, had taken considerable care in selecting the troops. Commanding the cannon and newly promoted to company sergeant-major was Henry Armstrong, the scarred veteran from the north-east of England. Clive and Nicholas had sought him out knowing that Arcot would likely be besieged after they'd taken it and believing his experience of the siege of Fort St. David at Cuddalore would be useful.

Leading Clive's scouts were the two who had, a couple of years earlier, located the Tanjorean camp before it could disperse. Although the crocodile bite had left a livid scar on his calf, the taller of the two, Vikram Narayan, swore he could still ride and run as well as ever. Neither Nicholas nor Clive had reason to doubt him. Riding just a little behind Nicholas and Clive was Thomas Saunders's aide Thomas Ponsonby, resplendent in a new scarlet Company uniform but with a nervous expression on his face. Clive and Nicholas could only assume that Saunders's insistence that he accompany them 'to gain experience in warfare' was in reality to keep an eye on them.

Tuhin Singh was not beginning the journey with them. While Clive had concentrated solely on recruiting and drilling the troops, Nicholas had also worked with Tuhin Singh writing letters to their contacts among Chanda Sahib's officers and courtiers, promising rewards if they retained their previous loyalty to the Company. Given his greater ability to move undetected behind Chanda Sahib's lines, Tuhin Singh, travelling in the guise of a northern merchant, would deliver the letters. His mission would require great care given the risk that one of those he approached might betray the plot to Chanda Sahib. But if all went well Tuhin Singh would rejoin the column not long before it reached Arcot.

The monsoon rains – the first of the autumn – fell intermittently as the column progressed along its 70 mile journey, turning part of the well-trodden road into liquid mud. Even starting at dawn, and despite all of Clive's cajoling – alternately promising rewards and threatening punishment to the drivers of the baggage carts – the column made little more than 10 miles a day.

Towards evening on day five, as they approached the junction where the road to Kanchipuram diverged from that to Arcot a great thunderstorm burst overhead with sheets of rain so heavy that no one could see more than a few feet ahead.

'We can go no further tonight sir,' Henry Armstrong reported to Clive, riding up from his post with the cannon. 'The limbers are bogging down every 10 yards or so and we've already lost three oxen to over-exertion and another to a broken leg. More are showing signs of weakness or foot rot.'

'Very well,' Clive replied, as lightning flashed overhead. 'We'll get Vikram Narayan to ride ahead to look for the nearest suitable spot to make camp.'

Ten minutes later, through the sheeting rain, Nicholas and Clive heard rather than saw a horseman galloping up, splashing through the puddles which were swiftly turning into pools. When they could discern him more clearly they realised it was not one of the scouts or pickets, but a totally drenched Tuhin Singh.

Despite the rain running down his face he was smiling. 'My mission went well. As you suspected, Chanda Sahib's arrogance has not won him many friends. Perhaps my most important news is that the commanders of the nearest significant body of Carnatic troops – they're encamped about 25 miles east of Arcot, just beyond Kanchipuram – assured me that they would delay reporting our advance to Chanda Sahib as long as they could. They also promised to take no initiative to move against us until they receive explicit orders giving them no choice but to do so. They also told me they will accept no payment but act in friendship to the Company and to Nicholas. They simply asked that in the aftermath they, their men and the lands around Kanchipuram from which they came should be spared ill-usage – a promise I was happy to make.'

'And one I will as happily honour,' Clive said, great satisfaction in his voice. 'Their action – or rather inaction, I should say – will allow us more than enough time to get to Arcot even in this foul weather and seize the fort. What else did you learn?'

'That the garrison at Arcot is no more than 300 – mostly local men with no French troops – and is likely to be little inclined to die for Chanda Sahib.'

'Better still!' Clive replied.

Two days later, with the rains easing and the fort now in view about six miles ahead, the column prepared to make camp just as evening descended. Vikram Narayan and his fellow scouts, who a few hours earlier had entered Arcot posing as pilgrims, rode in. They reported that the garrison and townsfolk still appeared entirely unaware of the approaching Company troops. The gates of the fort were wide open. The large bazaar just inside them was doing good business. They had encountered no guard posts or pickets as they returned to the Company column.

After some moments' thought, Clive summoned Henry Armstrong and Nicholas. 'Sergeant-Major, if you harness up all the remaining oxen, could they haul the cannon the last miles to Arcot by dawn? With the rains easing there should be some moonlight to help us.'

Armstrong sucked in his scarred cheeks. 'If we borrow some extra beasts from the baggage carts we should be able to do it. But, sir, if we do, we'll lose even more animals. If we suffer any setback we won't have enough fit oxen to retreat with the cannon. We'd have to spike them and abandon them.'

'I'll take that risk,' Clive said. 'The cavalry horses would also be too exhausted for us to withdraw successfully. It's either victory or a choice between disgraceful surrender or heroic death, isn't it young Ponsonby.' He swung around to look at Thomas Saunders's aide, who was standing within earshot. The man had been troubled by diarrhoea for the last two days, frequently dismounting to slip behind roadside bushes. Ponsonby nodded weakly. Quickly, Clive began to give orders. The baggage train, with the exception of a few carts needed to carry the scaling ladders, the powder and the musket and cannon balls, would remain in the encampment with a detachment of men to guard them. 'You can command it, Ponsonby. It'll give you some of the military experience Thomas Saunders is so keen on for you! Pick thirty men for the task – choose those least able to march and fight because of injury or illness. Subedar Das should stay with you. Though weakened by his recurring fever, he's an experienced man. You can rely on his advice. Get to it now!'

Ponsonby brightened perceptibly, whether at the thought of responsibility or simply at not having to ride six more miles in his weakened condition and face a fight at the end of it. Sergeant-Major Armstrong hurried away in response to an instruction from Clive to make sure the powder they took had remained dry during the rainstorms. Clive himself went among his troops, ordering them to sharpen their swords, check the contents of their powder horns and not to forget to feed their horses as well as themselves.

Nicholas splashed through the mud and puddles to supervise the piling of three of the strongest baggage carts with scaling ladders and enough good rope to lash them together if increased height was needed. He also had six barrels of powder prepared with fuses and loaded carefully onto another baggage cart ready to be detonated against the gates of Arcot if they found them closed against them.

Just after midnight the column set off beneath scudding clouds that sometimes obscured the pale moon, which was no more than half full. It provided the only light except that from the lanterns which Clive had issued to each of the officers and sergeants.

All went well for the first three miles or so as they struggled over the ridge of a small hill to see the Pilar river glinting silver in the moonlight. An hour later they were moving confidently across the stony plain to reach the river and follow it the last mile and a half or so to the fort, which still lay out of sight beyond a tree-lined bend in the river. But then, as clouds obscured the moon, the two oxen leading the team pulling the second of the four cannon limbers, stumbled over some rocks and fell, each breaking a foreleg. Armstrong quickly cut them from their yokes and traces and killed the animals, now bellowing in pain.

Cracking their whips, he and his artillerymen urged the remaining beasts on but another collapsed to its knees, exhausted. With that one too freed from its traces, the rest struggled to start the cannon moving again even when the gunners also set their shoulders to the limber. Inspecting the remaining animals and the teams pulling the other three cannon by the flickering lantern light, Clive and Armstrong saw that several were clearly weakening, tongues lolling and heads low.

'Let's abandon this cannon here, Armstrong.' Clive said. 'Share any oxen still capable of hauling between the other three teams.'

Dawn was fast approaching as the column rounded the bend in the Pilar to see in front of them the walls of the fort of Arcot meandering around the top of a small hill on the south side of the river. They had passed no habitation during the night except a few scattered palm-thatched huts whose occupants had stayed out of sight. Now they saw buildings clustered beneath the fort's walls and spreading a little along the road down which they were approaching. The gates had already been opened for the day.

'It can't be more than half a mile. Let's get the vanguard through the gates before the garrison have time to close them,' Clive shouted to Nicholas who nodded and spurred his horse on. Tired though it was, the willing animal began to gain speed.

So, too, did those of the other leading riders forming a packed phalanx as they galloped down the muddy road sending great clods of earth up from their hooves. As they passed the first dwellings, several of their startled inhabitants, preparing to take their animals to the fields for the day, jumped back in surprise. With Tuhin Singh now leading, they were only 200 yards from the heavy iron-studded gates and charging up the twisting ramp towards the walls when they heard the first cries of alarm from the wakening soldiers on the battlements of the fort. Two figures appeared outside the gates, trying to help their comrades inside to heave them shut.

Arriving first, Tuhin Singh, bending low from his saddle, hacked one man down. The other ran back inside. Moments later, the other leading Company horsemen including Nicholas and Clive were swerving through the now only half-open gates after Tuhin Singh. When just fifteen were inside, another rider tried to turn his mount too quickly to get through the closing gap into the fort. The animal fell heavily, blocking the gates and preventing others from entering. Musket fire from the battlements knocked one of the riders waiting behind from his saddle. Moments later another horse and rider crashed from the ramp after the animal was hit in the head and shoulder.

More defenders began to appear, firing down from the battlements at those already inside, causing more casualties. All was not going well, Nicholas thought, as he aimed one of his pistols at a defender who had just emerged from the gatehouse. Hit in the belly, the man turned and staggered back inside, doubled up and clutching at his wound. Another defender, hit in the shoulder by Tuhin Singh's pistol ball as he attempted to reload his musket, twisted around and fell. A musketeer toppled headfirst from the battlements above the gates to spatter his brains across the flagstones. His fall was quickly followed by that of another musketeer who – more fortunate – landed on the palm-thatched roof of a shack built against the wall, which collapsed under the impact.

Seemingly unnerved by the fate of their comrades, several defenders rushed down the stone steps from the ramparts and fled past the stalls of the bazaar that lined the street sloping up towards a tall central tower. Two or three paused in their flight to fire wildly at the Company troops now pushing through the gates in increasing numbers. Hit by a musket ball, one of the fleeing defenders collapsed sideways onto the stall of an early-arriving vegetable seller who had just set out his produce, sending onions rolling down the slope.

Urging his horse into the bazaar and ducking beneath the awnings of the stalls as he rode, Nicholas galloped towards the tower. He soon emerged into a small square fronting it. Looking up at the crenulated top of the tower he saw several musket barrels levelled at him. Then, as he looked for somewhere to take cover, a turbaned officer from the Carnatic army emerged from the small doorway at the bottom of the tower and shouted, 'We surrender!'

Moments later, as a relieved Nicholas wiped sweat from his brow with his neck cloth, a troop of blue-uniformed horsemen – obviously French – emerged through a gateway from a building beside the tower, swords drawn. Seeing the fight already lost, they rode off down another broad alley lined with stalls. Galloping after them, Nicholas saw they were headed for a second open gate opposite the one the Company troops had attacked. As he went through the gate, a rider at the rear turned and fired his pistol at Nicholas. The ball ricocheted off a stone wall and caught Nicholas a stinging blow on the cheek, drawing blood, while some stone splinters hit his horse and caused it to skitter sideways into a vegetable stall piled high with purple aubergines. By the time Nicholas had regained control of his mount, the fleeing French horsemen were already beyond pursuit.

A short while later, the fort of Arcot was the Company's. A couple of hours after that nearly all the Carnatic soldiers were trooping down the ramp having handed over their weapons and sworn never to fight against the Company again. A few, including some sub-officers, asked to join the Company forces claiming they had never had any wish to fight against their friends in the

Company. Clive ordered Armstrong to take their names, telling them their requests would be considered when more about them was known.

From them, Clive and Nicholas learned that the troop of French cavalry whose presence they had not expected had arrived only two evenings previously. They had been on their way to Kanchipuram and had been intending to start for their destination that morning after resting their horses for a day. 'We can be sure that Chanda Sahib will learn of Arcot's capture as fast as those horsemen can ride,' Nicholas told Clive.

'Of course,' Clive replied. 'We need to make our preparations to defend the fort quickly. I'll make an inventory of the weapons, ammunition and stores we've been left with and have the three cannon which have arrived manoeuvred into position. Why don't you and Tuhin Singh ride back to the baggage train and bring that and the fourth cannon into Arcot?'

Nicholas and Tuhin Singh covered the six miles to the baggage train in less than an hour. But when they were still about half a mile away, they saw smoke rising from the vicinity of the train and realised that something was wrong. Approaching cautiously, their pistols drawn, and alert for any ambush, they discovered the smoke was coming from three of the baggage carts that were now almost burnt out. Two wheels and some large pieces of wood scattered over the scorched grass indicated that a powder wagon had exploded. The corpses of several men and animals lay sprawled on the ground. Most of the dead men were wearing Company red but two or three were wearing blue. The French cavalry must have paused in their flight to warn Chanda Sahib of the capture of Arcot to raid the baggage train. As Nicholas and Tuhin Singh neared the centre of the silent camp, Subedar Das and his surviving troops emerged from behind two overturned baggage carts.

'What happened, Subedar?' Nicholas shouted. 'Where's Mr Ponsonby?'

'D... dead, sir.' The man's voice was shaking. 'It was all very sudden. The French attacked about three hours ago, overwhelming our pickets and sentries before they could pull back. Mr Ponsonby and I had the men turn over these two carts as barricades. The Frenchmen ignored us and fired on some of the other carts.' Subedar Das paused and rubbed his forehead, looking dazed.

'How did Mr Ponsonby die?' Nicholas asked more gently.

'He... He was a hero. At first he looked terrified – his whole body shaking with fear. But seeing a French officer about to toss a blazing log from one of our cooking fires into a powder wagon, he seemed to rally himself. Drawing his pistol, he rushed towards him and fired. He brought down the officer before he could hurl the log. But another Frenchman rode at Mr Ponsonby and slashed him to the ground with his sabre. Then, bending from the saddle, the Frenchman seized the blazing log and threw it into the powder wagon which exploded. Less than a quarter of an hour after they'd appeared, the French rode off. I'm glad to say, sir, I killed one with a musket shot as they departed.'

'You did well. Are you injured?'

Subedar Das shook his head.

'Where's Ponsonby's body?'

'Over there.' The subedar pointed to behind one of the over-turned baggage wagons. 'When we reached him we found he had a deep gash in his chest. We carried him back but he was conscious for only a little while. He asked us to tell Captain Clive he hoped he'd done his duty. Then he died very quietly.'

Dismounting, Nicholas and Tuhin Singh walked over to where Ponsonby's body was lying. His face, relaxed in death, betrayed his youth – he was perhaps no more than eighteen or nineteen. Brushing away the black flies already clustering round the corpse, Nicholas felt inside Ponsonby's clothing and took from a pocket a bloodstained locket. Wiping it clean with his neck cloth, he opened it to find a picture of a pretty young woman with dark curly hair. A sister or a sweetheart, Nicholas wondered. He would get it back to Ponsonby's family and let them know Ponsonby had died well – whatever small comfort that might bring.

'Subedar,' he said. 'Let us perform the funeral rites of all our dead, according to their religion, and then get what remains of the baggage train into Arcot.'

–

The next day Clive, Nicholas and Tuhin Singh reviewed their situation, almost certain that an attack from Chanda Sahib could be no more than two or three weeks away. They had only lost twenty men during the capture of Arcot and the attack on the baggage train. Perhaps double that number were wounded, but most were likely to recover. A bigger problem was the number of men falling ill with dysentery and the number of horses suffering from colic.

On the credit side they had brought in all four of the 18-pound cannon they had set out with from Madras. Nicholas had feared that the French horsemen might have spiked the one abandoned two miles from the fort but to his relief he'd found that – thanks to Armstrong's suggestion to cover it – they'd either missed it or thought it unwise to pause so close to Arcot in case of pursuit. Additionally, the previous occupants had abandoned six cannon in the fort. They varied in size and antiquity but none were modern and most were rusting. Armstrong was already at work with his men cleaning them and reinforcing their worm-infested wooden limbers. An investigation of the arsenal building had brought good news. The fort was well-provided with powder and cannon balls and had a casting mould together with a large quantity of lead to make many more musket balls.

'One of our biggest problems,' Clive said, 'is the size of the fort. I calculated the walls to be about a mile in circumference. What's more, they're crumbling in many places. We've scarcely enough fit men to defend them.'

'We could use dummies again to deceive the attackers,' Tuhin Singh suggested.

Clive nodded in agreement while Nicholas added, 'We should have enough time to shore the walls up in places. We can use logs, overturned baggage carts, rocks from the plain, sacks filled with sand from the riverbank, anything we can find in fact. And we should block up all the gates except the main one we entered by.'

'Yes. You take care of all that, Nicholas. I'll see if there are places where we can pull the perimeter back by constructing a second line of defence. I'll get Armstrong to advise on anything we can do to increase the cannon's field of fire. The final problem is food and water and that's what I want you to deal with, Tuhin Singh. Assess what we've got, then take some men and buy up everything you can from Arcot and the surrounding countryside. Don't worry about paying over the odds. It'll only make the local people look kindlier upon us. And when you're out in the countryside find out as much as you can about the terrain and the mood of the inhabitants.'

'I will,' Tuhin Singh replied. 'And when I'm buying food I'll make sure we respect both Hindu and Muslim diet restrictions. It's more important for morale than you Europeans might think. As for water, the monsoon has filled the fort's small reservoir and the townsfolk say the two wells rarely run dry. But I'll still have as many barrels filled from the Pilar River as we can find or fashion – the problem will be keeping the water in them sweet.'

–

Clive's and Nicholas's estimate of how long Chanda Sahib would take to reach Arcot proved accurate. Seventeen days later, they watched from the walls of Arcot a long column of Chanda Sahib's troops appear on the stony plateau. The defenders of Arcot had had good warning from the scouts of their approach. Vikram Narayan had captured a deserter who, in return for his freedom and a few coins, had informed them that Chanda Sahib's son Rana Sahib commanded the army which numbered about 2,000 men, a hundred of whom were French. According to the deserter, many of the troops from the Carnatic had, like himself, no appetite for the fight.

About an hour after the column had reached the Pilar and begun to make camp on its banks, the watchers on the walls saw a blue-coated French officer ride towards the fort. Behind him were two troopers carrying white flags of truce. When they reached the bottom of the ramp leading to the gate, Clive shouted down from the battlements for the officer alone to ride up to it, which he did. Calmly reining in before the closed and barred gates, he dismounted, clearly expecting to be admitted. Instead Clive addressed him again, this time from the roof of the gatehouse. 'Tell me your business.'

'I would prefer to discuss it privately with the commander,' the officer replied in good if accented English.

'I'm Robert Clive. I am the commander,' Clive said. 'I have no secrets from my men, so state your business.'

'I am here to offer you the same honourable terms to depart as you gave to the soldiers of the Carnatic when you took the fort. Surrender Arcot and your arms and you go free, every last man of you. My offer is that simple. Will you accept it?'

'My answer is even simpler. No.'

'Sir, you are outnumbered and outgunned.'

'I repeat my answer. No. We did not occupy Arcot to surrender it meekly at the first appearance of danger. Didn't the French outnumber and out-weapon the English at Agincourt? Like the men of Henry V, we will rely on our comrades and form a band of brothers to see you and the usurper Chanda Sahib off. Is that a clear enough answer for you to take to your commander?'

'It is, but you will regret it,' the officer said before remounting his horse and riding down the ramp to rejoin his two troopers and return to the camp by the Pilar.

'That was a brave speech,' Nicholas said to Clive, 'if relying heavily on Shakespeare.'

'We must live up to it,' Clive responded, frowning, failing to register the humour in Nicholas's voice. 'We need to do something to dissuade our enemy from launching an all-out assault once they've positioned their cannon and readied their troops, which will only take them a day or two.'

'We've plenty of powder, and cannon and musket balls, so we can afford to keep up disruptive fire when any enemy comes even remotely within range. And we should make sure our sentries remain vigilant,' Nicholas suggested.

'And we can fire cannon randomly, day and night, to unsettle the enemy,' Tuhin Singh added.

'All good thoughts and we should put them into action,' Clive replied, 'but what is it that the attackers least expect from us, outnumbered as we are?'

'An attack on their camp not so different from the one we made at Cuddalore, perhaps,' Nicholas mused.

'That's a better idea than you may think,' Clive replied. 'They're too strong for us to attack in daylight while they're forming up for an assault on us, as we did at Cuddalore. However, if we launch a night raid, it'll have maximum surprise and effect. We'll be through their camp and back in the fort before they can even reach their weapons.'

'To forestall an early attack, the sooner we act the better. What about tomorrow night?' Nicholas asked.

'Yes, why not? Let's start our preparations now. There's no time to lose.'

Over the next thirty-six hours they selected the troops to go on the raid, had tar-soaked rags wrapped round pieces of firewood to serve as torches and the horses given an extra ration. Those not going were ordered to stand on the battlements to provide covering cannon and musket fire as the raiders withdrew.

An hour after midnight, to the hooting of owls and on an order from Clive, the chosen troopers bending from their saddles lit their torches from braziers burning brightly in an inner courtyard. Then, as some of the foot soldiers heaved open the iron-studded gates, with Clive, Nicholas and Tuhin Singh in the lead, they charged in a clatter of hooves down the ramp and across the stony plain towards Rana Sahib's camp less than a mile away.

One of the troopers somersaulted from the saddle as his horse stumbled over unseen rocks. The horse next to it shied away from the fallen man's burning torch, unseating its rider, too, but the rest pressed on. They had almost reached the enemy camp before the first cries of alarm went up and one of the few alert sentries fired a musket shot, toppling another rider from his saddle. Then they were in among the enemy tents, some throwing their fiery torches onto them while others slashed at guy ropes and then at the occupants as they struggled from the burning, collapsing tents. The defenders were running hither and thither in complete bewilderment, most half-awake and half-dressed, and desperately seeking their weapons as their enemies rode among them. Yelling their battle cries to add to the confusion, the Company soldiers slashed and cut at them. With a single stroke of his sword, Nicholas levelled to the ground a tall French officer as he tried to marshal his men. Riding deeper into the camp, he tossed his burning torch into what he believed was a large powder wagon before urging his horse away.

Moments later the wagon exploded in a sheet of flame, throwing pieces of wood, packing cases and the bodies of two men who'd been sleeping beneath it into the night sky. Nicholas felt a blast of hot air propel him from the saddle – he'd been too close. Landing with a crash on the earth he lay winded as sparks and embers began to burn holes in his uniform. Rolling rapidly over and over on the ground he extinguished them and scrambled to his feet. Looking wildly around for a horse, he saw two tethered outside what appeared to be a deserted officer's tent – larger, better constructed and a little removed from the rest.

He raced towards the horses, pulling his dirk from his sheath as he ran. Reaching them he quickly cut the tether of the first animal and threw himself onto it. The horse had no saddle. Surprised by the unexpected weight on its back it bucked and threw Nicholas to the ground. Just as he stood up, gasping for breath, and was preparing to attempt to remount, he saw by the flash of a second exploding ammunition wagon another horse no more than 10 yards away already saddled, reins dangling. Despite noise and chaos all around, the animal, which had clearly lost its rider, was quietly eating from a spilled sack of grain. Rushing across to it, Nicholas swung himself into the saddle.

Almost at once, three trumpet calls – the prearranged signal to withdraw – sounded and turning his new mount, Nicholas headed back towards the fort. A few musket shots followed him and the other raiders but then the musketeers on the walls of Arcot opened up with their covering fire and Armstrong's cannon began to boom out, banishing all thoughts of pursuit from the minds of Rana Sahib's men.

Within half an hour of starting, the raiders were back in the fort and Clive began to take their reports. Tuhin Singh described how he and his men had made for the main animal lines, as agreed, and cut the ropes of at least four ranks of horses, sending them galloping off into the night with slaps to their rumps. He'd also released from a pen several baggage oxen, which had charged into the camp, bellowing with all their might. 'A most satisfactory addition to the mayhem,' he said.

'And what about you, Nicholas?' Clive asked, a smile on his face at the sight of Nicholas's singed, bruised and muddied appearance.

'Well, I destroyed a powder wagon.'

'But not without it fighting back, I see.' Clive began to laugh and was joined by Tuhin Singh.

When Clive and Nicholas woke the next morning, Subedar Das, who had commanded the watch from the walls over the enemy's devastated camp during the rest of the night, made his report. Rana Sahib and his men were departing under cover of a protective screen of horsemen and foot soldiers.

'Should we sally out against them again, I wonder?' Clive asked Nicholas.

'No, definitely not. It's daylight. They still outnumber us. They're alert and their weapons are loaded. Their retreat might even be a ruse, a trap. Even if not, we'd lose a lot of men if we attack.'

'You're right, though in a few days, once they've got over their shock, they'll be back.'

'Maybe. But we've gained time to allow the Company forces despatched from Bombay and Calcutta to reach Madras and set out to relieve us as planned.'

'Let's just hope they're not as slow as they usually are in organising themselves – and once we're sure Rana Sahib and his men have truly departed for the present let's inspect what remains of his camp and see what stores we can salvage.'

–

A month later, as autumn began to fade into early winter, Nicholas wiped the sweat from his powder-streaked face as he helped Henry Armstrong and his gun crew – much depleted by both disease and wounds – push their 18-pound cannon back from its firing position to be reloaded for at least the twentieth time that morning as the defenders of Arcot attempted to frustrate yet another of Rana Sahib's onslaughts.

'We'll need to wait a minute or two, sir, before we reload,' Armstrong said. 'The barrel's too hot. We don't want the powder charge exploding as it's rammed home.'

'Of course, Sergeant-Major.'

Armstrong was right. Such an explosion had already destroyed one of the old cannon left in the fort. Its red-hot barrel had burst while being loaded, hurling pieces of metal and bloody hunks of artillerymen's flesh far and wide. Looking along the battlements from the cannon position, Nicholas saw the head of one of Rana Sahib's soldiers appear above the parapet of a weakly defended portion of the walls. Then the man began to scramble from a scaling ladder over the parapet. Drawing his sword Nicholas ran towards him, legs pumping, but before he could reach him a sepoy thrust his sword into the attacker, knocking him from the ladder to crash, arms flailing, to the ground below. Using all his strength, the sepoy heaved the scaling ladder away from the wall. It slid slowly sideways, taking with it two more of Rana Sahib's men, who had been climbing after their comrade.

'Good work!' Nicholas shouted to the sepoy, who made him a small bow. He must remember to recommend the man to Clive for reward, he thought, as he returned to the cannon and heard Armstrong report, 'Ready to fire now, sir.'

'Then, do it.'

A loud roar and flash followed almost immediately and the cannon recoiled, only prevented from crashing into the interior of the fort by the ropes with which the gun crew restrained it. As the white acrid smoke cleared, Nicholas saw that some attackers were retreating back towards the Pilar river. In several cases, three or four unwounded men were supporting a single injured man as he limped away – always a sign that the enemy was losing heart. Sure enough, only a few minutes later Nicholas heard a trumpet blast and all the attackers turned away towards their camp. The defenders of Arcot had defeated yet another of Rana Sahib's attacks, but it had been the closest run thing yet since Rana Sahib had returned ten days ago with even more superior numbers – perhaps four thousand men in total.

Half an hour later, Nicholas sat with Clive and Tuhin Singh in the shelter of one of the few surviving trees in the fort, gulping water from the fort's wells, which fortunately still showed no signs of running dry. The expressions of all three were grim as Clive voiced their shared concern. 'Today's attack was the fiercest yet and the enemy came the closest to succeeding. We need those promised reinforcements from Madras soon if we're not to be overwhelmed...' The other two nodded as he continued, 'The only scout we've sent out who's returned safely said they'd not even started yet. Damn the Company for their procrastination! And he couldn't seem to make them understand our predicament.'

'We need to send someone more senior,' said Tuhin Singh. 'I'm prepared to go.'

'I'm not sure even you could succeed, Tuhin Singh,' Nicholas said. 'Some of the officials are so bigoted they think all Hindustanis exaggerate.'

'Not just Hindustanis,' Clive said. 'Look at how they treat my own concerns! For greater credibility, you and Tuhin Singh should both go.'

Nicholas and Tuhin Singh exchanged glances, then Nicholas said, 'Well, that's agreed then!'

That night Nicholas and Tuhin Singh, both dressed in black tunics and pantaloons, with daggers and pistols tucked into their belts, prepared to enter a small tunnel about two feet wide and tall. It was a disused drain leading outside from some latrines positioned near an outer wall. It still smelled of its previous usage – sewage. A sepoy handed Nicholas a sturdy iron bar to knock out the stones inserted just before the siege began to block the tunnel's exit; others had already removed those blocking the entrance from the interior of the fort. To Tuhin Singh, who was to take the lead, the sepoy handed a lighted lantern.

Crouching and holding the lantern before him, Tuhin Singh entered the tunnel and began to crawl over hard rocks and sometimes through dried faeces. As he followed, Nicholas felt one rat and then another run over his legs and scuttle away. At least the drain wasn't long. After about 20 yards they reached the stones blocking the exit to the outside. Tuhin Singh put down the lantern carefully and Nicholas passed him the iron bar. Tuhin Singh began to lever away the stones, manoeuvring them backwards for Nicholas to stow behind them. He was making good progress when, as Nicholas reached for a particularly large stone, he caught the lantern. It was only a glancing blow, but still enough to turn the lantern on its side and extinguish the flame before either man could reach it to right it.

Now they were alone in the stinking darkness with rocks behind and in front of them. Stupidly, neither of them had brought a tinderbox. However, Tuhin Singh continued to pull at the stones, feeling for them in the dark. After he'd removed four or five more and passed them back to Nicholas, both men badly grazing their hands and splitting their nails in the process, he whispered, 'I think I can smell fresh air. Give me a little space and I'll try and turn and kick the rest away.'

Nicholas squeezed back against the stones they'd already removed while, contorting himself, Tuhin Singh managed to turn. Moments later he began kicking at the remaining stones with all the strength he possessed. Now Nicholas could smell cool night air too. Another two or three kicks and they saw moonlight. To reduce the noise they again began to move the rocks individually by hand. Soon both men had wriggled from the tunnel and were lying flat on the ground, scanning the terrain dropping away from the fort to Rana Sahib's camp by the Pilar river still over three quarters of a mile distant. Pinpoints of light showed the likely positions of sentry posts and pickets. One appeared to be close to the riverbank where, from observations from the battlements, they knew were the horse lines from which they intended to steal mounts.

After waiting long enough to be certain their exit from the drain had not been observed, they set out, bending low and sometimes crawling on already bruised and grazed knees over the stony ground. When they came close to a dead ox killed in the fighting, two stray dogs gorging on the putrefying flesh of the animal's belly turned and growled at them. But no sound came from Rana Sahib's camp. By the light of flashes of nocturnal sheet lightning occasionally illuminating the riverbank they saw that there was indeed a small sentry post by the horse lines. Creeping closer they heard two voices coming from it, one complaining in French about his bowels. 'Diarrhoea like hot water stinging my arse every few minutes...'

'Count yourself lucky you don't have piles like a bunch of grapes, like I have,' the second voice replied.

'It'll be almost a kindness to relieve their suffering,' Nicholas said, gesturing to Tuhin Singh to circle the post one way while he went the other.

'At least with their own bowel problems they won't smell us coming,' Tuhin Singh murmured as he crept away into the darkness.

Less than a minute later, both sentries were dead. Quickly removing their uniform jackets and putting them on, Nicholas and Tuhin Singh moved towards the now unguarded horse lines. Three or four of the animals were saddled, presumably for the use of pickets in the early morning. Mounting, they headed towards the exit from the camp to the Madras road only for two sentries to challenge them and demand their business. 'Ordered to check if any reinforcements are approaching for those damned Englanders,' Nicholas replied, hoping his French accent would be passable.

'Proceed. Be safe!' one of the sentries – a stubble-chinned corporal – replied.

Two hours later, they stopped by a pool. Carefully scanning the banks and the shallows for crocodiles, they discarded their French uniform jackets and plunged in to wash the filth from themselves and their remaining clothes. Now much sweeter smelling, they rode hard towards Madras. By evening they were beyond the junction of the roads to Madras from Arcot and Kanchipuram. Concealing themselves in a coppice to rest themselves and in particular their horses for a few hours, they took turns to keep watch.

Neither saw anything other than the occasional deer until at dawn a small group of travellers leading donkeys loaded with merchandise appeared from the direction of Madras. Tuhin Singh – on watch at the time – walked out to greet them and asked whether they had encountered any large bodies of troops. As he reported back to Nicholas, their answer was, 'Yes. Just after we left Madras we passed a large column of Company soldiers making slow progress.'

'Even allowing for the time it's taken these people to get here, that means the reinforcements are still 40 miles off. Even so, if we push the horses to their limits we can reach them by evening,' Nicholas replied.

Stopping only twice to water their horses they in fact met the leading scouts of the column by mid-afternoon. 'Who's in command?' Nicholas asked.

'Captain Kilpatrick,' a scout replied.

Nicholas smiled at Tuhin Singh. Kilpatrick was a no-nonsense soldier who would understand the urgency of their mission.

–

And so it proved. Only three nights later, the relief column was passing the burnt-out wagons of the baggage train and the graves of Thomas Ponsonby and the Muslim sepoys who had died with him. Both Nicholas and Tuhin Singh were riding among the vanguard. As they topped one of the last low hills before the Pilar river, Nicholas saw vultures circling in the sky in the direction of Arcot. Were they too late? Had the fort fallen, the defenders finally buckling under the weight of attacks from overwhelming numbers? Had his friend Clive found not glory but the death to which he had so often claimed indifference? Had he allowed himself to be drawn into Clive's hubristic and, yes, self-serving scheme and had his own advocacy unnecessarily sacrificed Company lives?

No. He had been truly convinced that the seizure of Arcot could succeed and he didn't yet know it hadn't. There could be many causes for the vultures to mass. Nevertheless, their appearance in the sky had unsettled him. He needed to know Arcot's fate and spurred his horse forward towards the screen of pickets which Kilpatrick had wisely thrown about the vanguard.

With Tuhin Singh at his side, Nicholas was passing through the pickets when he saw two advance scouts hastily descending a small hill in front of them. Reining in before Nicholas, one of them reported breathlessly, 'Rana Sahib seems to be retreating. He's broken his camp. Most of his men are skirting Arcot and making for the south-west, back towards the Carnatic heartlands. But a small squadron of blue-coated cavalry are heading in this direction, perhaps wanting to get the news of the retreat to Chanda Sahib's headquarters. At the moment, they seem unaware of our presence.'

'Then let's make them aware,' Nicholas shouted, elated that Arcot was safe. Calling some troopers to his side, he galloped up the hill that the scouts had just descended. Yes, there were French troops half a mile away, riding diagonally across the path of Kilpatrick's approaching column. Yelling loudly, the Company troops were soon in pursuit of the French riders who, now realising the danger, bent to their horses' necks and were galloping hard away amid increasing clouds of red dust. Slowly the leading Company troopers, foremost among them Tuhin Singh, overhauled the laggards among the French. One Frenchman at the rear turned in his saddle and fired his pistol. The ball only grazed Tuhin Singh's temple. Then, as Tuhin Singh continued to gain on him, the Frenchman reined in his winded chestnut horse and raised his hands in surrender. So, too, did several others.

Only the five leading riders were now pressing on, their horses' hooves pounding the ground. Nicholas, who was fast gaining on them, guessed they'd already fired their pistols. Rather than use his own and risk missing at the speed at which he was galloping, he waited until he drew level with the rearmost rider – an officer – and threw himself sideways onto the man, pulling him from the saddle. As they hit the ground Nicholas lost his grip and they rolled over separately. The Frenchman recovered and scrambling to his feet ran at Nicholas with his dagger drawn. Grabbing a handful of grit and dust as he got to his feet, Nicholas threw it into his opponent's face. As the officer let out a surprised yell and raised one hand to clear his eyes, Nicholas grabbed the other hand that held the dagger and wrenched his arm back with all the force he could muster. There was a pop as the man's elbow dislocated, forcing him to drop his weapon. '*Je me rends!* I surrender!' he shouted, his face contorted with pain.

Now all but one of the French cavalrymen were down or had given up. Tuhin Singh was about to continue the pursuit of the lone remaining rider when Nicholas shouted, 'Let him go. There's no harm in Chanda Sahib learning quickly of our victory. Knowing we will soon be heading for Trichinopoly can only encourage him to break his siege of the city.'

That night, as they sat around a large fire in the courtyard of the fort, Clive regaled Nicholas and Tuhin Singh with stories of the later defence of Arcot. Rana Sahib had bought up war elephants in an attempt to batter down the gates, but Armstrong's cannon had wounded the leading elephant, causing it to rampage and panic its fellows. Rana Sahib had then tried a night-time sortie to plant barrels of gunpowder against the gate, which vigilant sentries had thwarted. Rana Sahib's final throw, no more than forty-eight hours ago, had been a simultaneous assault on all parts of the walls. Although a dozen or so of his soldiers had actually succeeded in entering the fort, Clive and his men had repulsed the attackers. Upon this – and doubtless learning of the approach of the Company column – Rana Sahib and his French advisors had decided to withdraw.

'One thing I can tell you,' Clive said as they raised a toast to victory and survival, 'is that those damned dullards in headquarters will never be able to ignore me again.'

'And isn't that what we've all fought so hard for,' Nicholas replied winking at Tuhin Singh.

16 – The Rift

'Gentlemen, I give you "the heroes of Arcot"!' As Colonel Wheeler raised his glass in the officers' mess in Fort St. George, an answering roar went up, 'The heroes of Arcot!'

Nicholas and Clive exchanged grins. There'd been no way of avoiding something like this. As soon as they'd dismounted in the courtyard, junior officers had rushed forward and borne them shoulder-high to the mess. Nicholas had envied Tuhin Singh for being able to slip quietly away. By rights he should have been with them but he knew Tuhin Singh had no more taste for being lionised than himself – unlike Clive, now standing on a table, holding forth about the defence of Arcot.

With every eye on Clive, now was a good opportunity to get away himself. Out in the street, Nicholas hailed a pony-drawn tonga, his thoughts focused on seeing his son again after so many months. As the tonga jolted to a halt outside his bungalow, Nicholas handed the driver a few coins, jumped down and ran inside. Passing beneath a low arch into the inner courtyard, he saw Sohini seated at the far end on a bench, his son on her lap. James was playing with her long hair that she had loosened from its customary plait, entwining his small fists in it and laughing.

Preoccupied with their play on this beautiful summer's day, neither Sohini nor James realised Nicholas was there. He drew back a little, into the shadow of the arch, content just to watch for a while. How much his son, nearly two years old now, had grown during these past months. He couldn't help imagining it was Meena's beautiful hair James was tugging at, her voice that was jokingly chiding him. Then squaring his shoulders, he stepped forward into the sunlight. Moments later he was swinging James high into the air and his son was squealing with delight.

In fact, over the months that followed, Nicholas had plenty of time to spend with James, reading simple stories to him beneath the mango tree – it astonished him how quickly James's vocabulary in both English and Bengali was growing – and holding him on the back of a pony as he took his first ride along the riverbank and all the time thinking how proud Meena would have been.

The reason for his new-found leisure, Nicholas knew, was that the victory at Arcot had bought the Company the luxury of time to consider its strategy. President Saunders had no major tasks for him and he was left to his own devices. Nicholas didn't even see that much of Clive until one January day, returning from the early morning ride he liked to take along the shore, he was surprised to see him descending from a tonga outside his bungalow.

'What brings you here this early? Not that I'm not glad to see you!' Nicholas called out. Dismounting, he handed the reins of his horse to his groom, then slapped his friend on the back.

'The truth is I've something I want to tell you as my friend – something important and private.' For once, Clive sounded a little uncertain of himself, slightly embarrassed even.

'Come inside.' Intrigued, Nicholas led the way to his small study. As usual at this hour, Sohini was with James in his nursery and the servants were still in their own quarters so the bungalow was quiet around them.

'Well, go on then,' Nicholas said as soon as he'd closed the door behind them. 'What is it?'

'I'm to be married. You're the first person I've told,' Clive said looking at the floor.

'When are you intending to tell the lady in question?' Nicholas asked, laughing.

'You know perfectly well what I mean.'

Nicholas said nothing. The thought of the ebullient Clive – a man so restless, so tormented by his sense of destiny that he needed opium to sleep – entering domesticity rendered him speechless for a few moments. Then he said, 'Well, that is news... good news. I hope you'll be very happy. Even though it's so early, we must drink to it – but first – who is this fortunate lady, your bride-to-be?'

'Miss Maskelyne.'

Nicholas's smile stiffened. 'Who?'

'Margaret Maskelyne. You look surprised?'

'I am... I don't see you as a sober married man...' Nicholas said hastily, trying to force a smile to his lips.

'I know what you mean. I can hardly credit it myself. I'm not entirely sure how it happened. Margaret and I haven't known each other long – just these past few months since we returned to Madras. But there's something about her... I saw it the first time I met her. She's clever, and she has a shrewd nose for Company politics. Do you know, she was the one who first told me Martingdale would be pushed out, and she was right? He's packing for home now.'

'You say you don't know quite how it happened. What do you mean? When did you ask her?'

'Three evenings ago, at dinner at her cousin Anna Mulgrave's. She told me she'd decided to go back to England... It took me by surprise. I realised how much I didn't want her to go. I acted instinctively, just like in battle. I asked her there and then to be my wife. What would have been the point of thinking about it too hard anyway? If I'm going to take a risk – and allying yourself to another person can only be that – I thought it better to plunge straight in. And I could have done worse, couldn't I? She's good-looking, well-connected, got money of her own. I'm only surprised no one else snapped her up... Now, what about that drink you were going to get!'

'Of course,' said Nicholas. Going to the cupboard where he kept his alcohol, he took his time selecting a bottle of the Canary wine Clive enjoyed as he pondered his friend's news. Clearly Margaret hadn't said anything about what had passed between them. What was in her mind? Had she set her cap – or rather

her bonnet – at him? Did she love Clive or had she accepted his friend out of pique because Nicholas himself had turned her down? Surely not. More likely it was ambition, simple as that. Clive had been the toast of Madras since his return from Arcot. Perhaps Margaret foresaw a great future for him with herself at his side, guiding him, as preferable to returning alone to Britain. If so, she and Clive might do very well together. And now that he thought about it, Clive hadn't mentioned anything about love…

Pouring two glasses of wine, Nicholas turned and held one out to his friend. Then raising his own glass he said, 'Your health, Clive. I wish you both every happiness!'

–

Quick to act, as he always was, once he had made a decision, Clive lost little time in setting a wedding date. Or perhaps Margaret Maskelyne herself was keen to see the knot tied quickly. The well-attended ceremony took place in the elegant, high-spired St. Mary's Church in Fort St. George.

From what Nicholas saw of his friend in the days that followed, marriage seemed to suit him unexpectedly well. He moved with his new bride into a large, elegant house near the fort and acquired a grand carriage, the doors emblazoned with both the Clive and the Maskelyne coats of arms. Most evenings he and Margaret, dressed in their best – Clive in a tricorn hat and Margaret with pearls or diamonds in her ears – were to be seen among the fashionable people of Madras parading in their carriages along the waterfront to take the evening air. It amused Nicholas to see his friend – a man who had never paid much attention to his appearance – turning into a dandy. He also noticed the slight paunch developing beneath Clive's magnificent brocade waistcoats.

Without making it too obvious, Nicholas did his best to avoid Margaret which was not difficult. Since the wedding, several intelligence-gathering missions had taken him away from Madras for which he was grateful. When he was in the city, he had plenty of opportunity to see Clive at Company meetings or when they went duck shooting or riding together. But now Margaret had decided that she wished to become a horsewoman, and Clive had asked Nicholas to join him at Jinkses, the dealer who supplied most of Madras's grandees with their mounts. As they leant against the wooden fence around a sand-strewn ring, a young lad led in a grey mare with a white blaze on her forehead – the third horse they'd been shown.

'Well, what do you think of her?' Clive demanded. 'Just the thing for Margaret, I'd say – spirited but good-mannered. Just like her!'

Nicholas ran a critical eye over the grey mare as the lad put her through her paces. 'I'm not sure. She's a bit long in the back. And I'd like to take a look at that scar on the right front fetlock.'

Entering the ring, Nicholas patted the mare's neck then bent to examine the scar, running his hand gently over it. 'She's fine. The scar's not deep – just a scratch – and it's healed well. What are they asking for her?'

Clive glanced at the expectant-looking ferret-faced dealer at his side. 'Twenty guineas you said, Jinks?'

'Too high. She's worth no more than eighteen guineas,' Nicholas said firmly.

Shooting Nicholas a look of dislike, the dealer said to Clive. 'Very well, sir, eighteen guineas it is.'

'You'd have done better to ask Tuhin Singh's advice,' Nicholas said once Clive had paid Jinks and he'd gone off jingling his sovereigns. 'You know he's a far superior judge of horses than either of us.'

'I do know that. To be honest, the real reason I wanted to talk to you somewhere out of the public eye has nothing to do with horses – not that I don't value your opinion on the topic. Let's sit in that shade over there and I'll explain.'

Clive and Nicholas settled themselves on some straw bales beneath a banyan tree. 'What I'm going to say is for you and you alone,' he said. 'I've had an idea. If it works, it will be the grandest scheme I've pulled off so far.' Clive leant forward, hands interlinked and an eager expression on his face. 'You know about the disagreements between the Raja of Biralpur and his neighbour, the Raja of Sonur? Their territories lie north of here.'

'Of course I know. They hate each other. Only last year skirmishes broke out between them as they squared up to each other. The Political Department's been keeping a close eye on their affairs because of the risk of disruption to our trade.'

'That's just my point. Those two rulers are too volatile for the Company's good. We need order and certainty because that's what's best for trade.'

'And we in the Political Department try to achieve that because we make it in those rulers' interests to be quiescent,' Nicholas replied, amused that his friend thought he needed telling.

'That costs money, time and effort. There's a much better way of bringing that entire region to heel – permanently.' Clive leaned forward, brown eyes sparkling with the almost messianic enthusiasm Nicholas knew well. 'If we could only encourage the Raja of Biralpur and the Raja of Sonur to go to war against each other, the Company could intervene. We could offer support to one of the rulers in return for a treaty of alliance and a guarantee of a monopoly in trade within their territories.'

'But you'd be provoking a war with all its chaos.'

'The "chaos", as you call it, would give the Company the perfect excuse to move in – and all in the name of good order. What could be more logical or more legitimate?'

'I don't think even the Council would be hypocritical enough to see it that way...'

Clive grinned. 'I don't intend to consult the Council. My plan is to provoke the war myself, in secret and using my own money... You can be assured I'll more than compensate myself later! As for the Company, once my plan succeeds – as it will – and they see the profits they won't want to know how the war began, if, indeed, they ever suspect it was contrived.'

Nicholas sat for a moment, stunned at what his friend had just said, then burst out, 'How can you think of provoking bloodshed just because the results might benefit you and the Company, Clive! People will die – not just soldiers, but ordinary people!'

'I know,' Clive said, frowning. 'The innocent always suffer in times of conflict. It's a fact of life. You can't make an omelette without breaking eggs, Nicholas. But the Company will quickly stop the fighting, won't it? The people will enjoy lasting peace, lasting protection and that will have been worth the sacrifice of a few of their number.'

'That's twisted, self-deluding logic. These "people" you speak of are not one amorphous lump. Each is an individual. Why should any one of them be forced to sacrifice anything for your benefit? I think…'

'No. Just hear me out as you've always done before. The way I see it, the one to approach is the Raja of Biralpur and I need your help. Don't you see, it's perfect! You're in the Political Department. He'll listen when you tell him the Company has secret intelligence that his neighbour is planning to attack him. Then you offer him money – my money – to strike the first blow.'

'I can't believe you're seriously suggesting such deceit. Have you been drinking or taking too much of that opium you're so fond of?'

Clive flushed. 'No, I am serious. Never been more so. You're just being squeamish, Nicholas. You said yourself that the Rajas of Biralpur and Sonur are unreliable neighbours for the Company in Bengal and are sworn enemies. They're bound to go to war at some point. I'm just accelerating things.'

'No. This is wrong and immoral – as immoral as the French encouraging the Jacobites to rebellion in the '45. Look at the harm it's caused the Scottish people. This is one thing about which you won't change my opinion. I won't get involved and nor should you!'

'For God's sake, Nicholas, you're being priggish again,' Clive replied, a sharp edge to his voice. 'Why do you think the Company's here in the first place? How many times have I had to tell you? It's profit, profit, profit! Not for some higher good. If you think it is, then you're a fool.'

'Of course I know the Company's motivated by self-interest, but that doesn't mean it doesn't also have the power – and the obligation – to do good in Hindustan. You cannot do that by dishonest warmongering but by promoting peace and prosperity by lawful means, even if it takes time.'

'That's fine when time's on your side but here in Hindustan it isn't. We've given the French a kicking but they'll be back. We must use the period before they're up to their old mischiefs to strengthen ourselves. That's why these past months I've been turning over in my mind how best to advance the Company's interests.'

His anger rising, Nicholas stood up. 'Advance your own interests you mean, Clive? Are you sure that isn't what this is really about? Wasn't Arcot enough? You were brilliant there. You helped the Company in a time of terrible danger – danger not of our making. It wasn't our fault Chanda Sahib went over to the French any more than that after we defeated him the Hindu subjects he'd so despised captured and killed him – useful though that was. It just happened. You can't fabricate another crisis simply to give yourself a crack at even greater glory or because you're bored!'

Clive stood up, face flushed even deeper. 'I'm beginning to think Margaret was right about you! She warned me you were jealous of my position – the power and influence I have. She said you'd been belittling my role in the defence of Arcot... That you were the source of rumours going round that I'd enriched myself by taking plunder that should have been handed over to the Company. I thought better of you than that. I told her not to be ridiculous. I told her she didn't know you, that such thoughts would never even enter your head. But now I'm beginning to see that perhaps I was wrong. I'd been wondering why you don't come to my house as often as you used to, but I understand now. It's because you know that Margaret sees through you! I've noticed you never spend time with her if you can help it... I've been a fool but at least she's had the eyes to see the truth...'

For a moment Nicholas was speechless, then he too stood up. 'Clive, I don't know what you're talking about. Neither do you.

I don't envy you anything. I wish you all the success you crave. But as your friend – your true friend – I can't stand aside and say nothing when you seek to embroil yourself and the Company in a shameful escapade.'

Clive shook his head and his tone was colder, more formal, than Nicholas had ever heard it as he said, 'I'll remind you that everything I've said was in confidence.'

'You don't need to remind me.'

'Don't I? I'm not so sure… Goodbye Nicholas.' Dusting some wisps of straw from his coat, Clive strode away.

Over subsequent weeks, Nicholas saw little if anything of Clive. When Company business made meeting inevitable, Nicholas watched for any sign that his friend regretted their argument. He hoped Clive had at least thought about what he had said. Or perhaps he hadn't. Perhaps even now he was seeking someone else to be his emissary to the Raja of Biralpur? What had made Clive even consider such a scheme and had Margaret Maskelyne encouraged him? Was it his need to prove himself to his new wife?

Such thoughts gnawed at Nicholas but loyalty prevented him from confiding in anyone – even Tuhin Singh. All the time, he hoped to hear from Clive, but weeks turned into months with still no overture from his friend. Again and again he wondered whether he himself should take the initiative. But he didn't regret a single word he had said. In any case, knowing Clive, his friend would interpret any approach from him as an admission that he'd been wrong. But he missed their shared confidences. Everything they had experienced together had created a bond he, at least, had thought unshakable…

One evening, returning home, Nicholas found a note from Clive waiting for him. But any hopes he had that it signalled a rekindling of their friendship were dashed as he read Clive's brief message.

I thought you should know that Margaret and I are sailing for England on the Pelham. *We'll have left Madras by the time you read this.*
    Yours,
    Robert Clive

Had Clive abandoned his 'grand scheme', or had something urgent called him home? Nicholas wondered. If only either of them could have swallowed their pride enough to talk before Clive's departure... But greater than Nicholas's regret at that was his disappointment that the man who'd once been his friend – his good friend – hadn't had more faith in him. Clive's new wife had been astute in making him feel threatened by Nicholas. Yet, despite everything, he felt in his bones that Clive would return. He knew, just as Clive must, that only Hindustan could provide the glory and fortune his friend still craved so passionately.

The Ballantyne papers contain few references to Robert Clive between his departure to England with Margaret in 1753, until his arrival back in India, without his wife, in July 1755. However, letters and diary entries suggest Nicholas's continuing friendship with Tuhin Singh. They also reveal that in early 1754 Nicholas was recalled from Madras to Calcutta where he continued to serve the Company on various 'political' missions. The fact that Nicholas was reluctant to commit very much to paper about these activities suggests clearly that they were clandestine intelligence exercises.

However, there is one notable exception. In 1755, the Company sent Nicholas, with Tuhin Singh, into one of the wildest, remotest regions of Hindustan to report on the growing pirate menace there. In a small notebook bound with buffalo hide I found Nicholas's notes detailing what happened. As it later transpired, the events he describes not only changed his life but shaped the destinies of future generations of Ballantynes.

What follows, pieced together from Nicholas's own words, is what I believe happened.

A.R.

17 − *Lucia*

The midday sun in one of the remotest regions of the great wide muddy delta of the Ganges seemed hotter even than in Calcutta, nearly 300 miles away. With the monsoon fast approaching, the air was heavy with moisture and the extreme humidity made it even more oppressive as Nicholas and Tuhin Singh walked side by side down the dusty main street of the small port. They had left their horses with a fisherman two or three miles away. He had been too frightened to accompany them but had told them that here they would be sure to find their quarry − pirates.

'We're hearing stories that a local ruler has joined the pirates who've long infested the backwaters of the delta and has organised them into a more powerful fleet. We need to know if they're true,' St. John Casson, a senior council member, had told Nicholas. 'Undoubtedly more of the craft bringing produce to our outlying stations are being attacked and there are unconfirmed accounts of the enslavement and sale of crewmen, local people and even Burmese taken from across the frontiers. Rumours are also doing the rounds that a couple of the chief pirates are Europeans who've moved on from the Caribbean and Madagascar in search of easy pickings. Take Tuhin Singh with you, as you usually do. Find out what you can and report back as soon as you can. And Ballantyne, take care!'

And so Nicholas and Tuhin Singh had set out on their long, uncomfortable journey from Calcutta, first travelling by boat and then onwards by horseback.

Nicholas wiped the sweat from his forehead with the loose end of the head cloth he was wearing to conceal most of his face. 'Don't show too much of yourself. You're scarcely better at disguising yourself as a Hindustani now than you were when we escaped from Madras with Clive,' Tuhin Singh whispered.

'Well, you can hardly talk. You stand out as well! You're taller and bigger than most local people,' Nicholas retorted quickening his pace. He felt Tuhin Singh's hand on his shoulder.

'Slow down or we'll draw more attention to ourselves. The pace of life here isn't as quick as in Calcutta.'

In truth, most of the local people were inside their mud brick huts. One or two men were lying on charpoys in the shade, sheltering from the sun and an occasional near-naked child could be seen playing in the dust near the doorway of a home. A pale-furred dog ran barking towards them but after pursuing them a short distance wheeled away, seemingly satisfied it had performed its guard duty.

As they drew nearer the quayside they saw two men, sticks in hand, standing in the middle of the road about a hundred yards ahead of them. A third was gesturing towards one of the few other pedestrians – an itinerant hawker from the looks of him – to go no further. 'Quick! Duck down the next alley, before they take too much notice of us,' Nicholas said.

They did and soon emerged into an open space at the back of some of the dwellings with a couple of middens in it. By the side of one an old woman in a red sari, which, like her, had seen better days, was fashioning dung cakes and slapping them against a wall to dry for fuel. When she saw them, she got creakily to her feet and disappeared into a hut. So, too, did another woman who had been pounding grain and, more surprisingly, a man chopping firewood.

'It's as if they know they must keep out of our way,' said Nicholas, speaking now in Bengali to avoid suspicion in case they were overheard.

'Or are simply frightened,' Tuhin Singh responded as they moved quickly down another alley parallel to the main street. Several of the houses along it were dilapidated and unoccupied.

It opened onto the riverbank where, on rows of racks, hundreds of filleted and flattened fish were drying, buzzing with flies. The stench almost made Nicholas retch, but the racks formed the ideal cover from which to observe the quay.

There, sure enough, was a large dhow with two tall masts moored about 40 yards away. A heavily bearded man with a club at his side was lounging on a charpoy beside the gangway. Then, at a cry from a voice somewhere on the deck, he sprang up and spat extensively. Seven or eight figures appeared at the head of the gangplank and began to edge their way down it. Shading his eyes against the sun with his hand, Nicholas saw some were children but most were women. All had their wrists bound and attached to a long rope joining them together. A burly man at the rear of the column held the rope's end.

'They must be slaves, those the Company and the fisherman talked about, mustn't they?' Nicholas whispered over his shoulder, still speaking Bengali.

'Of course,' a voice answered from behind him, and it wasn't that of Tuhin Singh!

Nicholas's hand immediately went to the dagger concealed beneath his clothes.

'No need for that,' the voice said. 'I mean you no harm – in fact quite the contrary.'

Turning, Nicholas saw the speaker was none other than the man who'd been chopping firewood. 'Come with me,' he whispered, 'and I'll explain myself.'

Nicholas and Tuhin Singh exchanged nods and, with Nicholas's hand still on his dagger as he was sure Tuhin Singh's was too, followed the small, wiry man into an empty hut filled with nothing but flies and a few goat droppings.

'My name is Ram Das,' he said. 'When you came into the alley I could immediately tell you were strangers from beyond the delta. I followed you and when I heard what you said I hoped you'd come to do something about these pirates and slavers. They first appeared about three years ago, only infrequently at first.

But recently they've made this place their base and they treat the people here as their possessions. We are afraid. The women live in constant dread of being violated. Six months ago they took my eldest son – a boy of ten – just because I objected when they seized some of my grain. It may be too late for my boy but I'll do anything to protect my wife, my other children and, indeed, the village.'

'You're right,' Nicholas replied. 'We have been sent by the East India Company to discover the truth about reports of piracy and slavery in the delta.'

The man looked relieved, then grew thoughtful. 'You can do more than that. Help us free those captives you've just seen and destroy that dhow and its evil captain – a white man, as I think you are,' he said, looking directly at Nicholas.

Nicholas and Tuhin Singh again exchanged glances before Tuhin Singh replied, 'If we do, the rest of the pirates may descend on you and your fellow villagers to exact reprisals before we can return to Calcutta and alert the Company to send forces to protect you.' Thinking of Cumberland's actions in the Highlands, Nicholas added, 'they may burn your houses and kill anyone they choose, whether they're involved in our attack on the dhow or not.'

'Let them come,' the man responded. 'We should have time to go further inland to hide until the Company's troops arrive. It will be worth it if we no longer have to live in fear.'

Their orders were merely to observe and report back, but Ram Das's words had moved Nicholas. Glancing at Tuhin Singh, he could tell his friend felt the same. 'Very well, we'll return tonight and do our best to help you,' he told the man.

That evening, after sunset, the fisherman who had kept Nicholas and Tuhin Singh's horses rowed the two of them and Ram Das downriver towards the port. Encouraged by Ram Das, who had accompanied them back to their horses, and the news that most of the port's inhabitants were united in their mission, the fisherman had overcome his fears and agreed to join them.

The plan of attack they had worked out was disconcertingly simple. In the middle of the boat – an old, decaying one and not the fisherman's own – was a barrel containing pitch. In the dark, the fisherman would manoeuvre the craft beneath the stern of the dhow. Many of the crew, Ram Das 'had assured them, would be ashore, preparing for the auction of the captives which, so he'd heard, would take place in an old abandoned fort just outside the town the next morning. The only crewman likely to be in any way alert would be the watchman at the gangplank. Unseen in the darkness, Nicholas and Tuhin Singh would scramble aboard the dhow, whereupon Ram Das, who was sitting quietly in the bow of the rowing boat, would ignite the pitch and set the stern of the dhow on fire before he and the fisherman dived overboard. As the crew rushed to investigate, Nicholas and Tuhin Singh would deal with them while Ram Das – after swimming ashore – would muster the waiting villagers to free the captives in the fort.

Now the rowing boat was rounding a bend in the river. By the light of the rising moon, Nicholas could just about make out the shape of the moored dhow. Letting the current do most of the work for fear of the splash of the oars rousing suspicion, the fisherman skilfully manoeuvred his craft towards the dhow's stern. Lights flickered in the dhow's cabin and the sound of raised voices drifted towards them in what sounded like a discussion about the division of the spoils from the sale of one of their captives. Now the boat was beneath the stern, on the side away from the riverbank and the guard, and bumping against it with still no sign that they had been seen or heard. At a gesture from Nicholas, he and Tuhin Singh stood and began to climb onto the large wooden rudder of the dhow. Balancing there, they reached out and grasped some of the ropes of the rigging and began to heave themselves upwards.

One of the ropes Nicholas was grasping snapped and for several moments he was left clinging, one-handed, above the water until – kicking his feet upwards – he wrapped them round a larger hawser and was able to secure another handhold. A few moments later he was on the deck and joining Tuhin Singh who had his back to the rear wall of the lit cabin which had no portholes. From within they heard voices talking about a woman captive.

'A dish fit for a prince's table or rather his bed,' one voice said.

'A pity about her temper but he won't find out about that until too late,' a second voice replied, chuckling.

'Anyway, maybe she'll cool down a bit when she's been locked in that crate for another night. We'll keep her in it until we get her to the market in the fort and then sluice her down with water so she looks a bit nearer her best,' a third voice said, and then, 'Damn! I need to piss!'

As Nicholas peered round the corner of the cabin a figure appeared on the deck, loosening his clothing as he came. With a grunt of relief he unleashed a stream of urine into the river.

Nicholas drew his hand across his throat in a gesture to Tuhin Singh and advanced towards the man, dirk drawn. By this time, Ram Das had completed his work and the blazing pitch was beginning to eat into the stern of the dhow. Before the man at the rail could even turn to look, his throat was gaping open and he pitched head-first into river. As flames began to lick around the rudder, the remaining four pirates hurried out on deck to investigate.

Nicholas and Tuhin Singh were ready and waiting for them. With his pistol Nicholas despatched the first with a ball to the brain. Tuhin Singh killed the second with a single dagger thrust to the neck as the man's head appeared at the top of the stairs. Nicholas's shot with his other pistol only grazed the third man. He and the fourth pirate who, by the light of the now brightly blazing stern, Nicholas saw was a European – a hefty man with a ginger beard – were quickly on the deck. Tuhin Singh grappled with the third man while Nicholas reversed his pistol and struck at the ginger-haired pirate. The butt caught him on the cheekbone. He cursed but still came on, seizing Nicholas round the waist and dragging him to the deck. There they rolled over and over, struggling for advantage as the heat of the fire grew closer.

Nicholas finally succeeded in straddling the man, and hitting him several times in his face, but he brought his knee up hard into Nicholas's groin. Nicholas fell backwards, groaning, but managed to roll out of reach. Both men now scrambled to get to their feet and faced each other again. 'Surrender!' Nicholas shouted in Bengali. 'Be damned if I do. I'll die first,' the reply came back in English.

Both men now had their daggers drawn. The pirate lunged at Nicholas but missed and then, as Nicholas made his own thrust, seized Nicholas's arm and by striking it against the rail made him drop his dagger. As he attempted to kick Nicholas in the groin again, Nicholas caught hold of his foot and upended him to fall backwards onto the deck. His ginger hair was caught by the advancing flames as he lay momentarily stunned. Pulling himself to his feet with his hair burning, he launched himself at Nicholas who was standing by the rail. Nicholas dodged aside, and with all his strength, helped by the momentum of the pirate's own charge, pushed him overboard. With a great splash, the man disappeared into the river.

Meanwhile, after a long struggle, Tuhin Singh had finally disposed of the third man who was now lying sprawled on the stairs down to the cabin with a great cut to his face which exposed his teeth. But the watchman was now on deck, club raised. His first swing missed and so did Nicholas's first with his fist. The watchman's second attempt, though, caught Nicholas a glancing stinging blow on the arm but Nicholas succeeded in hitting him hard and full on the point of the chin, knocking him unconscious.

Shouting to Tuhin Singh to tie up the watchman, Nicholas ran towards a large box roped to the deck at the bow and what he now recognised as the crate the pirate had been talking about, in which the woman must still be imprisoned. The crackling flames were increasing all the time, fanned by the breeze. Getting closer Nicholas saw that the crate – about five feet by four – had small holes cut roughly into its sides and a hatch secured by two strong metal bolts. Nicholas slid back the bolts and peered inside. His eyes took a moment to focus. In the dark he made out a huddled female figure and a pair of eyes wide with fear peering from behind a tangle of hair. Instinctively he put his head further inside and reached out only to feel fingernails scratch his face. Blood dribbled into his mouth tasting metallic and salty.

'I don't mean you any harm,' he shouted, again in Bengali, grappling with the woman. 'I'm trying to save you!' But she either didn't believe him or didn't understand, as she continued to claw at him with her nails. Realising he must be quick or they would both be caught by the flames, he grabbed her, pulled her from the crate through the hatch and dragged her towards the gangplank. She was still struggling when they reached it and he picked her up to carry her down. Almost as soon as he'd got both feet onto the gangplank, he felt the plank turn and twist beneath him. Looking down, he saw the burned face of the ginger-haired pirate, strips of skin hanging from it. The pirate's hands were jerking at the plank. Then he began yanking at Nicholas's feet so that he lost his balance on the swaying gangplank and fell into the water, letting go of the woman in his arms.

Struggling for a foothold on the shallow, muddy bottom, Nicholas saw the pirate reach the woman and, despite her struggles, seize her head and hold it under water. Launching himself forward, Nicholas grabbed the man by his burned head. The man yelled in pain and let go of the woman but then lashed out at Nicholas with his elbow, catching him with a blow in the mouth. Nicholas clung on to him and forcing his head below water, held it there as he kicked and struggled until his body went limp.

Looking round Nicholas saw the young woman huddled against the muddy bank, half in and half out of the water. He scrambled from the river, slipping on the mud and once he got a firm foothold on the bank held out his hand to her. After hesitating for a moment she took it. As he pulled her up, by the light of the now fiercely burning dhow he saw that she, too, was European.

–

The following evening, at the end of the first day of their journey towards distant Calcutta, Tuhin Singh, Nicholas and the young woman were encamped beneath a dark velvet sky on the banks of a stream. How very lucky they had been, Nicholas thought looking up at the infinity of stars splashed across the peaceful heavens. Not only had their attack on the dhow succeeded but at the same time Ram Das and his fellow villagers had overcome the pirates in the old fort and freed their captives.

Of course, he himself had exceeded his orders. He'd probably have some explaining to do back in Calcutta, but glancing at the young woman he had saved from the crate, now sitting quietly on the other side of the fire, he had no regrets. For the first hours after her rescue, she had seemed totally stricken by her experiences, hunched with knees drawn up to her chest and arms clenched around herself, against the mud wall of one of the villagers' huts. When anyone came near she cowered away. Slowly she had seemed to recover a little of her wits, but her only response to Nicholas's gentle questioning in English had been looks of wild-eyed incomprehension. Finally, after trying to communicate with her in Bengali and a number of European languages of which he knew the rudiments, Nicholas had attempted Italian, of which he had some knowledge from reading Dante's poetry at university.

As soon he had begun to speak it, Nicholas realised she had understood. Her green eyes had widened and she had begun to nod. Yes, she had said, yes, she came from Italy, from Venice. Her name was Lucia Vendramin. Visibly relaxing a little, she had accepted water from one of the village women but still remained wary, eyes flickering around the hut. When Nicholas approached her, offering a plate of rice and dal she had shrunk back. All she wanted, she said haltingly in Italian, was to be left alone to sleep.

But this morning, when Nicholas had told her that he and Tuhin Singh intended to leave within the hour for Calcutta and asked what she wanted to do, Lucia had unhesitatingly asked to go with them. Some of the women had taken her down to a secluded stretch of the riverbank to wash and when she returned clothed in some rough garments they had given her, Nicholas had realised why the pirates had been talking about her looks. Even though still marked by her ordeal, she was strikingly beautiful, with curling red-blond hair, full lips, high cheekbones, and was tall for a woman.

During that first day's journey, Lucia had ridden alternately behind Nicholas and Tuhin Singh, clinging tightly as they rode hard towards the port where Nicholas hoped they could take a ship for Calcutta. He wanted to return as quickly as possible to ensure that Company forces reached the delta in time to prevent the local ruler and any pirate henchmen from taking revenge on Ram Das and the others who had dealt them such a blow. Once, as she'd ridden behind him, Nicholas had felt Lucia's body convulse and heard her sobbing heavily, but when he'd reined in and looked around to ask if she was all right, she had simply rubbed the tears from her face and gestured for him to ride on.

But now, as the three of them sat shrouded in semi-darkness, illuminated only by the soft glow of the camp fire, Lucia herself broke the silence, saying to Nicholas, 'You and your friend saved me. You have a right to know my story... It is not pretty... and I won't find it easy but I want to tell you.'

Still speaking hesitantly and pausing frequently to gather herself and to take deep breaths, Lucia told her tale. Her pauses gave Nicholas time to search his memory of Italian vocabulary as well as to translate briefly for Tuhin Singh. Early one morning, off the north-east coast of Ceylon, the pirates had attacked and boarded the Venetian trading vessel on which she and her merchant father were returning from a voyage to China. Her eyes brimmed with tears and her voice shook as she related how after stripping them of their valuables, including any good clothing, the pirates had thrown the men into the sea to drown. She would never forget the last look of love and fear that her father Marco – by then dressed only in his shirt – gave her as the pirates pulled him away from her and seizing him by his arms and legs tossed him overboard. The pirates had kept the women to sell as slaves, shamelessly examining and probing their bodies and calculating the prices they would fetch.

The days of her captivity had been the worst in her life, both terrifying and degrading. The pirates' red-haired leader – the 'Red Devil', his shipmates called him – had seemed to relish the suffering of others. He had deliberately humiliated the women, allowing them no privacy to wash or fulfil their natural functions but forced them to do everything in full view of the laughing crew. Though he himself showed no sexual interest in the women, which she had thought strange, he'd allowed his crew to force themselves on some of them. She guessed she'd only escaped that fate because she was the youngest and the 'Red Devil' expected a high price for her virginity. When a drunken pirate had tried to violate her, he had drawn his dagger on the man.

She had vowed never to submit passively to whatever fate he intended for her but to fight against it with all her might and until her last breath. One night, when the boat was near the shore, seeing village fires burning on the riverbank, she had scrambled onto the rail but as she was about to dive in and attempt to swim ashore, the watchman had grabbed her ankles. In response, the 'Red Devil' had devised the crate to confine and control her. But then, and she thanked the heavens – '*Sia lodato il cielo*' – Nicholas and Tuhin Singh had appeared out of nowhere and saved her. It seemed like a miracle.

Ending her story, Lucia looked down as Nicholas translated the final portions for Tuhin Singh. For a while, all three sat in silence. What inner strength and courage she had shown, Nicholas thought, what resilience... 'We'll get you safely to Calcutta, I promise,' he said quietly. 'Once there, we'll do our utmost to find a ship to take you back to Europe.'

Lucia nodded and for the first time since her rescue managed a faint smile, but Nicholas knew that her road to recovery, to feeling any kind of happiness or even security, would be long and hard after all she had suffered.

Part Five

Siraj-ud-daulah, 1756–1757

18 – The Mission

'Ah Ballantyne, good. Sit down.' Roger Drake – tall, lean and with a long face reminiscent of a highly-strung greyhound – gestured Nicholas to sit down. It was the first time the President had asked to see him alone; Nicholas usually received his orders from an aide.

Drake remained standing, pale fingertips resting on his desk. 'You've performed many useful tasks for the Company over the last few years but what I'm about ask you to do may be the most important yet. Alivardi Khan, Nawab of Bengal, is dead. His officials say he died of dropsy and it's quite possible he did since he was eighty years or more. But we've also heard reports suggesting he was murdered. Perhaps it's just the usual bazaar gossip but our relations with the Nawab of Bengal are important to us, so we can't discount such talk. We must know.'

'If he was murdered, who do you think was behind it?' Nicholas asked.

'It could be the French, of course. As you and your colleagues in the Political Department well know, despite their setbacks in the south, they've not abandoned their ambitions in Hindustan and are looking for an opportunity to expand their little station at Chandernagore up the Hooghly from here. But more likely it could have been some internal intrigue – you know how Byzantine Hindustani court politics can be...'

Nicholas nodded, the memory from years past of the assassin suddenly lunging at Anwaruddin Khan as they'd sat eating melons vivid again. 'Who'd benefit from the Nawab's death? Who is to succeed him?'

'His grandson, Siraj-ud-daulah. Apparently, he was always the Nawab's favourite – the family's so-called "fortune child". He's about twenty-three but, apart from that, pretty much an unknown quantity to us… And that's dangerous. The old Nawab was a man with whom we knew where we stood. He was not always our friend but a mature ruler who recognised where our interests coincided, where there was a mutual profit to be had by trading treaties, the lease of land, all that sort of thing. Everything he did was considered – no surprises, good or bad. And that's what the Company likes – certainly what I like. What little we know suggests that his successor has the rashness of youth combined with a high opinion of himself and a poor one of us. That's why I want you to go to his court. I need to know for sure. Assess the man… his character… his ambitions… where you think his loyalties lie, if he has any… And, above all, make him understand it's in his interests to keep good relations with the Company – to be a man we can do business with and share a profit with.'

'So this is to be an official mission?'

Drake straightened up and examined the gold-embroidered right cuff of his blue coat. 'Ostensibly, yes. We're promoting you to the rank of captain and you'll go as my envoy with official letters of accreditation from me. No disguises, no subterfuges. Siraj-ud-daulah's currently holding court in the Nizamat Fort in Murshidabad. You'll go there to convey the Company's congratulations on his accession and to present him with gifts.'

'When do I leave?'

'The day after tomorrow at first light – we must act quickly before the French get to him and try to bribe him. I'll give you an escort of twenty soldiers. And, Ballantyne, whatever you do, whatever you find in Murshidabad, commit nothing important to writing. We can't risk any despatches falling into the wrong hands. As soon as you've formed a view on Siraj-ud-daulah, return quickly to Calcutta and report to me in person. Is that clear?'

Nicholas nodded. 'Of course.'

'In that case, it only remains for me to wish you good luck. Let's hope you return with the good news about Siraj-ud-daulah's attitude that the Company wants to hear.'

As Nicholas made his way from the President's high-ceilinged, wood-panelled chamber through his outer office where clerks were labouring at their high desks and out into the street to hail a tonga, he was already reviewing everything he'd need to do over the next thirty-six hours including having to explain to his son that he was going away again. At least, Tuhin Singh, still recovering from an infected bite from one of his hunting dogs, would be there to watch over James, along with Sohini, who guarded him as carefully as his own mother would have done... There was also Lucia, still recovering from her ordeal, to whom James seemed to be growing very attached. Sometimes she sang softly to him in Italian, and he had heard his son trying to mimic some of the words. The thought of Lucia reminded Nicholas that he must soon find a way to honour his promise to her to send her home to Italy. This was no easy task considering the recently renewed war between Britain and France. Though it had first broken out in North America, it was now spreading eastward, disrupting sea traffic.

Jumping into the tonga, Nicholas reflected how in the old days the first thing he would do when assigned a mission was to consult Clive. He'd always have a view, even if sometimes cynical or outrageous, but as often as not pertinent. Over three years had passed since their argument and in all that time there'd been no contact between them. Just as he had expected, Clive had indeed returned to Hindustan. He'd arrived back a year ago, alone. According to what Nicholas had heard, Margaret had recently had a son and chosen to remain with the child in England. Clive had been posted to Madras and had gone directly there from Britain. Nicholas hadn't been sure whether he was sorry or relieved not to have a chance of seeing him in Calcutta and trying to salvage something of their former friendship. While Clive had been in England, he'd several times been on the point of writing to him but something – pride, obstinacy, or a mixture of both – had held him back. So had the thought that Clive would interpret any overture as an admission that Nicholas regretted what he'd said. He didn't.

–

Two days later, shortly after dawn and after kissing his sleeping son's forehead, Nicholas set out at the head of his escort of Company troopers on the 140 mile journey north to Murshidabad. At the rear rumbled two baggage carts. Beneath their oilcloth covers were presents for the new Nawab of Bengal. Hiralal Das, one of the senior clerks from the Treasurer's office to whom Nicholas had often chatted when withdrawing cash for his missions or drawing his salary, had made Nicholas sign a detailed inventory recording every item entrusted to him from a full-size portrait of the bulbous-eyed King George II to a huge mechanical clock and a telescope for star-gazing. Given that the Nawab was one of the wealthiest rulers in Hindustan, Nicholas doubted the gifts would either impress him or win him over. He could only hope his advocacy on the Company's behalf would be more effective in gaining the Nawab's favour.

–

The ponderous pace dictated by the bullock carts, one of which splintered a wheel on a rock, made the journey maddeningly slow. Not until dusk on the fifth day did Murshidabad at last come into view on the eastern shore of the Bhagirathi river, whose waters glinted rose in the dying light. The iron-studded gates were still open as Nicholas and his escort approached the town walls. The red and white striped Company flag carried by one of the troopers was a familiar sight and the watchmen waved them through.

Directions to the Nizamat Fort were unnecessary. Sited on a low, flat-topped hill in the heart of the town, square-built with thick stone walls and a tower at each corner, it seemed to squat over Murshidabad. Leading his little column up through the narrow streets out onto the sandy parade ground that surrounded the fort on all sides, Nicholas signalled his men to halt and looked around. Torches were already burning on either side of the high gateway leading into the fort which was guarded by two soldiers. Another soldier, green-turbaned and, judging by his gold sash, an officer, appeared on the parapet above the fort gateway and peered down through the gathering gloom at Nicholas.

'Identify yourself,' he yelled.

'An envoy sent by the President of the East India Company in Bengal to pay the Company's respects to His Highness, the Nawab Siraj-ud-daulah, on his accession to the throne. These men are my escort.'

'I have not been notified of your arrival,' the officer replied.

'I did not realise there needed to be formal arrangements between friends.'

'Wait there while I consult my commander.'

Time passed and the first bats began flickering overhead before Nicholas, whose tired mount was fidgeting fretfully, saw the officer appear in the gateway. With him was an elderly man, quite bald but with a wispy beard, whose bearing as much as a gold chain of office proclaimed him as a person of some importance.

Nicholas dismounted. Holding his reins with one hand, he swept off his hat with the other and made what he hoped was a suitably courtly bow. 'My name is Nicholas Ballantyne, personal envoy of the Company's President in Bengal.'

'And how is our friend Mr Roger Drake?' the bald man asked. 'I had the happiness to meet him when the last Nawab of Bengal was his guest at Government House in Calcutta. I was his vizier – a position his grandson, His Highness Siraj-ud-daulah, has done me the honour of asking me to retain. My name is Naraigan Singh.'

'The President is well, thank you.'

'Excellent news. It is my honour on behalf of the new Nawab to welcome you and your men, however unexpected your visit. Follow me. Servants and grooms have already been put to work to ensure you are all comfortably lodged and your horses and oxen stabled, watered and fed. Tomorrow, I will introduce you into His Royal Highness's presence.'

So far so good, Nicholas thought, following the vizier through the gateway into the Nizamat Fort, but let's see what tomorrow brings.

–

Naraigan Singh was as good as his word. Nicholas's apartments – the walls hung with brocade, floors covered with velvet-soft carpets and air scented with frankincense burning in silver saucers – were more than comfortable. He slept well on a thick mattress stuffed with soft down, only waking as the early morning sun filtered through a woven screen covering a doorway onto a small balcony overlooking the parade ground and, beyond it, the meandering streets of Murshidabad.

Eating some hot bread, honey and figs brought to him by a servant, Nicholas contemplated his coming meeting with Siraj-ud-daulah. What would he be like? And how easy would it be to form the judgements Drake was so eager for? During the journey, the more he'd thought about his mission the more naïve it had started to seem. After all, if the new Nawab was contemplating changing his state's relationship with the Company, he'd hardly make it obvious. The best he could achieve would be, as Drake had said, to convince the Nawab that cutting loose from the Company wasn't in his best interests. As Clive had so often said, 'Self-interest is the way to men's hearts – and to their minds and actions as well!' and there at least he had been right.

Nicholas wasn't kept waiting for long before Naraigan Singh himself came to escort him to the Nawab. Remembering his great-great grandfather's description of the English ambassador being received by the Great Moghul, Nicholas pictured himself greeting the young ruler before his assembled court, but the room into which Naraigan Singh ushered him was small and plainly furnished, almost like a Company office. Its only occupant was a tall, hawk-nosed young man with a neatly-trimmed black beard studying some drawings spread on a trestle table.

'Highness, here is the British East India Company's envoy, Nicholas Ballantyne, come to pay his respects.'

Siraj-ud-daulah was dressed in green robes edged with gold. A dagger hung from a steel belt round his waist. For some moments he continued to contemplate the papers before him, then as Nicholas rose from his bow the Nawab looked up at him.

'Welcome to my court,' he said, before continuing immediately, 'you see these plans? They are for the new fortress I'm going to build here to be called the Nizamat Imambara. I intend it to be the symbol of my rule. I already have the materials to begin and I will lay the foundations with my own hands to show my people I do not shirk from hard work to benefit my state.'

Nicholas nodded but said nothing. Clearly Siraj-ud-daulah was not a man to waste time on formalities.

'But I'm not the only one interested in building something, am I?' the Nawab continued, standing motionless and scrutinising Nicholas's face as acutely as he had been the drawings. 'I hear the Company has been strengthening its fortifications around Fort William in Calcutta, digging out that old moat and starting construction of strong points for cannon. Is this true?'

'Yes, Highness.'

'But why? Who are you so afraid of? Not me, surely!'

'Certainly not, Highness. It is merely a prudent precaution. The Company desires only peace and tranquillity in which to trade but who knows when and from what direction trouble may come?'

'I take it you mean your rivals in Hindustan, the French?'

Nicholas shrugged. 'Perhaps, though they should have learned by now not to meddle in our business... But we also wish to discourage others who bring trouble wherever they go – like the Marathas whom your grandfather so successfully kept out of Bengal, but who, as Your Highness knows, are on the rise again and may seek to attack us both.'

At the implied compliment to his grandfather, Siraj's expression softened just a little.

Emboldened, Nicholas continued, 'Above all, the Company wants stability in Bengal just as you do, Highness. Indeed, we share common aims. We want to promote trade, make Bengal even richer. These practical reasons make us natural allies – something your grandfather appreciated, as he often told President Drake.' But even as he spoke Nicholas realised that this time invoking Alivardi Khan's memory had done no good at all.

The Nawab's eyes flashed with scarcely concealed hostility. 'You speak as if the Company treats my state as an equal partner in their schemes. They do not! They are never satisfied, always asking for more. Like leeches you are sucking my land dry. The terms of the trading privileges you have extracted from my predecessors mean that the Company and its officials – not I and the people of Bengal – are the ones to prosper. All the Company wishes is to grow rich and carry off our wealth to your rainy islands – something my grandfather – mighty and respected ruler though he was – did not always realise. The Company must understand he and I are different people.'

Taken aback, Nicholas paused to collect his thoughts then replied as calmly as he could. 'I will certainly convey your views to the President who I know will wish to explore and resolve your concerns. But, Highness, you aren't being entirely fair. You profit too from the increased trading opportunities the Company offers you. Many members of your court invest heavily in joint trading enterprises with us – cargos of indigo, silks, spices. They would not do so if the financial returns were poor. They also have the assurance that the Company's strong fleet will protect their goods from pirates when they ship them by sea... Perhaps the bargain is not as one-sided as others may have led you to believe.'

'Hypocrisy is a vice of you British. You find it easy to convince yourselves that what suits you is in the best interests of everyone else as well, even when it clearly isn't. However, I concede there is some truth in what you say about the Company's fleet, but don't the French at Chandernagore also have strong vessels? Why shouldn't I rely on them? They would ask less in return.'

'Perhaps, but only because they have less to bargain with than the Company – less money and less power.'

The Nawab gave a half smile. 'Yes, I know you've defeated the French. All I mean is that the Company should never take me for a fool nor take my friendship for granted. You will need to convince me of your good intentions and take time to get to know me, as I will need to take time to know you. Therefore, do not rush to return to your colleagues in Calcutta. Remain at my court for a while – three or four weeks at least, so that we may talk further.'

'Er... I... Thank you, Highness... I should be pleased to... And I hope that in due course you will do the President the honour of examining the gifts he has sent to mark your accession.'

'Yes, in due course.' The Nawab waved a hand to indicate the audience was over and turned back to his drawings.

Nicholas followed the vizier, who had not spoken a word during the discussions, merely nodding vigorously to support everything his master had said, down the long arched corridor leading back towards Nicholas's own quarters. As he went he reflected on the brief meeting. Siraj-ud-daulah's invitation to stay had surprised him but he could scarcely refuse. Also, it might prove useful. The Nawab had been blunt and his resentment towards the Company seemed genuine. If he remained a short while in Murshidabad he might manage to convince Siraj-ud-daulah that any grievances he had – and he could well believe some were genuine, given the personal avarice of some Company officials – could be dealt with and that an alliance with the Company, rather than with the French, would be more beneficial than not. Clearly the Nawab was not yet the Company's friend, but that did not necessarily make him their enemy.

–

The elephant fight on the banks of the Bhagirathi river staged as part of the Nawab's birthday celebrations was heating up. Two bull elephants – tusks painted scarlet, and grey hides criss-crossed with scars – roared at each other across the eight-foot-high earth wall separating them in the large stone-walled compound which they had just entered. The mahouts perched behind their torn ears had slipped down and run through the wooden gates in the compound wall which had been quickly shut and barred after them. The elephants hadn't needed any coaxing or goading to confront each other. To the cheers of Siraj-ud-daulah's courtiers, who like Nicholas were watching from stepped platforms erected around the compound, they'd immediately charged towards the earth wall dividing them.

As the elephants continued to hurl themselves at the wall, their great heads swinging from side to side as they frenziedly attempted to batter it down to get at one another, a tall, grizzled man, diamond rings on his fingers sparkling in the sunlight, edged past other spectators to Nicholas's side. Nicholas recognised the new arrival at once – Mir Jafar Khan, the Nawab's commander-in-chief. At the feast held the previous night as part of the Nawab's birthday festivities, he'd been among the first to receive the traditional gifts and robes of honour and was clearly much in Siraj-ud-daulah's favour.

Mir Jafar nodded affably at Nicholas. 'Their names are Ranabijoy, "the winner of mighty battles", and Bajradaman, "the conqueror of thunder". A mighty contest and a fitting part of the celebrations.'

'Indeed.'

'I've wagered an emerald on Bajradaman – that's him on the right. Although he's the smaller of the two, he makes up what he lacks in height and weight with speed and courage. He's never let me down! Have you seen many such fights?'

'Yes, while I was seconded to the court of Nawab Anwaruddin Khan of the Carnatic. It's an amazing spectacle but I wasn't sure I liked to see elephants pitted against one another for our sport.'

'I'd heard some of you British are sentimental about animals...'

At that moment the top of the earth wall began to give way, crumbling slowly at first and then more quickly. Bajradaman lunged through the debris and the rising red dust towards his opponent, ripping into Ranabijoy's leathery hide above his right eye with the tip of a tusk and immediately drawing blood. The crowd roared its approval, as trunk raised and trumpeting furiously, Bajradaman's great feet trampled what remained of the wall to get at his enemy. Though blood was pouring into his eye, Ranabijoy stood his ground and got in two slashes of his own before, rearing up on his hind legs, he hurled himself forward. Glancing at Mir Jafar, Nicholas saw that his entire attention was on the two animals, attacking each other with their tusks and kicking up more clouds of choking dust.

Bajradaman seemed to be getting the worst of it now. With blood running from a wound in his left shoulder to drip into the dust, he backed away into a corner of the compound. Ranabijoy saw his chance and charged forward, head down. But Bajradaman – gasping so heavily that Nicholas could hear him – swerved sideways at the very last moment. Ranabijoy hit the wall with such momentum that the tip of one of his tusks snapped. For a moment he staggered and then he crumpled to the ground, stunned as his enemy began trampling his prone body, pausing occasionally to jab at his victim with his tusks.

'I knew it!' Mir Jafar raised his fists high above his head in triumph. His smile was exultant as the two mahouts ran into the compound, each carrying a flaming brand to drive Bajradaman from his victim. Other men followed carrying bundles of grass – further inducements to lure the victor away. Within just a couple of minutes, men were tending Ranabijo's many wounds, while others were feeding the heavily breathing victor and attempting to staunch his deep shoulder wound.

Nicholas had felt a visceral excitement at the contest but was relieved to see Ranabijoy slowly raise himself to his feet. As he joined the spectators descending the platform and making their way along the riverbank to the next attraction – a wrestling contest between two court champions – he heard Mir Jafar say,

'I've been looking for a chance to talk to you properly.' Putting a hand on his arm to draw him aside, Mir Jafar continued in a low voice, 'It's hard to find places away from curious ears...' He was still smiling but there was purpose in his tone.

'What is it you need privacy to discuss?' Nicholas asked as Mir Jafar halted in front of one of the small, silk-draped pavilions erected to shelter the nobility from the sun and gestured him to enter. During the ten days since Nicholas's arrival in Murshidabad few had wished to converse with him, many hurrying off at his approach. Those who were prepared to talk had kept looking around to see if they were being observed, even while uttering the greatest banalities. Much to his frustration, everyone, from the sometimes taciturn, sometimes oleaginous, vizier to the attendants appointed to serve him, had seemed cautious and non-committal. Other than gaining a sense of mutual distrust among the courtiers and a fear of displeasing their autocratic Nawab, he'd learned little of significance and his hopes of further audiences with Siraj-ud-daulah had been disappointed. Instead, he'd found himself expected to attend these seemingly never-ending celebrations for the Nawab's birthday.

Once they were inside, Mir Jafar said, 'I know why you've come... So does the Nawab... You're testing his attitude to the British. That we realise this won't surprise a man of your intelligence, I'm sure, and of course explains your cool, if courteous, reception. However, there are other things you and the Company should know about...' Mir Jafar's voice had fallen to almost a whisper despite their being alone in the pavilion. 'The Nawab's position on the throne is far from secure. Many think him too impetuous and hot-blooded – too inclined to overestimate his own strengths and abilities and to underestimate those of others. In their eyes he's not the wisest choice as the new ruler.'

'But he was chosen by his grandfather. Who'd dare challenge him?'

'His greatest enemy is Ghaseti Begum, his aunt. She wanted the throne for her adopted son. Some say she had the last Nawab, his Excellency Alivardi Khan, may peace be upon his soul, poisoned, hoping that her faction could profit from the confusion following his death to seize the throne for her son. They also say she tried to kill the new Nawab but his friends forestalled her. Instead it was her son who was found with his throat slashed... At present, Ghaseti Begum is licking her wounds in her palace, but like the tigress she is she will want her revenge. Rumour says she's already intriguing with Shaukat Jang, another potential rival to the Nawab who has his base at Purnea, even if Shaukat Jang is currently making a show of subservience to the new Nawab.'

'How much of this does Siraj-ud-daulah realise?'

'He is no fool. He knows he's at risk, knows his enemies, and that he needs allies to protect himself. That is why he is sending out feelers to other Hindustani rulers and also to the French. He knows they are hungry for revenge against the British and hopes they will offer him more generous terms than the Company whose ambitions he distrusts. I tell you all this to use how you choose. As I said before, I'm a gambling man and my money is on the British – not the French. The Nawab hopes the French will make him extravagant offers to favour them. However, I believe that others in Hindustan have even greater means to shape events and reward their friends. And, believe me, I am the Company's friend, if they wish it... and if their terms of friendship are generous. You understand me, don't you?'

Nicholas nodded. Mir Jafar could not have been clearer.

19 – The Black Hole

Shouting... Trumpet blasts... The clattering of hooves... The noise was coming from the parade ground. Were Siraj-ud-daulah's troops drilling? Surely not, it was barely light. Getting out of bed and rubbing his sleep-filled eyes, Nicholas stepped onto the balcony of his quarters high in the walls of the fort. What he saw shocked him instantly awake. A column of horsemen, banners embroidered with tigers fluttering, lances at the vertical, were forming up on the parade ground beneath him. Behind them were ranks of foot soldiers, some of whom had muskets strapped across their backs. A ten-strong ox team, appeared around the fort walls, heads bent as they struggled to pull an eight-wheeled limber on which a long-barrelled cannon was mounted. They were quickly followed by several other cannon limbers, each attended, like the first, by European officers, many wearing the blue uniforms of France. Barefoot gunners, some carrying ramrods, walked with them. Then came baggage and ammunition carts. Finally, when the column was complete, drums boomed in the gatehouse and Siraj-ud-daulah trotted onto the parade ground on a white horse. He was wearing a steel breastplate. His gauntleted left hand held the reins, his right a drawn sword.

Slipping back into his room, Nicholas dressed quickly, intending to find out what was happening. He was just buttoning his shirt when the door to his apartment opened to admit a grim-faced Mir Jafar.

'What's going on, Mir Jafar?'

The commander pulled the door closed behind him, then putting his arm around Nicholas's shoulders drew him away from the door to the far side of the room. In a voice so low it was almost a whisper he said, 'For your sake and mine we mustn't be overheard. Siraj-ud-daulah is about to march on Calcutta...'

Nicholas's heart missed a beat as he glanced round for his sword. 'What! Two days ago, you said you were the Company's friend. If you are, why didn't you warn me earlier?'

'Believe me, I couldn't. The Nawab told his council only yesterday. He used the cover of his birthday celebrations to keep those of us he thought might disagree distracted, as well as you, of course, while he readied his forces and assembled supplies in a fort a few miles away. He's allied himself with the French. It seems his vizier Naraigan Singh conducted the negotiations in secret. They've agreed that, with one of the Company's British regiments already departed from Calcutta and its replacement not due for some time, this is the moment to strike. For another thing, they think that while you're still at the Nawab's court, the Company will not expect an assault on Calcutta. The Nawab has even patched up a truce with the Afghan Rohillas to the north. He believes that he has enough resources to defend against any incursions by the Marathas in the south and west, provided his campaign against Calcutta is a quick one.'

Mir Jafar, who had been speaking very fast, paused to take a breath, then continued, 'I argued an attack on the Company was folly – any victory would only be temporary – but the Nawab wouldn't listen. Then, with a look of steel, he told me to trust his judgement as any loyal subject should. He kept me busy for the rest of the day and night making final preparations. I was conscious of being watched by officers he had deputed to assist me. This was my first chance to slip away to you – I had no messenger I could trust...'

Was Mir Jafar telling the truth, Nicholas wondered. The pouches beneath his eyes suggested a man who'd not slept for a while and his anxiety seemed genuine. Yet, almost as likely, by cosying up to him at the elephant fight and coming to him now, when it was too late for him to warn the Company, the general was seeking to protect his position in case Siraj-ud-daulah's attack should fail.

'What's to happen to me and my men?'

Mir Jafar looked down at the floor as he spoke. 'You'll all be kept prisoner as useful trading counters in case the attack breaks down. Guards are already stationed outside your room and your men are also confined... I'm sorry – truly – but in the days ahead remember what I first said at the elephant fight. I remain the Company's friend, whatever you may think and whatever may happen. However, for the moment, I can be nothing other than the loyal servant of the Nawab.'

There was no point in protesting. As Mir Jafar hurried from the room, Nicholas glimpsed two guards in the corridor outside before the door swung shut again and a key grated in the lock. Cursing himself for a fool, he went out onto the balcony again. Why hadn't he suspected the reason behind the Nawab detaining him for so long at Murshidabad? At that moment, a bugle sounded and he saw Siraj-ud-daulah urge his horse forward ahead of his men, his sword now raised above his head and a banner bearer on either side of him. The column was on the move now and anger and regret were pointless. His priority must be to think of a way to get a warning to Calcutta without delay. The problem was how to do it.

The apartment that had seemed so comfortable was, Nicholas now realised, in reality a prison with only two exit points – the balcony 40 feet above the parade ground and the single door outside which two guards were stationed. Nicholas spent the day pacing in frustration, feverishly conjuring wild escape plans and just as quickly discarding them, damning their stupidity. With effort, he forced himself to calm down and think more rationally. But not until the evening did he come up with an idea that he thought might just work. It wasn't brilliant and would depend considerably on luck but he didn't have the luxury of time.

By dawn, for better or for worse, he was as ready as he could be. Not long after, an attendant accompanied by a young guard brought a dish of food for Nicholas's breakfast. Once they had departed, Nicholas swallowed a few mouthfuls of dal and chewed quickly on some naan. Then he threw the dish and the remainder of the food onto the floor and put his fingers down his throat, forcing himself to be sick. 'Poison! I've been poisoned!' he shouted, retching loudly for effect. 'Help me!'

Nothing happened. Going to the locked door, Nicholas beat on it with his fists, continuing to cry out that he had been poisoned in a voice as hoarse and agonised as he could make it. More minutes passed during which Nicholas heard the two guards talking outside but couldn't catch their words. He was beginning to lose hope when, finally, the key turned in the lock and he slid quickly to the floor amidst the spilled food and vomit, writhing and clutching his stomach in simulated agony.

Both guards entered. The elder, a heavy, dark-bearded man, bent over him and none too gently yanked back his hair to stare hard at his vomit-streaked face. Breathing heavily, Nicholas rasped, 'Get me... Get me water for the love of God. I'm burning up...' The guard hesitated, then barked at his companion, a youth of sixteen or seventeen, his face scarred by smallpox, 'Don't just stand there gawping, Kasim, you numbskull. Give him some water. I suppose I'd better fetch a hakim.'

As the older man's footsteps receded down the corridor, Kasim filled a brass cup from an ewer and knelt beside Nicholas who was still flailing and retching. Before he could put the cup to his lips, Nicholas sat up and said in a low voice. 'No need for that, I'm not ill. Just listen. We don't have much time.'

Panic in his eyes, Kasim reached for the dagger in his sash but Nicholas was quicker and gripped his wrist. 'Don't! And don't call for help. I promise I mean you no harm. But I must get away from the fort. Help me and I'll reward you. Look!' Nicholas pulled out the gold pocket watch his uncle had given him on his eighteenth birthday and swung it temptingly back and forth.

Gazing at the watch, the youth shook his head. 'No. I cannot. It's too dangerous.'

'But this could be the moment that changes your life – such an opportunity might never come again.'

Kasim once more shook his head, but couldn't take his eyes off the watch. It reminded Nicholas of the times he'd gone fishing with his uncle in Scotland, waiting patiently for the salmon to take the bait. But how was he to make Kasim bite?

'I've gold coins as well,' he urged, gripping Kasim's wrist more tightly. 'You'll be wealthy enough to buy yourself a piece of land, build a house, pay dowries for your sisters. You'll be a man of consequence instead of being kicked around by that other guard. I heard how he speaks to you. What's his name?'

'Abdul.' Instinctively the youth looked round at the door then turned back.

'Is this Abdul always on guard with you?'

'Usually. He's supposed to be training me.'

'Couldn't you find some way of distracting him?'

'I... I don't know. I can't see how.'

'Perhaps Abdul would be willing to help me as well? I've enough gold for you both.'

The youth shook his head vigorously. 'No, no. He would never agree.'

Nicholas hesitated. Was that true, he wondered, or was Kasim unwilling to share the bounty? If the latter, he must be seriously tempted. Recognising a glimmer of hope, Nicholas pushed hard. 'You're thinking about it, aren't you, and you'd be a fool not to! Come on Kasim!'

Kasim took a deep breath. 'Yes, I'll think about it.'

'Do. You won't regret it.' Kasim's eyes followed the watch as Nicholas tucked it away again.

Suddenly the young man's expression changed from one of longing to fear. 'Quick, lie down again. I think I hear Abdul and the hakim coming.'

Kasim was right. Almost immediately, the older guard ushered in a small, middle-aged man in a brown robe and white turban, carrying a leather satchel. The hakim felt Nicholas's pulse, examined his eyeballs and tongue, and peered at the vomit on the floor. 'It's nothing. The food may not have suited him, that's all,' he pronounced in an exasperated tone. Taking a small green glass bottle from his bag he poured out a small amount. Then he raised Nicholas's head, put the cup to his lips and ordered, 'Drink this! It will make you feel better.' Nicholas obediently swallowed the puckeringly bitter liquid. Then he lay back and closed his eyes. 'He'll be fine in a few hours. Just leave him to rest,' he heard the hakim say. Moments later the door closed and the iron key turned in the lock. He was alone again.

Would Kasim have the courage and the guile to help him, Nicholas wondered as the hours slowly passed. Somehow, he doubted it. But he had underestimated the young man. Shortly after nine o'clock that evening, he heard the key turn and in the arc of light cast by an oil lamp he had lit, made out Kasim's slight figure in the doorway. He was holding a large bundle. Glancing back into the gloom of the corridor to reassure himself that no one else was there, Kasim pulled the door shut, then thrust the bundle at Nicholas.

'Clothes for you. Put them on – quick as you can! I persuaded Abdul to rest for a while but he could return at any time.' Kasim's voice sounded nervous and Nicholas noticed his hands shaking as he handed over the bundle.

Unwrapping it, Nicholas found pantaloons, a tunic, a sash and cloth for a turban. Heart pounding, he tore off his army tunic and trousers, which he pushed out of sight under the cushions on the bed, and dressed quickly in the new clothes. Hands cold as ice, Kasim helped him tuck in the loose ends of the turban. Then, he said, 'With the Nawab's army marching on Calcutta, only a skeleton garrison has been left guarding the fort. If you're lucky you'll get away without anyone seeing you. Now, before you go, give me my reward.'

'Aren't you coming with me?'

'No. That would be too dangerous for me.'

'But how do I get out of the fort?'

Kasim held out a piece of paper. 'I thought of that. This drawing shows the way to a side gate that opens onto the parade ground. It is rarely used and you will find it unlocked, I promise.'

Nicholas hesitated. For all he knew Kasim could be planning to betray him, but he had no option but to trust him. 'Very well. Here you are.'

Kasim's eyes gleamed as Nicholas counted gold sovereigns into his palm and handed over the watch, all of which the young man tucked quickly away in his sash. Then he said, 'It will cost me my life if anyone suspects me, so now you must knock me unconscious. I'll say you seemed to be ill again and that when I came in you attacked me.' Kasim's face clouded, as if a new and unwelcome thought had struck him. 'You won't take back the money and the watch when I'm unconscious, will you?'

Even under the circumstances, Nicholas smiled. 'No. You have my word.'

'Then do it quickly. We've already taken too long.'

Nicholas obliged, delivering a swift upper cut that sent Kasim flying back to hit the floor with a thud. Pulling back his eyelids, Nicholas satisfied himself that the young guard was indeed unconscious, then went quickly to the door, opened it and peered cautiously down the shadowy corridor in the direction indicated in the sketch. For a moment he hesitated – the temptation to try and find his men was strong. But every minute counted if he was to get to Calcutta in time. The longer he stayed in the Nizamat Fort, the greater his risk of recapture.

Kasim's map was accurate. Without encountering another soul, Nicholas located the side gate that was indeed unlocked and slipped out into the darkness. Slowly, he edged around the parade ground before, his heart pounding ever faster, he turned down what he recognised as the winding main street of Murshidabad leading down to the city gates. Forcing himself not to run for fear of attracting attention he set off down the street. As it was, none of the few people he encountered gave him a second glance.

His luck was holding. Not long now and he'd be out of the city. But ten minutes later, by the flickering orange light from two braziers lit on either side of them, he saw the gates a hundred yards ahead and his heart sank. They were closed and unlikely to reopen till dawn. Nicholas ducked down a side alley and adjusted the dun-coloured turban that was already starting to unravel. No disguises, no subterfuges, Drake had promised, but who would have guessed anything like this would happen, Nicholas thought, as he considered what to do next. He couldn't wait for the gates to open. Perhaps he could find a place to climb out... Murshidabad's outer walls weren't that high. But where would be best to try?

Crouching behind a cart, Nicholas was still puzzling over it when a voice cried out, 'Night soil! Night soil!' Glancing round he saw four men pushing and pulling a giant handcart loaded with half a dozen large clay pots along the street towards the gate. Four more followed, each hunched beneath the weight of the large round basket on his back. As they drew nearer he caught an appalling stink. Of course – these must be the collectors of the town's human and animal shit, urine and other rotting rubbish, carrying it out of the city to the farmers who'd buy it for their fields. Every town had them. The nightwatchman wouldn't lose any time letting them through.

Looking around, Nicholas saw behind him in the alley an old basket. A bit too small but it would have to do. It was half-filled with what looked – and smelled – like rotting vegetables. Grabbing its two fraying handles he hoisted it onto his back then waited in the shadows in the entrance to the alley until first the night-soil cart and then the basket-bearers passed by. Slipping out into the street he fell in step behind the last of them – far enough away for the others not to be aware of his presence but, he hoped, close enough for the nightwatchman to assume he was one of them.

Reaching the gates, one of the cart-pushers called out again, 'Night soil!' this time adding, 'Open up!'

'You're late again, you stink merchants!' a cry came from a gate-keeper sprawled on a charpoy. 'I've told you before, if you can't get here before I turn in I'll make you wait till morning.'

'All right, all right, we're sorry,' the man just in front of Nicholas shouted. 'Now, just get on with it please. This basket's crushing the life out of me.'

The gate-keeper – a tall, burly man – rose from the charpoy and, still grumbling to himself as he scratched at his crotch, pulled out a large key on a chain round his neck. Going to the gates, he unlocked an inner door set into one of them, then stood back, holding his hand over his nose. 'Go on, out you go!' Nicholas quickened his pace and was right behind the last bearer as the man bumped his basket against the sides of the door, spilling some of its evil-smelling contents – maggoty cabbage leaves and slimy, rotting onions. The gate-keeper turned away with an expression of disgust and didn't see Nicholas as, sidestepping the spilled refuse, he slipped quickly through. Moments later, the door clanged shut behind him.

Still unaware of his presence, the night-soil and rubbish collectors shuffled away into the gloom. Nicholas turned in the opposite direction, quickly reaching the shelter of an abandoned and roofless mud hut a little way from the town walls, put down his basket and stopped to think out his next move. If he could find a horse he might still be able to overtake Siraj-ud-daulah's main force, encumbered as it would be by baggage and artillery wagons, though whether he could outstrip the vanguard was doubtful. Everything depended on the Nawab's strategy. If he intended first to rendezvous with French forces before moving on Calcutta there might still be time. If not… No, Nicholas told himself, there was no point in thinking about that. To have any chance he must concentrate on finding a horse and quickly.

If he remembered correctly, within a mile or two down the road towards Calcutta he should come to a small village – the first of many dotted along the highway, whose inhabitants made a living by supplying travellers and their pack animals with food and drink. With luck, he might be able to find a mount there. He started to run down the road, thanking the heavens that the waxing moon was only two or three days from being full. He would have some light to guide him.

Half an hour later, he was approaching a cluster of huts to one side of the road. Nothing, not even a dog, stirred as he entered the village which, with its scantily thatched mud-walled dwellings looked a poor place. But a hundred yards or so ahead was a building larger than the rest, a barn or granary perhaps. The double wooden doors were closed but when Nicholas gave a gentle push, to his surprise, one creaked open. Slipping inside he pulled the door shut behind him. His eyes took time to adjust but he caught a musty animal smell from the interior. Moving towards it, he saw two pairs of bright eyes in the dark.

Pulling out his tinderbox, Nicholas struck a light to see a calf in one rough wooden stall. In another was a horse. But what a horse it was – old, and so thin he could count nearly every rib. It would have to do, though. Picking up a discarded piece of jute sacking from among the straw, Nicholas quickly tore it into strips. Then, entering the horse's stall and giving a reassuring pat to its scraggy neck, he wound strips around its hooves to muffle any sound they might make. A quick glance confirmed the only way out of the barn was the door through which he'd entered. Taking a rope halter from a hook, he put it on the horse and led it from the stall. A thought struck him: decrepit though the horse was, it was doubtless some poor villager's prized possession. Digging into his sash, he found the cotton pouch in which he'd secreted the coins he had left. Pulling out a few – more than the nag was worth – he placed them on a wooden ledge where they'd be seen. Next he helped himself to an old blanket from a peg near the door.

Still whispering soothingly to the horse and holding one hand over its muzzle to discourage any whinnying, he led it outside. The animal was obligingly docile and the sound of its muffled hooves on the sandy ground was barely audible as Nicholas led it towards the exit from the village. Suddenly his foot caught the leg of a stool positioned in the shadow of a hut and he fell to the ground with a thud. But he kept his grip on the halter and was soon on his feet again, moving quickly away from the village. Reaching the cover of a large mango tree a hundred or so yards from the last hut, he looked back. To his relief he saw that the village slumbered on and that there was no sight or sound of pursuit from the fort. Then, jumping onto the horse's bony back, he rode off into the night.

Over the next forty-eight hours, the old horse proved more resilient than it looked though its pace was agonisingly slow. Twice Nicholas tried and failed to exchange it for a better one – the only animals for sale along the road seemed to be pack mules and donkeys. Perhaps Siraj-ud-daulah's commissariat had appropriated any available horses for their use. At least he looked the part, Nicholas told himself – a farmer shrouded in a blanket riding his old nag to the market. None of the few other travellers or villagers he had encountered had even given him a second glance. From what he saw, there could be no doubt that a large force had passed along the road towards Calcutta. The ground was marked with cart tracks and hoof prints and littered with animal dung and the other debris that an army usually left in its wake. Everything suggested the Nawab's army was making straight for the city.

In the afternoon of the third day, Nicholas decided he must get off the main road and find alternative routes through fields and byways. If Siraj-ud-daulah's troops were indeed somewhere between him and Calcutta – now a mere 15 miles away – remaining on the main highway was no longer safe. A pity. On the highway he might have overheard conversations in the increasing number of wayside eating places about what was happening in the city. The little he'd heard earlier in the day had been ominous, suggesting that Siraj-ud-daulah had thrown a cordon around Calcutta and intended to have his troops advance on the city from several directions at once.

After pushing on as fast as he could along paths and through muddy fields – for what, having given Kasim his watch, he could only surmise was two or three hours – Nicholas spotted through the gathering gloom two or three large fires in the distance, in the direction of Calcutta. What could they mean? Urging his mount, whose flanks were heaving with every breath, to one last great effort, he rode on, alert for possible enemy pickets but disturbed by nothing more than the shrieks of a few late-roosting peacocks fluttering into the trees.

After what could have been another two hours of slow progress, Nicholas approached the city's north-western outskirts. He had still seen nothing of the Nawab's troops or indeed of any Company outposts. However, on two or three occasions in the last few minutes he had heard what might be the distant sound of musket shots. Realising that from now on he'd be safer on foot, he slid down from his exhausted, sweat-scummed horse, unfastened its halter and with a slap on its bony haunches sent it off into the night. As the sound of its hoofs slowly receded, he stood where he was, listening intently. He heard nothing at all now, which was peculiar. He was only a few hundred yards from the first habitations. Even at this late hour, there'd normally be sights and sounds of life from them. Yet, everyone seemed to be inside and scarcely a light was showing. It was as if people didn't want to draw attention to themselves.

Keeping to the shadows, Nicholas hurried past the huts and beyond the milestone that read 'Fort William – 4 Miles' to enter the city proper. Sticking to narrow alleys rather than using the broader thoroughfares and on alert for the slightest sound, he'd covered about three quarters of a mile before he finally heard voices. Ahead of him, two men were squatting beside a glowing charcoal brazier beneath a tree. In the flickering light, he saw a musket leaning against the trunk – soldiers.

'That taught them a lesson they won't forget – we didn't lose a single man,' one said. At this the other laughed. 'The cowards! I thought they'd put up more of a fight when we came at them, not just run away after scarcely firing a shot.'

They were speaking in Bengali but were they Company men or the Nawab's? Nicholas heard the first man continue, 'The Nawab deserves his title. He's indeed "Fortune's Child", and I hope he passes some of that good fortune our way!' Both men laughed.

Nicholas's heart missed a beat. So he was too late. Calcutta had already fallen. His thoughts turned at once to his son, and then to Sohini and Lucia. Were they safe? They had Tuhin Singh to protect them but who knew what might have happened... Giving the soldiers a wide berth, he broke into a run in the direction of the river and his bungalow which he knew couldn't be more than a couple of miles away.

Twenty minutes later, rounding a bend, Nicholas nearly collided with a group of Siraj-ud-daulah's soldiers, laughing and joking as they swaggered through the wrought iron double gates of what Nicholas recognised as the Company Treasurer's mansion. The men were laden with gilded chairs, swathes of brocade – doubtless they were curtains ripped from windows – and armfuls of other booty. Some had what looked like women's jewellery round their necks. In their revelry, they paid no attention to the grimy man in the dun turban, who stood back to let them go by.

After dodging another group of the Nawab's troops – this time a disciplined patrol, muskets at the ready – Nicholas at last saw ahead of him his own white-washed bungalow. One of the gates was half-hanging from its hinges. Clearly looters had been here, too – perhaps they had lit the lamps whose light flickered through the windows.

He ran inside, almost falling over a French soldier sprawled face down, his blue coat stained with blood, clearly dead. Another was spread-eagled in a doorway, a scorched round hole made by a musket ball above his open unseeing eyes. Broken plates and bits of furniture were strewn across the tiled floor. A trail of blood drew Nicholas's eyes to a shadowy corner where another body lay. Grabbing an oil lamp he hurried over. It was Sohini. The ayah's sari was soaked with blood from what looked like a bayonet wound to her stomach. Her large dark eyes, usually so full of warmth and life, now stared sightlessly back at him.

'James? Tuhin Singh? Lucia?' Nicholas ran from room to room, frantically shouting their names. But there was no response until finally from the direction of the back veranda a voice called faintly, 'Nicholas? Over here…'

Nicholas ran out to find Tuhin Singh lying on the veranda, his clothing blood-stained and his eyes half closed. He had obvious wounds to his right shoulder and to his leg. Seeing Nicholas, he tried to raise himself but fell back. Nicholas knelt beside him. 'Tuhin Singh, what happened? Where's James?'

'French soldiers burst into the house in the late afternoon... The first person they found was Sohini. I heard her screams as she tried to warn us. They killed her before I could reach her...' Tuhin Singh's breathing was ragged. 'Lucia... She seized James from his bed and escaped with him over the back wall. I tried to hold the looters off and after I'd killed two they finally made off... But by then I... I'd been hit by two pistol shots and was too weak to go after them. I'm sorry, I don't know where James and Lucia are. You must go. Leave me. Find them.'

'In a moment.' Nicholas hurried inside, snatched a cotton tablecloth and tore it into strips that he used to tightly bind Tuhin Singh's wounds. Next he fetched a pitcher of water and after his friend had gulped some down took him as gently as he could by the armpits, dragged him inside and propped him up against a wall. Placing the pitcher of water beside Tuhin Singh, he said, 'Stay here, out of sight, while I go and look for them. I'll be back...' Tuhin Singh nodded weakly and closed his eyes.

Nicholas ran out into the street. Where would Lucia have taken James? To the fort? To the harbour? Both lay in the same direction and he headed for them, ducking down alleys or into shadowy doorways to avoid groups of the Nawab's loot-laden, sometimes drunken soldiers. Almost as dangerous were the group of stray dogs he came upon round one corner, feasting on the corpses of a fallen Company cavalryman and his horse. As Nicholas drew nearer, they lifted their snarling blood-encrusted muzzles towards him, growling in warning, but soon, to his relief, lowered their heads and went back to their meal.

Nearing the city's centre, Nicholas turned into a street lined with small shops. Several had had their shutters forced open and their merchandise lay scattered on the ground. A bow-legged old man was standing over something on the ground. Approaching him, Nicholas saw four or five rolls of coarse, unbleached cotton lying higgledy piggledy in the dirt. If they belonged to him, the cuts to his face showed he'd put up a fight to protect them.

The old man squinted up at him. 'What do you want? Who are you? No Bengali, by the looks of you!'

'I'm a Company man just returned to Calcutta. I'm looking for my young son. Please... Tell me what you can about the attack...'

With a heavy sigh, the man replied, 'It began early this morning. The first we knew of it was the booming of their cannon. Then they came swarming in — French officers among them... Some of us tried to protect our homes and a fat lot of good it did us! As for your fine Company soldiers, they did nothing!' He turned his head and spat a gob of phlegm onto the ground. 'I had it from my nephew, who'd taken some goods of mine into Fort William and was waiting for a receipt, that when they realised Calcutta was being overrun the garrison couldn't get away fast enough, running like rats from a flood down to the Hooghly to board boats to take them downriver to safety, the President and his high and mighty officials among them...'

Nicholas was aghast. 'Everyone...? Did everyone escape?'

'Only those who were quick enough... My nephew said the Nawab's forces occupied the riverbank. After that very few boats got away and the Nawab's troops rounded up any British they came upon. Some were taken to the fort. And then the looting began — destruction for destruction's sake. That's all I know.' He paused as though about to break down, but when he looked up Nicholas saw resentment not tears in his eyes. 'Go now! Leave me be! I've had enough of the Company, the French and Siraj-ud-daulah. None of you care about us, the common people whose land this is... You never have, you never will. A plague on the lot of you.' He spat again and turned his attention back to the rolls of cotton.

Nicholas hesitated. Had Lucia managed to get James onto one of the departing boats? He could only hope so. Yet, the old man had described abject panic on the riverbank, with soldiers and officials all scrambling to get away. What chance would a young woman and a child have stood in such madness? Perhaps Lucia had taken refuge with James somewhere in the city... Her previous experiences with the pirates had shown her to be resourceful and brave... She wouldn't panic... Already a survivor, she would be one again, wouldn't she?

But wondering was pointless. He had to find them, or at least to be certain that they'd got away. All he had to guide him was what Tuhin Singh and the old man had said – and the evidence of his own eyes. The fires he had seen burning from a distance, he now realised, were some of the Company warehouses along the Hooghly going up in flames after being looted.

Hurrying on, conscious of occasional frightened eyes peering at him through shutters and lowered rattan screens – few were as brave as the old shopkeeper – Nicholas realised he was less than three quarters of a mile from Fort William. Siraj-ud-daulah's patrols were becoming more frequent, protecting the approaches to the fort. And what was happening inside Fort William? He could picture the Nawab reclining in the President's high-backed chair in his panelled office beneath the large painting of the Court of Directors in London and laughing up at their sombre, sober faces beneath their curled wigs...

A few hundred yards on, Nicholas made out, silhouetted against the flames from a burning building, a man approaching quickly from the direction of the fort, clasping a bundle protectively in his arms. A child perhaps? He was too far away to see clearly. Nicholas took a few steps towards him but he wasn't the only person to have spotted the man. Two figures suddenly burst out of a side alley just behind the man. One had a pistol, while the other held a bottle in his hand from which liquid was spilling. 'What are you doing outside?' Nicholas heard one shout in broken Bengali. French soldiers! 'There's a curfew on till dawn. And what have you got there?'

The man turned to flee but the soldier with the bottle threw it aside to smash against a wall and ran after him. Grabbing his shoulder, he spun him around and lunged for the bundle. The man resisted, holding on with surprising tenacity. But the second assailant clubbed him to the ground with blows from his pistol butt. 'Stop!' Nicholas yelled in Bengali, and drawing his dirk from his waistband ran forward to the man's defence. Hearing his voice, the soldiers looked around at him. Then, perhaps not relishing a fight, they turned and ran off, though not before one aimed a kick at their victim lying curled on the ground, arms still clutching whatever he was so keen to protect.

Reaching the crumpled figure, Nicholas helped the man up. Surely he recognised that face – the Company clerk from the Treasurer's office. 'Hiralal Das?' he asked. The man nodded, brushing away blood from a cut on his cheekbone. As he peered more closely at Nicholas through eyes almost closed by swelling from the assault, he asked in shocked tones, 'Captain Ballantyne?'

'Yes, it's me. Are you all right?'

'I think so. Thank you, Captain. I don't know what would have happened if you hadn't come along.' Hiralal Das sounded almost as calm now as when he was sitting at his high wooden desk, authorising transactions in the Treasurer's office.

'What are you protecting?'

'Only notebooks, but precious to me… When Company business has been slack I've been writing a history of my family. When the fort was captured and Siraj-ud-daulah's men and the French began to ransack it, I grabbed them and hid in the fort grounds and waited until I thought it safe to try to get home – my house isn't far from here.'

'Come on. I'll get you back safely! Give me the books to carry.'

Cautiously they made their way through the streets, still dark except where fires burned, the clerk limping a little. 'Das – I'm looking for my son. A young woman who was caring for him fled with him from my bungalow when the soldiers came. I don't know where to begin my search… They may not even still be in Calcutta.'

'They might have got away – some families did – but Siraj-ud-daulah's men imprisoned others in the fort. From my hiding place, I saw mostly men but some women and children being herded past. I don't know where they were being taken but there were quite a number – fifty at least, and perhaps many more… It was hard to tell.'

'My son's six-and-a-half years old – dark hair, dark eyes. His mother was a Hindustani. He's with a young European woman with long red-gold hair. Did any of the prisoners look like that…?'

'I didn't have a very good view though I did recognise some faces – like Mr Holwell's.'

Nicholas nodded. John Zephaniah Holwell was a member of the Company Council, a no-nonsense man who had been a military surgeon.

'But a young woman with red-gold hair, you say? Well… now that I think about it, I might have seen such a woman among the prisoners – her face was bruised… But I don't recall a child with her…'

Five minutes later, they'd reached Hiralal Das's modest white-washed house on a narrow street shaded by a banyan tree in a part of the city where many of the Company's more senior Bengali employees lived, whether they were clerks, port officials or non-commissioned officers of the Company's army.

'Good luck with your search, Captain Ballantyne. If there is anything I can do to repay you for saving me from the soldiers, tell me. What's more, when you find your son, as I hope and pray you do, you will need a refuge. Remember where I live…' the clerk said, gripping Nicholas's hand.

'Thank you, I will, Das. I have two requests to make, please. First, my friend Tuhin Singh is badly wounded. He is at my bungalow. Can you find a hakim to attend to him? Second, can you find a Hindu priest and ask him to arrange the cremation of Sohini, my son's ayah, killed by French soldiers? Her body is also at my home. She took very good care of my son after his mother died and I owe her that at least…'

Hiralal Das nodded. 'I will.'

'Thank you.' As he turned towards the fort again, Nicholas asked himself what more information he now had to go on in his hunt for James and Lucia. Nothing as far as his son was concerned and only a brief sighting of a woman who might or might not be

Lucia… He might be able to learn more around the fort. But perhaps he was too late. The thought that James might be dead, taking with him the only part of Meena he still possessed, was unbearable. He must know what had happened to him…

Reaching the fort without incident, Nicholas concealed himself in the shadows. All seemed quiet. In the light of torches burning in sconces three sentries lounged beside the closed main gates. After a while – Nicholas guessed it must now be about three or four o'clock in the morning – a clatter of hooves snapped the guards to attention.

'Name and business?' one shouted to a dark-clad rider as he galloped up.

'Messenger from Murshidabad, with despatches for the Nawab from his vizier, Naraigan Singh.'

'Show me them – and your face!'

The rider pulled down his face cloth and produced from his saddle bag a packet which he held out. 'See, it carries the vizier's seal.'

'Very well, but give it me to take inside! Our orders are that no one enters the fort until daybreak.'

The rider surrendered the packet, then turned his horse away.

So much for any idea – however wild – that, somehow, he might be able to get inside the fort through the gates during what remained of the night… Still sticking to the shadows Nicholas circled the walls of Fort William, searching for a spot where he could climb in. Although the tops of the walls were crumbling in some places, they were still too high and sheer for him to scale. He returned towards the main gates. What now? There was nothing he could do but wait until dawn.

Wracked with guilt at not having figured out sooner a way to escape from Murshidabad, he squatted behind some sacks of straw – probably fodder for the Company horses abandoned by grass cutters bringing them to the fort when the attack came. Perhaps, once the gates were opened, he could load one of these sacks on his back and pretend to be a grass cutter, coming to sell his wares. Common sense told him his disguise would fool no one in daylight, but if he could think of nothing better he was determined to make the attempt.

Each minute seemed more like an hour until, at last, the sun began to rise and a few cockerels to crow in the streets behind him. Though exhausted, Nicholas had not shut his eyes for a single moment. Shouts from within the fort followed by the sound of heavy wooden bars being drawn back behind the gates alerted him that something was happening. The gates slowly opened and a minute or two later three heavily laden carts rumbled out. Nicholas rose from his hiding place to get a better look. In the half-light it was hard to see what was piled on the carts, but when he realised what it was he almost exclaimed with horror. Corpses – limbs and heads dangling off the sides! The clothing – coats, buckled shoes, muslin dresses – were European. The bodies could only be of those who had been imprisoned. As the leading cart came closer he saw the corpses better, unable to take his eyes off them. Not only were there adults among them but also one or two children. None had obvious wounds. What had the Nawab, or the French, done to them and why?

Nicholas watched stupefied as the carts rolled by. But then, he saw a small group of people, also European by the looks of them, come stumbling through the gates after the carts. Nearly all were men – three or four of them soldiers. It took him some moments to recognise a dishevelled figure in a torn shirt and stained breeches as the usually fastidious Zephaniah Holwell. Behind him, a drooping older woman was supporting a young girl. Compared with the number of bodies on the carts, they were only a handful – just over twenty perhaps? Suddenly, among the last to emerge, Nicholas spotted a tall young woman staggering beneath the weight of a child in her arms – Lucia and James.

Without another thought, so overwhelmed he could scarcely breathe, Nicholas rushed towards them. Taking the half-conscious James from her, he said to the blank-faced Lucia in Italian, 'Quickly… This way!' She scarcely seemed to understand, but as he pulled at her arm she nodded and followed him. None of the soldiers, nor a French officer who'd followed the group through the fort gates, intervened. If anything, they appeared to be relieved to have at least two of their embarrassing charges removed.

Once they were out of sight of the fort and the troops, Nicholas paused in the corner of a small square. Looking down at his son's semi-conscious face, he began to breathe more deeply again. Glancing at Lucia, he saw her whole body trembling. Even so, she found strength to whisper, 'I kept him safe in there... I didn't fail him...' For a brief moment, Nicholas felt her hand on his shoulder, as if he, not she, was the one who needed comfort and reassurance. What had happened to his son and to Lucia inside the fort?

But this was not the time for such questions. The immediate problem was where to find refuge. James was starting to stir in his arms, groaning softly. His brow was dry and hot, and his face flushed. Nicholas tried to clear his head. He must think fast. As a Company officer known to Siraj-ud-daulah, he could not return to his home, nor live openly anywhere in the city. Suddenly, he remembered Hiralal Das's offer of shelter. He had seemed sincere and it might be their only chance...

The journey to Das's house took longer than he'd expected. Big for his age, James was no light burden and Nicholas had to stop occasionally to recover his breath. Lucia, too, could only stumble along, often stopping to cough and twice to bend over and vomit. Reaching the house at last, Nicholas knocked on the door. No answer. He knocked harder. Was Hiralal Das pretending not to hear? Or perhaps he wasn't there? He knocked yet again. Finally, the door opened and Das himself appeared. Immediately grasping the situation, the clerk stepped back to admit them, calling out urgently to his wife, and beckoning them through to a small inner courtyard. 'Lay the child down here. I'll fetch water,' he said pointing to a cotton rug beneath the shade of a neem tree.

He returned quickly, accompanied by his wife and carrying a brass pot. As Nicholas gently raised James's head, Das splashed water on his face and, filling a ladle, put it to his lips. James moaned faintly but would not open his mouth and the water just ran down his chin. Nicholas had never felt more helpless as he stroked his son's burning forehead.

'Nicholas… Let me try,' he heard Lucia say. 'Give me the ladle…' Taking it, she knelt beside James and began to whisper to him. As he continued to cradle his son's head, Nicholas caught the Italian word *caro*, 'my dear one', again and again. But there was no response from James, whose breathing seemed to be growing shallower. Lucia continued to whisper endearments, gently stroking the child's cheeks and forehead. At last, he gave a faint sigh, his eyes flickered open and he looked up at her. At once, Lucia put the ladle to his lips. He drank only a little and turned his head away, but she persisted, and a few moments later he took another sip, then another and another, until finally he shook his head.

James's forehead was cooler now, his face less flushed. Lucia got to her feet and stepped back as Nicholas laid his son's head down on the rug. 'James?' he said softly. 'It's me.' James looked up and seeing his father's face, at first appeared bewildered but then he smiled. That look released Nicholas's pent-up emotions and he could barely hold back his tears.

Eventually, when Das's wife had taken Lucia away to wash and rest, and Das had helped Nicholas to make James comfortable on a charpoy, Nicholas and the clerk sat in silence in the courtyard, watching James sleep. But as the minutes passed, Nicholas knew he could not avoid the question gnawing at him. 'I know that our presence here puts you and your wife in danger but my son and Lucia both need time to recover. How long may we stay here?'

'As long as you need, Captain Ballantyne,' Das replied.

Nicholas grasped his hands in silent gratitude.

Nicholas hadn't expected to see Lucia again for some hours – after helping to revive James, she had looked utterly drained in body and in mind and he'd urged her to rest. But shortly after noon she came into the courtyard where Nicholas was now alone with James. Nicholas smiled at her as she sat on the edge of the charpoy, looking down at his son.

Though he badly wanted to know what had happened to James and her, looking at her strained face, he hesitated to ask. Yet, he found he had underestimated her strength, as he had after rescuing her from the pirates. After only a few minutes, speaking slowly in Italian, though by now she had learned a little English, she began to tell him of the night of horror she and James had spent.

'When we were rounded up and taken to the fort, the soldiers... they forced us into a small room. I heard some of the Company officers call it the "black hole".'

'The "black hole"? That's what the soldiers call the room where drunk or ill-disciplined troops are confined to cool off. It can't be more than 15 feet by 20 feet or so.' Nicholas's eyes widened as the implications of what she was saying dawned. 'You mean that's where they kept *all* of you...'

Lucia's stricken expression answered his question. For a moment Nicholas wondered if he should stop her from reliving her suffering, but he sensed her need to continue. Her words came more rapidly now. 'James and I were among the first into the room, but they kept cramming more people in. As the pressure built up behind us, we were pushed up against the back wall. That's where the room's only windows were – well, not windows so much as two small barred grilles. At first, I felt the same breathlessness and panic as when those pirates put me in their airless box, but I was determined that I would survive and so would your son. I lifted James up and fought to get him as close as I could to one of the grilles.

'I would never have been able to hold him up for all those hours but I didn't really need to... So many of us were squeezed in – at least sixty people... It became impossible to move. I did everything I could to shield James from being crushed. At first people were screaming and sobbing... I suppose I was too... We could hear guards laughing outside. Some people were calling out to them, begging for water, and offering them large sums of money to be released. Not one guard answered.' Lucia's green eyes shone with tears.

'Later I heard people beseeching God for his help. But as the hot night drew on the sounds grew less as people suffocated. I saw the faces of those crushed up against me turn purple, eyes bulge and tongues protrude... I heard some fighting for breath... Others became delirious and lost control of their bowels. The room smelt as if all of us – the living and the dead – were putrefying... I tried to focus on just one thing – keeping myself and James alive...' Her voice broke as she brushed away the tears that had begun to run down her cheeks. 'But that is enough for now. I... I can't say anymore...'

His mind full of the horrific images Lucia had conjured, Nicholas could not speak for some moments. Then he got up and, going over to the charpoy, gently drew Lucia to her feet. 'I'll never forget my debt to you. You saved my son,' he said.

At that moment, James woke and called out, 'Lucia.' Quickly wiping away any trace of tears, she knelt down beside him and smiled. 'I am here, James, *caro*, don't worry. I am here.'

20 – Escape

'How are you feeling?' Nicholas asked, squatting beside Tuhin Singh who was lying on a charpoy in a small room off the court-yard in Hiralal Das's house.

'A bit sore and stiff – but that's probably because of the way the hakim's bandaged me. I feel like a trussed chicken,' Tuhin Singh smiled.

Nicholas wasn't deceived. His friend's face was drawn and he was clearly in considerable pain. But he was safe. The previous night, together with Hiralal Das and one of his servants, Nicholas had returned to his bungalow to fetch Tuhin Singh. The hakim's assistant had still been with him. 'Hakim Sahib told me not to leave him till you came. His wounds are deep, but they are clean and he will live,' the assistant had said. 'If the pain gets bad, my master said to give him these opium pellets dissolved in milk.'

'What are you going to do, Nicholas? Try to get out of the city?' Tuhin Singh asked.

'No. I'm not going to leave James or Lucia, not even you, at least not until you've recovered enough to take care of the other two... Besides, I'm not sure where I would go. The only thing I can be certain of is that when the Company have called up reinforcements they'll try to retake Calcutta. If they don't, they're finished in Bengal... But perhaps they deserve to be for their complacency and stupidity.'

'What do you mean?'

'Everything I've seen and heard since reaching Calcutta shows the feebleness of the Company's efforts to defend the city! Roger Drake allowed the Company's forces to be depleted. When the attack came he must have had some warning of Siraj-ud-daulah's approach and known how badly he was outnumbered. Why didn't he immediately order everyone into Fort William and wait for reinforcements? Instead, he tried to throw up a defensive line some distance from the fort. I've seen where he stationed cannon and set up flimsy barricades. It's hardly surprising that when the enemy stormed in, the few defenders quickly abandoned their hopeless positions and joined the stampede to get away, quickly followed by Drake and others who should have known better. The city fell like a ripe mango from a tree – it didn't even need to be plucked!'

'It's easy to be wise after the event, Nicholas.'

'I suppose so. But not when I think of the lives of Sohini and all the others that have been lost, very nearly yours among them. Of what James, Lucia and the other captives endured. Of all the lives still to be lost in the battles to retake Calcutta... But you're right. There's little point dwelling on the past and determining who was responsible. What matters now is what happens next. Siraj-ud-daulah and his French allies aren't fools. They'll be expecting a British attack on Calcutta. The most useful thing I can do is lie low here and gather all the intelligence I can. Then, when the time comes, I'll find a way to get out of the city to wherever the Company's troops are assembling...'

'You'll need to be careful. You need to pay attention above all to your own safety and to that of James. You should not concern yourself so much with your duty to the Company. You are more loyal to them than they would be to you, as they've already proved when they sent you from Calcutta to Madras after news of the Jacobite rising reached Bengal. You know as well as I do that the Company puts its own interest and profits above those of any individual, whether British or Hindustani. Equally as bad, it turns a blind eye to the massive corruption amongst some of its officials. Hiralal Das has been telling me how much of it he sees from his desk in the Treasurer's office.'

'I understand what you're saying,' said Nicholas, 'and there's some truth in it, but rather than just abandon the Company I want to do what I can to make it better. You know that corruption is anything but restricted to the British – we at least have laws against it and offenders can be brought to book. Besides, why are so many Bengalis of whatever rank happy to trade with the Company or be employed by it?'

'Self-interest isn't restricted to the British either, Nicholas. The Bengalis seek opportunities for enrichment and to better themselves and their families wherever they can. But I'm sure they have no particular love for the Company. Don't you think they'll be as happy to trade with the French if they establish themselves in Calcutta?'

'The French are as alien to Hindustan as we are and Hindustan would do well to be rid of them. Their king is as great an autocrat as any Moghul emperor. He knows no restraint, makes and unmakes laws as he wishes and unjustly imprisons anyone who displeases him. He brooks no true debate at all of the kind we have in our Parliament. He is ruthless in achieving his ambitions, resolute in his attempts to foment dissent and to obtain more territory, whether in Europe or Hindustan. I am in no doubt that I am right to resist the imposition of his unfettered will and unpredictable whims on Hindustan, just as I'm right to oppose it in Europe.'

'I admire your belief in law and justice, despite the sufferings of your uncle and others during the Jacobite rebellion. British law and justice are all very fine in theory but are they really always applied even-handedly in practice? I remain to be convinced. However, those were two long speeches for you, Nicholas, and I will not challenge you further. Although I will always remain loyal to you, do not expect me not to speak my mind about the Company's many failings after all I've seen of them.'

'And I would be more than a hypocrite not to wish you to do so. One of man's great freedoms is to be able to say without fear whatever he wants to whomsoever he wishes...'

Nicholas paused briefly and then continued, 'Now back to practicalities, I think. Hiralal Das permits us to stay here. I'm indebted to him. It's far safer than anywhere else we could go.

But in doing that we're all taking a risk, Das and his family included. Siraj-ud-daulah I'm sure has his supporters in the city, ready to curry favour by reporting any suspicions. We'll need to take precautions – I'll be careful when I go out. James and Lucia mustn't leave the house at all! Though James speaks Bengali and could pass as a Hindustani child, at his age he might say or do something that could betray us.'

'Well, you needn't worry about me. I can't go anywhere for a while. But is there anything at all I can do to help you?' Tuhin Singh sat up with a slight grimace of pain.

'Not yet. Just concentrate on getting better. Once your wounds have healed a little, you can go about the city more easily than any of us and see what you can find out. Or else you can come with me. As you're so fond of telling me, when I'm in disguise I'm much less likely to be caught when you're by my side...'

'That's certainly true,' Tuhin Singh replied.

–

In the fading light, Nicholas walked along a narrow street towards the Hooghly. He was wearing the uniform of a French lieutenant Hiralal Das had bought from a contact of his in the bazaar. The trader had produced it from a jute sack after satisfying himself that Das was not a French agent. Das had sewn up the large slash in the breast of the jacket through which the previous owner had probably received a fatal wound. The uniform had proved useful on Nicholas's cautious sorties around the city these past few months. He'd avoided times of day when patrols were frequent, only going out in the shadows of dusk or the pale, misty light of early morning.

So far, no one had challenged him, though he'd had his story ready – that he was a Scottish Jacobite exile in the French army.

There was no question that Siraj-ud-daulah's forces had Calcutta in an iron grip. After the capture of the city, the Nawab himself had lost no time in giving orders for strengthening the fort, repairing the tops of the walls Drake had let crumble and for the positioning of new cannon batteries. Then he had left one of his generals, Manik Chand, in command at Calcutta, departing himself, so it was said, to confront his internal rival Shaukat Jang who had now assembled a large army and come out in open rebellion against the Nawab. The latest rumour was that the Nawab had already defeated and killed Shaukat Jang.

Tuhin Singh, now well on the way to recovery though still walking with a limp, had been out in the city the last few weeks. His recent visits to the Nawab's camp in the guise of a tonga driver had been particularly productive. The troops had readily believed in the loathing he'd expressed for the English who he said had wounded him by their random fire as they fled Calcutta in panic and so had been less discreet about themselves and their regiments.

Yet, what interested Nicholas most on this particular night was something Tuhin Singh had overheard in the bazaar. He'd only caught fragments of a conversation between two of Siraj-ud-daulah's soldiers buying ghee at a stall but it had been clearly about a new munitions and gunpowder storehouse they were guarding. He'd followed them back to a new brick building on the banks of the Hooghly, seemingly capable of storing a large quantity of munitions. Nicholas wanted to see the building for himself and assess its importance so that he could pass the information on to the Company forces when the time came.

A Company attack was clearly coming. These past two weeks, talk in the city had been of British forces massing in the Hooghly delta. Accounts of the number of troops varied wildly. Some even claimed the British king had sent a great army of one million to avenge the Company. Nonsense, of course, but something was clearly afoot. According to Hiralal Das, some Bengalis were sending their families to safety in the countryside. Others were burying their most prized possessions, hoping to preserve them from the whirlwind to come.

A quarter of a mile later, Nicholas rounded a corner and there, just as Tuhin Singh had described, was the storehouse – a large red brick building some 20 feet high. It had a single gateway and its only windows were small and set just beneath the eaves. Behind the storehouse, the Hooghly glinted metallically in the light of the fast sinking sun. Some guards were squatting by their cooking fires – placed well away from the store. Others were talking and laughing and one was playing a flute-like instrument. All were Hindustanis. Good. They'd be less likely to suspect his identity than Frenchmen. He walked confidently towards them. Eyeing him without interest, they continued what they were doing.

'What have you got in that pot there?' Nicholas asked in Bengali a young man stirring something over a fire.

The man started at being addressed in his own language by a foreigner, then grinned up at him. 'Brinjal and dal. A tasty combination. Want some? You're welcome to join us but if you do, you'll have to wait a little.'

Nicholas shook his head. 'Thank you but I'm wanted back at the fort soon. I thought I'd just stroll down to the river.'

'You foreigners are lucky. You can come and go as you please.'

'Can't you? How many men does it take to guard a warehouse? Especially when there's no one to guard it against? The British have fled with their tails between their legs. I don't believe these stories that they're planning an assault... it's nothing but bazaar gossip, if you ask me...'

'Our officers don't see it like that,' another guard who'd overheard the conversation interrupted. 'They're hastening their preparations for the defence of the fort. They say Company soldiers have set up a big camp downriver at Fulta... Their new commander's called Clive and he's brought up reinforcements from Madras to join Drake and those cowards who fled our attack. We've also heard reports of a fleet of British warships in the delta.'

'Hah! Don't worry. They've probably come to take the British home... Whatever your officers may say, I doubt they've any stomach left for a fight,' Nicholas replied, hiding his surprise at hearing Clive's name.

The guards laughed and the young man stirring the cooking pot jerked a thumb towards the storehouse, 'Well, if they do come, we've enough gunpowder and cannonballs here to blast them all the way back to Britain, if not to hell…'

'Same place, I'd say! Enjoy the food,' Nicholas said, as he moved away, remembering to curb his impatience and head for the riverbank, as he had told the soldiers, so as not to arouse their suspicion. Afterwards, making his way back to Hiralal Das's house, he thought about what the soldiers had told him. Clearly the moment had arrived for him to leave Calcutta for the British camp and if Robert Clive was indeed in command, it was to his erstwhile friend that he would be revealing what he had discovered about the enemy defences.

In the inner courtyard of the house, lit by clay oil lamps, Lucia was playing with James, helping him feed crumbs to a gecko. Since his ordeal, Nicholas's once boisterous and lively son had become quiet and withdrawn. He often woke in the night screaming that he couldn't breathe and calling for Nicholas. Almost every day he asked for Sohini. Nicholas thanked the stars his son had not witnessed the ayah's murder. He had told James the white lie that Sohini had had to go back to her family but James had loved the woman who had been with him all of his young life. Her sudden absence bewildered and distressed him and he insisted on knowing when she would return. As for Lucia, James would scarcely let her out of his sight. As Nicholas approached, unfastening the high neck of his grubby uniform jacket, both of them looked round. James's attention turned quickly back to the lizard, but Lucia smiled and got to her feet. 'I'm glad you're back. I'm always worried something will go wrong…' she said. 'Did you find out much?'

'Enough,' Nicholas replied, looking at her.

How young she was, Nicholas thought – far too young to have experienced so much danger and unhappiness. Not for the first time it struck him that if he'd fulfilled his promise to send her home to Italy, she'd at least have been spared what had happened to her in Calcutta. He couldn't be sorry about that – she'd saved his son's life. Yet, that made it even more important that he kept his word to her.

'Lucia,' he said softly, taking her hand in his, 'when this is all over I will find a ship to take you to Venice. Believe me, I will...'

Lucia was silent for a moment. Then, raising her chin, she looked at him with her large green eyes and said simply, 'I think I no longer wish to go.'

—

'You will take good care of James – and Lucia too, won't you?' Nicholas asked as, a day and a half later, Tuhin Singh limped along beside him. They were heading in the pre-dawn hours through the almost deserted back alleys of Calcutta for the little harbour a mile or so from Fort William where the local fishermen anchored their small boats. Each day at this time the men took out their boats to catch the fish that the citizens of Calcutta eagerly bought at the quayside morning market. Tuhin Singh had had the idea of using the daily exodus of the fishing fleet as cover for Nicholas's escape downriver from Calcutta and had made the arrangements. Together with Hiralal Das, he had assembled some fisherman's garments and dyed any of Nicholas's skin that was exposed with a mixture of henna, clothes dye and oil.

'Of course. You know I'll watch over them,' Tuhin Singh replied. After a slight pause he added, 'We seem to have got you better disguised as a Hindustani than on some past occasions. That bleary-eyed sentry we passed five minutes ago didn't give you a second glance. And, as the local people also tell me – and that's the true test – your Bengali is now so good that that shouldn't be a problem either.'

'Let's hope not,' Nicholas replied. 'I really can get down to the harbour myself you know. You still look in pain from the wound in your leg... I'll find your fisherman contact easily enough, I'm sure.'

'No. My leg's improving every day. I insist on coming. Better not to take any risks. With me you're more likely to be accepted as the fisherman you're pretending to be. The man whose boat is going to take you downriver towards Clive's camp has never met you. Without me there he might even suspect you're a French agent probing for malcontents.'

'You may well be right.'

Minutes later an increasing smell of fish and the raucous cries of early rising seabirds told them they were approaching the fishing harbour. Rounding a final corner they saw it stretching out in front of them – in reality just a collection of mud flats where at least two hundred small boats were clustered. Most were moored half in, half out of the water but some were completely beached on the mud. Tuhin Singh moved off as fast as his leg wound would allow in search of the fisherman in whose boat Nicholas would travel, leaving Nicholas to squat behind a pile of fishing nets and scratch at the bites early morning mosquitoes had inflicted on his bare calves and feet.

After what seemed to Nicholas a long time but was in fact no more than a quarter of an hour at most, Tuhin Singh returned with a small figure at his side. The man had a thin cotton blanket pulled about him against the morning chill in the same way that Tuhin Singh had draped its like around Nicholas.

'This is Rabi,' Tuhin Singh said. 'He'll take you beyond the French defences to a point from where you can wade across the mud towards our friend Clive's camp.'

'We should get moving soon,' Rabi said quietly. 'The other boats are already setting out.'

Standing up, Nicholas saw that there were already fewer boats on the mud flats than when they had first arrived. After briefly embracing Tuhin Singh, he splashed barefoot through the liquid mud after Rabi towards a small boat whose stern was now beginning to bob up and down on the incoming tide.

'Before we get in, help me push the boat further out,' Rabi said, 'and then scramble in.' He and Nicholas put their shoulders to the bow freeing it easily from the mud. Quickly, both men hoisted themselves aboard. Rabi set the single sail – a piece of thin jute matting – and then began to row, straining at the oars to move the boat downstream against the tide. Soon they were nearing a series of nets the Nawab and his French allies had strung from anchored boats to forestall any attempt by Company troops to attack Calcutta from the water. Looking across at the shore, Nicholas noticed cannon batteries positioned at each end of the line of nets.

Two French sentries, both smoking clay pipes, were sitting in a small boat moored where the nets had been lowered to allow the fishing fleet to pass through. As Rabi's boat approached, Nicholas hunched himself up and pulled his cotton blanket further around his face as if protecting himself from the cold. One of the two sentries – a corporal with a livid scar cutting through his left eyebrow – appeared to recognise Rabi. Taking his pipe from his mouth he said in broken Bengali, 'Got a friend with you today to help you then?'

Rabi nodded. 'The shoals of fish are good at the moment. I might need his help hauling in the nets.'

'Good luck, then,' the sentry said and waved them through.

The oncoming tide and the extra weight of Nicholas in the boat slowed their progress. Rabi refused all offers of assistance, pointing out that he had only one set of oars. Not until about an hour and a half later did he lower his sail and steer towards the riverbank. Then he jumped into the shallow water and holding on to the bow with one hand, pointed with the other away from the rising sun. 'The Company camp is in that direction. This is as far as it is safe to take you. You must get out here.'

Dropping into the warm muddy water, Nicholas felt the silt squeeze between his bare toes as he waded towards the bank. Reaching it and turning back to wave his thanks he saw Rabi's boat already heading for midstream. Nicholas began to walk across the mudflats in the direction Rabi had indicated. Several times, despite his best efforts, he startled waterfowl into the air as he pushed through reeds and long grasses. About half an hour after Rabi had dropped him he spotted a large number of tents some distance off beyond a further series of reed beds – this had to be Clive's camp. He increased his pace but when he was halfway through the last of the reeds he lost his footing and fell with a great splash into a small pool concealed among the vegetation, disturbing more waterfowl which rose shrieking before settling back again.

Scrambling to his feet Nicholas found that as he emerged from the reeds the ground became firmer, and he noticed one or two what looked like deserted fishermen's shacks dotted across the landscape.

'What may you be doing here?' a voice came from the nearest hut as Nicholas passed it. Moments later, two red-coated soldiers emerged, their muskets levelled and bayonets fixed. 'I'm a Company officer,' Nicholas replied. 'My name is Nicholas Ballantyne. I need to speak to Robert Clive.'

'Do you, now. First you're coming with us to see my sergeant and let's see what he thinks of that.'

A few minutes later Nicholas was standing, water still dripping from his mud-streaked garments, before the sergeant – a grey-bearded veteran – just outside the perimeter of the British camp.

'He says he's a Company officer, sergeant. Wants to see Colonel Clive so he does. He doesn't look much like an officer, does he?'

'Officer, eh? Why are you pretending to be a Bengali then, and not very well either?' the sergeant demanded of Nicholas, pointing to his calves from which much of the colour so carefully applied by Tuhin Singh had vanished, washed away by the Hooghly.

'To get out of Calcutta undetected, sergeant! I'm bringing vital intelligence about the defence of Calcutta. I am Captain Nicholas Ballantyne.'

'Oh, are you? Can you prove that? You could just as well be a French spy. By your accent you're a damned Scot and the French have enough Scottish Jacobites among their ranks. You wouldn't be the first to be caught spying.'

'No, I can't prove who I am. How could I? Just take me to Clive's quarters.'

'So you can assassinate him?'

'Don't be a fool, man.' Nicholas could no longer keep the exasperation out of his voice. 'Clive knows me. Tell him...'

But before he could finish his sentence the sergeant exploded, 'Don't call me a fool! We had enough of your Scottish treachery at Culloden. I lost two of my best comrades there.' Without warning he smashed his fist into the pit of Nicholas's stomach. As Nicholas doubled up, battling the temptation to start a fight he knew he couldn't win, he heard another voice behind him ask in a strong Northumbrian accent, 'What is the problem, Sergeant?'

'I think we've got a French spy here, sir. A Jacobite Scot.'

Twisting round Nicholas saw the scarred face of Sergeant-Major Henry Armstrong. Their recognition was instant and mutual.

'You fool, that's Captain Ballantyne. A good comrade of mine and of Colonel Clive. Release him at once.'

21 – The Drummer Boy

Robert Clive was standing in front of a large white tent talking to three junior officers clustered attentively around him as, led by Sergeant-Major Armstrong, Nicholas approached. Suddenly recognising Nicholas, Clive broke off his conversation, strode forward and embraced him awkwardly. 'I'm glad to see you.'

'And I you,' Nicholas responded.

'But what brings you here and in this eccentric costume?'

'I've come from Calcutta with as much intelligence as Tuhin Singh and I could gather about the strength of Siraj-ud-daulah's and the French forces.'

'Is Tuhin Singh with you?'

'No. While I was away on a doomed mission to Siraj-ud-daulah's court, he was quite badly wounded defending James and my bungalow when the Nawab and the French captured Calcutta. He's still there in hiding with James.'

'Ah, I see. Give me a moment to finish dealing with these three and I'll be with you. It's just commissariat stuff.'

Alone in Clive's tent Clive beckoned Nicholas, now washed and wearing borrowed clothes, towards a table on which a map of Calcutta was spread out. Looking at the floor rather than at Nicholas, Clive said, 'I've missed you. I've thought often about that... misunderstanding... we had. You know I didn't go ahead with that scheme of mine involving the Rajas of Biralpur and Sonur – nothing to do with your views, of course...'

Nicholas smiled, realising Clive might well not be being entirely truthful. 'I would never have expected it to have been, but whatever the reason was I'm glad.'

'Good. Well enough about that then. Tell me everything you know about the enemy dispositions. This map should help us piece together the best overall picture we can.'

Nicholas explained as concisely and logically as he could what he and Tuhin Singh had discovered about the number of Siraj-ud-daulah's troops his general Manik Chand had under his command, how many French forces he had to support him, where cavalry and infantry were disposed and the construction and positioning of the new munitions store and strong points. When he'd finished and after Clive had asked a few more questions – in particular about cannon numbers – Clive said, 'Admiral Watson and I are holding a council of war tomorrow morning to plan the assault on Calcutta and all this information will be a great help. You must join us.'

Their business finally over, Clive produced a flask of brandy. 'Come on, it's been a long time since we shared a drink together... and God knows we deserve it.' Pouring two generous measures he handed Nicholas a glass, then raised his own. 'What should we toast? The past? All the battles we've fought together, all the close shaves we've had...? But what am I saying? What matters most is the future... Let's drink to the victories to come!'

'The victories to come!' Nicholas smiled. His friend hadn't changed and he was glad of it. The level in the bottle grew lower as they talked into the night, an animated Clive, in fact, doing most of the talking. Characteristically he said nothing more about their quarrel. When he did talk about the past it was to reminisce about their voyage out to Hindustan and the victorious Arcot campaign. Any remaining tension between them seemed to ebb away. Later, as Nicholas made his way a little unsteadily to his sleeping quarters, he realised that neither of them had mentioned Margaret Maskelyne.

The next morning Nicholas woke early and dressed himself in a somewhat ill-fitting uniform Clive had lent him. He smiled as he remembered pointing out to Clive the previous evening that increasing success and fame were rapidly adding to his girth, now beyond Nicholas's own. After Clive's orderly, a Scot like himself, served him a breakfast of bacon and porridge – it was a long time since Nicholas had eaten porridge and it tasted good – he made his way to Clive's large white command tent. Clive was chatting to a slighter figure who had his back to Nicholas. Seeing Nicholas Clive said, 'You know Warren Hastings, don't you?'

'Of course,' Nicholas had met the young Company official a number of times in Calcutta and shook his hand. 'I'm glad to see you. How did you get here?'

'A long story, but briefly, as Calcutta was about to fall, I helped a party of women and children escape to an island in the Hooghly.'

'That's a very modest description,' Clive said. 'He was quite a hero. Now he's volunteered to fight with us and he's here, just like you, to add his knowledge of Calcutta and its geography to our own.'

As they were speaking several other officers were entering and seating themselves at the large trestle table partly covered with a white cloth that stood at the centre of the tent.

'You and Hastings take seats by me,' Clive said as he himself moved towards the table.

The meeting began with the officer commanding the various frontline pickets and scouting parties reporting that Manik Chand was well aware of the presence of the Company army and had his defences fully ready. Nicholas quickly confirmed this from his observations in Calcutta itself. Then he added details of his own, in particular of the nets strung across the Hooghly and the cannon positioned beside them to thwart any attack upriver whether by men-of-war or by smaller boats manned by sailors and marines.

Admiral Watson – a stoutish figure with a round face burnished copper by years at sea – immediately said, 'In that case I suggest I disembark my marines to join the land forces and we use the men-of-war to keep up harassing long-distance cannon fire to unsettle our enemies and to ensure they never know when an attack is imminent.'

'Thank you, Admiral,' Clive said, 'just what I would have proposed myself, so that's one thing agreed! But that leaves the big question of how, when and where we attack by land. Thoughts, anyone?'

Nicholas smiled to himself. Clive had at least learned to make a pretence of consultation.

But after only waiting a few moments, Clive continued, 'In my view, we haven't enough men to make a simultaneous assault all along the enemy line. We need to punch a hole quickly through in a place they'll least suspect us to attack. I suggest through the rice fields near the Hooghly.'

'But the area's full of canals and irrigation ditches,' a scrawny infantry officer protested.

'And that's precisely why they won't be expecting us that way. They'll expect us to attack further west where the ground is better,' Clive said.

'We could even attempt a night-time attack. We've used the cover of darkness successfully before, haven't we?' Nicholas put in.

'We have, but in smaller-scale actions when we didn't have to deploy so many troops,' Clive said. 'But yes, it would make sense to move the cannon and our troops in darkness, ready to go into action at dawn. The moon is sufficiently near full for that, I think.'

'I know I'm only a simple sailor,' Admiral Watson said. 'But what about a diversionary attack on another point of the enemy line?'

Clive nodded his agreement as others began to chip in with more detailed proposals. These included taking jute matting with them to place over particularly muddy patches to prevent cannon limbers bogging down in the rice paddies and wooden planks to bridge the deepest irrigation ditches. Clive accepted all these suggestions and began allocating tasks. Admiral Watson would command the diversionary attack that would be made by his marines – backed up by six cannon disembarked from the men-of-war – against a series of watchtowers west of the rice paddies. Both Nicholas and Warren Hastings would lead squadrons of mounted Bengali musketeers. To allow time for the required preparations, the advance would not begin until the following night.

In the thirty-six hours that followed, Nicholas took part in readying the army for the largest battle he'd yet been involved in. First he met the sub-officers of the mounted Bengali musketeers whom he would command and found them ready and eager for the battle and needing no detailed guidance from him to prepare themselves. Later, he and Clive toured the camp on horseback, giving words of encouragement or guidance, with Nicholas using his language skills to talk in particular to the sepoys who, as usual, made up the greater proportion of the troops.

When they visited the area occupied by the surgeons' tents orderlies were bringing buckets of water, tables were being scrubbed and knives and saws sharpened, and laid out ready for use, together with forceps designed to extract musket balls, packs of needles and thin twine to stitch wounds, bandages and splints. Other orderlies were setting up rows of beds inside the makeshift hospital tents for the inevitable casualties. Returning they passed Sergeant-Major Henry Armstrong drilling his gun crews – a combination of Hindustanis and Europeans – to increase their rate of fire.

'Good work, Sergeant-Major, but make sure they get some rest too,' Clive shouted to him.

'Yes, sir,' the Sergeant-Major replied saluting.

Riding on, they encountered a group of marines and sailors stripped to the waist and sweating in the heat as they dragged the cannon disembarked from the men-of-war across the mud flats to ready them for use in the diversionary attack. Next, Nicholas and Clive crossed to the camp kitchens where great iron pots were being filled with water and placed over piled firewood, ready to provide a hot meal for the troops just before they advanced.

'Your role is as vital as anybody's,' Clive told the chief cook, a bulky man busy chopping onions. 'It's no myth that soldiers fight better on a full stomach. Make sure the food is good and that there's plenty of it.'

As they rode back towards Clive's tent, they passed a red-coated regiment of British infantry cleaning their muskets and honing their sword blades. Among them were drummer boys practising their battle tattoo. Several were very young – little more than ten years of age. Nicholas's thoughts went back to the youth who had attempted to rob him as he'd made his way through the Wapping docks to the *Winchester*. Were these drummer boys' lives any better than that robber's? Reining in, he asked one of the youngest how he'd come to be in the army.

'My older brother's in the regiment,' he said. 'He's promised to take care of me tomorrow.'

'I'm sure he will,' Nicholas said, relieved that at least the child would not face the battle alone.

On the day of the attack, even before darkness fell, the first of Clive's forces began to move from the encampment – a company of Bengali scouts who had been ordered to check that the approach to the paddy fields was still entirely clear of the enemy and, if they were, to establish pickets and mark the route for those who were to follow. Two and a half hours later one of their junior officers returned to report that the area was indeed free of enemy troops and the easiest route – the one most free of ditches and other obstructions – had been marked.

Soon afterwards Clive ordered the artillery to advance. As their drivers cracked their whips and the double-teams of oxen strained at their yokes, the cannon began to move forward on their creaking eight-wheeled limbers, at first slowly, and then a little faster. Two ox-carts carrying the powder and the cannon balls for the big guns, all carefully secured beneath oilcloth covers, followed each cannon.

Together with one of the British infantry regiments, Nicholas and the Bengali mounted musketeers he was leading were designated to accompany the leading cannon. Nicholas rode beside the three cannon commanded by Henry Armstrong. The grizzled Sergeant-Major by turn cajoled and encouraged his men, and in particular those driving the oxen forward, one positioned by each pair of yoked animals urging them on. Fortunately, a gentle breeze was blowing from the sea meaning there were fewer mosquitoes than earlier to trouble the troops – although, the bites Nicholas had received during his journey to Clive's camp continued to itch and he found it all he could do not to scratch at them constantly.

After three hours of slow but steady progress the cannon had covered nearly half their four-mile journey but this had been the easiest section. After a brief rest for both men and animals, they pressed on again beneath the light of the three-quarters full moon shining from a clear sky. Soon they reached the start of the area of broken, muddy ground bordering the rice fields. After about only 100 yards, the two oxen leading the team pulling the first of the cannon sank up to their hocks in some deep mud. They had to be unyoked before they could be hauled free, too exhausted to be capable of further pulling. Nicholas ordered five of his men to dismount and walk ahead of the cannon, probing the ground to identify the swampiest places so the cannon could avoid them. Henry Armstrong had the jute mats taken from the ammunition carts, ready for use beneath the cannon wheels when they were needed which was almost as soon as the artillery moved forward again.

Their progress slowed dramatically, particularly when an ox in the second team broke its leg and had to be cut from the traces. Seeing how badly the oxen were struggling, Nicholas ordered half of his musketeers to dismount and push the cannon forward to ease the task of the oxen and joined them himself, putting his shoulder to the leading cannon limber. The extra assistance and the frequent use of jute mats and sometimes of wooden bridging planks helped increase the speed of progress a little. After another half mile Nicolas conferred with the officer commanding the British infantry regiment – a Lieutenant Rawlings – and some of his men replaced Nicholas's now increasingly exhausted musketeers in pushing the limbers.

In another half mile or so the remainder of the British infantry swapped places with their mud-spattered comrades. After they'd only gone a few hundred yards more, they had to use planks over a wide irrigation ditch. But as the full weight of the third cannon reached the middle of the creaking makeshift bridge, three of the five planks suddenly snapped. The cannon and three of the infantrymen pushing it toppled into the muddy, green-scummed water of the ditch, pulling the rear four members of the cannon's ox team down with them in a bellowing flurry of hooves and legs.

Armstrong, who had already crossed the plank bridge, immediately ran to the members of the ox team that remained on his bank and released them from the traces. His comrades soon had two of the infantrymen on their feet again after pulling them out of the ditch but they had to lay the third man carefully on the bank. His face was contorted in pain and his left leg bent at an unnatural angle, clearly broken. Tying a pair of ropes beneath the animals' bellies, the soldiers succeeded in hauling three of the four oxen from the water. To end its suffering they killed the fourth which appeared to have broken its back and was bellowing loudly in pain.

Armstrong jumped into the muddy water to inspect the cannon and its limber, using a makeshift torch consisting of oiled rag wound round a ramrod that Nicholas lit using his tinderbox. 'Two of the eight wheels and one of the axles on the limber are broken, Captain Ballantyne,' Armstrong shouted up.

Nicholas thought for a moment. Delaying any longer would hinder the whole advance. 'Abandon the cannon in the ditch,' he ordered. 'It's more important we get the remaining guns into position for the attack by the agreed time.'

There was a glimmer of pale light on the eastern horizon beyond the Hooghly as the troops – now guided by the local scouts – pushed forward again. An hour later, mud and sweat-soaked, they reached their appointed positions which the scouts had already marked out with strips of bright yellow cloth. As some of the troopers and infantrymen relaxed for a few minutes eating food from their packs or smoking clay pipes, Nicholas saw Robert Clive ride up followed by more horsemen and foot soldiers. His broad smile showed his satisfaction at his men's successful completion of their hazardous night-time advance. The assault would begin on time! He joined Nicholas on a low hillock, scanning the flat ground in front of them as a Bengali sub-officer pointed out, about half a mile away, a thin line of defences his scouts believed to be occupied by Siraj-ud-daulah's troops, apparently still unaware of the Company's approach. A few minutes later they could not but be aware. To the west, flashes and booms signalled that Admiral Watson and his marines were beginning their diversionary attack on the watchtowers.

'Time for us to advance,' Clive said.

A few minutes later the Company's cannon fired in unison at the defences and a regiment of red-coated British infantry began to move forward through the drifting cannon smoke, muskets levelled and bayonets fixed, flanked on either side by the mounted musketeers, including those led by Nicholas. As he rode, Nicholas noticed the young drummer boy he'd spoken to the previous day marching at the head of his company with his fellow drummers, beating his drum with a look of taut concentration on his face.

Scarcely a quarter of an hour later the troops were marching through Siraj-ud-daulah's front lines whose few and heavily outnumbered defenders had hurriedly fled scarcely firing a shot. However, although they had penetrated this part of the enemy line, Nicholas realised the real fight was still to come as Manik Chand moved troops – surely of a better quality than those who had abandoned their positions – from Calcutta or other more heavily defended sectors in the west, in an attempt to push back the British incursion.

Half an hour later with the sun now fully up, the Company infantrymen continued to advance in disciplined ranks through the rice fields to the beating of their drums. They were approaching a belt of dusty trees and scrub elevated above the rest of the low-lying, waterlogged countryside which Nicholas knew fringed one of the main roads leading into the heart of Calcutta when suddenly volleys of musket shots rang out from the roadside bushes ahead. Lieutenant Rawlings, advancing at the head of his men, sword in hand, spun round and collapsed, clearly hit. Several of his men also crumpled. Rawlings struggled to his feet after a few moments and tried to run after his men, only to stumble and collapse again into the mud and water of the paddy field. Two of his men ran back to him, seized him beneath his arms and carried him to the rear. Nicholas had meanwhile drawn his sword. Shouting to his men to leave their muskets slung across their backs, he charged, mud and water spraying from his horse's hooves, up towards the roadside trees and scrub concealing the enemy musketeers.

Yelling their battle cries he and his troopers reached the bushes, just as some of their opponents, quicker to reload than the rest, fired. Two of Nicholas's men pitched from their saddles, one to be trampled beneath the hooves of the horse following him which in turn crashed to the ground unseating its rider before recovering its foothold and galloping away, reins dangling and neighing loudly. Then the Company soldiers were hacking and cutting at their enemies who were now lunging at them with their bayonets. One succeeded in thrusting his weapon deep into the belly of a Company trooper's horse, only to be slashed down by its rider as he tried to extract the weapon before the rider himself jumped from the saddle of his collapsing, mortally wounded mount. Another of Siraj-ud-daulah's men pulled a Company trooper from his horse as he rode into the bushes. Together they rolled over and over in the mud and scrub until another cavalryman following behind succeeded in thrusting his sword into the attacker's back.

Nicholas ducked as a French officer rose from behind a nearby dusty bush and levelled his pistol at him. The ball passed over Nicholas's head as pulling hard on his reins he swerved towards the officer who, discarding his pistol, had his hand on his sword hilt ready to draw it. Before he could, Nicholas's own sword sliced through his blue-uniform coat and into his shoulder and he fell backwards into the bush from which he had so recently emerged.

Nicholas and his men pushed through the vegetation and out onto the elevated Calcutta road, driving their opponents before them some of whom soon broke ranks, running in any direction they could to escape. Others, however, fought on until, cut off and surrounded, they too had no choice but to surrender.

Riding back towards the paddy field to ensure that Lieutenant Rawlings's subordinates – his sergeant-major and sergeants – were marshalling their foot soldiers effectively, Nicholas saw the drummer boy. He had a bloody bandage round the knuckles of his left hand and was squatting in the mud, cushioning the head of a fallen comrade, giving him water to drink from a leather bottle. The left leg of the man's white trousers was torn and bloodstained. As Nicholas reined in beside him, the drummer boy looked up, eyes full of tears, and said, 'He's my brother, sir. He's been hit.'

'Cut a branch from one of the trees for him to use as a crutch and help him back to the surgeons. The sooner they attend to his leg the better,' Nicholas ordered. 'Tell anyone who asks that Captain Ballantyne gave you permission.'

As Nicholas continued his inspection he pondered the irony that the elder brother had expected to look after the younger but in fact it was the reverse. Quickly satisfied that Rawlings's men retained their discipline and were moving up to continue the fight, Nicholas returned to the Calcutta road. As he was preparing to lead his men down it into the city he saw a large cloud of dust moving fast along it towards them from the direction of Calcutta – clearly enemy cavalry riding to the counter-attack.

Immediately Nicholas ordered his musketeers to dismount, tether their horses to the nearest trees and line up with the infantry, half to one side of the road and the rest to the other all with their muskets loaded. As the dust cloud grew nearer Nicholas heard bugles blowing and saw shadowy figures of men and horses at its centre. 'Ready your weapons! Wait for my command to fire!' he shouted and heard his orders repeated down the line.

His men levelled their muskets as the horsemen, now clearly visible, galloping five abreast and with their lances lowered, approached within 100 feet. Two or three of Nicholas's men lost their nerve and fired wildly. Most, however, held off until the onrushing horsemen were no more than 60 feet away and Nicholas yelled, 'Fire!'

The crash of musketry was momentarily deafening. All five of the leading rank of enemy horsemen fell, together with many of the men and horses following, leaving the column in complete confusion with unwounded but dismounted men and those still in the saddle, struggling to avoid the dead, dying and injured – all impeding each other in their panic and pain and with riderless horses only adding to the chaos.

'Infantry, load and fire at will. Horsemen, follow me. Mount up and at them with your swords!' Nicholas yelled as loudly as he could so that his order could be heard above all the noise. He ran towards his horse, untethered it and leapt into the saddle. Urging his mount on, he galloped along the chaos of the enemy column until he reached near its end. Then with several of his men at his back he charged into it. They quickly cut down a number of men and horses whose fall half blocked the road back into Calcutta.

Fearful of being trapped, many enemy riders began to turn, pulling hard on their mounts' reins and desperately trying to avoid fallen men and the thrashing hooves of fallen horses, to flee back in the direction from which they had come. Not all succeeded in avoiding the bodies and themselves crashed from their saddles as their horses stumbled and fell. The muskets of the Company infantry shot down yet more as they fled. Soon, all the enemy soldiers still able to had galloped away and quiet was returning. Some Company infantry began marshalling those who had surrendered, making them squat on the road prior to being marched to the Company camp. Others tended to the wounded including Lieutenant Rawlings who, though he had two musket balls lodged in his shoulder, was conscious again.

While he was beginning to assemble his horsemen ready to pursue the fleeing enemy, Nicholas saw Clive approaching across the paddy fields with several more squadrons of cavalry. 'Good work, Nicholas,' he shouted as he rode up. 'Now that you've made the breakthrough, I will lead most of the troops with the artillery west to engage the bulk of the Nawab's forces. Our scouts confirm they remain in that area and we will drive them away from the city and harbour. I want you to take your own musketeers and two of these squadrons of cavalry behind me – the Madrasis and the Ninth King's Lancers – directly into the city. Probe how many enemy are still there and if you are not overwhelmingly outnumbered expel them.'

'Yes sir,' Nicholas replied, grinning at Clive who was already turning to tell the two squadrons they were now to be under Nicholas's command. Within ten minutes Clive and his troops were moving off west. Nicholas also prepared to leave. First he ordered the infantrymen of Rawlings's regiment to form a road-block to repel any enemy troops retreating that way. Then he commanded twenty of his mounted musketeers to precede his main force, fanning out to scout for enemy positions. After they'd cantered off, Nicholas with a wave of his arm set the remainder of his Bengali troopers, together with the Madrasis and King's Lancers, into motion down the road.

Quickly leaving the rice fields behind, they reached the outskirts of Calcutta without encountering any significant body of the enemy. A few disorganised and demoralised foot soldiers fled immediately on sighting them. Then one of his advance scouts galloped up, his long black hair streaming behind him. 'I got right into the city, sir. In the parade ground in front of Fort William there were a great number of the Nawab's soldiers and officials and also some French troops. All were preparing to depart in a hurry. It looked like they were separating, the French heading for the harbour and Manik Chand's men for the north-west. The latter were carrying large amounts of baggage and loot which will slow them down. We can cut many of them off if we take the left fork in this road a quarter of a mile ahead.'

Nicholas quickly despatched two British lancers to the main Company camp by the Hooghly to alert the naval officers to the probability of French ships attempting to break out of Calcutta down the river. Then, with his men behind him, he headed down the left fork in the road to intercept Manik Chand's retreating forces.

After about a mile they began passing some of the larger mansions formerly belonging to senior Company officials. Many had been ransacked, with furniture and linen thrown into the gardens and doors and windows flung open. The grand Greek portico of one white-painted house was streaked black with smoke from a fire started inside. Approaching a junction where a road crossed theirs at right angles, they saw the column of the Nawab's men moving along it out of Calcutta. There were soldiers on foot, others on horseback and yet others riding on baggage and ammunition carts. Few appeared to have their weapons readied for action. Their muskets were slung across their backs, their lances held at the vertical and their swords sheathed.

'Let's help them on their way and give them such a mauling they'll never want to return. Charge!' Nicholas yelled. His three squadrons urged their horses into a gallop. Quickly reaching the junction they crashed into what proved to be the middle of a long and disorganised column of Manik Chand's troops, knocking several riders from their horses and trampling some foot soldiers. At Nicholas's command the lancers swung towards the front of the column and the Madrasis towards its rear in an attempt to entrap the whole column, while Nicholas and his musketeers continued to enlarge the hole they'd punched in its middle.

Although some of the Nawab's troops attempted to fight back, firing from the cover of roadside bushes or baggage carts or thrusting at riders with their bayonets, they were either quickly shot or cut down or followed their comrades who were fleeing in every direction – all, that is, except a group of forty or so who formed themselves into a tight defensive position around three large baggage carts. Enough were holding their lances out in front of them to give the appearance of a hedgehog. Others had their muskets levelled and their bayonets fixed.

As Nicholas charged towards them, a half-spent musket ball grazed his thigh and a little blood immediately began seeping into his uniform trousers. Then he reached the first cart, slashing down with his sword a turbaned musketeer just about to fire. Suddenly his horse shuddered and stumbled. A defender's lance had penetrated its chest. As it collapsed beneath him, Nicholas flung himself on top of the baggage cart, dropping his sword in the process.

At once a defender started to climb onto the cart to confront him. As he scrambled up, the weaponless Nicholas kicked the sword from his hand, then grappled him onto the cart's oilcloth cover. His opponent tried to thrust his splayed fingers into Nicholas's eyes but Nicholas seized his wrist and twisted it back till he heard the bone snap. Then he brought his knee up hard into the man's groin. As he doubled up, Nicholas seized him round the throat, pressed both his thumbs onto his Adam's apple and squeezed as hard as he could until the man, with his eyes starting from his face, went limp.

Nicholas threw the body aside and jumped down from the cart. The fighting around the three baggage wagons was already over. Glancing round to make sure no last assailant lurked nearby, Nicholas raised the oilcloth covering one of the wagons and reached inside. He pulled out a large object well wrapped in an embroidered white cotton tablecloth. Inside was a magnificent three-branched silver candlestick embossed with the Company coat of arms and with drips of wax still sticking to it... Ah, that was why the Nawab's men had fought so hard around the carts – they were defending their loot from Fort William. 'Stay here and guard these wagons until I send word it's safe to bring them into the fort,' Nicholas ordered a section of his troopers.

He led his remaining men deeper into the city, searching street by street for any sign of hostile troops still capable of organised resistance. But they saw only small bands of stragglers who on seeing them threw down their weapons and surrendered. As they approached Fort William, Nicholas found to his surprise that the gates were wide open. Was it a trap? He signalled a halt, then, pistol in hand, scanned the tops of the walls, expecting any moment to hear the crackle of musketry from concealed enemies. Surely, he couldn't simply walk in...

He was about to send soldiers to reconnoitre the outside walls when a head appeared above the parapet. Wasn't that the governor's steward? The man was beckoning and shouting something Nicholas couldn't catch. Pistol still at the ready, he moved closer. Yes, it was the steward and he was smiling. 'I've been in hiding ever since the Nawab's troops came,' he called down. 'When I saw them leaving, I came to the fort to see for myself and found they really have gone, every last man of them... There's no one here but me!'

'Dismount and follow me!' Nicholas ordered his men. Together they moved cautiously forward, weapons at the ready. Once they were inside and, as the steward had said finding no opposition, Nicholas ordered the Company flag to be run up the flagpole once more, posted troopers to man the walls and told others to check every corner of the fort carefully to ensure that no hostile troops were hiding anywhere. Then he told three of his scouts, 'Go and find Colonel Clive. Tell him the city and the fort are secure. There's no threat from this direction. Then report back to me on our army's progress.'

Two hours later, Nicholas was back on the streets of Calcutta. The scouts had returned with news that Clive's men were victorious everywhere, driving Manik Chand and the main body of Siraj-ud-daulah's forces westwards, further and further from Calcutta.

His duty done, Nicholas's thoughts were no longer of battle but of James, Lucia and Tuhin Singh. As he turned into the narrow street with its familiar banyan tree sheltering Hiralal Das's home, all was quiet – doors and shutters closed, the inhabitants doubtless inside waiting for news of the fighting before risking themselves in the open. Reaching Das's door, Nicholas rapped hard but no sound came from inside. He waited a moment, heart starting to pound, then knocked again, even harder, and shouted, 'It's me, Nicholas! Let me in!' This time almost at once he heard footsteps and a key turning in the lock. The door opened and there was Tuhin Singh, cocked pistol at the ready, and behind him James gripping Lucia's hand and Hiralal Das.

Seeing his father, James let go of Lucia and pushed past the now smiling Tuhin Singh towards him. Kneeling down, Nicholas put his hands on his son's shoulders and said gently, 'Hello, James. You've been cooped up for far too long. Let's go for a walk. It's safe now...'

22 – Chandernagore

'Most of the Council wouldn't agree with me that we should take immediate action against the French and the Nawab before their forces can recover their full strength,' Clive told Nicholas as they gazed from the battlements of Fort William three weeks after the recapture of Calcutta.

'Why not?'

'Some of them are just plain cautious – both of us know that well enough. But others like our old friend George Braddock hanker after turning Siraj-ud-daulah into our ally against the French to ensure their complete destruction.'

'Braddock? Why should anyone pay attention to what he thinks?'

Clive smiled a little wryly. 'We always underestimated him. From what I hear, he's negotiated contracts with Hindustani merchants and rulers for shipping silks and muslins to Britain worth tens of thousands of pounds. That's made him a darling of the Company. When he and I were both in Madras, before he moved to Calcutta not long before its capture, I even heard him called the "King Midas of Madras"! You might prefer an alternative explanation for his success – the old saying "turds always float to the surface".'

Despite himself, Nicholas smiled as Clive continued, 'Anyway, the point is that two or three of the Council members – Braddock among them – think we should accept Siraj-ud-daulah's assurances that he deeply regrets the suffering and death in the "black hole" and that he himself never ordered the confinement of British men, women and children. The Nawab blames everything on the actions of an overzealous French officer.'

'Does he now? Does he name the officer? I don't think he can. Lucia and James were in the black hole and two of the few to survive. Brave as she was in protecting James, Lucia can scarcely speak about it and shakes every time she does. But when she does talk, it's Hindustani soldiers she identifies as herding them into the room and ignoring their cries for water and help during the night.'

'Couldn't they have been obeying the orders of a French officer?'

'Quite possibly, but the Nawab was in overall command and so he bears the responsibility.'

'I'm not questioning his guilt but others are – and they're influential people.'

'May I guess that most of them are among those like Braddock and Drake who panicked and fled the city at the first sign of danger and so have no first-hand knowledge?'

'You may and you would be right. But the Nawab's guilt doesn't dim his attractiveness to some as an ally against the French. They point out how small our forces are in comparison to his.'

'In numbers, yes, but when I was in Murshidabad I learned something of the divisions between the Nawab's immediate subordinates, his commanders and officials. There is no trust among them. Some are venal men, seemingly fonder of their harems and luxury than battle. Others are so unscrupulous and ambitious that they would desert Siraj-ud-daulah immediately if they saw advantage in it for themselves. These divisions are real. Mir Jafar, Siraj-ud-daulah's commander-in-chief and my chief informant, is one who I think might be easily persuaded to defect when the time comes. He assured me he was the Company's friend. He would make a more pliant Nawab to the Company than Siraj-ud-daulah and perhaps a less divisive and more just ruler of his own people.'

'I'm not entirely convinced, Nicholas,' Clive said, 'that I wish simply to replace the Nawab when we do come to fight him. It may be better to take some of his territory under our own rule.'

'Why on earth would you want to do that? Controlling and administering territory costs money unless you start to raise taxes and that raises antipathy. All such administration detracts from our main purpose – trade – and probably means a considerable decline in profits. I have great sympathy with some advice I found in my ancestor's papers, given by the English ambassador Sir Thomas Roe to the Moghul court over a century ago:

> 'Let this be perceived as a rule, that if you will profit, seek it… in quiet trade; for without controversy it is an error to affect garrisons and land wars in Hindustan.'

Clive nodded. 'That was, as you say, a long time ago. But rather than disagree about hypothetical situations, we should probably confine ourselves to the immediate future, to what measures we should take to ensure we can trade safely. Can you at least agree we should deal with the French, our long-time enemies and rivals, with whom we are formally at war across the globe and take Chandernagore before the French can reinforce it from their possessions elsewhere and that in the meantime we shouldn't commit ourselves one way or another for or against Siraj-ud-daulah?'

'In a word, yes.'

'Well, then, accompany me to the Council meeting tomorrow to help me argue the case. But on no account should you name those you suspect may be disloyal to Siraj-ud-daulah. The walls of the Council chamber have ears and I would not put it past some Council members even to tip off the Nawab to the danger, if they think they can profit from doing so.'

–

'Tell me why you have asked me to gather us all here today, Colonel Clive,' Roger Drake, the President, asked the following morning as they took their seats in the teak-panelled Council Chamber in Fort William.

'I propose to advance north along the Hooghly to capture Chandernagore and put a permanent end to French ambitions in Hindustan. With the Council's approval, I intend to attack the French as soon as I can assemble my troops and before either the French or the Nawab can recover from their recent defeat,' replied Clive who was sitting with Nicholas at his side in the middle of the long Council table opposite Drake.

Looking around the room, Nicholas saw shock, even consternation on several faces, George Braddock's among them. However, the first man to speak was Major Eyre Coote, a bellicose Irishman from Limerick with a fine military reputation from victories in the south of Hindustan and in the campaigns leading to the recapture of Calcutta and known to his men as 'Coote Bahadur' – 'Coote the Brave'. Nicholas well knew he was a long-time jealous rival of Clive for supremacy in military matters. 'Great soldier I'm assured you are, Clive,' Coote said in his gravelly Irish accent, his voice full of irony, 'but even you can't walk on water. Our numbers are insufficient and our troops are still recovering from the last battle. Surely, you must see that we should consolidate our position here first. Siraj-ud-daulah still has strong forces. If you take our army north he may seize the opportunity to attack Calcutta once more.'

Clive looked hard at Coote and Coote looked equally hard back. 'I grant you that Siraj-ud-daulah has the greater number of troops,' Clive replied, 'but many of the best are a great distance away on guard against the Marathas on the borders of Bihar or to the north-west against the Afghans. I believe some may be dissatisfied and at least one or two of his commanders are ready to defect if promised sufficient reward. Yes, our troops are a little tired but their morale is high after our victory, unlike those of the Nawab who must be at least equally tired as well as demoralised by defeat. If we act quickly against the French we have little to fear from them.'

'What evidence do you have, Clive, that any of Siraj-ud-daulah's senior officers are ready to desert him,' George Braddock asked, though a good deal less belligerently than Coote had intervened.

'Good evidence but to protect those concerned I can't disclose names.'

'Are you implying, Clive, that some of us here may be disloyal?' Coote demanded, his face turning as red as his uniform.

'No, of course not. But I'm sure both the French and Siraj-ud-daulah have their spies and agents, just as we have, and no one can even unwittingly betray what they don't know.'

'So even though you don't trust us weak wits and blabber-mouths with names, we must trust you?' Coote was now on his feet, chest thrust out like a turkey cock.

'Yes, if you put it like that. When the Company has trusted me have I ever failed it?' Clive stood up too.

'Success breeds over-confidence. Pride comes before a fall and on this occasion your fall would envelop us all,' Coote responded.

'Gentlemen,' Roger Drake said, raising a hand. 'This is not a personal issue. Coote is at least right in that this matter concerns us all. Our decisions over the next few months could decide the destiny of Bengal. Ballantyne, tell us what you found out on the mission I sent you on to Siraj-ud-daulah's court before he invaded Calcutta.'

With all eyes on him, Nicholas stood up to speak. 'His court is indeed divided, and not just between those who supported his aunt Ghaseti Begum in her failed attempt to put her adopted son on the throne or those who supported Shaukat Jang in his rebellion and those who remain loyal to Siraj-ud-daulah. Other deep fissures exist, some based on suspicion of the young Nawab's abilities and volatility – he's certainly a devious character – some simply due to personal ambitions and grudges, not to mention ancestral rivalries. Even the merchants and bankers in Siraj-ud-daulah's domains are fearful that he will suddenly seize their goods or impose excessive taxes to finance his ambitions and grandiose building plans. To sum up, like Clive I think the Nawab will be too preoccupied with other matters to act quickly against the Company if we advance on Chandernagore.'

'Unlike Clive, are you going to give us the names of some of these potential turncoats, Nicholas?' George Braddock asked.

'No, I know how quickly rumours or suspicions of treachery – even when, unlike in this case, they are unfounded – can spread and the effect they can have,' Nicholas looked hard at Braddock who, understanding his meaning, had the grace to blush.

Admiral Watson, who had been sitting slouched in his chair at one corner of the Council Chamber contemplating the punkha swaying above his head, now straightened himself and spoke, beginning with his usual refrain. 'I know I'm only a simple sailor,' before continuing, 'but I am prepared to trust Clive as I did in the preparations for the recapture of Calcutta and again I am willing to subordinate my naval forces and vessels to him to enable him to get quickly upriver to seize Chandernagore.'

Drake nodded. 'Your word carries weight, Admiral, and so I should add does Ballantyne's here. I could rarely fault his judgement when he acted as our agent. If we attack the French immediately we can maintain some low-key relatively friendly contacts with Siraj-ud-daulah to keep him uncertain of our attitude. Then, once we've dealt with the French, we can decide what to do about him, but still before he can put together a large army.'

Clive nodded his enthusiastic agreement and Major Kilpatrick said, 'I'm inclined to agree to endorse that Machiavellian scheme of yours, President Drake. Clive was right when he proposed to occupy Arcot to relieve the pressure on Mohammed Ali in the Carnatic. My only reservation is the possible effect of the monsoon rains. We must complete the campaign before they arrive.'

Nicholas answered, 'If we travel part of the way by Admiral Watson's vessels, we should easily complete our work before the rains.'

After more debate, Drake's and Watson's interventions supported by that of Major Kilpatrick sufficed to convince the majority of the Council members and the decision to go ahead against the French was taken for granted as the discussion moved to the military details. There, even Coote chipped in with pertinent and helpful suggestions, though prefaced by phrases beginning, 'Clive has perhaps forgotten...' or 'Clive, you may have overlooked...'

By mid-March, Clive, accompanied by Nicholas and Tuhin Singh, had led the land component of his troops 20 miles north up the Hooghly towards Chandernagore. They encamped some three miles south of the walled French settlement, sited on the low riverbank with a fine port fronting on the river and a fort at its centre to defend it. Admiral Watson had navigated his three large ships of the line, the *Tyger*, the *Kent* and the *Salisbury*, up the river and anchored them a little further downstream of Chandernagore where he disembarked some heavy equipment and provisions. In response to a command phrased as a request from Clive – 'There's no one better than you two for a mission like this' – Nicholas and Tuhin Singh had set out to learn what they could about the numbers and dispositions of the French forces.

Under cover of darkness they crept along the mudflats bordering the Hooghly which was low at this time of year, before the monsoon, keeping a careful watch for crocodiles and tigers as well as French troops, but they encountered nothing until a sudden loud rustling in the bushes stopped them in their tracks. But it had turned out to be only a solitary waterbuck coming down to drink. Resuming their careful progress, Nicholas and Tuhin Singh reached half a mile or so from the walls of Chandernagore. There, with the vegetation along the riverbank becoming ever more sparse and the dawn pinkening the eastern sky, they realised they could not safely venture further.

Tuhin Singh trained his brass telescope – a large, powerful instrument he'd borrowed from one of Watson's officers – towards the fort's ramparts. 'The walls don't look in too good a condition but from here I can't see much more and certainly can't get a view beyond them into the fort itself. We need higher ground.'

'Not much of that here,' Nicholas said. 'But what about that single tall banyan on the hillock over there? It should be easy enough to climb.'

Tuhin Singh nodded and together, keeping low, they crept through the long grass towards it. Quickly both men began to scramble up into it. As they did, they disturbed fifteen or twenty green parakeets roosting there which flew off into the morning air, squawking so loudly that Nicholas thought they might even wake the dead. Nicholas and Tuhin Singh froze but nothing stirred and they resumed their climb. When they were about 50 feet up in the tree, Nicholas put his foot on a branch which, too weak to take his weight, gave way. Tuhin Singh grabbed him by his belt as he pitched forwards. Once Nicholas had regained a firmer foothold, Tuhin Singh said, 'The branches are becoming too weak for us to climb any further up. Besides I think I can get a view over the walls from here. Hold me steady so I can use both hands on the telescope.'

Nicholas did as Tuhin Singh suggested. After moving two or three times to get different views, Tuhin Singh nodded in satisfaction. 'I can see where two of the main cannon batteries are and there don't seem to be any large ships in the harbour. From this vantage point the walls look even more in disrepair than we'd thought. I think that's the best we can do for Clive.'

'I agree,' Nicholas replied, 'let's climb down.' Reaching the ground without incident they began their return to the Company camp. When they had covered a quarter of the distance Nicholas noticed that a fisherman had drawn his boat out of the water onto one of the glistening mudflats and was mending his nets.

'Tuhin Singh, why don't you go and see if you can find out anything further from that man while I wait here,' Nicholas suggested. Tuhin Singh nodded and set off, picking his way through the mud and around the deeper pools to reach the man. He soon returned with news. 'He confirms there are no large ships in the harbour. From what he's seen from the river and heard from friends who've been in the settlement there's no more than 800 or so people in Chandernagore at present – less than 500 of them soldiers and sailors.'

By the time the two men returned to the Company camp the sun was well up and Clive was taking a late breakfast outside his white canvas tent. He looked up from his plate of bread and cheese as they approached. Reaching him, Nicholas picked up a piece of bread from Clive's plate and, after taking a quick bite, reported their news.

'Excellent!' Clive said. 'Nothing to stop us from attacking. Before we do, I will give the French commander, a man called Renault, I think, the opportunity to surrender.' Calling one of his ensigns to him, Clive dictated the following:

> *Sir,*
>
> *The King of Great Britain having declared war against France, I summon you in his name to surrender the fort of Chandernagore. In case of refusal you are to answer the consequences and expect to be treated according to the usage of war in such a case. I have the honour to be, sir, your most obedient and humble servant,*
>
> *R. Clive*

When the young man had dusted his work with sand from a horn to dry the ink, Clive signed the letter and ordered it to be taken under a flag of truce to Chandernagore. 'We'll give this Renault till 8 p.m. to reply, but I don't expect any,' Clive said.

Clive was right. He received none by that time and so called a brief and informal council of war to outline his plan for an attack the following day. Cannon fire would be key. He had already established a battery of 24-pounders capable of bombarding the settlement from the landward side and he described how Admiral Watson, who was not present, being with his ships, should bring them upriver and as far into the channel leading into the port as he could before turning broadside to open fire, while Clive's artillery opened a simultaneous barrage from the landward side.

Clive turned to Nicholas. 'I need to be as certain as I can that Admiral Watson understands his instructions. He should be in position abreast of Chandernagore to start his bombardment as near 10 a.m. as safe navigation allows. Therefore, I want you and Tuhin Singh to take my written orders to him so that you can ensure there are no misunderstandings and answer any supplementary questions he has.'

The next morning at 8 a.m., Tuhin Singh and Nicholas stood on the quarterdeck of the *Kent* beside the blue-coated Admiral, who had not been entirely pleased with Clive's assumption that he needed detailed guidance on his mission but had nevertheless quickly made his preparations. Just before dawn he had issued an extra round of rum grog to all his men. The decks had been cleared of all unnecessary clutter such as the sailors' hammocks and mess tables, the sixty-four gun ports opened, the wheels of the sixty-four cannon greased and stocks of powder and cannonballs readied, together with buckets of water and of sand to quench any fires that might break out.

Once this had been done to his satisfaction on all three ships, the *Kent*, *Tyger* and *Salisbury*, Watson had their boats lowered and tow ropes attached between them and each of the larger vessels. Then he gave orders for the three ships to get underway. Immediately, with the sailors bending to their oars in the boats, and the sails on the larger ships catching what little breeze there was, the three men-of-war began to move slowly upriver towards Chandernagore with the *Kent* in the lead.

After they had gone less than a quarter of a mile, the *Kent* suddenly juddered and swung violently sideways across the Hooghly, throwing Nicholas and several others to the deck. The vessel had hit a concealed mud bank and was stuck by the bow. Admiral Watson immediately flagged orders to the *Tyger* and *Salisbury* to drop anchor and send their ships' boats across to the *Kent* to try to pull her free. Within half an hour, the extra boats had their ropes taut and their sailors were straining at their oars but even after fifteen minutes of hard pulling the *Kent*'s bow remained firmly stuck.

After ordering the sailors in the boats to rest for a short while and then to try again, Admiral Watson discussed with some of his officers whether moving some cannon from the bow to the stern to change the weight balance might help free the bows. Then he said to Nicholas, 'If that doesn't work, I'll have no alternative but to jettison some of the cannon entirely, even though I know how your friend Clive will react to my reducing our fire power.'

Just then, a strong tremor ran along the hull of the *Kent*. The bow was free at last! Admiral Watson ordered his little convoy to proceed but with more frequent soundings of the water depth with the lead line by the accompanying small boats. Inevitably, this slowed progress further and it was nearer 11 a.m. than the 10 a.m. Clive had ordered when the three ships came abreast of Chandernagore. White smoke and flashes and bangs from Clive's shore batteries showed that they had been in action for some time.

So too were the guns of Chandernagore. As the *Kent*, still leading, nosed into the channel leading to Chandernagore's harbour, the garrison's first shots at the vessel fell short, raising great spurts of muddy river water, but with each yard the *Kent* progressed they got closer. Admiral Watson shouted to his gunners. 'Hold your fire lads. We need full visibility to make our way as close in as we can if we are not to go aground again. So the less cannon smoke the better.'

Just then, the first French cannon ball to hit its target struck the *Kent*'s rail, sending large splinters of wood across the quarterdeck. One struck the helmsman in the thigh and he collapsed by the wheel. Seizing the wheel himself, Watson called, 'Steady, boys, steady. It won't be long now.' Almost immediately two more balls hit the ship. One smashed a wooden water butt. The other carried over the side part of a spar and a sail and some rigging. At last Watson gave the order, 'Turn broadside and fire!' and himself swung over the helm.

Thirty-two cannon discharged as one, with a flash and a boom that temporarily deafened Nicholas. The gunners' muscles bulged as they held on to the thick ropes attached to the cannon to limit their recoil. Then, following their oft-practised drills, they began methodically to reload. Each member of the gun crew had his particular task, one inserting powder, another wadding, another – or sometimes two – inserting the heavy cannon ball, all of which were then rammed down before the leading gunner applied a lit taper to the firing hole. With a flash and a bang and a mass of white smoke, the now red-hot ball was flying towards Chandernagore. The gunners were again hauling on the ropes to contain the recoil and the whole process was beginning again.

Through brief breaks in the drifting smoke, Nicholas saw that the *Salisbury* was having difficulty moving into a firing position, but that the *Tyger* was getting into action and the *Kent's* broadsides had already collapsed portions of the fort's walls into the water. Nevertheless, the French gunners in the fort's batteries seemed to have found their range. As Nicholas watched, half a dozen cannon balls smashed into the *Kent* in quick succession. The first produced a stream of splinters that swept the deck. Another decapitated a young midshipman whose blond head rolled a little distance along the deck before coming to rest against the scuppers. Others injured several sailors. Yet another brought down part of the foremast and its spars and rigging. They crashed down to the deck, crushing a sailor and the wounded comrade he was trying to help. Their fall also dislodged a red-coated marine posted in the rigging to pick off any French gunners he could with his Brown Bess musket once the *Kent* got in range. He fell headlong, arms and legs flailing, into the Hooghly with a great splash. The worst damage, however, was done by a cannonball which smashed into the gun deck, and hit a bag of powder by one of the cannon, detonating an explosion that not only killed four of the gun crew, wounded the rest and blew the canon from its carriage but started a fire.

On the main deck, some sailors, seeing the carnage around them and the flames beginning to lap up the side of the vessel, panicked, fearing the blaze was about to set fire to the main powder store. Rushing to the ship's rail, they prepared to dive overboard. 'Don't panic lads. No need to fear,' Watson shouted from the quarterdeck, as calm as if sailing on a summer day down the Thames to London. 'The fire is well away from the main powder store and it's already dying down.'

His words were premature. After dipping their neck cloths in water and tying them round their mouths, Nicholas and Tuhin Singh led some of the less fearful sailors from the quarter- and main decks down the steep ladders into the smoke-filled area of the gundeck. Peering with stinging eyes to locate water and sand buckets, they seized them and threw their contents onto the fire. While the orange flames subsided for a little while, they soon began to flare up again. Quickly refilling their buckets from water butts and sand stores, the men tried again. This time the fire really did begin to die out amid a mass of hissing steam and smoke. The contents of a third round of buckets extinguished it entirely. Most of the *Kent*'s gun crews had continued to work their cannon throughout, despite the flying splinters and the choking smoke.

Their bravery was soon to have its reward. While Tuhin Singh remained on the gundeck to help tend the burns and wounds of some of the sailors, Nicholas returned to the quarterdeck, coughing and smoke-stained, where he found no further cannon balls had hit the *Kent* for some minutes. Then Admiral Watson, who had returned the wheel to a replacement helmsman and was squinting through his telescope through a gap in the smoke at Chandernagore, exclaimed, 'By God, I think they've raised a white flag.' More drifting smoke blocked his view before he could be certain but nevertheless he gave the order to cease fire. There was silence. No sound of cannon fire either from Chandernagore or from Clive's land forces. Chandernagore must indeed be the Company's.

Two hours later, Nicholas and Tuhin Singh took leave of Admiral Watson who, preoccupied with ensuring care for his numerous wounded, and making temporary repairs to the battered *Kent* which he feared might never be able to put to sea again, merely grunted, 'Tell Clive the navy's done its work again as usual.'

The two friends made their way towards the stern through the area where the ship's two surgeons with their assistants, all wearing red aprons, were busy treating the wounded. One surgeon, his hands and forearms covered with blood, was working as quickly as he could with his saw and knives to cut through the bone and sinew of the thigh of a red-headed sailor whose limb had been shattered by a cannon ball. Two of the surgeons' assistants were struggling to hold the man down as he twisted in pain. Turning his eyes away, Nicholas could only hope that the tumbler of rum usually given to those about to undergo such surgery before a wad of cloth was thrust between their teeth to prevent them biting through their tongues in their agony was having at least a little effect.

When Nicholas and Tuhin Singh had scrambled down a makeshift rope ladder from the *Kent*'s relatively undamaged stern into the only one of the ship's boats still intact, seamen rowed them the short distance to the shore. Disembarking on the remains of Chandernagore's ghats, they made their way past the smoking ruins of two large warehouses to the white-washed mansion which they were told Clive had made his headquarters. There they indeed found Clive. To the dirty and weary Nicholas he looked as clean and fresh as a daisy. He was in the middle of dictating a letter to the Company's Board of Directors in London:

> *We have dealt a blow of inexpressible significance to the French interests in Hindustan. We have captured Chandernagore and in so doing have deprived the French East India Company of their largest source of revenue. All trade with Europe from Bengal must now go through us in Calcutta to our great profit. Let me leave you in no doubt that I already have other measures in mind to strengthen our position in Bengal further of which I will inform you in subsequent correspondence.*
> *Your humble and obedient servant,*
> *R. Clive*

Nicholas smiled to himself. 'Humble' and 'obedient' were not the first adjectives that came to mind when he thought of Clive.

Having completed his task, Clive looked up. 'The Directors should be pleased with us, Nicholas. Our victory will mean the Company's stock price will surely rise a good few per cent. I hope, like me, you've already sent a message to buy more stock for yourself before the price rises when the magnitude and implications of our victory are fully appreciated.'

'No, I haven't,' Nicholas replied, restraining himself from adding that he had been more concerned with the opposite side of the balance sheet – the cost in human lives and other destruction which would lead to the increase in profits and share price of the Company and its privileged directors. In any case, he was probably being unfair. Clive was, and always had been, a self-confessed opportunist and an ambitious one at that. He was no hypocrite. He was brave, prepared to take a risk and to pay the price – even the ultimate one – if he failed, just as he expected his opponents to do.

Clive in the meantime was already beginning to dictate another triumphant letter, this time to the President of Madras, so Nicholas turned to Tuhin Singh, 'We must leave Clive to claim his laurels. Let's go to get ourselves some food and rest. Then perhaps we'll go back out into Chandernagore to inspect how much remains of what I've been told was an elegant settlement.'

Dusk was falling when the two men set out, refreshed, into Chandernagore. Most of the fires were out, the wide streets, nearly all set at right angles to each other, seemed deserted until Nicholas heard and saw a sight which brought memories flooding back of his journey through Calcutta on the night of its capture. A group of European Company troops emerged through the gates of a large pillared house. Two were swigging what was clearly wine from green bottles looted from the cellar. Three others were struggling to carry off a large gilded chair for which they could have no obvious use.

Nicholas immediately ran towards them. 'Don't you know looting is forbidden! Put that chair down and get back to the encampment at once!'

The men mostly just stared, but one put his hand on his sword hilt.

'Obey an officer's orders or there'll be a court martial and a field punishment flogging for you all,' Nicholas shouted. A long, tense pause followed as the men continued to stare aggressively at Nicholas, some swaying on their feet a little. Then one of the five – a burly corporal, the only non-commissioned officer among them, and perhaps less drunk than the others – growled, 'Come on, do as he says, lads. He may be a Puritan kill-joy, but he's an officer and I don't relish losing my stripes and even less the prospect of a flogging!'

The three men holding the chair abandoned it and the group staggered off, the corporal keeping to the rear, perhaps concerned the wildest of his comrades might suddenly decide to attack Nicholas.

Returning to Tuhin Singh, Nicholas said, 'How can they behave like that? Company soldiers should know better. What are their officers doing?'

'Perhaps rushing off messages to buy Company stock like Clive,' Tuhin Singh replied with a half-smile. 'How can you be surprised at these men's behaviour after what you've seen of that of the Nawab's and the French troops who captured Calcutta. And after all you've told me so often, about how English troops treated the ordinary people of the Highlands over a period of months, burning their homes, driving off their cattle, not even having the excuse of blood heated by battle. Both you and I should know by now that no man is better than another just because he was born in one place rather than another, to one rank rather than another.'

'You're right, I know. But it's up to those in authority like me to curb such excesses. I'm going to find the provost marshals and tell them to stop turning a blind eye to such doings and then I shall return to Clive and have him issue an order forbidding looting on pain of death.'

'I can only admire your idealism and wonder at your naivety if you think such an order will be fully obeyed.'

338

'Well at least it will be a start.'

When Nicholas retuned to Clive's headquarters, he found Clive in a more communicative mood. He immediately agreed to issue an order prohibiting looting. 'I agree there is no need to antagonise the inhabitants. We are too few to hold down a rebellious populace – or indeed to guard prisoners. Therefore, I've already given orders that the sepoys among the French forces should be freed to return home and the French troops to go where they will, provided in each case that they promise never to take up arms against us again. We need to give the impression to all of Bengal that we are magnanimous in victory, not vicious or vindictive. It should help us convince any waverers in the court of Siraj-ud-daulah of the benefits of siding with us in the conflict to come. I have discovered that the Nawab ordered one of his commanders, Nand Kumar, to march 2,000 men from Hooghly to aid in the defence of Chandernagore only for Nand Kumar to turn back on learning Chandernagore was already besieged. I've made up my mind. We cannot leave Siraj-ud-daulah on his throne.'

'You'll need to convince the Council in Calcutta of that,' Nicholas replied.

'I know and I will. I'm leaving for Calcutta tomorrow. There is no time to lose. You and Tuhin Singh must return with me.'

23 – The Bargain

Two weeks later, Nicholas was once more sitting beside Clive at the long table in the familiar Council Chamber in Calcutta, with punkhas working furiously, just as he had done when the decision was taken to attack Chandernagore. Roger Drake was once more in the chairman's splendidly carved high chair at the centre of the table. George Braddock, clad in cream linen, was whispering into his ear. Admiral Watson, in his gold-braided British naval uniform, was leaning back in his chair, with his usual look of slight disinterest, whereas both Major Kilpatrick and Major Coote seemed to be paying rapt attention. Perhaps the biggest difference from the previous occasion was the marked increase in heat and humidity as the monsoon drew nearer, Nicholas thought as he loosened his neck cloth.

Clive was already in the middle of laying out his case for proceeding against Siraj-ud-daulah before or even during the monsoon. 'I believe we can overcome all the issues of transport and supply to get an army up to Murshidabad, whatever the weather – with Admiral Watson's help of course.' Clive paused and turned towards Watson who looked up and nodded. 'If the Council agrees, the navy can always be relied on.'

Coote said to Watson, 'You do know, Admiral, that Murshidabad's at least 100 miles further north than Chandernagore, don't you?'

'Of course. I can read a chart or a map better than any soldier.'

'Gentlemen,' Drake interrupted. 'Before we get into such matters, Braddock here has reminded me of the fundamental question – what are our reasons for wanting to attack the Nawab? You've simply assumed we should, haven't you, Clive?'

340

'Well it seems obvious to me. However, to be clear, the main reason is that all the time that he has been sending emollient and conciliatory messages to Council members he has continued to intrigue with the French, even since we took Chandernagore. Despite their defeat, he has encouraged them to maintain a trading station at Kasimbazar near Murshidabad. He has welcomed the French officer Jean Law to his court and encouraged him to persuade the Marquis de Bussy to bring his army north from the Deccan. We know about the latter from a letter that we found in the possession of a French courier we captured. The Nawab has French officers training his troops and more French soldiers seconded to his army than he ever did before he captured Calcutta. His artillery is commanded by the Marquis de Frais and most of the gunners are French too. He ordered one of his officers, Nand Kumar, and two thousand troops to march to help the French to defend Chandernagore. They only turned back when they discovered that they would be too late. How many more reasons do you want?'

There was a pause while Drake and Braddock had another brief whispered conversation, then the President spoke again. 'Despite all your victories, battles involve risks and costs. I have two questions. The first is, might not a simple show of force followed by the opening of negotiations persuade the Nawab to desert the French and look more favourably on us? The second is what happens in the event that we fight and win? Do we leave an embittered Siraj-ud-daulah on his throne or depose and replace him? We must have a plan – not just leave chaos behind us.'

'The answer to both questions,' Clive replied instantly, 'is that we cannot trust Siraj-ud-daulah, either in early negotiations or if defeated. What's more, he cannot control his own commanders. They send messages to me, some directly, some through intermediaries, saying that they don't trust his temper or his promises, fearing a knife at their throat in the night. They go on to offer their support to me – at a price, of course! As you'd expect, my replies are warm, sympathetic and encouraging.'

'Perhaps these commanders should fear the Nawab's knife if they are willing to turn traitor,' Coote observed dryly. 'I'd execute any of my men I found conspiring with the enemy.'

'Conspiracy and bribery are a way of life in Hindustan,' Clive retorted.

'Not only among Hindustanis but Britons too in Bengal, from what rumour says about the private activities of some of you Company officials and what I hear from London of the vast fortunes they bring home,' Coote responded. 'Few in Bengal can claim to be like Caesar's wife "above reproach" or as pure as driven snow. The Nawab may have some reasons to distrust us just as we have to distrust him.'

'Let us leave personal slurs out of this, unless any of you can produce evidence, gentlemen, please,' President Drake interrupted.

Nicholas smiled. Drake was himself the subject of such rumours according to Hiralal Das.

'I don't deny some of what you say is true, Coote,' Clive continued, ignoring Drake's interruption, 'but we are where we are. If we can't trust the Nawab, we can't trust him, whether part of the reason is the behaviour of some Company officials or not.'

'I'm afraid I must agree with Clive, President,' Coote spoke again. 'Look at how the Nawab deceived us before his capture of Calcutta, stringing young Ballantyne here along as your envoy while making secret preparations for an attack.'

'On the rare occasions when Coote and Clive agree, so must I, President,' Admiral Watson said quietly.

'While there seems to be a consensus that we attack the Nawab and the French, rather than attempt to split them by diplomatic means,' Drake said, 'that still leaves open the question of what do we do with the Nawab after we've defeated him.'

'Replace him with one of his commanders who has been the most helpful to us or annex some part of his territories as a kind of buffer between us,' Clive answered immediately.

'The latter is well beyond your or my authority to under-take, Clive, remember that,' Drake said. 'Replaced by one of his commanders or officials he must be.'

When the meeting eventually broke up, the Council had agreed that Clive should lead twenty-nine hundred men – eight hundred Europeans including two hundred and fifty from the British 39th Regiment of Foot and twenty-one hundred Hindus-tani sepoys – and nine cannon up the Hooghly to confront the Nawab's reportedly far greater force, estimated to be fifty thou-sand, including twenty thousand cavalry with numerous batteries of French-manned cannon. Major Coote and Major Kilpatrick would both lead subsidiary columns.

Over the next days, Clive, with Nicholas's help, undertook careful preparations supervising the loading of the transport ships which, under the protection of Admiral Watson's men-of-war, would carry the army upstream on the first part of its journey towards Murshidabad. They took great care to ensure that the artillerymen who again included Sergeant-Major Armstrong took more than enough oilcloth sheets to protect their dozen cannon and their powder against the monsoon which had now arrived with flashes of sheet lightening and heavy rain which at its worst turned some of the streets of Calcutta into little rivers.

–

As Clive had predicted, the teeming monsoon rains did not impede the expedition's progress up the Hooghly. Indeed, the increase in the height of the river caused by the rain meant less danger of grounding for Watson's large ships as they moved upriver. Clive, leading the land forces, had also made good progress.

One evening, in mid-June, as Clive and Nicholas were eating a frugal meal of bread and tough and gristly stewed mutton, while rain pattered on the roof of Clive's tent, the sentry on guard outside lifted the tent flap. 'Sir, a messenger has arrived from Kutwa and wishes to report to you urgently.'

343

'Show him in then,' Clive responded.

Kutwa was a strategically important town, five miles north of Clive's present camp on the banks of the Hooghly, 100 miles from Calcutta and 40 miles south of Murshidabad. The walls of the town's fort, a mile in circumference and with eight strong bastions, occupied a dominant position over both the Hooghly and the road to Murshidabad. Clive had sent Coote in advance of the main column with seven hundred men and two field guns to seize the fort and, thus, to safeguard the passage of the remainder of the Company army.

Shaking the water from his oilcloth cape, the messenger – a young ensign – entered, saluted and then handed Clive a letter bearing Coote's seal. 'Major Coote's report, sir.'

Clive broke the seal and read the letter aloud.

> *18 June 1757*
> *Kutwa*
>
> *Sir,*
>   *We have taken Kutwa. When we approached the fort the defenders opened fire on us. Nevertheless, I sent a Hindustani subedar under a flag of truce to demand that the fort be handed over and to state that if the commander refused I would immediately storm the fort and give no quarter. The commander's reply was that he was resolved to defend the fort to the last. I gave orders for some of my sepoys to make a mock attack on the front of the fort while the British regiment crossed the river to attack from the rear. At their combined approach the defenders fled.*
>   *Eyre Coote*

'Excellent news,' Clive said to the ensign. 'Get something to eat, then take back the following message to Major Coote: *My column will march up the Hooghly early tomorrow morning, however much it rains, and we should be with you by noon.*'

Immediately on his arrival in Kutwa the next day, Clive called a council of war. As the officers assembled an hour later, monsoon rain was again beating down on the canvas roof of Clive's command tent and large puddles were forming outside. As soon as he arrived, Major Coote sat himself down opposite Clive. When all the officers, including Major Kilpatrick who seated himself among some of his more junior staff, were present, Clive began with a courteous compliment that Nicholas had suggested to him a minute or two earlier.

'I must congratulate you on your success in capturing Kutwa, Major Coote. A great achievement, with no loss of men or equipment.'

'No more than my duty. No more than any competent officer could achieve.'

'I remain grateful.'

Coote looked as if he wished to retort 'you should be' but remained silent.

Clive next asked for reports on the position of the Nawab's army.

'His forces are encamped about four miles north of us on the opposite bank of the Hooghly, not far from a village called Plassey,' the officer commanding the scouts reported.

'What do your estimate their strength at?'

'Roughly as we anticipated – about 50,000, including 20,000 horsemen.'

'Cannon?'

'Forty or perhaps more, but some designed for static deployment and so large they would be almost impossible to manoeuvre in battle. However, there are enough 18-pounders among them to easily outnumber our weapons. French artillerymen are manning most of the guns.'

'Any other enemy forces within marching distance?'

'Some French troops under their officer Jean Law are two or three days' march away from here.'

Clive looked pensive. 'Gentlemen, numerical odds of nearly twenty to one against would daunt even a hardened gambler. What d'you think?'

'God dammit, the time for thinking about such questions was when we were in Calcutta. Now we're here there's only one decision – attack!' Coote glared at Clive.

'That's what I was hoping to hear,' Clive responded. 'And the good news is that my friend Ballantyne here has his own plans to at least halve the odds against us by some judicious bribery. He will set off shortly with his old comrade Tuhin Singh to infiltrate Siraj-ud-daulah's camp. There he will follow up some promising contacts with some of the Nawab's commanders – those he made previously as an envoy to Siraj-ud-daulah's court and those I've received in letters from some of these same men. I've already signed promissory notes committing the Company to honouring any deals he may make.'

'What sort of commitments?' Coote asked.

'I shouldn't say too much but they involve eye-watering sums in terms of both cash and territory, I can assure you.'

'Necessary commitments?'

'Yes, the reward they'll bring to the Company will make them pall into insignificance. The Company will become the most powerful force in this part of Hindustan, supplanting the remnants of the Moghul Empire and reducing the French presence to insignificance.'

'And, of course, bringing you not a little fame and reward too, Clive,' Coote said, but for once there was a hint of a smile on his face as he continued, 'but I'm sure that's a burden you'll be content to bear for the greater good. When do you propose we make our advance?'

'To allow Ballantyne a little time to work his magic, I suggest we cross the river on the twenty-second of June and make our assault on the following day. Does anybody disagree?'

No one did.

That evening as they ate together in Clive's tent, Clive suddenly said to Nicholas, 'I worry that you may not be able to convince Mir Jafar to come over to us, now that decision time is near... Even that he may have been playing us along, perhaps even in collusion with Siraj-ud-daulah...'

'You shouldn't. You should trust in my powers of persuasion and in my instincts. I believed what he said to me before the attack on Calcutta about wishing to support the Company, and although we thought it unwise to discuss it at the Council, we both know he has written to you in recent weeks congratulating you on defeating the French at Chandernagore and, unlike the Nawab, stating that the victory is to the benefit of all Bengal. He's ripe for the picking.'

'I do trust you. But just answer me this. I would be right, wouldn't I, even if you did not succeed, to attack such a large force as the Nawab's with my much smaller one?'

'I won't fail – and what is it that's unsettling you, Clive? It's not like you to lack confidence. Besides, as Coote said this afternoon, it's too late now. One thing I do know is that you're a good commander and, perhaps what's more important, a lucky one. I supported you in taking the risk at Arcot and we got it right, didn't we? Take this one last great risk. You've always said how cautious I am, but now we've come so far, I urge you to do it! You can banish the French and their machinations from Hindustan and all the fame and fortune you've ever wanted will be yours. It's in the aftermath, in the arrangements you make for the governance of Bengal, that I urge you to show caution and respect everyone, whatever their origins. Don't let the innocent – the ordinary people – suffer.'

Clive took a deep breath, his expression grave. Then he said, 'You are a true friend. The only one with whom I can discuss my doubts or even reveal them. Whatever our fates in the coming battle, nothing can change that. I will take the risk. I will defeat the Nawab and drive the French out of Bengal.'

Early the following morning rain was streaming from Nicholas's oilcloth cape as he rode with Tuhin Singh through mud pools and dripping vegetation. Beneath his cape he had on the full dress uniform of a French captain – blue tunic with white facings, brass buttons and gold trim and white trousers tucked into highly polished knee-length riding boots. Tuhin Singh was equally finely dressed as a subedar in a French Hindustani cavalry regiment. Together they had crossed to the east bank of the Hooghly below Kutwa to avoid detection and were now taking a circuitous route designed to enable them to approach Siraj-ud-daulah's camp from the north. Their story which had already seen them past one small group of Siraj-ud-daulah's pickets, sheltering from the monsoon in a palm-covered shack at a crossroads, was that they belonged to the forces of Jean Law and had been despatched as emissaries to Siraj-ud-daulah's camp to discuss British intentions and possible rendezvous points with the Nawab for an attempt to retake Kutwa.

An hour later with the rain ceasing, and the sun beginning to peep through the purple clouds, and their resplendent uniforms now as mud spattered as their mounts, they had reined in and were repeating their story to a lushly bearded Bengali sergeant commanding one of the entry points to Siraj-ud-daulah's vast camp. Nicholas, thankful to be speaking Bengali in which he might be expected to have a foreign accent rather than French in which he wouldn't, assumed an expression that he hoped combined authority and impatience. 'Quickly sergeant!' he said, 'there is no time to lose. Point me the way to Mir Jafar's tent. I've important matters to discuss with him.'

'It's a quarter of a mile away, sir. The one over there with the two orange banners outside,' the sergeant responded, then saluted and waved them through.

Nicholas and Tuhin Singh faced no further challenge as they made their way deeper into the camp past cooking fires newly lit now that the rain had stopped and smoking as wet wood dried, past soldiers drilling, past the elephant lines where mahouts were feeding their animals with bundles of grass and past the monstrous 36- or 40-pounder cannon about which the scouts had warned. The greatest impression Nicholas had of the camp was of its sheer immensity.

Mir Jafar's tent was surrounded by a low palisade with two sentries guarding the single narrow entrance. Nicholas again repeated his story.

'Very well. You may enter. But you must leave your weapons here. Our commander is a cautious man, ever alert for treachery,' one of the guards said.

'And so he should be,' Nicholas said as dismounting he unbuckled his sword and handed it over together with his pistols before, as was appropriate to his assumed status, instructing Tuhin Singh to remain with the horses. As he squelched through the muddy puddles the short distance to Mir Jafar's tent, Nicholas once more went over the arguments he had framed. The conversation he was about to have might affect the destiny not only of the Company but of Bengal and Hindustan. He must be both authoritative and convincing – there would be no second chance.

The tall sentry at the entrance to Mir Jafar's large tent admitted Nicholas without any further checks. The commander was alone, sitting cross-legged at a low table studying a book. As Nicholas removed his tricorn hat Mir Jafar gave a start of recognition. 'What are you doing here, my friend?' he asked, remembering, despite his surprise, to keep his voice low.

'I'm here on behalf of the East India Company. When we last talked in private you told me you were the Company's friend and a powerful man that we could rely on, despite appearances at the time. I believed you and have convinced others of your good will. I bring you an offer from Robert Clive and the Company. It is simple. If you will desert Siraj-ud-daulah and come over to the Company with your men and those of your associates, the Company will put you on the throne of Bengal.'

'Are you sure? I know you believe what you say but is it really in your power or even that of Robert Clive to dispose of the throne of Bengal?' Mir Jafar asked, looking quizzically at Nicholas.

'I think you know that it is within that of Clive, whose emissary I am, even if it is not in mine. His authority in Calcutta is now unrivalled. We have captured the French settlement at Chandernagore and are now seeking a ruler of Bengal who will be a more reliable friend to the Company's interests than we consider Siraj-ud-daulah could ever be. I have a document making the formal offer, signed by Clive and with the official Company seal, sewn into the lining of this jacket, together with promissory notes for any other leaders you think might join us. Do you want to see them?'

'There is no need for that... but are you sure about what you call Clive's unrivalled authority? The Nawab has repeatedly assured us in his council that the British are divided. He admits that some like Clive are ambitious for the Company to seize more power but, according to him, most only care about being able to go safely home with the riches they've already amassed at Bengal's expense. They have told the Nawab in correspondence that they will not object to his territorial ambitions in Bengal provided they can be assured of that, particularly if Calcutta is left to the Company so that it and the British Government do not lose face entirely. One or two of them seem to believe the Nawab will triumph in any case and drive the Company out. They have even been seeking to make private deals with him, offering help and information in return for rich rewards and future trading concessions.'

'I can scarcely believe that anyone could be so foolish. And if they have, they can only be junior officials disgruntled about their progress or prospects.'

'Hardly. Even now, one of the Company's Council members who has privately been supplying this army with muskets since before the capture of Calcutta is with the Nawab negotiating for trading rights for himself when the Nawab expels the Company.'

'What do you mean?' Nicholas asked, taken aback. 'None of the Council members would be so treacherous. Give me a name.'

'I will do better than that. I will conduct you to a place close to the Nawab's tent so that you can see him and identify him for yourself. Then you will know that I am telling the truth. Come now. As I think you British say, there is no time like the present!'

Ten minutes later a still disbelieving Nicholas, and Mir Jafar were standing as if in conversation 20 yards from Siraj-ud-daulah's large scarlet tent with its gold-coloured awning. The still watery sun was beginning to set as a sentry pulled back the tent's entrance flaps and a burly figure dressed in a brown European jacket emerged with his back to Nicholas, followed by the Nawab. A voice Nicholas found familiar was saying loudly enough for him to hear, 'Of course, Your Highness, if you insist I will accompany you into battle to prove my good faith.'

'I do,' replied the Nawab, as Nicholas strained to hear. 'I've learned to trust no one from the Company, whatever their protestations.'

As the burly man finally turned to go Nicholas saw his face – George Braddock! For a moment or two he was too shocked to speak. He had thought Braddock an obnoxious bully and braggart but not a man who would betray his country – the country of his grandfather the Earl of Marlow. His mind in turmoil, Nicholas suddenly remembered Braddock's vainglorious boasts about his 'ingenious unprecedented deals' in the Carnatic and the Irish Jacobite O'Sullivan's comments about Britons selling arms to the French. Mir Jafar's whispered warning to him, 'We must go. We don't want you to be recognised,' interrupted his thoughts.

As Mir Jafar ushered him back to his tent, Nicholas began to recover his wits. By the time they were inside, he had fully regained his composure. 'Braddock', he began, 'that is his name, and any more like him, are weak, selfish, greedy and pliable men. The Company and the British government have spines of steel. Robert Clive, their undefeated commander and my friend, epitomises that strength. His will cannot be broken. He defeated Chanda Sahib in the Carnatic and as you well know recaptured Calcutta. In this campaign he has taken Chandernagore from the French. He is so confident of his success that he has advanced against Siraj-ud-daulah knowing he is outnumbered. You should join this all-conquering hero now. An early adherent is always more welcome and well-rewarded than a vacillating latecomer.

'After you and Clive together have conquered Siraj-ud-daulah, you will be certain of the throne of Bengal. Fight on the Nawab's side and, in all probability, you will lose. Even in the unlikely event you help the Nawab to victory do you believe that unreliable volatile man would reward you as you deserve? Wouldn't he be jealous of your fame and see you as a potential rival? Might he not seek to rob you of your power or even to kill you? After all, he almost certainly had the adopted son of his aunt Ghaseti Begum killed. However great the jealousies among Company officials – and of course there are some – have you ever heard of any of them murdering each other?'

'I know all that,' Mir Jafar allowed himself a smile. 'And I know how well-equipped Clive's forces are and how stubborn the British can be... That even if Siraj-ud-daulah defeated Clive they would be back. By showing you the traitor I simply wished both to test your resolution and determination as Clive's emissary and to show you where my own loyalties lie. I will commit my forces to the Company. So also, I'm sure, will two friends of mine among the commanders, Lutuf Khan and Rai Durlabh, provided of course that you produce your promissory letters from Clive and that the terms of the rewards are as generous as you say.'

Relief spread through Nicholas but he said calmly, 'I – and, more to the point, Clive and the Company – will be grateful. And you, my friend, will be Nawab of Bengal.'

After a short silence, Mir Jafar asked, 'When should I and my associates desert Siraj-ud-daulah? The latest report I received from him, just before you appeared, was that Clive's troops are already crossing the Hooghly, taking up positions two miles away in a large grove of mangoes we call the Lakash Bagh and that the Nawab is making his own plans to repulse their attack.'

Nicholas thought quickly. 'To have the greatest effect, your defection should take place during tomorrow's battle. The sight of your forces turning away from the fighting will demoralise the rest of the Nawab's men ensuring his defeat. As token of my good faith I will remain with you so that if you suspect treachery you will have the power to kill me instantly.'

24 – Plassey

After Mir Jafar had left the tent to talk to Lutuf Khan and Rai Durlabh, saying he would return soon, Nicholas slipped out too and returned to the sentry position in the palisade. There he found Tuhin Singh waiting patiently in his guise as a French cavalry subedar, holding the reins of their two horses. Taking him well out of the sentry's hearing he asked him to find his way back to Robert Clive and report to Clive, and Clive alone, the apparent success of their mission and also to warn him of the possibility of treachery among some Company officials. He said nothing even to Tuhin Singh about Braddock. Braddock was to stay with the Nawab in his camp. Nicholas himself would deal with him and it would be his personal pleasure to do so.

As one hour turned into two and Mir Jafar did not return, Nicholas, back in the commander's tent, began to wonder if he had changed his mind. It was all he could do to not pace as manically as he'd sometimes seen Clive march up and down when angry or anxious. Instead he took a swig of brandy from a flask which he was carrying on the assumption that no self-respecting French officer would be without one.

Rain was beginning to fall again when at last Mir Jafar re-entered the tent, wiping some raindrops from his face and beard with his palm. As he lowered his hand, Nicholas saw an expression of triumph on his face. 'Lutuf Khan and Rai Durlabh are with us,' he announced, 'and are eager for the promised advancement.'

'Good,' Nicholas replied.

Sensing the relief behind his understated reply, Mir Jafar said, 'You must learn to trust me.'

'I do – but you were away longer than I thought you'd be.'

'I was trying to learn more about the Nawab's plans for tomorrow and I was successful.'

'What are the details?' Nicholas asked, regretting that he'd not waited longer before despatching Tuhin Singh.

'"Details" is perhaps not the right word. His plan is very simple. There is no subtlety at all. With the support of his cannon he will make a frontal assault in what he anticipates will be over-whelming force on Clive's position in the Lakash Bagh mango grove. His aim is to drive the Company's forces back to the banks of the Hooghly and massacre them there as they attempt to reboard their boats to cross back to the river's west side. His advance will start half an hour after sunrise. However, I am to command the right wing while Lutuf Khan and Rai Durlabh are to fight on the left. This is to our advantage. When we three defect we will expose Siraj-ud-daulah's centre to flank attack from both sides and to encirclement.'

Nicholas, was relieved. There was nothing about the Nawab's plan Clive would not have anticipated and made his dispositions accordingly.

Soon afterwards Nicholas retired to sleep on a divan in a curtained portion of Mir Jafar's tent. He tossed and turned for the first hour or so as lightening flashed and thunder boomed across the camp, presaging the battle to come, and rain rattled on the tent roof. However, he was sound asleep when Mir Jafar's elderly steward woke them about an hour before dawn. Nicholas and Mir Jafar ate a simple breakfast, then dressed carefully for battle. Nicholas, still in his French captain's uniform, tucked the pistols his uncle James had given him into his belt and ran his finger along the blade of his cavalry sword to check its sharpness. Next, he tucked his dirk in its scabbard into the top of his boot.

As dawn rose to reveal a leaden sky, the two men crossed the still muddy ground to the palisade outside which the tall war elephant from which Mir Jafar was to command his men in the action to come was waiting. As he walked over to it, Nicholas was careful to draw his neck cloth across the lower part of his face and to pull down his blue tricorn hat to be certain he could not be recognised.

The two mahouts – one white-haired, the other a young man with a straggly beard – who were sitting on the elephant's neck behind its ears encouraged the great beast to kneel down. Nicholas and Mir Jafar climbed into the open howdah on its back, using the animal's bent knee as a step. Two trumpeters followed them into the howdah. Their brass instruments would be essential to conveying Mir Jafar's orders. Four horsemen, each bearing one of Mir Jafar's banners, would precede the war elephant. Four of his qorchis, mounted on swift black horses, would follow as further insurance that his orders could be swiftly carried to his commanders. More horsemen and foot soldiers began to assemble around Mir Jafar's elephant.

Nicholas couldn't help noticing how few had the same quality of weapons as Company soldiers. Most of the infantry were barefoot and carried only spears or bows, not the swords, muskets and bayonets which the Company sepoys carried. The soldiers also showed a lack of urgency and discipline as their officers attempted to marshal them into ranks. Nicholas began to realise more clearly why the Company's forces so often triumphed over their numerically superior opponents.

Soon, however, Mir Jafar's troops, numbering at least 15,000, were in some semblance of order and had begun to move forward to join up with Siraj-ud-daulah's other forces. Then towards the centre of the newly formed line those of Siraj-ud-daulah's soldiers commanded by Mir Madan Khan – a man whose bravery and loyalty to the Nawab, Mir Jafar had told Nicholas, were unquestioned – started to advance to the sound of trumpets and drums. They were followed by the Nawab's personal regiment – the elite of his army and much better equipped than Mir Jafar's men. With these troops and the French-manned cannon already in position, Nicholas realised that despite Mir Jafar's intended treachery, there could be no certainty of a Company victory. What's more, the sword of treachery was a two-edged blade. How trustworthy could any potential traitor be? It would only take Lutuf Khan or Rai Durlabh to return to his loyalty to the Nawab to bring all of Mir Jafar's plans to dust. Everything was still to play for.

Straining his eyes, Nicholas could see the silhouettes of four men in the howdah of Siraj-ud-daulah's war elephant. However, at that distance he could not tell if one was George Braddock, as he anticipated. At a command from Mir Jafar, his men too began to move forward to the beat of their drummers, churning the ground into mud. Only a minute or two later Nicholas heard the boom of cannon from Siraj-ud-daulah's artillery. However, to his ears fewer of them were firing than he would have expected given the numbers of cannon he knew the French and the Nawab had at their disposal. As Mir Jafar's men continued to advance slowly and to pass through one of the cannon batteries which consisted of twelve large cannon, each on a sixteen-wheel limber, Nicholas saw a bald-headed French artillery officer on top of an ammunition wagon staring into an open wooden case containing powder bags. '*Maudites soient vos bêtises! C'est mouillé!*' he yelled.

Nicholas smiled. The French had let their gunpowder get wet. The artillerymen had by their carelessness already reduced the Nawab's chances of victory. No matter how much he waved his arms, yelled and cursed his men, it was the now red-faced and ranting French officer's fault. He must have complacently taken for granted that his men would cover the wagons properly and failed to check them himself when the monsoon rain had begun yet again the night before. Only two of the twelve cannon in his battery were in action and by the still only sporadic sound of cannon fire along the remainder of the Nawab's line, this was not the only battery whose powder the rain had ruined. Nevertheless, Madan Khan's and the Nawab's troops were advancing apparently undaunted.

Now Nicholas heard Clive's cannon begin to reply and by the booming sound of it their powder had remained dry. Two of Siraj-ud-daulah's war elephants at the centre of his line turned away from the battle trumpeting and bellowing in pain, one shedding its howdah full of musketeers, but the centre of the Nawab's army continued to press resolutely forward, men from the rear ranks running to take the place of those in the front line who had fallen.

Peering through the drifting patches of white smoke Nicholas saw lines of red-coated Company infantry emerging from the mango trees of Lakash Bagh now less than half a mile away. Led by their officers with their swords in their hands and with their drummer boys to the fore, they advanced steadily, muskets held at the ready. After they had covered a few more hundred feet and at a command from their officers they stopped, levelled their weapons and fired. Nicholas was sure some of the front line of Siraj-ud-daulah's troops must have been hit but all he could make out was the continuing advance of the line in front of the Nawab's elephant. Then through another gap in the smoke he saw that at least two of the mango trees in Lakash Bagh had collapsed, their trunks splintered by fire from some of the heavy cannon that Siraj-ud-daulah's men and the French had at last got into action. The bodies of several red-coated infantry were sprawled on the ground, shot down during their advance.

Meanwhile, at the centre of Siraj-ud-daulah's vast army, cavalry including a squadron of French horsemen, all mounted on white horses, was beginning to canter forward, banners fluttering, lances lowered. Facing them, Clive's foot soldiers suddenly halted and hastily began to form squares. The squadron of French cavalry enveloped one and even at the distance Nicholas could see the red-coated wall begin to waver, although some of the white horses's riders were down. Company horsemen now began to gallop forward, passing through the gaps between the surviving squares to engage their rivals, unhorsing several by the sheer weight and momentum of their charge. The crunch point of the battle was approaching.

'Time for us to make our move,' Nicholas called to Mir Jafar.

Mir Jafar didn't appear to hear.

Nicholas shouted again. 'Commander, time for us to act.'

Still no response. Nicholas now yelled into his ear. Mir Jafar turned towards him, his face closed and his brows knitted, as if in thought. Could he be making a last minute reassessment of the situation, Nicholas wondered.

Then Mir Jafar smiled and seeing Nicholas's doubtful face said, 'Yes, I know. I am committed. Trust me, I will not change my mind.'

Turning to the two trumpeters behind him in the howdah he ordered, 'Sound the halt!' Then he waved the four mounted qorchis behind him to the side of his elephant. 'Ride hard and order my commanders to cease fire and turn to the right, away from the flank of Siraj-ud-daulah's own forces, and then to retreat while maintaining good order. Repeat my orders to any officer who queries them and tell them I will reward them and their men well.'

Ten minutes later, the gap between Mir Jafar's and Siraj-ud-daulah's troops was becoming clear and from the commotion on the left it was becoming more and more apparent that Lutuf Khan and Rai Durlabh were following Mir Jafar's lead and making their own moves. Clive's horsemen had already seen the gaps emerging in Siraj-ud-daulah's army and were charging for them as hard as they could, intent on attacking their enemies' increasingly exposed flanks and rear before the Nawab's and Madan Khan's troops could change direction to protect themselves.

Then Nicholas saw a French officer galloping on a black horse towards Mir Jafar's elephant, mud flying from his mount's hooves. 'What are you doing?' he yelled in bad Bengali as soon as he was near enough to be heard above the noise of battle. 'Get your men back into the line at once and resume your advance!'

'No!' Mir Jafar shouted. 'I've renounced my allegiance to the Nawab and to you, his French allies.'

Even before Mir Jafar had finished speaking, the French officer had tugged a pistol from his belt and pointed it at him. 'Retract your orders and continue the advance or you'll be the worse for it,' he yelled.

Nicholas too now had one of his pistols in his hand. The French officer fired first. His ball missed Mir Jafar but hit one of the two trumpeters behind the commander who, dropping his instrument, fell backwards from the howdah, arms whirling, into the now almost liquid mud. Nicholas's aim was more sure. His shot hit the officer in the middle of his forehead. He collapsed onto his horse's neck and then, as the animal bolted, subsided from the saddle. From his vantage point in the howdah, Nicholas saw that to his right, while some of Siraj-ud-daulah's forces were continuing to retain their discipline and to resist, despite the weight of Company cavalry attacks washing over and around them like waves on rocks, other of the Nawab's formations were beginning to disintegrate into chaos.

Horsemen were pulling hard on their reins and heading for the rear. Some collided with the mounts of their comrades still advancing. Others trampled foot soldiers too slow to get out of their way. Elsewhere, infantrymen had thrown away what weapons they had and were running as hard as they could, legs pumping, through the thick, sticky mud to escape. A French officer spurred his horse towards one group, slashing down two of the fugitives with his sabre in an apparent attempt to make the rest halt and return to the fight. One of the foot soldiers succeeded in ducking beneath another swinging stroke of the officer's sabre, seized his booted leg and dragged the Frenchman from his horse to sprawl on the ground whereupon the foot soldier followed his comrades in their headlong rush to the rear.

With victory becoming certain Nicholas knew it was time for him to deal with George Braddock. Without telling the mahouts to make the elephant kneel, Nicholas quickly dropped from the howdah into the mud. Throwing off his French officer's jacket and tricorn hat, he mounted his horse with which an attendant had been following Mir Jafar's command elephant. As quickly as he could, he urged the animal through the descending chaos towards Siraj-ud-daulah's banners and the spot where he could occasionally see the neck and shoulders of the Nawab's war elephant and its howdah.

As he came within 200 yards of the elephant he saw it slowly turn away towards the rear, still with four men in the howdah, and still surrounded by twenty of Siraj-ud-daulah's mounted body-guards. From the bulky profile of the single European in the howdah, Nicholas was increasingly sure it was indeed George Braddock. However eager he was to confront the traitor, he knew that the bodyguards would thwart any attack he made at present. He must be prudent, he told himself and follow the group at a safe distance.

After what must have been a mile, the Nawab's elephant halted, knelt and the burly figure climbed clumsily from it to swap places with one of the Nawab's bodyguards who in turn climbed into the howdah, while Braddock swung himself into the saddle of the guard's horse. Then the group set off again. After a few hundred yards more, George Braddock turned his mount away from the rest and, now alone, guided it west instead of north. Nicholas suspected he planned to circle round behind Clive's forces and return south to Calcutta to feign rejoicing at the Company's victory and to see if there was any way he might profit from it.

Nicholas continued to follow Braddock unobserved until, leaving the noise and chaos of the battlefield well behind, Brad-dock came to the bank of a small river, doubtless a tributary of the Hooghly, where he reined in, perhaps wondering whether it was too deep to cross. Seizing his chance, Nicholas urged his horse on with hands and heels and galloped towards Braddock to get within about a hundred feet of him before he looked round. As Braddock recognised Nicholas, who by now had his remaining loaded pistol in his hand, his sweat-scummed face turned pale. Tugging at his reluctant horse's reins, he urged it towards the gently lapping water.

'No further,' Nicholas said. 'And for God's sake George, for once have a little self-respect. Don't try to make excuses, to pretend you're in the wrong place at the wrong time, caught up in the middle of a battle when you were on a trading mission. I saw you with Siraj-ud-daulah by his tent last night. Mir Jafar told me what you were up to and I've just followed you from the battlefield.'

'Wait,' Braddock's voice shook a little as after a short pause he said, 'Nicholas, haven't... haven't you ever been tempted? Can't we come to some arrangement? I'll give you any amount of money you wish if you'll let me go.'

'No, I want nothing from you. Nothing you can say or offer will turn me into the traitor you once called me.'

'What are you going to do with me? Take me to Calcutta for trial and public disgrace? No, I'll not have it – either for myself or my family!' George Braddock was almost shouting now. He jumped from his horse and scrambled towards the water, throwing off his jacket as he did so, and plunged in, trying to reach the other side.

Kicking his horse into the water, Nicholas got himself in front of the wildly thrashing Braddock. 'If you won't face trial, face me like a man,' he said. 'Draw your sword and let the best man win.'

'No!' Braddock cried, as he turned and stumbling in his agitation splashed back to the shore. He looked frantically around. Then, realising he could not escape, he drew his sword and stood dripping wet *en guard* at the water's edge, the expression on his face the same as when he'd faced Nicholas in their duel in Madras.

Nicholas rode back up onto the bank, dismounted, pulled his sword from its scabbard and said, 'Come on then, George, let's finish it now!'

Twice Braddock lunged at Nicholas with his sword but on each occasion, Nicholas jumped aside just in time. Breathing heavily, Braddock rushed forward again. This time his aim was better. The tip of his blade cut through Nicholas's white shirt and into the muscle of his upper left arm before he succeeded in parrying the stroke. Nicholas then aimed a cut at Braddock who took a pace back to avoid it before thrusting forward at Nicholas again. With blood running down his arm, Nicholas knocked his enemy's sword away and then, right arm extended, thrust his own weapon deep into Braddock's ample belly. Dropping his sword and clutching his wound with both hands, George Braddock staggered into the river and after only a few paces collapsed face down into the muddy water.

Nicholas stood and watched the current slowly carry Braddock's lifeless body off, arms and legs outstretched, downstream towards the Hooghly and Calcutta. Minutes passed, the silence broken only by the occasional distant bird call and the lapping of the water at his feet. Then he turned away, bound up the wound in his left arm as best he could with his neck cloth and washed George Braddock's blood from his sword. After a few minutes of further reflection, he remounted and rode slowly and reluctantly back towards Clive's camp – his mood one of melancholy and introspection, rather than of the uncomplicated elation and victory he knew he would find there.

25 – 'Remember You Are Mortal...'

As the sinking sun streaked the darkening sky pink and gold and a dozen Company flags, specially raised along the walls of Fort William, rippled in the evening breeze, a long procession slowly approached the fort gates. In front marched military drummers, beating out a joyous tattoo, and behind them trumpeters who every few paces vigorously sounded their instruments. Then came an elephant draped in gold cloth that glittered in the leaping flames of the flambeaux that Governor Drake had ordered to be lit along the route. Sitting alone in the silver howdah on its back was a familiar figure, turning this way and that as he waved to the cheering crowds.

From his vantage point on the battlements, Nicholas smiled. What was it Clive had said as they'd stood together on the decks of the *Winchester* as it sailed up the Hooghly all those years ago? '*I mean to grab every opportunity to make my name and fortune. If the chances don't come quickly enough I'll engineer them.*' At the time, the determination in Clive's voice and his desperate hunger to succeed had astonished and alarmed Nicholas in equal measure. But Clive had lived up to his words. All the fortune and glory he had ever craved were now his and this great victory parade must surely be the moment he had been waiting for all his life.

Nicholas's smile broadened as he watched Clive's elephant draw nearer. Clive had asked him to sit by his side in the howdah, but he had declined, insisting this was Clive's moment. But perhaps he should have done. From his studies of the Classics he knew that during Roman Triumphs, a slave had stood behind victorious emperors in their chariots as they rumbled through the streets of Rome, his task to whisper repeatedly into the imperial ear the warning 'remember you are mortal' – a warning against overweening pride. He could have done the same for his friend, not that Clive would have been likely to listen.

Reaching the fort gates, the military band formed up to their left, continuing to play as Clive's elephant approached. Ranks of Company soldiers, both British and Hindustani, drawn up to the right side of the gates, stood to attention and saluted. Nicholas hurried down from the battlements to the courtyard in time to see Clive's elephant make its stately entrance into the fort. As it did so, Nicholas caught a new sound – the wailing of bagpipes, something he had not heard for a very long time. Three pipers dressed in Scottish plaid had struck up on a balcony projecting over the courtyard. Nicholas guessed they must belong to a newly-arrived Scottish regiment.

Standing well back, Nicholas watched as the mahout seated on the elephant tapped its shoulder with his anka to bring it to his knees. Then a bearer hurried forward to assist Clive as he stepped down from the howdah. Beneath his white-plumed hat, his broad face was flushed and smiling as, with a flourish of his hand, he turned full circle to acknowledge the cheers of the Company officials gathered in the courtyard. Then, a guard of honour stepped smartly forward and its commanding officer said, 'Colonel Clive, sir! On behalf of Governor Drake we are honoured to welcome the victor of Plassey!'

By now the rest of the procession was entering the increasingly congested courtyard. First came elephants carrying others who had commanded in the recent fighting – Major Coote, smiling for once, Major Kilpatrick and others. Admiral Watson was not among them. A sudden fever had recently carried him beyond any earthly glory. Riding four abreast behind the elephants came more officers of the regiments that had fought at Plassey. They were followed by mounted musketeers and then foot soldiers, every item of their equipment from the buttons on their uniforms to their swords and muskets gleaming. Among a group of gunners

Nicholas was pleased to see the scarred face of Sergeant-Major Armstrong.

Looking around, Nicholas realised that Clive had already gone inside. Straightening the collar of his dress uniform, he too made his way indoors to the banqueting chamber where, as the culmination of the victory celebrations, Governor Drake was hosting a grand dinner in honour of Clive to which one hundred of the Company's most senior soldiers and officials had been invited.

The high-ceilinged hall looked truly magnificent, with Company flags hanging all around the walls, tall vases of lilies scenting the air and crystal and silverware shining on the long mahogany table. The light from many candelabras softened the austere features of Company officials whose portraits hung from the teak-panelled walls. The most recent – so recent, in fact, that the paint could scarcely be dry – was one of Clive himself. He was depicted standing in the foreground while pointing triumphantly towards the mango groves of Lakash Bagh where ranks of advancing Company soldiers were shown surging forward in pursuit of a fleeing enemy. Not an entirely accurate portrayal, Nicholas thought wryly, considering the real cause of the victory had been Mir Jafar's defection rather than Clive's daring and brilliance.

Would Mir Jafar also commission a painting of Plassey, Nicholas wondered. More likely the new Nawab would not relish a depiction of his treachery even if it had delivered to him everything the Company had promised. After Plassey, Mir Jafar had quickly established himself on the throne of Bengal and as quickly executed his erstwhile master. Siraj-ud-daulah, the man who had once dreamed of transforming his city, now lay buried in a simple tomb in Murshidabad.

Nicholas made his way towards the centre of the table, where Clive, already seated, was receiving slaps on the back and congratulations from those clustering around him. Looking up for a moment Clive spotted him and called out, 'Nicholas! Over here!' As Nicholas pushed through the throng, Clive rose from his chair and embraced him. 'As the host, Drake's sitting on my right, of course, but I insisted you should be on my left,' Clive said. 'I've hardly seen you since we got back to Calcutta,' he continued. 'These endless receptions and celebrations have taken up so much of my time and I know they're not to your taste but I wish you'd attended more of them...'

'Well, I'm here now,' Nicholas smiled. Clive's note, delivered to his bungalow the same day the invitation from the Governor had arrived, had insisted that Clive would not take no for an answer on this occasion.

'Seriously though, even if you hadn't come, I'd have winkled you out of your seclusion. I've something important to ask you,' Clive said.

In all the hubbub it was some while before they had the opportunity to talk. The dinner was the most magnificent Nicholas had ever attended – bearers in new livery of cream and gold circulated with bottles of champagne, kept cool in blocks of ice carved to resemble Fort William and which, Governor Drake smugly informed his guests to cheers, had been 'liberated' from the cellars of the French East India Company in Chandernagore. After the champagne came clarets, moselles, hocks and burgundies. The food was equally luxurious as course followed course – cream soups, consommés, patés, delicately sauced river fish, roasted pheasants and quails, curries and pulaos, cheeses transported in barrels from Britain, sherbets and jellies and, that greatest of luxuries in Hindustan, ice creams – mango, pistachio and guava.

The mood was one of fervent celebration. Some, like Clive, deserved it, Nicholas mused, but what about some others? Looking along the table his eye fell on several Council members who, though now lauding the courage of the victors of Plassey, had themselves fled Calcutta before its capture and demanded alliances with Siraj-ud-daulah after the city was retaken. Cowards and hypocrites all, and one or two very probably traitors like George Braddock. Yet, that did not stop them leaping to their feet as the banquet wore on to make increasingly grandiose speeches or propose extravagant toasts. Governor Drake had proposed they drink to 'courage under fire', yet he had fled Calcutta without a thought for his responsibilities – no 'black hole' for him.

As the evening wore on the din grew louder and louder, and the faces redder and redder. Nicholas felt more and more detached from the scene around him and drank little, merely sipping from his glass at every toast. As the port circulated, Clive, whose attention for most of the banquet had been claimed by Governor Drake, stood up and said, 'Gentleman, while I still can, I have one final toast to make.' Raising his glass of ruby-red port he proclaimed, 'To the gods who have smiled on us! To our future wealth and glory! To the Company!' For the umpteenth time that evening, there was a scraping of chairs as every man stood. 'The Company!' they roared as one, before draining their glasses.

Despite the open windows and the punkhas, the chamber was growing ever hotter. Sitting down again, Nicholas was just turning to ask the servant behind him for a glass of soda water when he felt Clive's hand on his arm. 'I'm sorry, Nicholas, Drake's been boring on and on… But listen, I want to talk to you,' he lowered his voice.

Nicholas smiled, 'Yes, earlier this evening you said you wanted to ask me something. What is it?'

Despite all he had drunk, Clive's face was suddenly serious. Lowering his voice even further he said, 'The thing is, I don't plan to stay in Hindustan very much longer.'

His words stunned Nicholas. 'Why on earth not when it's given you everything you've ever wanted?'

'That's exactly the point. It has – well at least for the present. Grateful gifts from Mir Jafar for placing him on the throne of Bengal have made me wealthy enough to pursue other ambitions and I have many… I've put an end to French ambitions in Hindustan. Now I want to command an army against them in Europe, and then perhaps to enter Parliament. With the fame and fortune I've amassed here, the connections I've made, I'm perfectly positioned for a political career. And Margaret agrees with me. She thinks that one day I could even be prime minister.'

Leaning closer, Clive put his arm around Nicholas's shoulder. 'The thing is, I know myself. How I sometimes get carried away... All these years, even though I've not always listened to you, you've been my conscience. I know I'd be a much better man – a much better politician too – in every respect if you'd come home to Britain with me to advise and counsel me. You will, won't you, Nicholas?' Clive's expression as he fixed his brown eyes on Nicholas suggested he had no doubt that Nicholas would agree.

His friend's confidence made it all the harder for Nicholas to give the answer he knew he must. Finally he said, 'I'm grateful to you for asking me but, I'm sorry, Clive, no, it's not possible.' Clive opened his mouth to speak but before he could say anything Nicholas continued, 'Whatever you say, you won't make me change my mind. You're not the only one who has thought about his future since Plassey. I have too and I've decided there's nothing left for me in Britain. With my uncle exiled I still don't know where and Glenmire confiscated, it's no longer my home. I long ago honourably repaid any debt I owed to my uncle or anyone else. For the first time since I arrived in Calcutta, I've realised my life's finally my own, to live as I choose, and I choose to live it in Hindustan, not Britain.'

'So you're going to stay with the Company then?' Clive said.

'No, definitely not! The truth is that I've had enough of making compromises, even for the best of reasons, and of acquiescing in Company decisions I don't always agree with. I've decided to resign and this time I won't let you dissuade me.'

For a moment Clive looked thoughtful, then he said, 'I won't. I know I couldn't even if I tried. But can't you see resigning is even more reason for you to come with me. I understand why you don't want to return to Scotland, but you won't be there – you'll be with me in London, the nation's political heart. Think of the opportunities we'd have!'

Nicholas shook his head. 'Clive, you want power, wealth, position, honours, everything the world can offer... But I think we both know that however much you achieve, it'll never be enough for you. Don't be offended when I say that, to me, the desire for such things often clouds men's judgments and sullies their reputations. My needs are simpler and very different. When Meena died, I thought I'd never love again. But I was wrong. I've come to realise that I'm falling in love with Lucia – a more gentle kind of love, perhaps, but deep and deepening every day. If she's willing – and I think she will be – I will make a new life with her, James and Tuhin Singh in Hindustan. You see, you have your dreams, but so do I. Mine are to build a new Glenmire in the foothills of the Himalayas, not too distant from Tuhin Singh's homeland, but far, far away from Calcutta's heated rivalries, divisions and self-serving ambitions. There, I plan to lead a quiet life, cultivating my land, reading, riding and playing that violin you've always teased me about...' Nicholas took a deep breath and reached for the glass of soda water the bearer had meanwhile placed on the table before him.

'That was some speech,' Clive said, a half-smile on his face. 'Will such a quiet life really satisfy you? Somehow, I doubt it!' He paused. 'But I can see you've made your choice, as I've made mine.' He turned away for a moment but when he looked back at Nicholas any hint of a rueful smile had faded from his face and his expression looked sadder than Nicholas had ever seen. 'Whatever happens to us... whatever fate brings... do you think life will ever be as good as when we were on the *Winchester* with the whole world before us...?' Clive asked. 'I sometimes think that the longer we live, the more complex our hopes and desires become... the more risk there is of disappointing ourselves or others...'

For some moments he fell silent, then said quietly, 'We should make a private toast – one we will always remember when we look back...'

'What do you suggest?' Nicholas asked, thinking his friend would toast success or good fortune or the future, but he found he was entirely mistaken.

Clive lifted his eyes to Nicholas's and said simply, as he half raised his glass, 'To true friends.'

Postscript

Among the Ballantyne Papers is a large, plainly bound notebook. The pages have yellowed; some are so badly mottled that the writing is near illegible, while others have crumbled away, leaving only fragments. Yet, enough pages remain to indicate that the notebook contained memoirs written by Nicholas Ballantyne many years after the events described in this book. The inside cover bears a simple inscription:

> 'For my wife and children, so they will know how Hindustan became my home and theirs, and for my great-great-grandfather who also loved this land – Nicholas Ballantyne, May 1780, New Glenmire, The Himalayas.'

In one of the surviving passages Nicholas candidly describes his relationship with Clive from their first meeting as naïve, eager young men through the often turbulent times they shared. I was especially moved by the following paragraphs:

> 'As events turned out, Clive was, of course, proved right about my future when many years later, after his death, I returned to the Company's service in Calcutta. But that is another story.
>
> As for Clive, what can I say? I mourned his death by his own hand in London at only forty-nine-years old. Sometimes, as I lie by Lucia in the quiet hours of the Himalayan night, I wonder whether, if I had stayed by his side, I could have saved him from becoming so deeply enmired in corruption, intrigue and controversy in both Hindustan and Britain. During our years together he already showed some

evidence of the flaws which later overwhelmed him. My studies both of the Classics and of the more modern history of the world show that power inevitably corrupts. If I had remained with Clive – as he wanted – perhaps power might not have corrupted him so absolutely and things would have been different. Who can judge? And who can tell what would have been the consequences for Hindustan and Britain?

All I can say is that, right or wrong, Clive was my friend. I am glad to have known him and to have fought by his side and I pray for his soul to rest in peace.'

A.R.

Historical Note

Although some characters are fictional, as indicated in the cast list, this historical novel is based on historical fact, some of which is outlined below.

The East India Company

The East India Company (also known as the English or British East India Company) was founded in 1600. By the time Robert Clive arrived in India it was Britain's largest and most important trading company. The Court of Directors, which comprised twenty-four stockholding members under a chairman and deputy chairman, managed its activities from East India House in Leadenhall Street in London and accrued great wealth for themselves and their investors. The directors, some of whom were Members of Parliament, maintained a close relationship with the British Government to which the Company made loans.

The centres of Company activity in India were three settlements – the Presidencies of Calcutta (Kolkata), Madras (Chennai) and Bombay (Mumbai). Here, Company trading was conducted within a hierarchy. At the bottom were the 'writers' – the junior rank at which Robert Clive joined the Company – then 'factors', then Junior Merchants, then Senior Merchants. At each settlement, a President and Council guided and monitored Company activities and reported back to London.

The settlement in Madras in southern India, based around Fort St. George and established in 1640, was the oldest of the three. The Company acquired Bombay in 1668, when the Portuguese princess Catherine of Braganza married Charles II of England, bringing a dowry that included the deep water port. Charles rented Bombay to the Company for just ten pounds of gold a year and it quickly supplanted Surat as the Company's main establishment on India's west coast. In 1690, Company employee Job Charnock identified the then village of Kalikata in Bengal as a suitable site for what became known to the British as Calcutta. Fort William was completed in the very early years of the eighteenth century and rebuilt in the years after Plassey when the buildings around it were cleared and the maidan was laid out.

By the mid-eighteenth century Madras was the wealthiest town on the Coromandel Coast with a population of four hundred Europeans and forty thousand local people. The President of Madras was formally a zamindar – tenant – of the Nawab of the Carnatic, who was in turn a deputy of the Nizam of the Deccan, the Moghul Emperor's viceroy in southern India.

During the period covered in this book, the East India Company's purpose was to trade and to produce dividends for its shareholders. Its Directors in London had no wish to spend money on administering territory and it had no territorial ambitions. At that point, it only desired to secure trade advantages in India and to eliminate its main European trading rival, France, from India, and thus to produce a profitable monopoly of trade with the subcontinent. However, in the years following Plassey, with French interests very much diminished, this stance would begin to change – initially under the influence of Robert Clive.

At the time of the events described in this book, the three Presidencies were functioning with increasing independence and confidence. They enjoyed a great deal of autonomy from London due not least to the long time it took – four to six months – to sail from India to Britain which meant that it took up to a year to send a report to the Directors in London and in turn to receive their instructions with regard to it.

Throughout the period of this book, the number of Britons in India was very small. The population of all the Company's establishments was overwhelmingly Indian. In particular, very few

British women were in India. The years of the 'fishing fleet' of women arriving in India to seek husbands were still to come.

The East India Company Armies

To protect its activities, each of the three Presidencies recruited its own infantry, cavalry and artillery troops from local populations. These sepoys were equipped with modern weapons, officered by Britons and well paid compared to their peers. Over time the Company introduced some all-European regiments. Sometimes, British Army regiments were sent to India to serve alongside Company troops, particularly in the period of this book during times of conflict with other European powers. They were often referred to as 'HM's Regiments' or 'Royal regiments' (Eyre Coote's 39th Regiment of Foot was the first regular British regiment to serve in India). In all the campaigns described in this book, the Company's armies consisted mainly of Indian troops.

The Moghul Empire and the Indian subcontinent in the Mid-Eighteenth Century

Aurangzeb, the last of the six great Moghul emperors – each the subject of one of the books of the Empire of the Moghul series – died in 1707. He had spent much of his life campaigning in the Deccan and southern India. A strict Muslim, his religious policies had divided the people of his empire. He had alienated the powerful martial Rajput leaders, major supporters of his predecessors. After his death, the Moghul empire had begun its slow decline and disintegration – a fact underlined when in 1739 Nadir Shah of Persia sacked Delhi and stole the fabulous Peacock Throne, which had been created to showcase the best gems of Emperor Shah Jahan. Though the Moghul emperors still exercised some control in the north and east – Bengal for example – through their vassals, in the south their suzerainty over powerful vassals such as the Nizams of Hyderabad was growing ever more theoretical. The resulting power vacuum encouraged jostling for power between local rulers and gave European rivals like the British and the French a chance to intervene in hopes of winning trading and other concessions.

In the period of this book, the peoples of the Indian subcontinent were at least as diverse and disparate in terms of spoken language, script, religion and culture as those of the Europe of the time.

Military Campaigns

The military campaigns described in this book all happened, although in many cases the detailed action is imagined. The actual chronology is as follows:

First Carnatic War, 1744–1748 (an extension into the Indian Subcontinent of the European War of the Austrian Succession, 1740–1748, in which Britain and France were on opposing sides)
21 September 1746 – East India Company surrenders Madras to the French.

1746/47 – East India Company aided by Anwaruddin Khan, Nawab of the Carnatic, defeats French attempts to capture Fort St. David, Cuddalore in southern India.

1748 – Stringer Lawrence takes command of Fort St. David.

1748 – East India Company unsuccessfully besieges the French in Pondicherry but Clive distinguishes himself in the action.

Spring 1749 – News reaches India of the signature of the Treaty of Aix-la-Chapelle in 1748 ending the war and providing for the return of Madras by the French to the East India Company which took place later in 1749.

The Tanjore Campaign begins, March 1749
The East India Company, at the invitation of one of the contenders – a usurped former ruler – and on his promise of substantial reward including the gift of the port of Devakottai, intervenes in the struggle for the throne of Tanjore.

Second Carnatic War, 1749–1754 (in part a proxy war between the British and French East India companies, sparked by the death of the Nizam of Hyderabad in 1748 and subsequent rivalry over the succession to his throne and that of the Nawab of the Carnatic)

1749 – Anwaruddin Khan, Nawab of the Carnatic, killed while fighting French troops and those of his rival, Chanda Sahib.

September–November 1751 – Siege of Arcot. News of the town's successful defence by Clive made him a national hero in Britain.

1755 – Britain and France sign the Treaty of Pondicherry ending the Carnatic War.

Conflict with Siraj-ud-daulah and His French Allies, 1756–57 (overlapping with early stages of Third Carnatic War, 1757–1763, itself an extension of the Seven Years War that began in Europe in 1756 and ended in 1763)

9 April 1756 – Mirza Muhammad Siraj-ud-daulah succeeds his grandfather as Nawab of Bengal.

20 June 1756 – Siraj-ud-daulah captures Calcutta.

2 January 1757 – East India Company under Clive retakes Calcutta.

23 March 1757 – East India Company under Clive and Admiral Watson capture Chandernagore from the French.

18 June 1757 – Eyre Coote captures Kutwa.

23 June 1757 – Clive defeats Siraj-ud-daulah's forces at Battle of Plassey following the treacherous defections of Mir Jafar, Lutuf Khan and Rai Durlabh. That year Prime Minister William Pitt the Elder called Clive the 'heaven-born general'.

2 July 1757 – Siraj-ud-daulah is executed in Murshidabad on the orders of Mir Jafar, his successor as Nawab of Bengal. (His simple but elegant mausoleum is at Khushbagh, Murshidabad).

The Jacobite Rebellion (sometimes called 'The '45')

The Jacobite Rebellion began in 1745 when Prince Charles Edward Stuart – 'Bonnie Prince Charlie' – landed with a few

supporters in Scotland's western isles and called on the Highland clan chiefs to support his bid to take the throne for the
Stuarts from his cousin, the Hanoverian King George II. (The
last Stuart king, James II had been deposed some fifty years previously.) Many Highland chiefs like Cameron of Lochiel, felt they
could not, out of honour, refuse the Prince's appeal even though
they suspected his campaign would fail. Others, in particular the
Campbells, supported George II.

At first the Prince's campaign prospered. With the help of
troops drawn from the Scottish clans, he defeated government
forces and seized Edinburgh. However, the troops promised by
King Louis XV of France failed to arrive and as the Prince led
his army south into England, the lack of popular support for
him became obvious to the Highland chiefs who, when the
army reached Derby some 120 miles from London, insisted on
a withdrawal back to Scotland. Meanwhile, the advance of the
Jacobite army had caused panic in London. King George II had
been preparing to flee aboard his yacht. Henry Fielding, author
of *Tom Jones* and other novels was among those who whipped
up hysteria against the Jacobites, publishing lurid and imaginary
accounts of atrocities committed by Highlanders, even suggesting
that they ate babies.

However, as one commentator wrote, 'No one is afraid of a
rebellion that runs away.' As the Highland army retreated to Scotland, nerves in England calmed and the government despatched
troops under George II's son, the Duke of Cumberland, north to
Scotland to destroy the Jacobite threat. The final confrontation
came on 16 April 1746 at the Battle of Culloden near Inverness,
the last battle ever fought on British soil. There the Prince's
army was defeated by Cumberland and his men and Charles
found himself forced into hiding until, after months of being
hunted across the Highlands, a French ship arrived to carry him
to safety. There was no such rescue for many who had supported
them. The estates of clan chiefs like Cameron of Lochiel were
confiscated, some Jacobite supporters were executed or imprisoned and Cumberland's troops drove many ordinary clansmen

and their families from their humble homes, which they burned, and expropriated their cattle and other possessions. Many of the dispossessed emigrated to North America.

Political and religious differences played a significant part in the Jacobite Rebellion. The Stuart kings had in general believed, like Kings Louis XIV and XV of France, in the 'Divine Right of Kings' to rule, make and change laws and impose taxes as they wished, unfettered by the views of those they ruled as expressed in Parliament and elsewhere. Many Britons found such behaviour anachronistic and unsustainable and the desire to entrench the rights of Parliament was key to the placing of the Hanoverian George I, father of George II, on the British throne in 1714 with significant restrictions on his powers. Thereafter, the British Parliamentary system began to develop with Robert Walpole becoming the first prime minister in 1721.

Besides which, both Prince Charles Edward Stuart, and his supporter King Louis XV of France, were Roman Catholics. King George II was a Protestant. Many Britons were deeply suspicious of Catholics, suspecting them of being in league with foreign powers against Britain.

Points on Specific Chapters

In some cases time scales have been changed and some events omitted or simplified to fit within the ambit of this book.

Chapter 2

Robert Clive was born on 29 September 1725. He indeed first arrived in India on the Company's East Indiaman *Winchester*.

The description of the sights, sounds and smells of sailing up the Hooghly and how Calcutta looked come from accounts of the time.

Chapter 3

The account of how and why Job Charnock chose Kalikata as the site for the settlement the Company would call Calcutta is based on fact.

Tuhin Singh's homeland of Nokila is fictitious.

Chapter 4

The novelist Henry Fielding indeed published warnings about the Jacobite threat and allegations about the Highlanders' brutality in *The True Patriot*.

Chapter 5

Jeanne Dupleix, wife of Joseph François, Marquis Dupleix, Governor-General of French territories in India, indeed had a reputation for seducing local Indian rulers to further her husband's ambitions. In India she was sometimes known as Joanna Begum.

Chapter 7

Elihu Yale was born in Boston, Massachusetts, but brought to England by his parents at the age of three. He made a considerable fortune in India where he was removed from office by the Company for enriching himself at the Company's expense – and later in the diamond trade in London. He was also a philanthropist who made significant donations towards the funding of a college in New Haven, Connecticut which was later named Yale in his honour – today's Yale University.

Chapter 9

Clive's military skill and administrative talent so impressed Stringer Lawrence that he made him his protégé and at one point his quartermaster. Lawrence later claimed that 'Clive's early years' suggested he was 'a born soldier with courage and judgment much beyond his years'. He would later become highly disillusioned with his protégé.

Anwaruddin Khan's reminiscences of Aurangzeb's austerity and self-denial are entirely accurate according to the many accounts of Aurangzeb's reign, as are those of Aurangzeb's affection for his sister, Jahanara.

Chapter 11

Clive was indeed promoted to lieutenant around this time. The tribute to his bravery that he quotes proudly to Nicholas are the actual words of his commanding officer.

Chapter 12

The intense and bitter rivalry between Admiral de la Bourdonnais and Marquis Dupleix was common knowledge at the time.

Chapter 13

Margaret Maskelyne was born in Shropshire in England. Portraits depict her as an elegant, fine-featured, intelligent looking woman. Her brother Dr Nevil Maskelyne in fact became Britain's fifth Astronomer Royal in 1765, after the events described in this book. She did not die until 1817.

Chapter 16

Chanda Sahib, birth name Husayn Dost Khan, was Nawab of the Carnatic from 1749 until, after the defeat at Arcot, in 1752 a Tanjorean general captured and beheaded him.

St. Mary's Church, where Clive and Margaret Maskelyne were married, was consecrated in 1680 and is the oldest Anglican church east of Suez and the oldest surviving British building in India. It is sometimes called 'the Westminster Abbey of the East'. The first marriage registered there was that of Elihu Yale to Catherine Hynmers, a widow, in 1680.

Chapter 17

Piracy in the Ganges delta and the wild reaches of the Arakan close to Burma was a serious problem at this time.

Chapter 18

The murderous rivalry between Ghaseti Begum and her nephew Siraj-ud-daulah described by Mir Jafar is well attested.

Chapter 19

The number of people who actually died in the 'black hole' is disputed, as is the matter of who was responsible. Most sources agree that the number of survivors was in the low twenties but estimates of the number of dead vary considerably from under twenty to well over forty. A monument to the victims is located in the grounds of St. John's Church, Kolkata.

Chapter 22

The quote from Sir Thomas Roe, ambassador to the Emperor Jahangir, is in Roe's own words.

The Company's Machiavellian interactions with Siraj-ud-daulah and those of the Nawab with the Company and with French officials prior to Plassey were more complex and complicated and involved more people, both British and Bengali, than described. Clive's negotiations with Siraj-ud-daulah and Amirchand, an intermediary between them, have been much criticised as duplicitous and amounting to fraud and forgery on Clive's part.

Clive's ultimatum to the French commander of Chandernagore is in his own words.

Chapter 23

Eyre Coote was celebrated for his capture of Kutwa on the eve of the Battle of Plassey.

Chapter 24

The Company's victory against the numerically vastly superior forces of Siraj-ud-daulah at Plassey was due in large measure to the defections at a critical point of Mir Jafar, Rai Durlabh and Lutuf Khan. Siraj-ud-daulah's loyal general Mir Madan Khan was killed in the battle by a Company cannonball.

Epilogue

Nicholas's words about power and its ability to corrupt foreshadow the celebrated nineteenth-century historian Lord Acton's comment that 'power tends to corrupt and absolute power corrupts absolutely'.

It was not until 1760 that Clive was, in fact, able to sail for England. He received generous personal reward from Mir Jafar after Plassey when Mir Jafar became the Nawab of Bengal. Clive participated in a defence of Bengal against an invasion by the son of the Moghul emperor for which he received, by no means unsolicited, further presents from Mir Jafar including a personal land grant. He became the Governor of the East India Company Presidency in Bengal and began to advocate that the Company should take control of territory as well as trade in the area. At the same time, he quarrelled with many of the Company's officials and army officers including, as he had before Plassey, with Eyre Coote but also with his former mentor Stringer Lawrence.

After his return to Britain in 1760, Clive had to defend his land grant against charges of it being against the Company's interest and obviously enriching him further. Although frequently debilitated by obscure nervous ailments and pains, he became a Member of Parliament. He subsequently persuaded the Company and Parliament that he should be sent back to Bengal to purge the administration there of corruption caused by the 'present taking' of officials – highly ironic in view of his past behaviour.

Once back in Calcutta, Clive's actions led to increasing de facto control of Bengal and its revenues. Despite his supposed anti-corruption remit, he was accused of what would now be called 'insider stock trading'.

Clive returned to Britain in 1767 with a personal fortune then estimated to be over 400,000 pounds sterling, a vast sum in those days, to find that his and the Company's activities had been subject to a Parliamentary Inquiry. He spent much of his remaining life defending himself. He died in London on 22 November 1774, aged only forty-nine, allegedly by his own hand but possibly from an inadvertent overdose of the opium he had taken for a number of years.

Acknowledgements

I would like to thank Poulomi Chatterjee and Thomas Abraham of Hachette India, and my agent Bill Hamilton and his assistant Florence Rees, for all their help and encouragement in writing *Fortune's Soldier*.

Alex Rutherford